"ONE OF THE BEST PSYCHOLOGICAL
THRILLERS OF THE SEASON!"
—*The Macon Beacon*

WAS IT MADNESS
for beautiful, talented Laura Wade to see herself as
a hideous creature of evil with the psychic power
to inflict injury and death on everyone around her?

WAS IT MADNESS
for decent, dedicated David Goldman to begin to
believe in something that violated all his training
and to yield to a desire that would destroy him as
a doctor?

WAS IT MADNESS
for both of them to play a dangerous game of
deception against a bulldog New York City police
inspector who thought Laura was a murderess . . .
and against a powerful, ruthless and jealous
husband who hated Goldman?

It might not be madness. It might be far worse . . .

A REASONABLE MADNESS

"A dynamite story. I couldn't put it down."
—Lucy Freeman, author of *Fight Against Fears*

"Tautly effective." —*Kirkus Reviews*

"Compelling . . . terrific suspense."
—Gloria Murphy, author of *Nightshade*

"Uncommonly good . . . imaginative, scary . . . a
wonderfully believable psychological thriller."
—*United Press International*

A
REASONABLE
MADNESS

A NOVEL BY

Fran Dorf

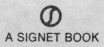

A SIGNET BOOK

SIGNET
Published by the Penguin Group
Penguin Books USA Inc., 375 Hudson Street,
New York, New York 10014, U.S.A.
Penguin Books Ltd, 27 Wrights Lane,
London W8 5TZ England
Penguin Books Australia Ltd, Ringwood,
Victoria, Australia
Penguin Books Canada Ltd, 2801 John Street,
Markham, Ontario, Canada L3R 1B4
Penguin Books (N.Z.) Ltd, 182-190 Wairau Road,
Auckland 10, New Zealand

Penguin Books Ltd, Registered Offices:
Harmondsworth, Middlesex, England

Published by SIGNET, an imprint of New American Library, a division of
Penguin Books USA Inc. This is an authorized reprint of a hardcover edition
published by Birch Lane Press.

First SIGNET Printing, September, 1991
10 9 8 7 6 5 4 3 2 1

Grateful acknowledgment is made for permission to reprint four lines from
"Desert Place," by Robert Frost. From *The Poetry of Robert Frost* edited by
Edward Connery Lathem. Copyright 1936 by Robert Frost. Copyright © 1964
by Lesley Frost Ballantine. Copyright © 1969 by Holt, Rinehart and Winston.
Reprinted by permission of Henry Holt and Company, Inc.

 REGISTERED TRADEMARK—MARCA REGISTRADA

Printed in the United States of America

PUBLISHER'S NOTE
A Reasonable Madness is a work of fiction. Names, characters, places, and
incidents are either the product of the author's imagination or are used ficti-
tiously, and any resemblance to actual persons, living or dead, is entirely co-
incidental.

For my parents.

And for Bob and Rachel,
who make it all worthwhile.

ACKNOWLEDGMENTS

I would like to thank Hillel Black at Birch Lane; my agent John Hawkins, for early support and faith; Drs. Marlin and Marcia Brenner, for professional comment; Dave King, John Maloney and Jane Rafal, for support, suggestions, jumpstarts and good advice.

Most of all, I would like to express my profound gratitude to the indefatigable Renni Browne— teacher, believer, friend.

They cannot scare me with their empty spaces
Between stars—on stars where no human race is.
I have it in me so much nearer home
To scare myself with my own desert places.

—Robert Frost

Prologue

No office should have been as hot as this one, no work as tedious, no building as quiet.

Lilly Dunleavy stopped typing and listened. Without the steady tap-tapping of her fingertips on the computer keyboard, there was no sound at all except for the muted hum of the computer terminal. Not even the air-conditioning system, normally a dirge of clanks and drones, made a sound. There had to be something wrong with the thermostat. She'd adjusted it downward three times now, and it was still sweltering hot.

Lilly glanced at the clock. It was after eight, and it was an oven in here. Maybe the whole system had been turned off for the night. Who cared about Lilly Dunleavy, working late on Allen Haverhill's damned report—was anything more boring than corporate divestiture—which had to be finished tomorrow, or goodbye job? Who cared about Lilly, the lowest of the low, secretary to a mere account executive who was pretty low himself? For nearly two weeks now, the mayor had been reminding the city daily: "Everyone pitch in. Save New York's energy during the heatwave." Maybe it was a decree from City Hall. No air conditioning at night. But everyone was long gone now, and there was no one to ask except maybe some janitor, whom Lilly might or might not find some-where on any of sixteen floors.

Lilly glanced back at the screen, flickering white letters on blue, then stood up to stretch her legs. She glanced over at the useless pane of glass. What the hell were the windows *there* for, always shut, not even a latch? Air-conditioned air. Which was okay, except when the air wasn't air-conditioned.

Absently, Lilly walked over to the window and glanced down at the sidewalk, two floors below. There didn't seem to be much traffic, no one out walking, but that was understandable this late in a nonresiden-tial neighborhood. It was dark now on the street. Only the light of a street lamp.

And something else.

At first Lilly couldn't make out what she was seeing. Everything seemed to have been washed, drained of color. A dark shadow on the sidewalk, a hulking, kneeling figure. No, *two* figures. One lying down. That one was a woman—Lilly could see the outline of a pair of high heels. Why weren't the feet moving?

The other figure was kneeling over her. But what was he doing?

Lilly put her palm up to the glass, trying to focus.

She saw the glint of a knife in motion, followed the blade with her eyes.

Not stabbing. Slicing. Again. Again. Again. Small, slow, careful movements, a pantomime in black and gray, in motion and shadow. Up. Down. Then up again. The motion reminded her of carving. Like carving a turkey.

She understood.

She watched, struggling for an idea of what she might do. Open the window, scare him away? No. She remembered now. It was glued shut, and she was two floors up. Maybe she could pry it open. With what?

She began banging at the window with her fists, little fists on a huge expanse of glass. Later, she would remember pounding, pounding, screaming. *But she couldn't break the glass,* and he was still there, doing his killing pantomime.

She could throw the paperweight from her desk at the window, the one with the coins imbedded in it; or maybe she could smash the computer monitor through the window, ripping the tangle of wires and the plugs from the keyboard. She would scare him away.

But then he would see her.

She stopped banging.

Suddenly the hulking figure straightened up, and became a man. The other figure, the woman, lay on the sidewalk, motionless but for the slight twitching of one hand and the movement of a dark shadow—the pool of blood widening around her head.

He was walking toward Eighth Avenue now, slowly, as if he were strolling through the park. Why was he walking so slowly?

She wanted to back away, but she remained transfixed, her hand on the glass, her eyes on the man. She could still see him as he walked. But he had no *face*!

No. It was a mask, a *ski mask.* She could see the place where the eyes were cut out, almond shapes, black hollows for eyes.

The killer was looking around him as he walked, and then he looked up. Lilly was no longer safe behind the glass, safe with distance, and dark.

The killer's eyes looked at her, registered her face just for the briefest instant. The black hollows of eyes held her, as if the man had reached up through the glass, placed his hand on her shoulder, breathed on her face. She realized she was part of the scene in black and gray. Him. And his victim. And *her*. She heard her fingernails screech down the glass, shrill, cold. Teacher-nails on the blackboard. Twelfth grade, Mr. Larson. He loved to do that, watch the kids squirm.

PART ONE

Culligan:
Logic

1 For the first time in nearly a year, David Goldman's private line rang while he was in session. Only a few people had the number—his soon-to-be-ex-wife, his best friend, his parents, a few others— and they were all well aware that the only time to reach him was between ten of and ten after the hour, unless it was an emergency.

Forty minutes into the session, lulled by the rhythm and cadence of his patient's voice, mildly startled, more than a little annoyed, David picked up the receiver.

"Dr. Goldman?" A deep booming voice. "This is Sergeant Jake Ammonetti, Nineteenth Precinct."

"How did you get this number, sergeant?"

"I called your office a couple of times and kept getting that machine, so I tried your home. Your wife gave me the number."

What the hell was Allison doing in the apartment? "Yes, sergeant," David said, "how can I help you?"

"We got a patient of yours down here, I think you'd better get over right away. Name's Wade."

"Who?"

"Laura Gardner Wade. Says you're her . . ." He started to say "shrink," then said, "psychiatrist."

"But I don't have a patient by that name. I . . ."

Wait a minute. He didn't, but he did—almost. A Laura Wade had come in on a consultation earlier in the year, maybe back in January. Mild depression. Very lovely woman. David thought the session went well, wondered why she never came back.

"Dr. Goldman?"

"Yes. I know her." He glanced over at his patient, Pepper Moran. He had to be very careful what he said while she was sitting there listening.

"We have to send Mrs. Wade down to Bellevue if we can't get her out of here, Dr. Goldman," Ammonetti said.

Bellevue? "What happened?"

"Your patient confesses to a homicide. Woman murdered last night down on Seventh and Twenty-ninth. Maybe you heard about it on the news."

As a matter of fact, he had. He'd done some case reviews at home last night, then turned on the television news for a little while before going to bed. What were they calling him for? It sounded like Laura Wade needed a lawyer, not a psychiatrist.

"Yes. I heard about it, sergeant."

"Of course, I knew right away something was up the minute she walked in," Ammonetti said. "I never figured a woman could of done this thing anyway, not *this* woman. I mean, she comes in here—she's quite a looker, your patient, doc—wearing a three-piece pink number that must have cost eight hundred bucks if it cost a penny. And when she said she was Laura Gardner Wade . . . well, right away I recognized the name—I mean, we shop there all the time, you can get some real bargains in Gardners. And then she said she lived up in Connecticut, in Fairfield County. Pretty exclusive digs for a Manhattan street killer. I told Culligan she was a confessor right away."

A confessor? And who was Culligan? David sighed. "All right, sergeant, I'll be there as soon as I can."

He hung up. Pepper, her arms folded, was looking over his head at the wall behind his desk. David's credentials were hanging there—diplomas, certifications, a citation for a paper on anxiety—arranged in a mishmash of frames just to the right of the clock. The "hour," he noted, was almost up.

"I'm sorry, Pepper, there's an emergency. I have to cut our session a little short."

Pepper Moran stood up. "If you have to go, you have to go. I understand." Her expression was devoid of the slightest trace of understanding.

David took off his glasses. "We'll continue this next week, Pepper. Okay?"

"Okay, but next week let's do it without your specs," she said, smiling. "You look cuter that way."

He waited until she closed the door behind her before getting up. She was a difficult patient, Pepper—a hotshot advertising executive, and all she could think of was having a husband and a family before her biological clock ran out. David didn't like putting people in categories, but it seemed to him that Pepper Moran belonged to a growing one. And lately she'd been blatantly seductive, complimenting him at every turn, crossing her legs, giving him long meaningful stares, the whole bit. Did she think *he* was her answer?

He made a couple of calls to cancel his five and six o'clock patients, then went into the bathroom to splash water on his face, catching a glimpse of himself in the mirror before he flipped off the light. What was it Pepper had called him a few weeks ago? "Stop looking at me that way," she said. "You look like a brooding Adonis." Brooding, he may have been, but Adonis? At best it was a Semitic sort of look, large jaw, biggish nose, dark hair—but for the blue eyes. He was over six feet tall, but pretty skinny. Even at thirty-nine. Some Adonis.

On his way out the door, he ran into the ubiquitous Mrs. Frangipani, collecting her mail in the vestibule.

"Good afternoon, doctor. Everything all right?"

Mrs. Frangipani lived in an apartment over David's office, which occupied the entire bottom floor of the brownstone—a turn-of-the-century Greek revival intricately carved with a lot of very sooty gargoyles. Sometimes it seemed a little dingy for a place where psychological healing occasionally occurred. He tried to lighten up the place by keeping geraniums in the window boxes. Mrs. Frangipani occasionally took it upon herself to water them, that is, when she wasn't collecting her mail.

"Good afternoon, Mrs. Frangipani. Everything's fine."

He headed outside and stood for a moment on the sidewalk in front of the stoop. It was a quiet, shaded side street between Columbus and Amsterdam. Quiet and shady, but hot. Another broiler, the kind of day when you wish you were anywhere on earth but in Manhattan, in a jungle of sweating cement and flesh. The geraniums looked wilted, and the air stank, the legacy of a recently settled garbage strike. Heading east, toward Central Park, David had to walk around a man standing at the end of the block, insisting that he repent, for the hour was near.

He hailed a cab at the corner without much difficulty: it was filthy inside, and the driver kept cursing at the top of his lungs in a language David couldn't quite identify, and the guy drove like a maniac. None of which made much of an impression on David. He was trying to recall whatever he could about Laura Wade.

She lived in Connecticut—Easterbrook, a name he remembered because he and Allison had stopped there on their way up to Cape Cod one summer. One of those sedate Waspy towns along the coast where all the people walking along the main street of chic shops and eateries seemed to look alike, dressed in ultracasual, outrageously expensive sportswear. They'd had lunch in a sunny, plant-filled restaurant that featured the best stew he'd ever tasted and a view of a quaint harbor and Long Island Sound that was spectacular. The experience had not been enhanced by the three slack-jawed crows at the next table, wearing tennis whites, munching radicchio salad and trumpeting their mean-spirited gossip in loud, shrill voices.

He remembered thinking at the time that Laura Wade seemed somehow not right for that town. And there was something about her that had bothered him. He certainly couldn't recall anything she had said that might enlighten him as to why she would do something as desperate as walk into a police station and confess to a murder. Confessors were usually psychotics, and she hadn't seemed even remotely psychotic. Or had he missed something? Of course, a lot could happen in six months.

When the taxi pulled up in front of the police station on Ninety-fourth Street, he handed the driver his fare and headed inside, expecting the madhouse scene familiar to anyone who watched as much prime-time television as David had watched in the nine months since Allison left him. It wasn't anything like what he expected. The atmosphere was quiet, orderly—rows of battered desks, steel file cabinets, glass-enclosed offices along the back wall—although there was a young Puerto Rican couple making a loud fuss in Spanish to a uniformed officer just beyond the reception area.

The officer at the front desk showed David into one of the offices.

"Sergeant Ammonetti, this is Dr. Goldman. Says you called him."

"Yeah, be right with you." Ammonetti, who was on the telephone, motioned David into a chair. "He's down in court today, Dammon."

David had expected a large man to match that booming voice, maybe even a cigar. Ammonetti wore Coke-bottle glasses and was thin and pale, almost sickly. Didn't the police have strength and size requirements?

"Christ, you'd have to go way back in the files for that," Ammonetti was saying. "Maybe six, seven years. Computer might tell you something. Listen, I gotta go, someone's in my office. I'll call you later on that other thing."

Ammonetti stood up behind his desk, whose surface David could barely see for the clutter of files and papers, the butt-filled ashtray, the three empty coffee cups, the half-eaten donut, and the teddy bear with the sign around its neck that said, "Best daddy in the world."

David shook the man's hand. "Tell me what's going on, sergeant."

"Like I told you," Ammonetti said, "she's a confessor. We get 'em all the time. Came in, said she wanted to confess to the Harmon murder. She wasn't talking crazy or anything, like confessors usually do, so I called Culligan—"

"Who's he?"

"Henry Culligan. Detective in charge of the case. At first we really thought we had a break. I mean, it only happened yesterday. Sometimes this kind of case can go on for weeks before we get anything at all."

"What kind of case *is* this one?"

"Odds are it's a mugging. Random victim. Which is one more reason I spotted her for a confessor—she said she knew the victim."

"Why would you think it's a mugging? I thought most homicides are between people who are related."

"They are. But these circumstances are all wrong for that. Locale is wrong. And it was pretty brutal for someone who knows the victim. Still, wouldn't rule nothing out at this stage of an investigation. But you want to know my hunch? There's gonna be another one just like it. What we've got here is the first in a series—you know, a serial killer with a particular m.o. I hope I'm wrong."

"I hope so too, sergeant. Doesn't a person have to have a lawyer present to give a confession?"

"She waived her right to counsel, doc. That means—"

"I know what it means."

"Anyway, Culligan was all set to book her. She laid out the whole thing for us. How she told her family she was going to the movies and instead she went to the woman's house and followed her. Even gave us a motive—said her husband and the victim were having an affair. I'll tell you, we got a lot of confessors in here, but I never seen the likes of this one."

"What do you mean?"

"Well, she had poise. Usually a confessor will give you a story that's . . . well, you know, unglued. Like they'll say they got little antennae on the top of their head that send out signals to kill people. One time I had a guy come in here and confess to a rape by long distance. Told me his, ah, genitals . . . well, you must hear this kind of thing all the time. Being a psychiatrist."

As a matter of fact, now that he was in private practice, David didn't hear this kind of thing much at all.

"Anyway, doc, this Wade woman had it all worked out. I almost believed it myself, she was so good. Every element down. Place, time, date, method, motive. She really wanted to be booked. Even figured out a place she could say she threw the weapon and we'd never recover it. In the Hudson River. Usually they don't have the presence of mind to concoct such a believable story."

True enough. A person in the grip of a psychotic delusion, Variety B paranoid psychosis—in which they felt so evil they were compelled to confess to a terrible crime they hadn't commited—*would* probably appear crazy, might well be babbling, or hallucinating. Probably *wouldn't* have the presence of mind to concoct a believable story.

"So why didn't you believe her, sergeant? Any reason besides your hunch that the murderer is a serial killer—and Laura Wade is a confessor?"

"Why? Because not fifteen minutes after Culligan got her confession, we had a witness walk in downtown, at the Tenth. Said she saw the whole thing from above, from a second-story window, in an office building."

"And?"

"And the witness said the perp was a man. Wearing a ski mask, but definitely a man. Had the victim down on the sidewalk, straddled her, held her chin steady, sliced away at her face like it was a side of salami." He shivered. "Can you imagine, a secretary working late, seeing that from a window? The witness is pretty unglued herself. Not that I blame her. Said she couldn't even open the window and scream so maybe he would hear it and get scared and run away. You know those air-conditioned office buildings, how the windows are made so you can't open them. And by the time the witness got down there, it was all over. Like I said, I never thought a woman could have done this anyway. Have to be pretty strong.''

And very sick.

"So when we got word the witness came in, we knew right away the Wade woman hadn't done it. And *that* was when she got hysterical. Saying yes she had, saying the witness was lying. And then, finally, when she realizes we're not gonna book her, she really breaks down and starts saying she'd put a spell on the guy who did it, or something to that effect. Oh, I remember. She said she was poisonous. We asked her if she wanted us to call her husband to come get her, she said she didn't. Then she said she wanted you.''

"Where is Mrs. Wade now?"

"Downstairs."

"Will you take me to her?"

"Sure. Look, I don't want to tell you your business, doc, but don't you think this lady should be in some hospital somewhere, one of those nice places up in Connecticut? Money enough there, all right, since she's a Gardner.''

He led David down a flight of stairs at the back of the building, then through a long hall with rooms on either side, closed doors.

"She's in this one," he said, stopping in front of the second door on the left. He put his hand on the knob, but turned back. "There's one thing I maybe should have mentioned.''

"What's that?"

The sergeant let go of the knob. "Well, it's the thing that really got us going when she first confessed. Really thought we had a suspect. Murder two, maybe one. Would have been a lucky break. Course, witness or not, Culligan's not convinced the Wade woman isn't involved somehow. He says—''

''What *was* it that got you going, sergeant?''

''Well, Mrs. Wade knew something about the murder. It had to do with how many wounds there were, a detail we deliberately held back from the press. Sometimes we do that.''

''So I've heard. How many were there?''

''Ten. Vertical on the face. Parallel. Coroner says it reminds him as if an animal had clawed her with all ten claws. Only, most of the wounds are pretty neat. Like a surgeon might of done it. Had to be some psychopath to do that kind of thing—get a woman down and take the time to make ten neat slashes, right there on an open street corner, where anyone could of come along. Course, I don't suppose the killer would have been counting, do you?''

2   Laura Wade was sitting alone in the small room, arms folded on the table, hands clenched into white-knuckled fists. She was sitting up very straight, perfectly still, staring at the wall.

''Dr. Goldman is here for you, Mrs. Wade,'' Ammonetti said, speaking from the doorway.

David stepped around the sergeant and into the room.

''Laura?''

She wiped her eyes before she turned to look at him.

"I'm sorry for having them call you, Dr. Goldman. I didn't know what to do. I'm all right now. Really."

He took a good look at her. Her lips and her eyes were a little swollen from crying, but she had obviously repaired her makeup. Lipstick. Blush. Mascara. Even eye shadow. Her hair was cut and styled in one of those fashionably layered cuts, and her outfit was simple but very expensive. Slim, pleated slacks and a matching sleeveless shirt and jacket, which was hung over the back of the chair. All pink linen.

She looked to be in top shape, the kind of shape a woman in her thirties has to work for. Her arms were well-muscled and smooth. Her purse was sitting on the table, pink snakeskin, with pastel patches. It struck David as odd that a woman upset enough to do such a thing would look so . . . well, *groomed.* Even her nails were perfectly manicured, not long but filed round and painted with a mauve polish.

She collected the jacket, stepped out from behind the table.

"Really, Dr. Goldman, I'm all right now. I do appreciate you coming here. You needn't have."

"Why did you tell them to call me, Laura?"

She glanced at Ammonetti, who was still standing in the doorway.

"I don't know. I was pretty upset. I couldn't think of anyone else to call."

"Your husband?"

"I could have, I guess. But after I thought about it a while, I realized I didn't want him to know." Her eyes started to fill up with tears. He saw a struggle for control.

"All right, Laura, why don't we go back to my office, where we can talk?" David looked at Ammonetti, who shrugged.

"She's free to go."

"No, really," Laura Wade said. "I'll be fine. I'll just go home, I guess."

He looked at her. Could he just let her go this way?

"Why did you confess, Laura?"

"Because I'm guilty. I killed her."

"When did you kill her?"

"Two weeks ago."

"Not last night?"

"It doesn't matter when she actually died. It only matters that I killed her."

She was staring at him, eyes hard, dark. Her irises were brown—almost black. She was a beautiful woman, in the modern style: tall and thin, long-limbed, wide shoulders, small breasts, narrow hips for a woman so tall. And very dark, olive skin, dark hair.

Suddenly she said, "I'm a mutation, doctor."

"What?"

"You know. Like a blue lobster."

"I don't understand, Laura."

She sighed. "Mutation. A sudden genetic alteration from the parent species. I was born with an extra set of senses. I hear what people are thinking."

David heard the police sergeant make a movement behind him. "What are we thinking?"

"*He's* thinking I'm a nut. Not that I blame him. I really did get pretty upset before. I'm sorry about that." She looked away. "And you . . . well, you're trying to come up with a diagnosis. You've never heard anyone say they were a mutation before. That's what you're thinking."

She was right. Once, back in his residency, there was a schizophrenic who said he was an alien, but no, David had never come across a mutation delusion.

"Well, now you've heard it," she said. "Here it is.

I have an extra set of eyes, and ears. I see things no one else sees. I know things other people don't. And now I have the power of life and death in my mind.''

There were tears spilling down her face now.

"Come with me, Laura," David said.

She closed her eyes for a moment, took a deep, prolonged breath. Then she opened them and nodded assent, wiping her eyes.

David put his arm on her shoulder and led her up the stairs, with Ammonetti trailing behind.

It took almost twenty minutes to find a cab in the rush-hour traffic, another half hour to cross town. Laura was silent in the taxi, and it was nearly five-thirty before David got her back to his office.

She glanced around for a moment, still silent, before she took a seat in the tweed chair across from his desk. He remembered that she'd tolerated a very long silence the other time, too. It had surprised him, since it was always his experience that new patients, especially women, had a little opening speech prepared, which might or might not have any bearing on their problems. He pulled up another chair, sat across from her.

She was still staring at him, looking at him with such intensity that he was taken aback. *That* was what had bothered him—the way she looked at him. Also, he remembered, her looks had bothered him, too. Close up, her features seemed oddly disparate, as if they might have come from different faces: the jaw firm and wide; the nose long, maybe too long, but straight; the lips carved, almost thin; the eyes with a slight upward slant, almost Oriental.

She still had not broken her gaze. Most patients,

most people, couldn't look at you so directly for so long.

"Why *did* you call me?" he said finally. "You never came back after the consultation."

"I hope you weren't offended that I didn't come back. You're very intelligent, you seemed very caring, very compassionate . . ."

"But you didn't think I could help?"

"It wasn't that, exactly. It was . . . well, as the session went on, I realized that to go on with you would mean I'd had to, well, tell you certain things about myself. In real life it's easy enough to keep from talking about yourself, or at least from revealing yourself—but in a psychiatrist's office, what else are you going to talk about?"

David had to smile. "And you were afraid to look inside?"

"No. That's not it at all. I've always been very . . . self-aware." She looked away for a moment. "I guess I realized I didn't want to talk about certain things because I knew you wouldn't believe me. I guess I've always thought it best to keep it all to myself."

"About being a mutation?"

Silence.

"Do you mean you feel there's something terrible inside you?" It was a guess, a pretty good one under the circumstances.

Silence.

"Lots of people think there's something terrible inside them, Laura. That there's something wrong with them, that they're not normal, even that they're evil. But what's inside is good, not evil. You have to find the courage—"

"Courage? Believe me, doctor, you don't know anything about courage.'' Tears started spilling down her face again.

''Why do you say that, Laura?''

She looked at him, drew herself up in the chair again the way she'd been sitting in the police station when he came in. Dignified. Stoic.

''My pain is my own, doctor. It always has been.'' She stood up and went over to the wall by the window that faced Seventy-fourth Street, leaned against it. ''I'll *give* you the diagnosis, not that I understand it. I never have. But I was born with certain extraordinary powers, powers of prescience, and sense and control, and feeling and cause. It's very hard to describe. I guess you could say I have second sight, but it's so different from what you read about—far stronger. Most of those people you read about are fakes. They used to be ladies with hoop earrings who told you to look for a stranger; nowadays they're more likely to be trans-channelers. Sometimes you get a person who occasionally gets *flashes* of the sixth sense, who may *sense* current and crosscurrent. But even then, they get involved in these media circuses and they're forced to perform on cue and they end up faking, after all.''

''But you're not a fake?''

''No,'' she said. ''I'm the genuine article. My dreams have often predicted the future. I hear things no one else hears—''

''Voices?''

She scowled. ''Not the kind of voices you're thinking about. It's more like other people's inner voices.''

''What do they say?''

''The things people don't say aloud.''

''Like what?''

''It's almost like pre-thoughts. The thoughts people screen out before they speak. So that they won't hurt someone's feelings, or because saying what they're really thinking is inappropriate in a particular situation.''

''Do people think bad things about you?''

''Don't look for paranoia, doctor. I'd say most people tend to think my motives are suspect. I do make an effort to be even-tempered in my dealings with people. Of course, I have an advantage since I'm privy to their thoughts. Not that other people's thoughts aren't difficult to interpret. I mean, inner thoughts—people's motivations—can be *very* stark, even horrifying, because they're uncensored. And, of course, everyone's psychological makeup is different, you know what I mean?''

Christ! How could he have missed this?

''And this is what you didn't want to tell me back then?''

She looked at him for a moment, then turned away, inhaling a deep breath, nearly shivering with the effort to keep from crying again. He went over and put his hand on her shoulder.

''Laura, let me help you.''

She looked at him, crossing her bare arms over her chest, huddling in, as if an arctic chill had invaded the room—then stood up straight again, her nostrils flaring slightly, looking away.

''You can't help me, doctor. No one can help me.''

''I can try, Laura.''

''Maybe six months ago you could have helped me . . . I don't know, live with it better. But everything's different now. It's too late. Believe me, Dr. Goldman, you don't know what you've got here.''

''What is it you're trying to tell me, Laura?''

Her eyes were filling up.

''I guess maybe it *was* the thing I was afraid of then,

to *really* look inside. You see, I'm reverting, changing, my structure is altering. My genes, my chromosomes, or something. It's all changing somehow.''

"Into what?"

She was crying in earnest now, so hard that it took an effort to understand what she was saying.

"It never used to be this way. I used to predict. I could never *cause* things before. My God! It's all out of control. I feel it inside. And it's growing. I'm afraid to think, I'm afraid to feel, I'm afraid to be.''

"Laura. Tell me what happens.''

She wiped her eyes. "I *try* to hold in my anger. Because now, sometimes horrible things happen when I get angry.''

Obviously, she didn't feel entitled to her feelings, specifically her anger. Very common in women, though of course not to this extreme. The delusion had developed perhaps as self-punishment for having inappropriate or unwanted emotions, emotions she couldn't deal with, had always repressed. Ladies didn't *get* angry. And if they did, they didn't express their anger. And if they did express it, they were truly evil, therefore responsible for bad things that happen to the target of their anger. Circular reasoning. Psychotic reasoning. The kind of reasoning it was difficult to poke holes in without some real work.

"You think I'm psychotic, don't you?''

"What do *you* think, Laura?''

She shrugged. "I suppose it sounds like some kind of crazy delusion. I mean, thoughts don't make things happen, right? The world doesn't operate this way. To me, of course, the truth is apparent. But, then, that's what makes a delusion, isn't it? That the person who has it doesn't think it's a delusion. Isn't that right, doctor?''

It was a pretty goddammned lucid statement for a woman as delusional as this one. She'd apparently had at least some form of these beliefs all her life. Yet she'd also managed to function. Got married. Had children. Came in six months ago and spoke reasonably, even thoughtfully, about her life.

"Yes, that's right," David said softly.

"Fine," she said. "Then listen to this, and you just tell me, doctor. Tell me what *you* would think if this happened to you. Two weeks ago my husband and I had a dinner party. Five couples, acquaintances from Easterbrook. I seated Rita Harmon next to Zach—that's my husband—and she was, well, coming on to him."

"Was she having an affair with him, like you told the police?"

"Probably not."

"But you suspected."

"No. I made that up."

"Why?"

"Well, it wouldn't have been very logical to go in there and tell the truth. They wouldn't have believed me, and I wouldn't have gotten what I wanted. An affair seemed like a good motive. I guess I wasn't thinking too straight. Anyway, Zach isn't the type to have an affair. At least I don't think he is. He's very involved with the business. My father made him president when he retired. He's expanded it, and he's building a new store already, up in Boston. And in the free time he has he plays tennis, or exercises, or is with the kids—he's a devoted father. Of course, he travels all over the world, so he certainly *could* have affairs."

"Would it bother you if he did?"

"Of course. I love my husband."

"And he loves you?"

"Yes. I think he loves me very much. Maybe too much."

"Let's go back to the dinner party for a moment. What happened?"

"She kept on flirting with him."

"Was he responding?"

"Not really. He was just being polite. But I couldn't help it. I got so angry. My God, when I think about it, it could just as easily have been *him* I had the thought about. Or my children. Don't you see? It's a danger to know me."

He couldn't let her go off on another tangent.

"What happened at the dinner party?"

"I went into the kitchen and tried to calm down, but then I had to go back. I have to *act* normal, you see. I've always been very good at it. But now I can't seem to act anymore."

She buried her face in her hands for a moment, then rubbed her temples, massaged them, as if she were in terrible pain.

"Oh, God, I never meant to really hurt her. But once I have the thought, I can't take it back. It gets out—like a gas, like a poison."

"What was the thought, Laura?"

"Well, I looked down at the table, at my hands. I had red nail polish on. It reminded me of blood, blood on the white tablecloth. And I thought of scratching at her face, like an animal would. Or a demon."

"I see."

"Then, when I read about it in the morning paper today—multiple cuts to the face, and that it was Rita Harmon . . ."

It was certainly something of a coincidence, assuming the dinner party or her "thought" had actually taken place.

"Of course," she said, "when I heard the name, I *knew* it had happened again."

"What happened, Laura? A witness saw a *man* commit this murder."

She stopped crying and just stared at him. "You don't understand," she said finally. "Now do you see why I'm so alone? Who would believe me? I sound like a lunatic. Still, murderers deserve to be punished, don't they? So I confessed."

"Do you *remember* killing this woman, Laura?"

"Of course not. I've never been able to stomach violence, of any kind. I went to the movies last night."

"What did you see?"

She shrugged. "Oh, some film about a secretary who changes places with her boss."

"Laura," he said, "there was a witness who saw the whole thing. She said a man did it."

"Maybe she's lying."

"In which case you may have stabbed the woman and just not be remembering it?"

"No. She isn't lying. It probably was a man. But don't you see, it doesn't matter who actually *did* it? What matters is that my thought caused it."

"Couldn't your thought and the murder just be a coincidence?"

"I abandoned that explanation long ago," she said, scowling. "Maybe a few months ago I would have thought it was another precognitive vision. I've always managed to live with the precognitive visions, with the dreams, with other people's thoughts in my head. Well, maybe I haven't managed according to your standards, but I managed. Once or twice I've saved someone's life. It's not much, considering the scope of my powers, but it's something. But now that I've changed, I don't know how I'm going to go on. The things that happen now are different, they're more from . . . inside me. You know, my *own* pre-thoughts.''

"Manifestations of your anger?"

"I guess so. Or maybe it's just my perception that's different."

"Are you saying you somehow put a hex out or something?"

"I just don't know. I have never pretended to understand my powers. How they work, why they work. Even as a child, I used to wonder which part of my body my extra senses came from. It's not like I have an extra set of eyes, or something that you can see in a physical examination. To the eye, my body looks pretty normal. Too tall, maybe. Maybe too skinny. And my face is, well, strange-looking. But overall, it's pretty normal. Of course, once I'm finished altering in this way I'm going now, I could end up looking like God-knows-what.''

David wasn't at all surprised at this description of her body. He wouldn't even have been surprised if she told him her body was rotting. The woman was clearly and seriously delusional, possibly schizophrenic. The grandiose delusions of power and evil, even the claims that she was poisonous, were characteristic. He had to decide what to do.

He asked her if she wanted to be hospitalized. She looked at him as if he'd suggested sending her to the moon.

"It doesn't matter where you put me. Poison seeps through walls." She stopped. "You can't force me to go into the hospital, can you? I have to go home. I have children. I have things to do for my children, I have a meeting on a charity event tomorrow. Tuesday I have a tennis game—God, if I stand up those women again this week, they'll know something's wrong with me. No one can know." She grabbed his arm. "You won't force me, will you?"

"Of course not, Laura. I'd like you to come and see me. We can start you on some medication—"

"You mean one of the psychotropics? Thorazine? Prolixin? Haldol?"

Psychotropics?

"Laura, have you taken this kind of medication before?"

"I've never told a soul about this, certainly not a doctor. Oh, except when I got pretty hysterical after the police said I was free to go, I may have screamed something about it. But they thought I was a nut. You think I'm a nut, too."

"Nut isn't a word I would use, Laura. I think you probably are suffering from some form of schizophrenia. It's a *disease,* a chemical imbalance, not some terrible shameful thing. We can treat it, Laura. There are new drugs. We've made tremendous advances—"

"Magic pills won't help me, doctor. You want proof, I'll give you proof. You were just thinking that you were surprised I know the word 'psychotropic.' Right?"

He looked at her.

"Don't be surprised, doctor. I've read a lot of things in my life. Psychology books. Parapsychology. Medical dictionaries. All kinds of things."

It was a *very* disconcerting habit she had, to make guesses about what he was thinking and be *right!*

"Do you always try to guess what people are thinking and answer their questions before they ask them?"

"No. I keep my knowledge to myself."

"Why are you doing it with me?"

She hesitated a moment, then said, "Well, I've told

you everything, anyway. Why not prove it to you? In a way, it feels good to finally tell someone.''

"You've never had yourself tested, then? In a parapsychology lab?''

"I've thought about it many times. I know there's one close by—in New Jersey, the Rockman Institute— and once I came pretty close to calling them. Then I thought, 'Why should I?' I've never liked being on display. And then, I've always thought I should have been able to . . . well, that there should be some *purpose* to it all, that I should be worthy of it. But how can I be worthy if I have the same petty emotions, the same jealousies, the same everything as all the rest of people? And now . . . God, if all this was destined to happen, why was I given reproductive organs? I have children, for God's sake. Three children. What about *them*?''

"Can you demonstrate your powers for me, Laura? Make me stand up and turn circles, something like that?''

"The powers that have always been with me I can demonstrate.'' She looked at him. "Like right now I hear you thinking that for a person to be this delusional she should be a lot less logical.''

It was pretty goddamned close. Of course, she could have guessed it. She was obviously well read on the subject.

"How about your ability to cause events in the real world?''

"I *did*, didn't I? I'm here, aren't I? I told you about my vision.''

"You told me *after* the fact, Laura.''

"Yes. I suppose that's true. I guess you'd have to know me a longer time to get the sequence of events—''

"I'm a good psychiatrist, Laura."

"You'd have to be a miracle worker to help me. Maybe even a god."

"Miracles are not my business, Laura. Let's start with what *is*. There are psychological explanations for the sequence of events as you've described them, this murder you've confessed to. Think about it. Maybe you had the anger then, at the dinner party, but only thought you'd had the specific vision *after* you heard about it on the news. The mind can make funny associations like that, can trick us. Or maybe you feel guilty about having such an angry thought, no matter what the specific content of the thought."

"Believe me, I wish that were it," she said. *"I'd rather be crazy* than the monster I've become."

"Getting angry doesn't make you a monster, Laura. Why do you think you aren't allowed to have your emotions?"

"How can I be *allowed* if people die when I have them? Dead is dead."

The argument was completely round. He'd been up against round ones before.

She was staring at him. "You're thinking about finding the tear in the loop of my argument, right? Something that will break down the delusion."

For Christ's sake, it was *exactly* what he was thinking.

"You can't," she said. "And now that it's all changed . . . You see, that's the horror of it, I never know when, or which thought is going to make something happen. I'm afraid to think *anything* negative. You know what I mean?"

"I want to help you, Laura."

"I know you do," she said softly.

"All right, then, why don't we make up an appointment schedule, let's say three times a week to begin. I have a few hours free now. And we can explore some of these feelings; we can begin to sort some of this out. Would you like to do that, Laura?''

She studied him for a moment; then a light shudder passed through her body, delicate as a cat's whisker. She stood up. "I guess I owe you that."

"You owe it to yourself, Laura."

"Do I?" she said. "No. You only *think* I do."

3 Detective Henry Culligan didn't like coincidences, and this one was a whopper. Twenty-five years a cop, and he'd never heard of a case where an ordinary confessor had described a murder so accurately.

Rita Harmon had been slit across the throat, nearly ear to ear—that was the wound that killed her. That much Culligan had known last night, at the scene. The rest of the wounds were all icing. Ten razor-thin cuts on the face, all superficial. Vertical. "I know this is wild, Henry," Pat Carle had said that morning on the phone, "but you know what it reminds me of? Animal claws. All ten of 'em."

And Laura Wade knew, described those ten wounds perfectly. Even said it looked like claws. Mother of Christ! Only six people, tops, knew the number of wounds on Rita Harmon's face. Jones; Compton; Pat Carle and Ed Reilly, of the Medical Examiner's office; Ammonetti, McGee and Donaldson. Culligan had also mentioned it to Betty, who called him around lunchtime to remind him to pick up pastries at Dalworth's Bakery near the precinct. Not even DeWitt and Dennis, who'd gotten to the scene first, knew. There was too much blood at the scene to count wounds. The woman hardly even had a face anymore. It was only this morning, after Carle had a chance to look her over in the morgue, that he'd told Culligan.

And yet the witness said the killer was a man.

"Okay, Lilly, let's go over it one more time."

Lilly Dunleavy shifted slightly in the chair across from Culligan's desk, adjusted her skirt. Culligan watched her silently for a moment, waiting. He was an extremely large man, tall and bulky, with a drooping mustache and aviator glasses, and he was well aware of the effect his formidable presence and continued interrogation—nearly two hours of questions—were having on the girl. She still looked pretty shaken, just as she had when he'd spotted her last night, at the scene.

She'd been leaning against the side of the building, just outside the cordoned-off area west of Twenty-ninth and Seventh, young, frightened, pale as dough. Onlookers after the fact were either horrified or merely curious; Lilly Dunleavy had been terrified. Yes, he'd noticed her standing there, but after he'd made his way into the fray—past the gathering crowd, into the huddle of uniforms and the glare of lights to inspect the carnage on the street and listen to the tale of the man who had found the body—he'd looked up and Lilly was gone.

"Lilly?"

The girl looked up at him.

"All right, let's go back. Now, what were you doing at the window?"

She sighed. It was the third time she'd gone over it.

"I was working late. I got up to stretch my legs. I happened to look down at the sidewalk—"

"What time was that?"

"Eight-seventeen."

"You told me you looked at the clock. Is that right?"

"Yes. As I got up from the chair, I was thinking about finishing the report. I wanted to go home."

"What kind of clock is it?"

"I don't know."

"I mean is it a digital clock?"

"Yes."

"Okay, so you looked down at the sidewalk at eight-seventeen. What did you see?"

She hesitated a moment. "I . . . I saw him killing her."

"What were the positions of the people you saw?"

"He was . . . like, straddling her—"

"So when you looked down, he already had her down on the sidewalk. Is that right?"

"Yes."

"And how long did the whole thing last?"

"I already told you. It was like a dream. I don't really know how long."

"Guess."

"A minute or two."

"What did the weapon look like?"

"Shiny. A knife."

"Big or small?"

"It didn't seem big."

"Okay, Lilly, while this was going on, did you look anywhere else? Did you see any activity on the street?"

"No. I kept looking at them, and I was banging on the window."

Culligan lit a cigarette, stood up and walked over to the far side of his office. Damn. There had to be something *useful* the witness remembered. Culligan could see Compton sitting at his desk just outside the office. From the look on the man's face it was obvious that he didn't have anything. A whole day talking to the shop owners, restaurateurs in a three-block area around the murder, people on the street. Where the hell had the perp gone? He had to be covered with blood. A man comes running by, wearing or carrying a bloody coat, ski mask, and nobody sees anything?"

"Lilly, were there cars parked on the street?"

"I guess so. Yes. They were parked all along the sides."

"Both sides?"

"Yes."

"Any empty spaces?"

"I don't know."

"Anyone double-parked?"

"I didn't notice."

"Think, Lilly. Even the most minute detail might be important."

She shook her head. "I just can't remember anything else. I was scared."

"Okay, what happened then?"

"I told you. He s-stopped. And he stood up. And he started walking toward Eighth."

"And you watched him go around the corner?"

"No. I told you. He looked up at me for a minute. And then he walked on."

The arrogant son-of-a-bitch. "Didn't you think it odd that he simply walked away after he'd done this thing?"

"I wasn't thinking about that. I was thinking that he saw me."

"But you didn't watch him after he passed on?"

"No."

"So you just assumed he turned the corner. You didn't see him do it?"

"Yes, I guess."

"What were you looking at while he was going around the corner?"

"I was looking at her."

Culligan took a drag on his cigarette. "Why didn't you come over and tell us last night, Lilly?"

Lilly ran her fingertips through her hair, flattening it against the top of her skull. "By the time I got to the street, there was already a crowd. And you were all there. All the lights and everything. I was scared. I went home, like I told you. I just ran and got on the train."

Poor kid. Not even twenty-one years old. Fresh out of high school. Culligan's own daughter probably would have done the same thing.

Lilly Dunleavy crossed her arms over her chest and looked at him. A serious look. "I'm afraid, detective."

"I know you are, Lilly. But you didn't see the guy's face. He was wearing a mask. It's not like you can identify him. Right?"

She shrugged. "Yes, but he's crazy. Maybe he doesn't realize I can't identify him."

"Lilly, even if he did see your face, it was only a face."

"I know, but still, he *saw* me. He knows where my office is. I can tell you one thing, I'm never going back there. But what if he . . . I don't know, looks through the records and finds me after I get a new job?"

Culligan told her that he was hardly likely to go to the trouble to look up records of a witness who couldn't identify him. Lilly was not reassured.

Neither was he. In fact, Culligan didn't know much of anything about this guy and what he might go to the trouble of doing. Nor even that it *was* a guy.

He looked at the girl in front of him. Maybe he'd acted hastily, letting Laura Wade go so easily. Maybe Laura Wade just changed her mind, suddenly got scared and started acting like a crazy woman to throw him off the track. After all, it was a whole different number thinking about confessing and actually being in a police station. Just maybe when she realized they were going to actually book her, she tried to get out of it by making up a story so they would think she was crazy. On the other hand, why had she sounded so sane before they told her a witness had come in saying it had been a man, and only freaked out *after* they told her she was free to go?

"All right, Lilly," Culligan said, stubbing his cigarette out in the ashtray on his desk, "I want you to think. From your position in the window could you guess how tall the person was?"

"It was hard to tell. I was so far away."

"Guess."

"I don't know. Five-ten maybe."

Laura Wade was tall, maybe even five-ten.

"Lilly, what made you think the killer was a man?"

She stared at him.

"If he was wearing a ski mask, how could you tell if it was a man or a woman?"

"I guess because he was wearing men's clothes."

"Describe the clothes again."

"Dark pants. Jeans, I think. A short black jacket. I don't know. It was dark."

"What about shoes?"

"I don't know."

"Was he big shouldered, like me?"

"Not really.

"How about the way he walked? Was that like a man?"

"Is there a difference?"

"Show me how he walked."

She got up from the chair, went over to the other side of the office, by the file cabinet, and began walking across the room. It was a brisk walk, but definitely not a run. It could not be characterized as either male or female.

Lilly stopped at the other end of the office.

"So you just assumed it was a man, then," Culligan said. "Why?"

"A woman couldn't do that."

"*Could* it have been a woman, Lilly?"

Lilly Dunleavy's eyes flooded with tears.

"I don't know, detective," she said. "Maybe."

"Thank you, Lilly," he said. "You can go now."

Culligan picked up the coroner's preliminary report from the corner of his desk, glanced at it for what seemed like the hundredth time. Female. Death apparently caused by a single knife wound across the throat, which severed the artery.

He could still picture that woman lying there on the sidewalk, all dressed up in her black patent leather shoes and her green silk cocktail dress with the puffed crinoline skirt. It was low-necked, that dress, torn at one sleeve, covered with blood. The expanse of neckline, stained red, revealed the tips of the woman's breasts. All dressed up for an evening out with her husband at St. Germain. All dressed up in her finery, with her diamond-encrusted gold bracelet. The stones had shimmered in the glare of police lights. All dressed up, and the fucker nearly sliced her face off.

Culligan glanced back at the report. "Additional wounds . . ."

Pat Carle had thought it was a mugging, a random thing, but he was wrong. That had been Culligan's own initial reaction, too, but not for long. What kind of street mugger did that to a woman, then left her lying there with her purse full of credit cards beside her, not to mention the sixty-seven dollars and change in the wallet, or the diamond bracelet Jones had had appraised at nearly three thousand dollars? No, this one was a true psychopath, maybe at the start of a series. Probably got his rocks off on the blood. No sign of sexual assault, though. In fact, except for a few bruises, the body was remarkably clean. Except for the face. Culligan could still see Carle kneeling over the body: "Christ, Henry, these guys are getting mean."

"These guys" had always been mean. But Carle wasn't a detective, he was a doctor, and green to boot, a transfer last year from Brooklyn North: "these guys" could not, did not, mean ordinary muggers.

The phone was ringing. Culligan tossed the report on the corner of his desk and picked up the receiver.

"Henry, it's Eric." He heard Detective Jones's familiar nasal twang. "We found the car."

"Where?"

"At the West Side tow dock. It had been parked on Forty-ninth and Lex. Last night, when she parked it, it was legal. They towed it away this morning."

Which explained why they hadn't spotted the car in any of the garages around St. Germain. Culligan had been there once, with his wife, for her birthday, a celebration that had set him back a hundred bucks. Place was for Wall Street types, interior decorators, rich folks who enjoyed paying fourteen bucks for three stalks of asparagus arranged artfully on the plate. So what the hell was Rita Harmon doing over on Twenty-ninth and Seventh, with her car parked at Forty-ninth and Lex and the restaurant even further downtown?

"Henry? What the hell was she doing over there?"

"Yeah, Eric. I was just thinking about that."

"Maybe she had some kind of errand?"

"Her husband said definitely not. She was due at the restaurant at seven-thirty." Culligan had talked to the victim's husband, George Harmon, at ten o'clock last night, in the morgue. God, he hated that part of the job. He thought the man was going to have a heart attack when he had to look at his wife, to confirm the identification. The poor guy had waited at the restaurant until eight-thirty before calling home and finding she'd left hours before, then called the police at nine. It wasn't until ten o'clock that someone at headquarters made the connection.

"Why don't you check around the area where the car was, Eric," Culligan said. "See if anyone saw anything there."

"McGee's already on it."

"Good."

"I think the guy knew her, Henry."

"Why?"

"I think he got her as she parked her car, and convinced her to get into his car, then drove across town to do it."

"Why would she get in the guy's car if she was supposed to be meeting her husband?"

Jones hesitated a moment. "I don't know. Maybe it's a lover. Making demands."

"Yeah. Or maybe a guy put a knife to her throat and insisted."

4 It was getting dark in the office now, as the sun set. David flipped on the desk lamp, altering the configuration of shadows on the walls, illuminating Laura Wade's face.

"Are you going to give me the magic pills now?" she asked.

He looked at her. Schizophrenia was a very tricky disorder, both to diagnose and to treat. There were many organic conditions capable of producing delusions and hallucinations that mimic schizophrenia, which meant the diagnosis was often a process of ruling out. The phenothiazines used to treat the disease were very serious medications with serious side effects, including the bizarre muscular disfigurement known as tardive dyskinesia, which would be devastating in her particular case.

"In order to give you precisely the right medication," David said, "I want to wait until more facts are in. I'm going to schedule a battery of physical and psychological tests for you. Personality tests, IQ—"

"I do pretty well on IQ tests."

"When was the last time you took one?"

She shrugged. "Back in grade school, I guess."

"We'll get a current score, okay?"

"Fine."

"And there'll be some physical tests, blood work, a CAT scan."

"Believe me, doctor, you can get all the facts you want. You still won't know what to do with me."

"Why don't we wait and see?"

"All right. I guess I'll go now." Tears again.

"Laura, how did you get here from Connecticut?"

She thought a minute. "I took the train. It was quite a ride. The man sitting next to me got up and changed his seat."

"I think you should have your husband come pick you up."

"No. I'll be all right."

He looked at her. She was clearly not all right. Obviously, she wanted condemnation, punishment. But she hadn't gotten what she wanted. Would she punish herself?

"Laura, do you ever think about suicide?"

She went over to the window, looked out for a moment, then turned back to him. "Yes."

"How often?"

She laughed. "Three thousand four hundred and sixty-one times a day. I have to get my daily dose of suicidal thoughts or I'm a wreck in the morning."

At last, a response. The first blatant sign of bitterness he'd seen.

"Laura, I'm trying to help you."

"You are *trying* to save me."

"All right then, I'm trying to save you."

"Why?"

"Because I think you're worth saving."

"Why?"

"Because you seem like an intelligent, warm and thoughtful human being. Because you have three children and a husband who loves you and a mother and father, a brother and sister. And friends.''

"I have one friend," she said, frowning. "It would be better to save all of *them.*"

No. Schizophrenia wasn't quite right here—perhaps he should start her on an antidepressant. This particular delusion . . . there was definitely an affective component, a severe depressive component. Of course, prescribing an antidepressant for a schizophrenic could make the symptoms worse. . . . Maybe he should force the issue of hospitalization.

"How often do you think about suicide, Laura?"

She ran her fingers along the broad leaf of the corn plant he kept by the window. "You really should dust these things, you know."

"How often?"

"If I decide to commit suicide, doctor," she said, "it will be because *I* decide. You could restrain me in a straitjacket and force me to a hospital, you could have me put on full-time watch—it wouldn't make any difference. If I decide, I decide."

She came over and sat across from him.

"Is that what you've decided?"

She thought about it a moment, then said, "No. This morning, maybe. But now, well, I'm not prepared to give up yet. I still believe there's some purpose to my life."

"I'm going to help you see that there is a purpose, Laura, that you don't *want* to end your life—because it's good, because it's worth living. That you are not some evil person who can propel your poison into the world. What do you think about that?" He wished he were as convinced as he sounded.

She laughed. "You know what? I hope you can. I really do."

A better response than he'd hoped for.

On that semiupbeat note—which did not in any way convince him that he was doing the right thing—he took a look at his appointment calendar. He had several free hours, including the two left open by Allen Davino, who'd informed him that he didn't need to come anymore, which he did; and the one left by Sue Weingarten, whose termination was a mutual decision David felt good about. (He had told Sue months ago that they should look toward an end, but she kept saying she liked coming in and talking to him, which was a nice compliment, but one hundred and twenty dollars an hour seemed like highway robbery if they were going to discuss movies, books and the situation in South Africa.)

So that left Tuesday morning, Wednesday and Friday afternoons. He told her he would try to schedule tests for the following day, then wrote out an appointment schedule, listing his home phone number.

"You can call me if you need me, at home, any time, night or day." He handed the paper to her. "And I want you to call me tomorrow and tell me how you're feeling, and then I'll see you on Friday. Now, how will you get into the city?"

She dropped the card into her purse. "I know how to drive, doctor. I've been doing it since I was sixteen."

"Perhaps it would be easier for you if you saw someone up in Connecticut. I could refer you—"

"No. I'm not about to tell anyone there about any of this. I'm going to go on with my life. Such as it is."

He thought: And when she decided "it" had happened again, what then?

Christ. She was crying. At least someone in her

family needed to be alerted to the situation. Patient confidentiality notwithstanding, David usually informed the family in the case of a severe disorder.

"Where's your husband's office, Laura?"

"Executive offices are downtown. But I don't want him to know."

"Why not?"

She took a cigarette out of her purse, and lit it with an engraved gold and tortoiseshell lighter. "I hope you don't mind."

Cigarette-smoking patients were an occupational hazard. He told her he didn't.

She took a long, deep drag, blew the smoke up in the air. "I could have his chauffeur come and get me. Would that satisfy you?"

"No."

She slumped into the chair. "That's a stupid idea, anyway. Go ahead. Call him."

"Would you rather call him?"

"No."

"What's the number?"

He jotted the number she gave him on his pad.

"He'll answer himself," she said. "That's his private number." She sat back in the chair with her cigarette and watched as he dialed.

Two rings.

"Zach Wade." The voice was deep, resonant.

"Mr. Wade, my name is David Goldman. I'm a doctor here in Manhattan and I have Laura here—"

"Is she all right?"

"Yes, she's fine. I'm a psychiatrist, Mr. Wade. I'd like you to come here to my office to get her."

"Come where?"

"I'm up on the West Side." David gave him the address.

"If I may ask, doctor, what is Laura doing in your office?"

"I'll explain it to you when you get here."

"Tell me now."

"Well, your wife is . . . in the midst of a crisis. She doesn't want to go into a hospital, but you should be aware of—"

"Mind telling me what you're talking about, doctor? My wife is perfectly fine. That is, she was fine when I last saw her."

"Well, Laura's behavior and thought patterns appear to be somewhat delusional—"

"Delusional? What the hell are you talking about? How did she get to you?"

"I'd prefer to discuss it—"

"I'd like to know before I come up there."

"Mr. Wade, your wife walked into the police station this afternoon and confessed to a murder."

Silence. "A murder? Doctor, are you sure you're talking about my wife? My wife wouldn't kill a roach. She doesn't even like to read a good crime novel, can't stand a movie where anyone gets killed, has never once so much as smacked any of our children. Violence is not my wife's thing, as they say. She's as timid as a cat."

Was a cat timid? "I didn't say she committed the murder, I just said she confessed."

"That's the most ridiculous thing I've ever heard. Is this a practical joke?"

"I assure you, Mr. Wade, it's no joke."

"All right, then, please explain it to me."

"Well, your wife believes she has certain . . . thought transference powers. It's really rather difficult to explain on the phone. I haven't precisely made a diagnosis yet, but she's going to need your help, your support—''

"I'll be right there."

He hung up. David put down the receiver and looked at her. "He'll be here in a few minutes."

"Was he angry?"

"What makes you think he would be angry?"

"No reason."

"Do you think anger would be an appropriate reaction, Laura?"

Suddenly she started to laugh—hard, loud, long. Inappropriate affect. More evidence for a diagnosis. Maybe she had no idea what an appropriate reaction *would* be, either in herself or in anyone else.

Her laughter stopped as suddenly as it had begun. "People should go with their anger, right?"

He looked at her; she was crying again. He reached out, put his hand on her shoulder. She pulled away, stood up, moved toward the sofa.

"Don't touch me. It's dangerous to touch me."

"No, it isn't, Laura. But if you don't want me to touch you, I won't."

She sat down, settled into the corner of the sofa.

"I feel very tired, Dr. Goldman."

She closed her eyes, and as she did she seemed to get smaller, darker. Very soon, she was sleeping.

He watched her for a moment, then went into the outer office to listen to his messages, closing the door softly behind him. There were six: the two from Ammonetti, one from a patient named Al Dunhill, who wanted advice on a new job he'd been offered; two from patients canceling appointments, and one from Allison.

He heard his ex-wife's small breathy voice: "David, I didn't know what to do. I was here getting the rest of my things when that police sergeant called. He said it was important, so I gave him your private number." And then, more like herself: "So you're in trouble with the police now?"

He wondered if the "rest of her things" included the parrot she refused to take when she left. They'd bought the parrot on a trip to Brazil six years ago. He thought spending six hundred dollars on a bird was ridiculous, but Allison really wanted it, and it was one of the up periods in their marriage, when they were both trying hard to respect each other's different approaches to life.

He was going to respect her BMW and her need to party on the weekends, and she was going to respect his seriousness (David had never thought he was so serious) and what she called his parsimony. David never understood the need to spend $40,000 on a car, even if you could afford it. And he didn't agree that he was a workaholic, either. It was true, he did care about his patients more than eight or ten hours a day. But spiritual stinginess had always struck him as far worse than the monetary variety. Which sounded self-righteous, but there it was.

He clicked off the machine and was just about to get Laura's old file out when the buzzer rang.

David couldn't really see the man too clearly—the light in the corridor was out—but he could see a stretch limo waiting on the street.

"You must be Goldman," Zachary Wade said.

David introduced himself, shook the man's hand and led him into the waiting room. Christ, he was a handsome man: tall, blond, green eyes, excellent build. David had never been one to notice another man's looks, but this was difficult to miss. His age was hard to guess. Maybe forty-five. And well turned out, of course, in a gray pinstripe suit that hung and fit . . . *perfectly*. Hand-cut. And Italian shoes. Butter-leather shoes, Allison used to call them.

"Why don't you tell me what's going on, doctor?" Zachary Wade said, taking a chair. The man was very authoritative, very precise, in both his movements and his attitude. Of course, he would have to be. Gardners was a very large business.

"Your wife asked a Sergeant Ammonetti at the Nineteenth Precinct to call me," he said.

"Where is Laura now?"

"She's fallen asleep in my office."

"I see." He was tapping his index finger on the arm of the chair, looking around. "Matisse." His eyes stopped at the framed print of *Harmony in Red* David had hanging on the wall. "I once met Matisse. In Saint Paul de Vence, in the south of France. He was very old. Beautiful place. Ever been there?"

"No." David sat down across from him and as easily, gently as he could, described the situation.

"Rita *Harmon*?" Wade said. "Are you sure?"

"Yes."

"I didn't even hear about it. She was at a dinner party we had a few weeks ago. Pity. So who do they think did it?"

"The policeman said it was early in the investigation to make a guess about that. Maybe a mugger."

He scowled. "Probably a crack addict. Good God, you can't even walk the streets anymore in this city. Quite a coincidence, though. Laura *was* angry with Rita. Of course, she had no reason to be."

"Did she tell you she was angry?"

"No. But right in the middle of the dinner party—

actually, it was all rather embarrassing—she suddenly said something that seemed to indicate she was.''

''What?''

''She said, 'Take your damned hands off my husband, Rita.''

''I see. She told me Rita was flirting with you.''

''Oh, she may have been. Rita was a silly woman. You know the kind.''

''What kind?''

''The flirting kind.''

''Mr. Wade, your wife told the police you were having an affair with her.''

''With *Rita*?'' He laughed. ''Hardly.''

''Why 'hardly'?''

''Well, I'm sorry she's been killed, especially this way. Terrible thing. But she was—well, let's say, not my type.''

''What *is* your type?''

He looked at David with a puzzled expression. ''Why, Laura is my type, of course, if it's any of your business.''

''Do women often flirt with you?''

''They seem to find me attractive.''

''And you weren't responding that night? At the dinner party?''

''I'm not on trial here,'' he said.

Who said he was? ''Were you responding, Mr. Wade?''

''What do you take me for? I'd hardly be inclined to dally with another woman in my own home, at my own dinner party.''

Dally? What a strange word.

''I was being polite to my guest, doctor. If you must know.''

''That's what Laura said.''

"She said it because it's true."

"Does she suspect you of having affairs?"

"I never thought she did. She imagines things sometimes."

"What kind of things?"

"Well, she's always trying to second-guess people's behavior, make excuses."

"Like what?"

"Oh, she'll say, 'So-and-so only said that because they were upset about something else.' That kind of thing. It all causes a lot of problems for her. But I never dreamed it would lead to anything like this. Why in the world would Laura think she killed Rita?"

"She's delusional, Mr. Wade. She believes she emits a kind of poison that affects the world. She believes her internal emotions—her anger, in particular—can harm people. Even kill them."

"What would cause such a bizarre notion?"

David gave him the standard speech about all the different theories put forward to explain what triggered an episode like this one, chemical imbalances, hormonal deficiencies, genetic factors.

"But there's nothing like this in Laura's family."

"Psychiatry is not an exact science, Mr. Wade," David said. Then he told him about the tremendous advances that have been made with new medications. "I think there's a good chance that with your support, and with extensive therapy and medication, we can begin to break down the delusions."

David didn't tell him how difficult he knew it was going to be.

"I know this is all very upsetting for you," he said. "Really, I do."

Zachary Wade was silent. Actually, he was taking it pretty well, better than David had expected from the phone call. Once David had the father of a schizophrenic patient he was hospitalizing knock him to the floor. He would never forget that guy. Herb Jorgansky.

"Do you have any questions, Mr. Wade?"

He said he didn't, so David asked *him* some questions.

"Has Laura been behaving oddly?"

"Not really."

"There's been a long history, Mr. Wade. These belief structures have been in place a long time. You never knew anything about it?"

"Well, my wife has always been a fairly quiet person," he said. "Very organized. A good mother, though she lets the children get away with too much. . . . I'd say Laura goes out of her way to be nice to people, nice to everyone."

"Out of her way?"

"Perhaps to a fault."

David asked him if there was anything he could remember at all that might have triggered the current personality decompensation and paranoid delusions.

"No. Nothing."

He didn't ask the question people usually asked—what to do if she started talking crazy—so David told him.

"The thing to remember is that she's very frightened, her mind has become her enemy. The best thing to say is that you understand that she believes these things but that it may be her mind playing tricks on her."

"Yes. That's a good idea."

David gave him a booklet on schizophrenia. Then, also because he didn't ask, David explained his reasons for not putting Laura in a hospital: she didn't want to go, and he really thought they would have to force her.

"Be patient with her, and don't be frightened of her symptoms."

Zachary Wade nodded. David had the feeling that he wasn't a man who scared easily.

He was drumming his fingers on the chair arm again. "I understand, doctor."

"Zach?"

Laura was standing in the doorway. He went over to her, put his arm around her shoulder.

"I'm sorry, Zach."

"Nothing to be sorry for. You'll be fine." He patted her on the shoulder. "We'll go home now."

And they left.

David sat down at his desk and put his head in his hands, suddenly realizing how tired he was.

There was a knock at the door. David opened it to find Zachary Wade standing there again, alone now, the limo behind him. Dark windows. He couldn't see Laura.

"I'd like to ask a question," Wade said.

"I'd be glad to answer it, if I can."

"Where is Laura's statement?"

"What statement?"

"The one she made to the police."

What a strange question. "I don't know. I guess they have it on tape. In the files."

Before David could ask him why he'd asked the question, he was gone. David decided he must want to know if Laura's confession had been given to the media. He didn't want a scandal.

David also decided he didn't like Zachary Wade very much.

* * *

In the file cabinet under W he found her folder, which was pretty thin. He put it in his briefcase, locked up and headed home. It was just past dark, and it was still hot. Broadway in the seventies was alive with people—jumping, the way it did on a hot summer night. So many different kinds of people, so many dialects, accents, features, shades of skin—the variety was endless.

Around the corner from David's building, a steel-drum band was playing on the sidewalk in front of a place called Phil's. No one stopped to watch or listen, but the band played on. The music reminded him of Laura: earthy, sad and oddly discordant.

5   David picked up a barbecued chicken from the Red Apple on the ground floor of his apartment building. All he wanted was a hot shower and a nice quiet chicken dinner, greasy but filling.

In the lobby of his building, walking toward the elevator, he ran into Allison. Preoccupied in his rush to get home he didn't see her until he'd practically knocked her over, which was fairly easy to do. She was a wisp of a woman.

"Excuse me—oh, David. Didn't expect to run into you here."

"Why not? I live here."

"I'm meeting Grace for dinner," she said.

Which David had already guessed. Grace Axelrod was a freelance copywriter who lived in the building.

Allison had confided in Grace as their marriage disintegrated; David didn't particularly like her, and Allison knew it.

He fell into step beside her, neither of them breaking stride.

"How are you, Allison?"

"Fine. And you?"

"Did you get that promotion?" Allison worked for one of the big midtown advertising agencies.

"Yes."

"Do you like the new job as much as you thought you would?"

"So far. My new boss seems pretty nice."

They went on like that for a while. David noticed, not without a twinge, that she looked beautiful, tanned and relaxed. Much more relaxed than she had ever looked when they were together. Her hair was even blonder than he remembered it.

"I was down in Barbados for the weekend," she told him, in that casual tone that let him know just how terrific weekend trips to exotic places were—and, at the same time, that it was really no big deal, she did it all the time. "We had a marvelous time," she said.

"You look beautiful, Allison." Not: Who's the other half of that "we"?

"Thank you. You look terrible." She giggled.

How would *she* look after a day like he'd had? This thought David kept to himself, because his work had always been a thing between them.

"Thanks a lot, Allison."

"Sorry, that was unkind. Bad day, I take it?"

"Let's just say, unusual day."

"I can imagine." She pushed the elevator button. She was waiting for him to tell her why a cop had called him, instead of just coming out and asking. The woman was never simply direct; with her, manipulation was an art form. He said nothing.

She smiled. "Isn't every day among the loonies unusual?"

He sighed. "Allison, my patients are mostly ordinary people with problems, just like you." How many times had he made a comment like that to her? She brought out the worst in him, and, he supposed, he brought out the worst in her.

"How fortunate for them that their *doctor* doesn't have any problems."

He didn't have to argue with her anymore. They were separated, practically divorced, although for some reason she seemed to be dragging her heels in getting the legalities wrapped up. But he didn't have to argue.

"I hope you're happy, Allison."

She gave the knife just one more twist. "Now I am."

He couldn't help getting into it with her just one more time. It was habit.

"I hope you took the goddamn bird on your little foray into my apartment today."

She touched her hair. "Bird doesn't fit into my single lifestyle," she said. "You keep him. Oh, here's the elevator."

Did possession count as nine-tenths of the law when it came to birds of no name?

They stepped inside. He pushed twenty, she pushed nine, then they retreated to separate corners, from which they turned and faced each other as the elevator started. David stood there looking at her, wondering who would finally get the bird in the property settlement and how, if he was the lucky party, he would get rid of it.

"Bye, bye," she said as she got off at Grace's floor.

"One of these days," he said to the empty elevator as it lurched upward again, "I'm going to sneak into your apartment and leave it there."

David was greeted by the usual screeching and screaming that heralded his daily arrival. Bird was sitting on its perch in the brass cage, cocking its head and squawking.

God, it was stifling. He turned on the air conditioner, then fed Bird and listened to his messages. There was just one: "David, it's your mother, please call me back." Her voice on the machine had that maddeningly sympathetic tone it had held ever since he and Allison separated. He decided he would call his mother back tomorrow.

His shirt felt soggy. He put the chicken in the oven on warm and took a quick shower. It seemed hotter instead of cooler when he came out. He turned some knobs on the air conditioner, pushed some buttons, and there was still warmish air coming out. He called the super, who said he would be right up. (Sure! Next *Thursday* he would be right up.) After opening the windows as far as they would open, he sat down again to eat while he read Laura's file.

The first page was her medical history. Nothing much there. The usual childhood illnesses. No history of mental illness in the family, at least none she'd listed. She got headaches, for which she took Fiorinal, a commonly given medication for migraines, prescribed by a doctor in Easterbrook.

The only other thing in the file was a one-page typewritten report. David recognized the font of his old electric. In May, he'd decided to go with the times and began entering his reports on a computer. Usually he divided a consultation report into distinct sections that included specific quotes from the patient he'd jotted down in his private shorthand during the session, non-verbal behaviors he noted, and anything else he deemed relevant. He scanned the section headings: Background, Presenting Problem, Current Symptoms.

Damn. The only clinical symptom he'd noted was a nonspecific depression, and a minor one at that.

She had described her birth family as "wealthy and uncommunicative, more like a collection of stones in a box than a family, and never very comfortable with all the money." Mainly she'd talked about her father, with whom she seemed to have a distant relationship, and whom she'd described as "aloof, detached, demanding." Nothing unusual there. Men like her father, men who built empires, were often detached and demanding. She also said she had always sought her father's love, wanted it, needed it, and so behaved exactly the way he wanted her to behave, never raising her voice in anger, always the little lady.

His notes to himself categorized Laura Wade as a very controlled woman, suffering from a loss of identity and lack of self-esteem. Having described herself as a "housewife" during the session, she had denigrated herself and her activities. "I try to be a good mother," she'd said. "Sometimes I worry about my children too much." But they had seemed to be normal worries—or, at least, normal neurotic worries.

"I try to make a good normal home for my husband," she'd said. "To make sure Zach is comfortable, that his needs are taken care of, that our parties are successful, that I'm charming when we entertain business clients." David remembered thinking it was odd, all of this. Usually the women whose lives revolved around such concerns wouldn't admit it, at least not in quite that way.

Her response when he asked if she had any other interests was odd, too. She said she played the piano ("pretty mediocre") and painted ("no one would buy my paintings").

Eventually he'd asked her if there was anything she actually liked about herself. She smiled and said, "Well, my ankles are all right." He asked her if joking helped ease her pain, at which point she'd burst into tears.

"I never cry," she said.

"Never?"

"My pain is my own, doctor. It always has been."

So. She'd said it then, too.

"Do you ever cry when you're alone?"

"Sometimes."

"About what?"

"About life. My life."

"Because you feel you've done nothing worthwhile?"

"Nothing worthy of my gifts."

David looked up. Damn. There it was. He'd assumed she meant her obvious gifts of intelligence, wealth, education. But she hadn't meant that at all. Having chosen him at random from the list of physicians in the Manhattan phone book, she had been testing him, perhaps deciding if he was worthy of knowing her secrets. In a way, she'd been telling him everything.

The phone in David's apartment rang.

"Hello, David? How are you? You sound tired. Are you getting enough sleep? Are you getting out?"

His mother was calling to invite him to a party the

following Saturday for his older brother, Ivan, who'd just received a large grant for his math research at Penn. She said she wanted to invite Stan Friedland; she missed having him around like in the old days. David was convinced that his mother still thought of him as the twenty-five-year-old he'd been when he and Stan were in medical school together in Philadelphia.

"It's fine to invite him," he said. "I'll see you then, Mom. I miss you."

He didn't tell her he wasn't particularly looking forward either to the drive down to Philadelphia or to the visit with her and his father, the latter being an event likely to bring up all sorts of green mold, even at thirty-nine.

"I'm making you an extra brisket to take home."

"Don't go to any trouble, Mom." David ate brisket three times a year, when his mother forced it on him.

"No trouble at all, David. I'm cooking for the party anyway. You can take home all the leftovers if you want. There'll be plenty. You can freeze them and have them for a month. I hate to think of you eating out every night."

Actually, Allison was the one who always wanted to eat out.

Christ! He must have left the oven on when he took the chicken out. Now the kitchen was filled with the burning smell of caked-on food. He turned the knob to off, then brought the file into the living room, where he sat down to finish reading.

There were only two paragraphs left in the report. The first he'd headed Generalized Depression—Existential (?), probably because, during the session, Laura kept interrupting herself. She'd talk about some aspect of her life, then suddenly move to another train of thought entirely—ask him if he believed in fate, in

God, in evil, in magic, in personal destiny, in man's ultimate isolation. He gave her the best short answers he could, then tried to discover why she was asking the questions. He figured it was because she wrestled with these issues as part of a general depression.

At one point, she'd suddenly asked, "Do you help people, Dr. Goldman?"

The tone of her question was so gentle, so refreshing, so utterly lacking in cynicism, that David had had to fight the urge to laugh.

"I try to, Laura," he said. "Mostly, I try to get people to see how they can help themselves."

"What if their problem is hopeless?"

"I don't think any problem is entirely hopeless. Life is complex and sometimes difficult, but people cope with all sorts of things. It's a matter of finding inner resources, I think."

"I understand that. But let's say someone comes in here and says he's depressed. You talk to him and try to find out what's wrong. And then you discover he's depressed because he has six months to live. You'd have to call that hopeless, wouldn't you?"

"You're not dying, are you?"

"No. I'm not dying."

"All right, then," he said. "We have this person who has six months to live. Of course, he certainly has a legitimate reason to be depressed, and I wouldn't try to tell him otherwise. I would try to get him to face his death, put his life in perspective, maybe do things he'd always wanted to do, say things to people he'd always wanted to say—that sort of thing."

"But the depression would still be there," she said, "because the reason for the depression is still there, and you couldn't get rid of that. Isn't that right?"

* * *

The last item in the report concerned a childhood dream she'd told him near the end of the hour. He'd recorded it verbatim: "I'm always tied down to a table, secured by straps of some kind, and there are suction cups attached to my head and some wires that go into a machine. And people watching me. I feel naked—or maybe I am naked, I can't remember. Then someone presses a button and there's a terrible pain. After that I always seem to be falling, but I'm not scared because I know falling will bring relief from the pain.

Odd dream for a child. But falling was a common symbol for losing control. He'd asked her what the dream reminded her of.

"Shock therapy."

"You haven't ever had shock therapy, have you?"

"No, but maybe I will at some point. So maybe the dream was precognitive."

"Laura, why would you think you'd have, or need, shock therapy. Even in its heyday, it was only used in extreme cases."

"And I don't seem like an extreme case to you?"

"Well, I don't know you, but no, you don't."

And that was it. He'd told her he thought there were some issues she needed to work out, and if she wanted to, they would try to work them out together. She said she would think about it.

And then she left.

He closed the file. Some consultation. He'd handled her as a garden-variety neurotic, with the usual identity crisis and some minor-league depression. Schizophrenic? It hadn't even occurred to him.

6

The man washed his hands three times, first with alcohol, then with a pumice stone, then with a strong soap. Finally, almost as an after-thought, he washed again, lathered with a per-fumed soap and rinsed. Then he took the wig and the mustache and the shoes, wrapped them in a small bundle, put them in their safe place. They would be used again, very soon.

Later, the clothes and the mask would be burned. The clothes were thick with blood, with death, but they were safe, beyond discovery. Al-ready, blood had turned to rust. Blood was bright red at first, then it turned a dull rust color. Soon it would be chocolate brown. Then ash. Not a trace of blood would remain. He had seen to that. It was only a matter of proper planning, of dis-cipline.

Very soon now, the Death Witch would die, a scourge wiped from the earth, wiped clean. The Death Witch, of course, could not be killed. She had to be defeated, outsmarted, tricked. Then She would take her own life. It was the only way; the proper way.

Staring at his image in the mirror, the man took a fresh towel from the closet, dried his hands. The image smiled. He did not feel sorry for the dead one, the sacrifice. The value of the sacrifice could not be underestimated, but the woman herself was unimportant; she had died easily, like a pawn. If there had been another way, a cleaner way, he would have used it. He had not liked the blood. Yet, there was a certain symmetry to the dead one's demise by knife. Corpse for corpse. Flesh for flesh. It reminded him of the way the Death Witch killed. In his mind's eye, he saw Her killing, then considered the difference between them: She had been wild, seized with fury and rage, striking out blindly, leaving ripped and jagged edges, torn shreds of flesh. Whereas he was calm. Practiced. Careful. His face would have registered no fury, he was sure, had anyone been able to see it under the mask, including that woman at the window, high up.

The man had to hurry now. He could hear the Death Witch coming, feel Her presence. Sometimes She surprised him by coming upon him before he had hidden himself. Carefully, quickly, he sponged out the sink, then washed again, toweled again, cleaned his manicured nails with a file, brushed them with a small brush, rubbed lotion into the skin.

Discipline. It was the only way to endure Her presence, to survive the touch of Her cold female flesh.

The man turned off the light.

Quick now. The Death Witch was appearing. He could see Her in the mirror.

7 Detective Henry R. Culligan had the videotape of Laura Wade's confession in his briefcase when he pulled into his driveway. It was against departmental policy to take the thing out of the file, but he'd done it anyway. He wouldn't say a word to Betty; he rarely discussed his work with her, even though she sometimes gave him good ideas when he did. Woman's intuition, or something like that. But he found that he managed life better keeping his work separate. And sometimes it seemed she didn't want to know.

He could smell cheese and tomato and garlic as he came in the door. Chicken parmigiana, he hoped.

"One more minute, and it would be burned," Betty said from the kitchen door. She had her Kiss-the-Cook apron on. Smiling, she pointed at the words and offered her cheek.

He kissed her.

"Had a few rounds at McKellen's?" she said.

No use denying it, since it was one of the reasons he was walking in at eight, instead of seven, as he had promised her. The other reason was that he'd finally gotten Ozzie Allen on the phone and it took him some time to give the man the background on the Harmon case. Allen was a Philadelphia PD detective with whom he sometimes traded favors. Culligan had met him years ago on a big drug case, when he was first made a detective, working in narcotics. He'd asked

Allen to run a check on the Gardner family, who hailed from Philadelphia, where the first store was located.

"It was only one round," Culligan told his wife.

Betty laughed, then slipped on her oven mitts and opened the oven door.

He watched her as she put the casserole on the table. She was a good sturdy woman, a bit full around the middle now, but she was still pretty in her mid-forties, especially with the new blondish look she'd gotten at the hairdresser a few weeks ago. She'd been a wonderful mother, even during Hayley's impossible adolescence; and she'd been an understanding cop's wife for twenty-five years, even seeing the marriage through the rough year that followed his misbegotten affair with Anna Grayboyes, a social worker he met on the job. And despite a severe Catholic upbringing, she was still interested in sex—more than interested, in fact. What more could he ask for?

They had a quiet dinner in the kitchen. Chicken parmigiana. Afterward, they watched a little television, some ridiculous awards show Betty wanted to watch, then went to bed at ten. Betty wanted to make love. She almost seemed to use sex the way men did, as a tension releaser, which was fine with Culligan. He had enough tension of his own to release, with this Harmon case. With Laura Wade. With Chief Hallahan, who was convinced it was the start of a serial.

In addition to Jones and Compton, Hallahan had assigned the case to a couple of guys from the homicide task force, up at the Nineteenth. Hallahan had also suggested Culligan give Doug Gray, the department's specialist in witness hypnosis, a call. Culligan had only met Gray once, a few years back, when he took the course Gray taught.

Hypnosis had seemed pretty far out to Culligan, who

liked things by the book—the old book—but Gray had surprised him. A career cop, not some fancy psychiatrist with his head in the clouds, Gray was the one who'd gotten the witness in the Johanson case to remember the detail—a green windbreaker—that led them to Eppie Duncan. Culligan certainly wasn't one to argue with success. If they didn't get a break soon, he might have to give the guy a shot at Lilly Dunleavy. Assuming he could get Lilly to cooperate.

As for Laura Wade, he'd changed his mind about her twice now. He'd believed her while he was listening to her confession. It was too complete, too accurate not to believe. But he'd completely reversed his opinion when she fell apart—although the speech wasn't jumbled nonsense, the content was. The fact was, she'd been equally believable as a scorned murderess as a crazy confessor. Now he was reconsidering her likelihood as a murderess.

Betty was asleep. He got up, took the tape out of his briefcase, pulled on his battered terry-cloth robe and went downstairs.

Every murder case he'd ever worked on was an exercise in logic and persistence. None of them made sense at first. The key was to identify the inconsistencies, then proceed in a logical, orderly fashion to explain them. The fact that this case had more inconsistencies than most meant he would just have to be more logical. He needed to think about the case without interruptions: no phones, no scuffle of cops' feet outside the office, no voices, no press of other cases. It was quiet in Brooklyn at two A.M.

Culligan made himself a cup of warm milk, took some Malomars from the cabinet and went into the den, where he fed the tape into the VCR.

He sat down on the couch and listened to Laura

Wade, to her flat monotone. Seeing the way she had stared at him again unnerved him. People always thought psychopaths had dead, merciless eyes. Some did. Some were amused. Others looked at you in a perfectly reasonable, normal way. That was their gift, to be able to look at you without giving themselves away.

Laura Wade's eyes fit into none of those categories. Her eyes were simply intense. Very dark brown—almost black. And her stare was . . . well, he'd never felt anything quiet like it. The camera had been positioned behind him, but she'd never looked at it, not once. She'd fixed her gaze on him, and so the confession on tape had a strange quality, almost as if she was a character in a television play, always looking *away* from the camera, never once appearing to acknowledge its existence.

He watched her tell her story again on tape, how she said she'd followed Rita Harmon, how she'd gotten the woman into the car. "What car?" Her own Mercedes. She took Rita over to the other side of town, she said, threatened her, then threw her out of the car. Then she got out and came up behind her, grabbed her around the neck, made her death slash, got the woman down on the sidewalk and destroyed her face. Ten slashes. "Because she was sleeping with Zach."

Simple motive. Simply told.

Why ten? "Ten claws. The way an animal kills."

What did you do with your clothes, with your knife? "I threw the knife in the river." Where? "I drove my car to the river, near the passenger ship terminal, got out, went over to the edge and threw it in, as far out as I could throw." And the clothes? There she hesitated a moment.

Culligan remembered thinking about a case about

nine years ago where the perp had burned his bloody clothes in his own fireplace. It was funny how people thought setting fire to something removed the residue of murder.

And it was exactly what Laura Wade said she'd done. "I wrapped them up in a plastic tarp I brought with me, took them home." What time was that? "About eleven." What did you do then? "I waited until about three A.M., and I took the tarp out of the car and I took it into my backyard. Then I poured lighter fluid on it and set it on fire." Right in your backyard? "On the sand." The sand? "We live on Long Island Sound. We have our own stretch of beach."

Maybe so. Bonfire on the beach at three A.M. What every suburban neighborhood needs.

Culligan sat there watching the blur of static on the television as the tape wound itself out. Logic. She knew about the ten cuts. Which meant she was involved somehow. But did she have the strength to do it? Maybe not. Hell, she could have hired someone to do it.

Culligan made a note on his pad. "Accomplice?" Jones was already working on her paper trail, bank transactions, credit card records, checking account. There were ways to hide large withdrawals, but they might get lucky unless she'd planned it all out for months, took a little out of her checking account at a time.

Culligan got up and set the tape to rewind. He would get subpoenas for her personal accounts if he had to, even if he had to bend the rules a little.

The question was, did he believe she did it? Possibly.

It was entirely possible that both the killer and the victim were suburban housewives who'd taken their murderous rivalry to another locale—his locale. It wasn't logical, but that didn't mean it wasn't possible.

New York City defied logic more often than not these days. There was a whole new class of killers now—drug-crazed psychopaths who roamed the streets looking for ways to support their habits, vicious punks without a reason in the world for living. Serial killers were rarer, and they usually preyed on strangers, too. But they gave themselves away eventually.

Anyway, if what he was thinking was true, this one wasn't a serial. This one was revenge, pure and simple. The revenge of a woman with a philandering husband. Old story. New twist.

She did the deed, felt guilty, confessed, then got scared and changed her mind. So she babbled on about putting a hex on the real murderer to make Culligan think she was crazy, throw him off her trail. He had to admit it was a pretty good act, if that was what it was, conceived and executed under pressure as it had been.

He would check out the philandering husband angle tomorrow. He hadn't yet been able to get Zachary Wade. Wade's secretary said he'd gone out of town on business. Some husband. His wife had either committed a murder or had a mental breakdown and he goes out of town on business not three days later. Which didn't mean the guy was a philanderer, but it certainly didn't show he wasn't.

Everything in the goddamned case was like that, which was what bothered Culligan about it. He didn't really have anything on Laura Wade, other than her knowledge of the ten cuts and her confession—a document undermined by her rantings about hexes. He would certainly have to testify to what followed the confession, so what the hell good was it? Especially since there wasn't even circumstantial evidence that Laura Wade had done it, let alone physical evidence.

Culligan himself had questioned the ticket taker who'd been at the Easterbrook movie theatre that night. The girl could neither confirm or deny. Compton had spent the past three days questioning shopkeepers and people on the street around the scene of the murder, and nobody had noticed a green Mercedes.

None of the night crew at the passenger ship terminal remembered a woman standing at the edge of the Hudson and throwing something in. The *Queen Elizabeth 2* had been in that night so they were tied up with that. And what about the ship's crew? "Well you could question them," one guy said. "Maybe one of them seen something. Of course, the *Queen* is just about in Southampton by now, and anyway, most of the crew gets the night off when the ship anchors, especially after the round-the-world cruise, and none of them would likely be hanging around here."

None of it proved a thing. Or disproved it either.

A partial footprint in the victim's blood, possibly the killer's, proved to be a man's size ten, but it was only a tip, not enough to get a weight or height. A blue cotton thread on the victim's dress matched the blue shirt worn by the man who'd discovered the body. A black hair found on the inside of the victim's sleeve was her daughter's.

The only real physical evidence they had so far appeared to exonerate Laura Wade. The perp was right-handed. Slashed from left to right, standing behind the victim. Laura Wade was left-handed; she had signed her confession with her left hand.

Culligan sighed, made another note on his pad: "Left-handed?" He'd been a cop a long time, and it had been his experience that appearances *were* often deceiving, even if he hadn't thought of an explanation for the apparent contradiction. Yet. And, of course, there was still the possibility that she had hired a right-hander to do it, told him to make ten cuts. But why would she give a specific number? So that she could confess to it?

"Henry?"

Betty was standing in the doorway, sleepy-eyed, hair tousled and damp. Backlit by the hallway lights, she looked almost naked standing there in her thin white cotton nightgown.

"Henry, what are you *doing*? It's nearly four o'clock in the morning."

He pushed the stop button. "Watching porno movies," he said with a grin.

She stared at him silently. He knew that look. He wasn't going to get away with a joke.

"You really want to know?"

She nodded. "Yes, of course."

He pointed to the couch and said, "Then sit down and take a look at this."

He rewound the tape the rest of the way, then pushed Play and joined his wife on the sofa. Maybe he needed her woman's intuition on this one.

8

"There's something wrong with my arm, Dr. Goldman."

On the following Friday, Laura Wade appeared in David's office at precisely three o'clock, wearing a

white sweater and white linen pants, her right arm
hanging awkwardly at her side. She explained that the
arm and her hand had suddenly gone numb—no, she
hadn't injured her arm—and that she was unable to
move either her hand or her fingers.

It sounded like some kind of a hysterical paralysis.
David made a cursory examination of her arm and
could find no evidence of a physical problem, not that
he expected one. For the first time, he really noticed
her hands. They were beautiful, long and slender with
tapered fingers, smooth dark skin without a blemish,
delicate yet strong. An artist's hands.

"It doesn't appear to be a muscle problem, or a
bone problem," he said. "Sometimes physical symptoms can convey things that psychological symptoms
don't."

"Zach says I'm a hypochondriac."

"The numbness in your arm is real, isn't it?"

"Yes."

"When did it begin?"

"Yesterday."

"Can you think of anything that might have caused
you to be upset yesterday?" (Other than that she still
thought she was a murderer.)

She hesitated a moment, then said, "My friend took
a job last week. She began work yesterday."

"Why did that upset you?"

She went over to the other side of the room, leaned
against the wall by the window. He could see tears in
her eyes. "Oh, God," she said. "I'm so afraid. I told
you I had one friend—she's it."

"What about your husband? Isn't he your friend?"

"It's different with a man."

"Why's that?"

"Oh, maybe because of sex."

"Why does sex preclude friendship?"

"I don't want to talk about this. Do we have to talk about this?"

"You brought it up, Laura."

"Well, I shouldn't have." She looked away for a moment. "Anyway, I enjoy having Ellen as a friend. She's a graphic artist. I think I may have told you, I paint, so we have that in common."

"You said painting was a hobby."

"Zach says my work looks like little gothic nightmares."

Now there was a male put-down if he'd ever heard one.

"What do *you* say?"

She smiled. "He's right."

Zach said this. Zach said that. David made an effort to concentrate on her story.

"Anyway, Ellen lives next door, and we used to have coffee together. We take—took—an aerobics class together, picked up the kids, all the usual things. But she decided to go back to work a few months ago. She got a job as a designer for an agency, and she was very excited about it."

"How do you feel about that?"

"Well, for her I'm happy. For me, I guess I'm . . . upset. I'm going to miss her."

"Do you feel abandoned?"

"Well . . . yes, I guess, sort of."

"Yes, you guess, sort of? Which is it?"

No response.

"Were you angry?"

She looked away. "Yes, I suppose I was. Isn't that unbelievable?"

"Why?" he asked her, but he knew the answer. This woman's entire personality—her beliefs, her way of looking at the world, her defensive modes, every-thing—had developed around an apparently long-standing delusional system. Like a person with a serious deformity, she believed herself to be so loathsome that she wasn't entitled to anything, least of all a friend she might count on.

"What right do I have to be angry at her?" Laura was saying. "To stand in the way of what she wants to do?"

"How could you stand in the way?"

She sighed. "Don't you see? My wishes come true . . . which wouldn't even be so bad, if—"

"Are you afraid something will happen *every* time you get angry, or just sometimes?"

She shrugged, shook her head.

"Why this time?"

"Because of the dream I had last night," she said. "You see, doctor, I'm afraid to feel *anything*. Listen! I had a dream about tigers. They weren't regular ti-gers, they were pure white. It was me and Sammy, my son, and Ellen, standing outside a tiger cage. I was watching one of the tigers groom the other, lick the fur with its tongue. I was holding Sammy's hand, and then suddenly Sammy was too close to the cage and I was afraid he'd get hurt. I panicked, and Ellen reached to pull Sammy away and one of the tigers lunged out and grabbed hold of Ellen, her right arm—and she couldn't get away. She was screaming, and he was clawing at it. Picking it clean. Licking it clean."

"A frightening dream," David said.

"You think so?"

"Don't you?"

"Yes," she said. "But it was only a dream, right?"

"That's right."

"I say that to my children when they have a bad dream. My mother said it to me."

"Did it help you?"

"No. My dreams aren't like other people's."

"Because they make things happen?"

"Well, my dreams have always been terrifying. Especially when I was a child. But it wasn't really so bad, then, because they only used to predict things. I always had the option of warning people if something bad was going to happen so that they could maybe avoid it."

"How could you warn people without giving yourself away?"

"There are ways to subtly plant a suggestion so that people think they've thought of the idea on their own. But, you see, if the fact that I have the dream is the *reason* the thing happens, then what good does it do to warn people?"

David stood up and came around to the front of his desk, leaned against it. It was very difficult to make distinctions with this woman. "Normal" as she perceived it—that is, before her breakdown—was almost as delusional as the "abnormal" she perceived now. Less threatening, perhaps. But had she always lived in a fantasy?"

"Laura, let's take a look at the dream. What does it remind you of?"

"We were going to go to the zoo on Saturday."

"Are you still going?"

"No. I can't."

"All right, then, you know the source for the dream, right?"

She stared at him, her eyes hard. "Doctor, I know what the *source* for the dream was. I also know about wish fulfillments and fantasies, and death wishes, and

manifest content, and latent content, and all the rest
of it. I know the *reason* for my dreams. I've always
known that. It's the consequences I can't control.''

"Wait," he said. "Let's talk about the reasons, first.
What were the reasons for this dream?''

"My anger, of course.''

He sighed, "Laura, you can't simply deny your feelings."

"What choice do I have?''

How could he get in?

"Does denying your anger prevent something from
happening, Laura?''

"No.''

"Do you think a tiger—?''

"It doesn't have to be that *exact* thing. Don't you
understand? If Ellen hurt her arm—her right arm—she
couldn't work.''

"And you will be responsible?''

"My anger will be responsible.''

And she would be doubly guilty, for having had the
anger in the first place and then for getting her wish,
that her friend would be home to keep her company.
Christ, this had to be the most convoluted delusional
system he'd ever come across, not to mention the fact
that it was accompanied by a hysterical conversion
right out of Freud. She repressed feelings of anger and
abandonment, which manifested themselves in a paralysis of her hand, then dreamed that her friend hurt
her drawing arm, then developed a delusion that this
would actually happen and she would have caused it.
Anger was inappropriate, no matter what the circumstances; and if she got angry, the delusion came into
play, quite possibly as a punishment for having the
anger in the first place.

"Laura, tell me," David said, "do you remember

the specific moment when you begin to perceive yourself as causing things to happen with your thoughts?''

''Not really. Well . . . I guess it was the fire.''

''What fire?''

She clasped her hands together in her lap. ''I am—
I mean I was—involved in a literacy advocates pro-
gram in Easterbrook. I was tutoring a little boy named
Josh Booker, every Tuesday in the school library. I
enjoyed doing it, and he seemed to like it. I was told
he was mildly retarded, but pretty soon I realized that
he was actually a very bright kid, who had some terrible emotional problems. I don't understand why the
people giving those IQ tests to kids aren't more . . .''
She cut herself off. ''Anyway, last summer Josh went
to visit his grandmother in South Carolina. All he
talked about when he came back was how much he'd
loved fishing off the pier, so about two months ago I
bought him a book about fishing, wrapped it up and
brought it to him in the library. Well, that day he came
in with some guy named Rapman on his mind—some
friend of his mother's—and when I gave him the book,
he went berserk. He was screaming that it was about
a white boy, and he was never going to be a fisherman,
that he was going to be in jail for killing that Rapman,
and what did I know about him, I was just some rich
white lady with nothing better to do. And I tried to
calm him down, but he wouldn't be calmed. Finally
he just grabbed my purse, which was sitting on the
library table, and ran.''

''Did you chase him?''

''I started to.''

''Were you angry at him?''

''I guess I was. I understood how he felt, and that
it was pretty much a reaction to something going on
in his own life, but still, I'd helped him and I thought

we were friends. We'd been working together since he was eight. He was eleven then. I tried to help him in every way I could. I gave him money, I was thinking of setting up a small trust for him.'' She looked at David. ''Oh, you're thinking it's just a matter of appeasing my own guilt about having so much when there are people who have nothing?''

''I wasn't, actually,'' David said, relieved to have her be wrong about his thoughts, for once. *''Is* that what it is? In part?''

She nodded. ''Yes.''

A reaction that seemed to fit within her delusional system. Not only was she so loathsome that she wasn't entitled to her feelings, she wasn't entitled to her money either.

''And also,'' she said, ''I guess because I've always thought a person with my gifts should be able to do something about these things, but I've never been able to figure out what.''

''All right, Laura, what happened with this boy?''

''I had a dream about him that night. We were in a large room and he was running away from me, and I was chasing him, and there were all these sparks—coming out of my fingertips—and then fire.'' She pressed her lips together. ''And in the dream, I set him on fire.'' Now there were tears spilling down her face.

David handed her a tissue. Where was it leading? He hoped she wasn't going to tell him that something had happened to the boy.

She was.

''And a few days later, Josh's house was destroyed in a fire. He went with his mother to South Carolina and I never saw or heard from him again.''

Good Lord! Which of the events she described were

factual and which were fabrications? Of course, the story was related after the fact. But was she inventing the entire incident or merely imposing the dream on the incident to punish herself for her angry feelings?

"Now do you see, doctor?" she said.

He decided to move on to something else.

"Tell me, Laura, when was the first time you became aware of your powers?"

She looked at him. "You're trying to find out whether this is a reactive-type disorder, or whether it's chronic. Isn't that right?"

Good God, she was at it again.

She told him that one of the first times she could remember was when she was eight. She'd "heard" her sister Carole planning, thinking about ruining a much loved doll of hers, then had a dream in which Carole hurt her leg. And the next day, her sister fractured her ankle.

"Children often believe their thoughts can make things happen. As you surely know, it's called magical thinking." He didn't say it was also characteristic of psychotics.

"But you see, I *didn't* think that. I thought I had only foreseen it. But now I have to reevaluate everything in my life. After all, I *was* angry at my sister. Maybe all along it was my perception that was faulty."

The look on her face made him wish he hadn't brought up the magical thinking. He asked her how she had managed to keep her special gifts to herself all her life.

"I told my friend Annie, once, a long time ago, but I don't see her anymore."

"How about your husband?"

"I think he's always suspected there's something wrong with me."

Really? He said he hadn't.

"If he suspected something, Laura, wouldn't he have talked to you about it?"

"We don't talk about these kinds of things. I've never understood why he married me."

"Why's that?"

"Well, you met him. He's the kind of man who could have any woman he wanted. Smart, charming, handsome, a good father. I'm lucky to have him."

She tossed out these statements—the most unliberated that David had heard from a woman in a long time—as if they were all one thought.

"Brilliant, too," she said. "My father thinks so, even made him president of the company over his own son. Not that my brother Greg wanted any part of the business."

"And is it his good qualities that make you feel you're not worthy of your husband?"

"I'm not worthy of any man—or any woman, for that matter. Don't you understand? There's something inside me, something evil, something poisonous."

"Laura, having angry thoughts doesn't mean you're a bad person. Did someone tell you it did?"

She stared at him for a moment, then said, "You're right, doctor. I did tell you once that my father insisted we control our anger."

He looked at her. Had she guessed again, or had he led her into that one?

"I *know* I don't feel comfortable showing anger," she said. "I never have. But it doesn't seem to matter now whether I show it or not. Why aren't I entitled to my private thoughts—my little jealousies and resentments, my dreams—like everyone else?"

Sometimes David found it helpful to try to put himself in the patient's mind, to imagine what it was like to live with the delusion. This one, of course, had told him that part of a delusion is that the person who has it doesn't think it's a delusion. But schizophrenics didn't *say* that kind of thing. Schizophrenics tried to convince you that the voices they heard on the radio were real, that there really were aliens in their soup, that they really did have this power, whatever this "power" might be. Maybe her comment only indicated convincement at work on a more sophisticated level.

"Laura, tell me. Is there a reason why you think this is happening to you now?"

"I don't really know. Maybe to punish me for being so unworthy of my gifts that I'm unable to control my emotions."

One thing she did have in common with a schizophrenic: terror.

Terror, of course, was a perfectly appropriate reaction to discovering there was a worldwide conspiracy against you, to realizing that the KGB had poisoned your drinking water, to discovering that you were Satan reborn. Or, as Laura would have it, to discovering that you were some kind of walking freak who had the power to strike people down with a passing thought or a dream, the kind everyone has sometimes, the thoughts with perfectly natural emotional content that cannot be tamed, changed or denied but eventually have to be accepted if one is to achieve psychological health.

"I took all your psychological tests yesterday," she said. "Over at NYU."

"Did it upset you to take them?"

"No," she said. "But it upset Dr. Duncan to give them to me."

9 The Wade Home was set far back behind a row of tall hemlocks lined up like soldiers along the edge of the street. Detective Henry Culligan glanced at his watch as he pulled into the long driveway and parked behind a mint-green Mercedes 500SEL. They were going to tear that car apart.

It was nearly nine-thirty. The ride up to Connecticut had taken longer than he expected.

Eric Jones, sitting in the passenger seat, let out a long, low whistle. "Some place, huh, Henry? How'd you like to have that as your private pool?"

Culligan turned off the motor. He could hear a dog barking somewhere nearby. It was a moment before he could take it all in.

The house was a massive white clapboard colonial with black shutters and two peaked dormers on either side of the roof. A wedge of sunlight illuminated a perfectly manicured garden directly in front of the house, but the rest of the lawn was in a dense dark shadow. A massive beech tree stood there, its copper leaves shimmering in the sunlight like dabs of metallic paint, its reach extending outward almost to the hemlocks. Between the Wade house and the more modest house next door, Culligan could see an expanse of lawn in the back, and the glimmer of water—Long Island Sound.

"Christ," Jones said, "we get an indictment on her and the media is going to eat it up. Money. Sex. Madness. Story's got everything. Who'd you say her father was?''

"Gardners Department Stores. Samuel Gardner. But he's retired. Her husband runs the business. I'm running a check on the whole family.''

"Anything there?''

"Father started the stores right after the war. Rags to riches, as far as I can tell. Seems to have come from nowhere. As a matter of fact, I haven't been able to find anything on him before he opened the first one.''

"That's odd.''

"I've got Ozzie Allen on it.''

Culligan glanced in the rearview mirror. Where the hell were Donaldson and LaRue? They'd been behind them in LaRue's tan Chrysler all the way. Probably driving around, checking out the houses. Not that he could blame them. This place was like paradise. Culligan, like Jones, had been born and bred on the streets of Brooklyn. Donaldson came from somewhere out west, LaRue was from the Bronx. Culligan had never actually been to Connecticut before, except to drive through. He'd heard it was loaded with money, this part of it anyway. But surely it couldn't all be like this.

Culligan glanced in the mirror again. Still no Donaldson. He glanced over at Jones, who gave him a nod, then both men settled into their own thoughts.

Detective Henry R. Culligan wasn't sure when he'd begun believing that Laura Wade was the perpetrator. Probably the night he took the videotape of her confession home and replayed it. Betty certainly thought so. After they watched the tape, she'd looked at him and said, "Why, she's as guilty as hell, Henry.''

He told Betty what the confessor said after she confessed, but Betty didn't buy it. "I can't believe an old pro like you would fall for that kind of malarkey. She's guilty, she admitted it, and you must be losing your grip. Now come to bed, Henry.''

''Here they are.''

Culligan could see Donaldson and LaRue pulling in behind them. He gathered up the papers from the seat between him and Jones. The warrants were really a hunting expedition, couched in legal terms, a favor from Judge Maxwell Wren. They didn't have probable cause on Laura Wade in the true sense of the term. It had taken some real work to get a search warrant; Chief Hallahan had had to make a personal call to Judge Wren. Wren agreed, but said they could search the house only for the weapon. ''You come out of that house with anything else, Henry,'' Hallahan had said, ''and you got nothing.''

They would also be permitted to scour the sand for evidence of a recent fire. Christ Almighty. They put so many goddamned obstacles in front of you, it was almost as if they wanted to let the killer get away with it.

At least the warrant for her car—the green Mercedes—was more flexible. No one could pull something like this, get back in a car and leave no shred of evidence, not a thread of fiber, not a microscopic drop of blood. And if she rented a vehicle, well, he would find that, too. Eventually. And if they didn't find that, the subpoenas for her bank records would surely produce something. First things first.

Culligan opened the car door and got out, motioning the other two to remain in the car until he gave the signal, then proceeded up the walk. Jones followed behind him.

Laura Wade answered the door. She was wearing jeans and sneakers and a short-sleeved white cotton blouse. She looked like any housewife during a day at home, more beautiful perhaps than most.

"Oh, Detective Culligan," she said simply. She wore no makeup and looked younger than he remembered. Faint dark rings around her eyes were the only telling feature of an otherwise unblemished face.

"We have a warrant to search your house, Mrs. Wade." He held out the papers. "And your car."

She nodded but displayed no emotion, just stepped aside.

Culligan motioned for Donaldson and LaRue to get started, then stepped into the front foyer. It was a large hall with a high ceiling and bleached oak floors polished to a high gloss. Along one wall in front of the chair molding stood a small Queen Anne table with a large cut crystal vase brimming with fresh flowers, brilliant red and pink roses, spectacular iris. Culligan recognized some of them from the garden at the front of the house. He wondered if she had cut the flowers herself.

Directly ahead, through the foyer, he could see the living room, a large sun-drenched room, filled with pricy antiques and plush chintz sofas laid over an oriental rug. Looking through the room, Culligan could see green lawn, a pool with a cabana off to one side, and beyond that the vast expanse of Long Island Sound, glistening in the sunlight.

At the edge of the yard was a dog pen and a small structure within it. And a big dog, a doberman. The dog wasn't barking anymore, he was just sitting there. Christ, why did people have dogs like that for pets? With kids around, yet.

"His name is Darwin," Laura Wade said. "He'd tear the throat out of a burglar, but he's very gentle with children."

How the hell did—

"Mrs. Wade, I—" A young woman of about twenty appeared in the doorway. Obviously not a daughter, perhaps a housekeeper or one of those mother's helpers.

"It's all right, Darlene," Laura Wade said. "Go on upstairs to your room."

The girl retreated up the curved mahogany staircase and disappeared on the landing above.

"Your housekeeper?" Culligan asked.

"Au pair," she said.

"I may want to ask her some questions."

Laura Wade sighed. "You're wasting your time, detective."

He looked at her, couldn't help saying, "Well, as long as we've gone to all this trouble, getting together all these legalities—"

"I didn't say I would try to stop you. Only that you're wasting your time."

"Why's that?"

"Because you're looking for a weapon, or some physical evidence that I was there at the scene of Rita Harmon's murder, and since I wasn't, you won't find what you're looking for."

Culligan shrugged. "But you still say you murdered her, is that right?"

"Not in the usual sense."

"By a hex of some kind?"

"Yes."

Culligan smiled. "And when did you place this hex on her?"

"At the dinner party where I became angry. I told you about that."

Which she had. She'd started screaming about the party after they told her she was free to go.

"So you now say that this murder effectively took place at this dinner party, rather than in the manner you described to me in your confession?"

"Yes."

"Mrs. Wade, do you know you can be prosecuted for giving false information to the police?"

"I only made it up so you would believe me."

"Which part did you make up?"

"All of it."

"Then your husband wasn't having an affair with Rita Harmon?"

"No. Rita was . . . flirting with him at our dinner party. That was when I got angry."

"I'd like you to provide me with the names of everyone at that dinner party."

"Do you have to tell them what it's about?"

"In connection with Rita Harmon's murder, of course."

"I mean—do you have to tell them . . ."

"About your confession?"

"No. About what I said *after* the confession."

The woman was obviously a lunatic, and hoping to keep that fact from her friends. She was one hell of a lunatic, too. The only question was what mode of lunatic—lethal or nonlethal. He said, "You are a suspect in a murder case, Mrs. Wade."

She closed her eyes, shook her head, then opened them again. "I'll go make a list." She turned and headed into another room.

Culligan began the search.

It took nearly two hours to go through the first two floors of the house, and by the time they got to the third floor, Culligan, too, had begun to think he was wasting his time. This woman, if she had done it, was too smart to leave evidence lying around here. But she wasn't that smart, or she wouldn't have gotten herself involved in the first place.

Laura Wade had been following them from room to room for maybe half an hour, watching as they inspected her things, opened her drawers, pulled apart her closets, saying nothing. They found nothing useful. They did find a gun hidden on a top shelf in her bedroom—a .38-caliber revolver, and a license with it.

"For protection," Laura Wade said.

The staircase to the third floor was at the end of the second floor hall. Culligan stood at the bottom step.

"What's up here?"

"Storage," she said. "And my studio."

"What do you do in your studio?"

"I paint. I'm an artist—sort of."

That figured. She had nothing to do with herself. Nothing except contemplate murder. Probably painted bad pictures of fruit.

Culligan followed her up a creaky flight of stairs, with Jones in tow. At the top, they came to a landing— Culligan had to duck so as not to bump his head—then an empty dark hallway with a ceiling barely high enough to pass beneath. No furnishings. No pictures on the walls. Not even a hall runner.

Laura Wade flipped a switch at the top of the stairs, which added some light, not much.

The storage area was off to the left. It took another hour to go through that, boxes and boxes of clothes, skis, roller skates, toys, old furniture (any piece of which Betty would have loved to have in their living room), and a cedar closet, also filled with clothes.

Back out in the hallway again, she said, "My studio is this way."

She led them to a door at the end of the hall and went inside. Culligan stood in the doorway for a moment. It was a large attic room, low eaves, unusual spaces, dormered windows.

The detective heard his partner gasp.

He stepped inside and looked around. She was an artist, all right. There were the easels, brushes, paints, sketchbooks, tubes of paint. And finished paintings, all over the place. Looked like the basement of a museum. He scanned the canvases, his eyes moving slowly from one to the next. There might have been hundreds of them—hanging on every square inch of wall, stacked up ten deep against the walls and against an old clawfoot bathtub. There wasn't a frame in the place, just the stretched canvases.

He exchanged a glance with Jones, who looked just as nonplussed as he. No pastoral landscapes, these. It was, in fact, the most gruesome collection of images Culligan had ever seen. Demons with extended claws, and blood, and wild animals devouring flesh, and more claws, and more blood. And they were all painted in such a realistic way that they practically looked like photographs, except for the subject matter. He lifted a muslin cloth from the work on the easel. It was the most gruesome of all. A demon standing over a woman, blood dripping from its claws. And the woman's face was . . . well, *clawed*.

He looked at Jones, who raised an eyebrow.

"You have a name for this one?"

She looked at the painting, then at him. *"Nightmare under the Moon."*

"Ever do any still lifes?" Jones said, with noticeable sarcasm.

Laura Wade didn't respond. At the moment, she was staring out the window, her back to the two detectives.

Donaldson and LaRue were probably out there now, taking sand samples.

Culligan looked at Jones again. He didn't have to ask what the other man was thinking. He was thinking the same thing: This was a woman obviously obsessed with violent images. It wasn't enough to charge her with murder, but it was something.

"You said you used a mat knife, Mrs. Wade," Culligan said.

She was still looking out the window. "Over there, third drawer." She pointed at a small chest of drawers in a corner.

Culligan went over and began opening the drawers. More brushes, bottles of turpentine, rags. Three small knives were lying amidst an odd assortment of things in the third drawer down—old keys, some papers, a sketchbook, old tubes of paint. Donaldson had said it was a small knife, very sharp, approximately one inch long, possibly a scapel. These knives looked rather dull, but the size was about right.

With a pincer, Culligan lifted them one at a time out of the drawer. Two were covered with paint, or perhaps putty; the third was cleaner. Maybe she had washed it. Maybe she wasn't so smart after all. He dropped the three of them into an evidence bag.

"I wouldn't go on any vacations just now, Mrs. Wade," he said. Then, with a quick glance over his shoulder at her back, he walked out into the hall.

10 Donaldson and LaRue had vacuumed every part of the Mercedes—rugs, upholstery; mats, even the inside of the ashtrays—into a special evidence bag, whose contents would be minutely examined later. Culligan joined them out in the driveway, clutching the list of names and addresses Laura Wade had provided him with.

"Find anything?" LaRue asked.

"Damned house is enormous," Culligan said.

Donaldson laughed. "I told you you wouldn't find anything, Henry. Lady's too smart for that."

"Wrong, Dan. Take a look at this." Culligan pulled the plastic bag with the three knives out of his case.

Dan Donaldson studied it for a moment, then said. "Might be. We'll just take it back to the lab and see."

"You two find anything?"

"We took everything out of the car, Henry," Donaldson said. "Got some good solid prints off the dash. A partial on the window. Doesn't look to me like there's been any kind of a fire on that beach. I didn't expect there to be anything. Salt water. Tends to eat things away. We took some samples, though. Might get lucky."

"Excuse me." There was a woman standing on the other side of the driveway. She was short, blond, rather attractive. "Is Laura home?"

"Are you a friend of hers?"

The woman was staring at what Donaldson was

holding in his hand, the bag with the three knives. It would have been hard for someone close by in a neighborhood not to notice two men vacuuming out a car in the driveway and taking samples of sand on a private beach. Of course, most of these homes were well shielded from each other: iron gates, fences, shrubs.

"Yes. I'm Ellen Lanier. I live next door. I just got home from work. Who are you?"

Culligan put the bag back in the case and glanced at the list Laura Wade had written out. Ellen and Jason Lanier. He took out his identification. "Detective Henry Culligan," he said. "New York City Police Department. Detectives LaRue, Jones and Donaldson."

The woman looked over the other three men, then looked back at him. "New York City . . . What are you doing here?"

"We're here in connection with the Rita Harmon murder."

She shook her head. "It's a terrible thing. I can't believe something like this could happen."

"Did you know Rita Harmon?"

"Yes, I—"

"Mind if I ask you some questions?"

She glanced uncertainly at the house. "No, I guess not."

Culligan got out his pad. "Can you confirm Laura Wade's whereabouts on the evening of August tenth?"

Her eyes widened. "Confirm Laura's whereabouts? Why?"

"It's all right, Ellen. Answer the questions." Laura Wade had come outside and was standing above them, next to the garden.

"Laura, they can't seriously—"

"Just answer, Ellen." She turned and went back inside.

Ellen Lanier turned back to Culligan. "Well, I . . . August tenth. Wasn't that the night Rita was . . . murdered? I think Laura had told me she had a meeting with Rita, about the March of Dimes ball."

"Anything else?"

"No. That's it."

"So you didn't know the meeting was canceled then?"

"No. I spoke to Laura in the morning and didn't speak to her again all day."

"What did you talk about?"

"I don't really remember. Laura and I often talk on the phone."

"How often?"

"Daily. At least we used to. But I began a new job a few days ago, so I haven't had the time."

"I see. Did you speak to her the following day?" That was the day Laura Wade had confessed. August eleventh.

"Yes, I heard about Rita's murder on the morning news and tried Laura right after that, but she was out. She didn't call me back until the following day, I don't think."

"Did you ask her where she'd gone on August eleventh?"

"I think she said she went shopping."

So Laura Wade had lied to her friend. "Mrs. Lanier," Culligan said, "Were you present at the dinner party Mrs. Wade had a few weeks ago? The one Rita Harmon came to as well."

"Yes. I was."

"Did something unusual happen at the dinner party?"

She hesitated. "Well . . . let's see, there was the usual conversation."

"Did something happen between Mrs. Wade and Rita Harmon?"

The woman cast a fleeting glance at the house, then looked back at Culligan. "Well, Rita was flirting with Laura's husband."

"In the presence of the other guests?"

"Rita didn't mean any harm. It was just her way."

"You mean she flirted with all the men at the dinner party?"

"Yes, but mostly with Laura's husband."

"So what happened?"

Another glance at the house. "Well, Laura was watching Rita come on to Zach the whole night, and she got quieter and quieter, and then suddenly right after dessert was served she stood up and said, 'Take your . . . hands off my husband, Rita.' "

"And?"

"And nothing. Everyone was very embarrassed. Laura disappeared upstairs, and the party broke up right after that."

"Is Mrs. Wade a very jealous person, Mrs. Lanier?"

"No. Not at all. It was very unusual. But I think if Rita had been coming on to my husband the way she was to Laura's I would have done the same thing. Laura is a wonderful person. She's probably the nicest person I've ever met."

"How so?"

"Well, she's genuinely nice. Sweet-natured. Probably the most patient mother I've ever seen. Almost never gets angry."

"How many children does she have?"

"Three. Detective, you can't honestly think *Laura* killed Rita Harmon."

"Why not?"

"Well, it just isn't in her nature. Laura's a good person. She couldn't be really mean to anyone, much less kill them."

Culligan wondered if the woman really believed she knew Laura Wade.

"Mrs. Lanier, to your knowledge, were Rita Harmon and Zachary Wade having an affair?"

"Well, I don't really know." She glanced at the house again. "But I doubt it."

"Why do you doubt it?"

"I don't know . . . My husband is probably Zach's best friend. And I think Zach would have told him about it."

"And he would have told you?"

"Yes. I think he would."

Culligan looked at her. Did these women really think their husbands told them everything? On the other hand, two people who were actually having an affair would be pretty stupid to actually flirt in the presence of their spouses. If anything, they would make an effort to keep a certain distance.

"Mrs. Lanier, how good a friend are you of Mrs. Wade's?"

"I suppose I'm her best friend."

"Did Mrs. Wade *think* that her husband was having an affair with Rita Harmon?"

"She never said anything like that to me."

"Would she have confided her feelings to you?"

"Absolutely."

"Mrs. Lanier, just one more question. Which hand does Laura use?"

She stared at him. "What do you mean, which hand?"

"Is she left- or right-handed?"

She looked down at her own hands. "Left, I think. She paints with her left hand. I know that."

"Yeah, I saw those paintings."

"You don't think they're good?"

"Good, I don't know. I'm no art critic. It's the subject matter that bothers me."

She shrugged. "But that's part of the reason why they're so good. Take it from me, detective. Laura's work is brilliant."

"Have you ever seen her use her right hand, let's say for writing? Or for cutting with scissors?"

"Why do you want to know?"

"I'm afraid I can't tell you that."

She stared at him for a long time, then said, "No, detective. I have not. Laura is left-handed."

And she smiled.

Well, it was worth a try.

Hours later, as the sun set in a haze of red-gray clouds over the city, Culligan turned off the Cross Bronx Expressway and headed over the Third Avenue Bridge. They were minus Arnie LaRue now. He'd taken the Chrysler for further questioning of the dinner party guests. Culligan had also told him to get to some of the neighbors and see if any of them had noticed a fire on the Wades' beach that morning. Another long shot. Interviewing the Connecticut gentry, a bloodless bunch of people if ever there was one, was probably a waste of time.

Damn. The FDR Drive was packed, practically at a standstill.

"Come on, Henry. Let's get going," Donaldson said.

Culligan looked at him. He wanted Culligan to put on the siren. "What's your hurry?"

"I got a wife at home, Henry." Donaldson said.

He shrugged, changed lanes. Donaldson slumped back in the seat with a loud, pointed sigh. Culligan got off at Ninety-sixth and took York. Amidst the working types, the women in skirts and sneakers, the men in suits, Henry Culligan spotted a man walking three dogs on three leashes. The guy was dressed in high drag. Skintight leopard-spotted pants and a black body shirt, blond hair, heavy gold makeup around the eyes. Not a familiar sight in this part of town.

"Get a load of that," Donaldson said. But Henry Culligan had already seen it. And moved on. Henry Culligan was thinking about Laura Wade, wondering why she had described everything so accurately but simply failed to mention the fact that she'd dressed up as a man. Maybe they were looking at it in the wrong way. Maybe she hadn't hired someone to kill Rita Harmon at all. Maybe she was one of those split personalities, who'd done it in one personality and didn't remember in the other. Of course, that still didn't account for her having the strength to do the deed, even if she was as fit as she looked.

But maybe, when there was more than one personality—a male personality—strength was increased. Pretty bizarre theory. Logical it wasn't. Still, he would check it out tomorrow. It wouldn't be logical to assume the illogical or bizarre *wasn't possible*. The whole thing was pretty bizarre, beginning with Laura Wade—suburban mother, wife, confessor, "painter," nut—as the prime suspect.

Culligan sighed.

"I think we're gonna get her with the stuff from the car," Donaldson said.

"Why?"

"Well, let's figure it. He—"

"I thought you're sure she did it."

"Just for argument's sake. If she did it, she was dressed up like a man. So we'll call her 'he.' Now, he's just finished his deed and he's got to get himself away. So he starts walking back to the car. But he's got to be covered with blood. He's wearing surgical gloves, otherwise he would have left us some prints. And a mask. Is he going to take the time to take off the gloves and the mask and wrap them in the tarp? Maybe. Is he going to take the time to take off his clothes and wrap them in the tarp before he drives away? I doubt it."

"Why not?"

"And get into the car naked? I doubt it. Which means he—or she—left us something in the car."

"I think he's got a point, Henry," Jones said, from the back seat, where he'd been reviewing notes.

"Unless he used another car," Culligan said.

"Unless she hired someone who used another car," Donaldson said. "Unless she rented a car."

There was a silence. Then Jones said, "So why doesn't Lilly remember a car?"

"I was just thinking that," Culligan said. "I talked to Doug Gray this morning. He says Lilly might remember a car under hypnosis."

"Will she agree to it?" Donaldson.

Culligan looked at him, shrugged. "Don't know. But I'm gonna call her."

Donaldson laughed. "Unless the perp got in a cab."

Snickers from the back seat. "Now that would be a lucky break, wouldn't it?"

"Come on, you asses."

"Well, what do *you* think, Henry?" Donaldson asked him. "that she hexed the perp, that she put some kind of voodoo curse on him?"

Jones, still giggling, started to hum the theme from *The Twilight Zone*.

It was starting to get to all of them. Culligan put on the siren and, in a few moments, a path began to clear in the traffic.

"So far, the only thing I can tell you is that the lady's rich."

Joe Lorenza, the ninth detective Hallahan had assigned to the case, had joined Culligan and Jones at a table at McKellen's. It was a boisterous place, particularly noisy tonight. The subpoenas on Laura Wade's bank records had come through, and Lorenza had spent the afternoon checking money records.

Culligan lit up a cigarette. "How rich?"

"Loaded." Lorenza motioned the waitress to come over, then watched her as she made her way through the crowd.

"Hey, Joe, how you doin'? What can I get you?"

"Bud. Thanks, Donna." He watched her walk away, then turned back to Culligan and Jones. "She owns eighteen percent of Gardners Inc. The husband is only a small shareholder in the company, with a big salary and the title of president. She has two irrevocable trusts, totaling almost four million dollars, both of which have grown substantially over the last few years. That's according to one Daniel J. Openwald. Park Avenue lawyer. 'Good investments,' he says."

"Ah, the rich get richer," Jones said.

"Anything on Openwald?" Culligan asked.

"Fancy offices. Only a few clients. He's been Gardner's personal business manager for years. For all of them."

Donna appeared with the beer and set it down on

the table. Lorenza nodded at her and picked up the mug.

"What about the interest on the trusts? Where's that go?" Culligan asked.

"As far as I can tell, the interest on the trusts, plus the husband's salary, are regularly deposited, divided between a couple of other investments, and five joint savings and two checking accounts in two different banks. Laura Wade has her own checking account, too, for household expenses."

"Anything useful there?"

"Far as I can tell, no. No unusual or particularly large withdrawals. Unless you count an average monthly MasterCard bill of nearly five thousand dollars, and monthly mortgage payments on each of four homes totaling almost twenty thousand."

Jones whistled. "Where are the houses?"

"There's the Connecticut home, a home in Florida, one in Spain, and an apartment in New York. On the East Side."

"What's she do with all that money," Jones asked, "besides hang out in Saks?"

"They donated over half a million dollars to various charities last year. And it looks like she does a lot of volunteer work on her own. Serves on a number of charity boards. More than a functionary, if you know what I mean. She really works."

"What's that prove?" Culligan said.

"Nothing. She doesn't appear to have any unaccounted sources of income, though. Dividends from stocks, part ownership in a California winery, ownership of a Japanese factory that makes private label electronic equipment for Gardners."

"Christ! It'll take days to unravel all of that."

"Even then," Jones said, "there are all sorts of ways to hide things."

Culligan could feel a heaviness in his chest. "Which means the conspiracy theory might never be disproven or proven."

They just couldn't get a break.

"What'd Lilly Dunleavy say?" Jones asked.

"She said she didn't want to be hypnotized. She wants to forget the whole thing."

Culligan glanced at his watch. His shift was long over and Betty had said Henry, Jr., was coming over with Edith. He'd probably missed them already. He took one last sip of his beer and stood up. "I gotta get going."

"Henry, for Christ's sake," Jones said.

"For Christ's sake, what?"

"You look like you just lost your dog."

He frowned. "I don't have a dog. We just can't get a break on this one."

"Do we ever get a break? That's the way it goes."

"Gotta be something we're missing."

Lorenza said, "Like she didn't do it."

Henry Culligan looked at Jones. "What about you, Eric? Think we're on the right track?"

Eric Jones shook his head. "After what we saw today in that house, all those paintings, I'd have to say—"

"What paintings?" Lorenza asked.

"She's a painter. Bloody stuff. Never seen anything like it."

"Did you get a load of that one on the easel, with the animal clawing the woman?"

"Looked awfully familiar to me."

"But we'll never be able to use it."

"Maybe we can. I'm gonna talk to the DA tomorrow."

Jones sighed. "Look, Henry, we'll either get her, or we won't. Just like all the rest."

"Maybe," he said, "that's what I'm afraid of. I don't think this case is just like all the rest."

PART TWO

David:
Belief

11

David Goldman's Tuesday eight-thirty appointment, Gerald Natulian, was droning on about vegetables. A puffy little pet products manufacturer from Queens, Gerald was walking through life with the ghost of his dead mother sitting on top of his head, which was bald. She perched up there all the time like a little nanny-goblin, telling him what to eat, where and how to spend his money, how often to screw his wife, go to the bathroom, visit his mother's grave. Forty-nine years old, and the poor guy still felt compelled to eat boiled vegetables, which he hated. It was pretty crazy, but to Gerald Natulian it was a big problem, and other people's ghosts would probably sound just as silly, even crazy, to him. Still, David was glad when he left, dragging his mother's ghost behind him.

Everyone had ghosts. Laura Gardner Wade, for example, had enough ghosts chasing her to haunt New York State. And each of her ghosts had the same name: the Ghost of Should. She should be beautiful, charming and witty; she should be kind, true and loving to her husband. She should give wonderful parties and always have a smile on her face. She should never miss her exercise class, or raise her voice in anger. Or be angry. She should be perfect. Perfect children. Perfect home. Perfect life. Poor Laura. All those should-ghosts sitting on her shoulders had to make for some mighty sore muscles.

Which seemed like the least of her problems. Or was it the root of her problems?

David took out the list he'd been compiling:

> *Patient: Laura Gardner Wade*
>
> * attractive, educated, intelligent
> * malleable personality, poor sense of self becomes lack of distinction between self and outside world/self-hatred forms delusional system—me powerful/me evil/me poison—expelling poison into the world
> * depression (precipitating crisis?)
> * physical symptoms, headaches, one known hysterical paralysis . . .

Slowly, he picked up his pen and wrote: "Split personality disorder?"

Maybe she had committed the murder dressed up like a man. One male psychopath, one woman psychotic. Possible, not likely. Split personalities were very rare. Of course, not as rare as mutations . . .

Anyway, while a split personality might explain her knowing about the ten cuts, it certainly didn't account for her increasingly disturbing habit of guessing what he was thinking. So, what did? ESP?

There had to be another explanation.

David Goldman was not a man who believed in witches or demons or ghosts or hauntings, except in the psychological sense. Nor did he believe in telepathy or psychokinesis, though a few years back his friend Stan Friedland had gotten involved in some dream experimentation down at the Rockham Institute with the famous Niles Martin. But it had always seemed to David that the popularity of such beliefs was like the popularity of religion. It rose dramatically during eras of stress, fear, uncertainty and disillusionment. And the stress/fear/uncertainty/disillusionment meter in this era was up dramatically—off the scale, in fact—for any number of reasons, not the least of which was the fact that the human race could blow itself off the planet the day after tomorrow.

Which might have been a big part of the reason why psychiatrists were doing such good business.

He had a few minutes before his next patient. The thought occurred to him that maybe he was being set up for something. He laughed. It was possible he had watched one too many suspense films. Noelle Duncan had left a message on his tape while he was with Gerald. He dialed her number at NYU.

She had called to give David the results of Laura's test battery. David often sent patients for psychological testing to Noelle. She was a good friend, a long-standing colleague, and she was highly skilled, particularly with disturbed patients. And Noelle herself was quite a charmer. David had asked her out about two months back, but when they got to the end of the evening and went back to her apartment, they both realized that their getting involved would never work. It was a rather uncomfortable moment.

He heard Noelle's voice. "Oh, David. Laura Wade's score was unbelievable. The highest Stanford-Binet score I've ever personally come across, one hundred seventy-one points, so far into the genius range it's almost off the chart. Of course, her MMPI score was over two standard deviations above the mean on both the paranoia and depression scales."

"I think she may be schizophrenic," David said. "She's certainly delusional."

"Delusional?" Noelle sounded flabbergasted. "You sure?"

"She believes she emits poison that kills people. Sound delusional to you?"

"Jesus, David, if I'd stopped at the IQ . . . well, I would have said she was brilliant, but perfectly normal. Christ, she didn't seem schizophrenic. That kind of delusion generally makes the IQ scores suffer. Interferes with cognitive functions. You know that."

He did. "Will you send me the written report?"

"Sure. Tell me, what does this woman do? She a theoretical mathematician? Particle physicist? What?"

"Housewife."

Noelle Duncan laughed. "Hey, let's have dinner sometime."

"Sure," he said. "You name the day."

She said she would call next week, but he knew she wouldn't. Neither would he.

He hung up the phone. Now he had all the results of the tests. Blood and urinalysis tests: no abnormalities, no drugs. CAT scan was normal. He could rule out hyperthyroidism, liver malfunction, brain abnormality. And what could he rule in? DSM-III—schizoaffective disorder with psychotic manifestations. With reservations. Exactly what those reservations were, he wasn't sure, but it made sense to be prudent. When Laura came in for her session, he started her on a two-week course of thioridazine.

A small dose to begin. If she responded, he would continue with a tricyclic antidepressant.

"Goldman? This is Detective Henry Culligan."

The detective Ammonetti had mentioned, the one in charge. "Yes, detective, how may I help you?"

"I'd like you to come down to the station for a talk. Tenth Precinct. Twentieth and Eighth. Mind?"

"I'd be glad to. When?"

"Today, if possible."

Was this a summons? David didn't know exactly what he could tell the detective; he'd seen Laura exactly five times—and gotten nowhere. The delusion that she was poison persisted. She seemed to have moved away from Rita Harmon's murder and was now obsessing about an imagined calamity befalling her friend Ellen.

"I've got two hours free between patients," David said. "I'll be down in twenty minutes."

"I suppose you know why I asked you here, doctor," the detective said as David took a seat across from his desk.

Completely surrounded by the glass walls of Culligan's office, David felt like a fish in a bowl. "I assume you want to talk about Laura Wade." The desk was remarkably orderly. There was a single file in the middle of it, a tape recorder in one corner, a neat stack of files in another. On top of a file cabinet sat a videotape monitor and a VCR player.

"Just what is the nature of Mrs. Wade's illness?" the detective said finally.

"Patient confidentiality—"

"This is a homicide investigation, doctor. I got a dead woman in the morgue. Maybe one of the most cold-blooded murders I've ever seen. Want to take a look? I'll show you her nice green silk dress, too, all covered with blood. It'll make your hair turn white."

David couldn't help himself. "Thank you, detective, I'd rather not."

Detective Henry Culligan clearly was not amused by David's attempt at levity.

"Now, I don't know anything much about your business," he said. "About the workings of the mind. But when the workings of the mind get sick enough to murder, *that* I know about. That I *want* to know about. And you know what I know? I know I got a maniac running around. And you know what else I know? I know I got a chief on my ass. And you want to know what he thinks? He thinks we're gonna have another one of these slasher killings. Just like it. Real soon. And we don't like that. Serial killers are bad news for cops. So you know what that chief on my ass did? He gave me a whole squad of cops to run around looking for clues. That's what we do, doc. But it's almost two weeks later and I gotta tell that chief on my ass the truth: we got nothing. Nothing at all. Except a witness. Now, that's pretty good in a case like this. We know it's a man. Unfortunately, we don't know much else. She said he was tall. Your patient is tall, now, isn't she?"

"My patient is tall for a woman."

"But, you see, looking down on the street from a window, even just a couple of stories up, it kind of distorts things. Tall for a woman might just look like a tall man. Especially if the perp was wearing men's clothes. Black men's shoes. Dark jacket. Jeans. And a ski mask. A woman could wear those clothes. A woman in those clothes could look like a man from a second-story window."

"Come on, detective. My patient is obviously a woman. A beautiful woman."

"Maybe a woman in a mask, doctor." He lit a cigarette, blew smoke in a puff out of his cheeks. "All right, let's leave it for a minute. Let's talk about the fact that even though we have a witness, which is nice, she doesn't tell us anything we can go on. There are lots of dark jackets in this world, lots of ski masks. So we still have nothing. But that isn't true, now is it? Because your patient *knew* something about this murder, *doctor*, something that we didn't tell a soul. Something specific. And so I want to know *exactly* what it is you're treating this woman for."

"She's suffering from a major schizoaffective disorder."

"What's that?"

"It's sort of like schizophrenia, but the onset of the illness and the clinical picture is different. Her illness has certain depressive features. I saw her once before this. Now I've taken her on as a patient."

"Could you tell me what exactly is this schizophrenia with certain depressive features?" He took another drag on his cigarette, held the smoke down a long time.

"Well, in this case the primary clinical symptom is the paranoid delusional system in which the patient feels evil, unworthy, loathsome. In particular, she feels so uncomfortable when she gets angry that, as a kind of punishment, she believes her angry thoughts are manifested—"

"Yeah, I know. She put a hex on the man who did it."

"That's about it."

"You believe in hexes, doc?"

"No, detective. I don't."

"Well, neither do I. I mean, my daughter got her fortune told once. And my wife reads the astrology column every day. And my son—well, who knows what he does? But I, for one, have never believed in hexes. So I think to myself, since we can eliminate hexes from the picture, how come your patient comes in and when we ask her to describe the murder, she knows about the ten wounds?''

"Did the witness say she saw him cut her ten times?''

"What's the difference what the witness said? Besides which, the witness wasn't counting. She was standing up in a second-floor window watching, screaming, banging on the window, and she's gonna *count*? She did say it was a small knife, maybe a scalpel. And she did say he took his time. Did it nice and slow. One. Two. Three. Four . . . like drawing stripes, could be his calling card. But sounds like a psychopath, for sure. Wouldn't you say?''

"I'd say." It was obvious where he was going. "But he'd have to be pretty strong to hold her down that way.''

"Yeah, he would. Do you know, doctor, that your patient Laura Wade works out five times a week? Daily workouts can make a person pretty strong. And the victim was on the small side, maybe five-four. And your Laura Wade is, what, five-ten or so?''

David tried to think how he might head the man off. "And weighs one hundred and thirty pounds.''

Culligan frowned, hesitated a moment, then said, "What goes down to make that kind of psychopath, doctor?''

Now there was a question. Even harder to answer than the other question: What goes down to make someone a schizophrenic? But the two were so different, they weren't even in the same universe. Most schizophrenics were harmless, except for the one who might lash out with a delusion that people were out to get him, which didn't describe Laura at all. And there were treatments for schizophrenia, even some that helped certain victims. A true psychopath, on the other hand, was probably not treatable. How could you treat amorality, viciousness?

"Doctor?"

"Essentially," David said, "a psychopath has failed to develop a moral conscience."

"I know that, doc. What I want you to tell me is what kind of things make a psychopath psychopathic, so he's got no conscience."

"I'd say it might be someone who perhaps wasn't even aware of what he was doing, maybe some kind of early trauma, maybe very early, so he might not even remember it. Or emotional deprivation in childhood. It's really hard to say."

"And your patient, did she have an 'early trauma'?"

"I haven't uncovered anything like that. And even if I had, it certainly wouldn't entirely explain the development of a psychopathic personality."

"You shrinks make me laugh," Culligan said. "First you say one thing, then you always qualify it, later. Then I get some other shrink in here and he'll contradict everything you said. Why the hell can't any of you guys admit that half the time you *don't know*?"

"Good Lord, it's not like diagnosing a leaky pipe, detective. Human beings are very complicated—"

"Give me a break," Culligan said. "Please."

"Look, detective," David said, "if I find out anything that indicates my patient is responsible, I'll certainly pass it on. If Laura Wade is a murderess, I certainly don't want her running around the streets any more than you do."

"Fair enough, doc. I asked her the other day if she—"

"You saw her again?"

"Searched her house."

David looked at him. "Did you find anything?"

The detective was silent.

"I guess you didn't or you wouldn't have called me in," David said. "What did she say then?"

"She said it was a hex. Which story do you think I should believe?"

"I'd say the confession story was a conscious fabrication and the hex story is the truth."

"Whose truth?"

"Hers. Obviously, it's still a fabrication. But it's an unconscious one. Consciously, she really believes it."

"Hmmm." Culligan got up and walked slowly across the room, then turned his back to the wall and leaned against it. "Now, we checked, and we know there *was* a dinner party. And the dead woman *was* flirting with Laura Wade's husband. There are eight witnesses to it, nine, including the husband. Your patient was angry about that."

"She overreacted, I would say."

"That's very interesting, doc. Wouldn't an overreaction to such a situation be a motive to kill someone—I mean, motive enough for a psychopath?"

"She isn't a psychopath, detective. Her delusional system doesn't fit the profile. Anyway, her husband denies having an affair with the dead woman."

"I know that. He denied it to me this morning. But we're talking about what *she* thinks. And maybe she thinks he was having an affair."

"She only said that, detective, because she wanted you to believe her, to punish her. She made up a believable motive."

"Or maybe that *was* her motive."

"She didn't do it."

"Then how'd she know about the ten cuts?"

This was getting nowhere. David considered telling Culligan about the possible paranormal aspects of the case, but immediately rejected the idea.

Culligan came back over to his desk, lit another cigarette from the first, stubbed out the first in a full ashtray.

"Maybe she's one of those split personalities, doc. Maybe one of them is a psychopath. That's the one that did it. Maybe the other one made up the story about the hex because she couldn't face what the psychopath part had done."

"So which one confessed?"

The detective stared at David for a moment. "Tell me, doctor. How different are these so-called split personalities within one person?"

"They can be very different. Tests done on multiples have even shown different brainwave patterns."

"Could one personality think it's a man, or at least dress like a man, and the other be a woman?"

"Possibly. Gender identification is a key personality issue."

"Could one personality be a left-hander and the other be right-handed?"

"Maybe." He'd never heard of it, but it was possible. He was about to say as much, but Culligan had moved on.

"All right then, what about this?' Maybe what we have here is a woman who confessed the truth, and then when she realized we were actually going to book her, she got scared and tried to get out of it by making up a story so we would think she was crazy."

The detective, David decided, thought he had just floored his visitor. Had he? Maybe it *was* all an act on Laura's part, because she got scared and changed her

mind—maybe she was setting him up to be her defender. Did he believe that? Good God. David had
been a psychiatrist for nearly ten years now, and if she
was setting him up that way, she had to be the best
actress in the world, working from one of the best
scripts ever written. No. Not a script. An improvisa-
tion—

"Doctor. Do you plan to respond to my question?"

David looked at him. He didn't, couldn't, believe
Laura was acting.

"Doctor?"

"All right, what about this?" David said. "What
about the fact that she didn't break down until *after*
you said you *weren't* going to book her, not like she
suddenly got scared and changed her mind about confessing."

Silence. Finally, "Yeah, that kinda bothers me, too.
Maybe you should have been a detective."

"I am, in a way."

Culligan looked at his half-smoked cigarette,
frowned, stubbed it out in the ashtray. "And yet we
can't find anyone who saw her at the movie theatre
that night up in Easterbrook. That's where she told her
family she was going."

"So who notices other people at the movies?"

"What I want to know, doc, is why you're defending
her."

"Because my patient is not a psychopathic killer. I
don't know what she is, but I know she's not that."

"What does that mean, you don't know what she
is?"

That had to be one of the stupidest things he'd ever
said. "It means . . . it means, I haven't exactly made
a precise diagnosis yet."

"Does it always take this long?"

"It's a very complicated case."

"Then how do you know she's not a killer?"

"I just know." How *did* he know?

"Then how come her alibi, and I use the term loosely, can't be confirmed? Miss Judy Wenct. Nice kid, spoke to her myself. She's the ticket taker who worked at the Easterbrook theatre the night of the murder. Says she never forgets a face. And she says she doesn't remember Laura Wade."

"How *would* she? Does she know her?"

Culligan opened the file on the desk, took out a snapshot of Laura in her pink pants outfit, a Polaroid.

"Got this photograph of her right here with her statement," he said.

"I'd like to hear that statement, detective."

"You can even see it, doctor," Culligan said. He took a videotape out of a pocket on one side of the file, went over and fed it into the VCR. Then he sat back in the chair with his fingertips touching each other and watched David while the machine wound forward. The tape began with file codes, dates, lists of police officers' names, then cut to a shot of Laura. She was sitting at the table in that small room he'd seen her in. There was a uniformed officer standing in the background.

The camera panned back to reveal Culligan, sitting across from her at the table. He identified himself, then explained her rights to her, asked her if she understood. She nodded, then began to speak, calmly, coherently. Too coherently.

When it was over, Culligan flipped off the machine, ejected the tape, looked at David and said, "Pretty convincing, huh?"

It was.

David took a deep breath.

"Where's the part where she broke down and said she'd put a hex on the murderer?"

"We didn't record it, doctor. We're not in the habit of making tapes of crazy people. That's your job." He shook his head. "It may have been a mistake not to record it."

David found himself wishing they had. It might have been useful to see what hysteria in Laura Wade looked like.

"Why do you think it was a mistake not to record it?"

The detective stared at him, stroking his mustache. "Because she may have done it, of course. We already know she's crazy."

"She's not that kind of—"

"Crazy is crazy, doc."

"She's the opposite of that, detective. She can't stand anger, much less violence."

"And maybe she can't stand it so much, she can't control herself?"

"She didn't do it," David said. His voice sounded like a screech.

"How do you know, doctor?" the detective said. "How do you know?"

12 Packing an overnight bag on Friday night for his trip to Philadelphia the next morning, David found himself thinking about Laura again.

Maybe she *was* setting him up to be her defender.

But she'd be trying to convince him that she *was* crazy, not that she wasn't. And exactly what was it she was trying to convince him of? That she was a mutation with powers far beyond even precognition? That she had the power of life and death in her hands—no, her thoughts?

David zipped up his case, left it on the chair in his bedroom, then went into the kitchen to make himself a cup of tea. He tried to think it through logically.

A person who had a dream or a thought that came true in the future might come to one of three conclusions. Most people would just write it off as a coincidence. If it kept happening, though, the person might well think there was some precognitive element to the dream or thought. And then there was the third conclusion, the *causal* conclusion. The psychotic conclusion. Laura had obviously decompensated somewhere along the line, shifted from the rather passive notion that her dreams and thoughts predicted the future to the more active notion that they *caused* the future. Which meant what?

As he set the water on the stove to boil, David reminded himself that he was a psychiatrist with a full schedule of patients, many of whom he believed he could help. He believed in psychiatry. He believed there were reasons for people's beliefs and behavior, even if they weren't always readily accessible: events in childhood, repressed fantasies, yesterday's dinner. He believed in natural, not supernatural, explanations for events. And so, when Laura talked about the power of her mind, a power she believed was uncontrollable and growing, he told her there were alternative explanations for these incidents. He had words to explain them all: selective attention, faulty memory, guilt, misinterpretation, coincidence.

What else should he be telling her? Patients often cited chance events in the real world to confirm a delusional belief system.

The teapot was whistling on the stove. He poured himself a cup and carried it to the kitchen table. Sipping it, he remembered the man he'd treated during his residency who was convinced that all airplanes overhead were really alien spaceships outfitted to look like airplanes. But when a patient walked into your office and told you aliens were after him, you didn't widen your eyes and say, "Really, what time is the spaceship landing?" That would be collusion. Psychiatrically defined as: agreement with (or promotion of) belief or behavior that is inappropriate, unreal or destructive. Believing the patient's delusions.

He finally went to bed at about eleven, resolved to get Stan Friedland aside for a private conversation at his parents' party the following night.

He dreamed.

He was standing on the edge of a cliff with his older brother, Ivan. There were mountains all around them, and a lake—the summer camp they had gone to in the Poconos. They were both young boys, the age they'd been then. He could see the mess hall in the distance. Suddenly they were fighting, scuffling, tumbling, punching each other. Finally he got Ivan down on the ground and said, "Give?" He said, "No." David said, again, "Give?" "No." So he gave him a push and he fell over the side of the ledge. He rushed to the edge to watch his brother fall, anticipating, wanting him to fall. But suddenly, David saw that his brother had sprouted wings. He backed away, turned around, and there was Laura. She was one of the camp counselors and had witnessed the whole thing.

Awakening, he realized that he hadn't dreamed the

dream in a very long time. It was a very old dream—a recurring nightmare, really, an unwanted visitor he had finally learned to live with, a reminder to him of just how stark subconscious wishes could be.

He lay in the dark. It was obvious why he'd had the dream—he would be seeing his brother, his family, at the party. But what was Laura doing in the dream? She was a new element.

Occasionally he had dreams about patients. That wasn't what was bothering him. What bothered him was the feeling he had in the dream, also a new element. He felt humiliated, exposed.

He closed his eyes and found that he simply could not get back to sleep. When morning finally came, he gave Stan a call to see if they could drive down together, but Stan had a meeting and said he couldn't leave that early.

The Volvo was in the garage on Eighty-first, a monthly space David had rented for nearly five years. It bothered him to pay over $200 per month to keep a car when he hardly ever used it, but there wasn't any alternative. He got inside and drove out.

It was a glorious late summer day, milder than the past few weeks, the sky cloudless and blue even over the city. He decided to enjoy the ride, rolled down the windows as he exited the Lincoln Tunnel and headed down the New Jersey Turnpike.

He turned up the radio. There was an old song on, "Born to Be Wild." He sang along, loudly. Then he laughed. He'd tried marijuana twice, and he'd had sex with a total of five women, including his wife. Not exactly wild.

He got to his parents' neighborhood around eleven-thirty. Named Sherwood Oaks, it was one of the ubiquitous suburban developments that had sprung up after the war: street after street of split-level homes, all alike except that some had three bedrooms, some four. And each house was painted and trimmed in the color of choice. The Goldman house on Robin Hood Lane was trimmed in pink: David's mother thought pink would make it stand out. It did.

His father was out in the garden, digging up weeds. Every time David saw him these days he realized he'd forgotten again how old his father looked. Old, but content. He'd always hated selling picture frames, though he'd done it all of his adult life. To David's father, something of an intellectual, not being able to go to college had probably been the major disappointment in his life. It was left to his sons to fulfill that dream for him. But now that he had sold his business, he read, he talked politics with anyone who would listen, he gardened, he did a little writing, he mourned again his uncles and cousins who'd been wiped out by the Nazis.

Abraham Goldman greeted his son with an enthusiastic bear hug, as always, then immediately began telling him about the night classes he was taking at Villanova: a course in Marxism and one in comparative religion. He confided that he knew more than the professors but was enjoying the courses anyway.

Lena Goldman was in the kitchen, cooking up a storm. She was preparing enough food for sixty, probably thirty-five more than were coming. The kitchen smelled of dill and onion, which she was slicing up for potato salad.

"I've already got a brisket for you wrapped up in the fridge," she said when she saw him. Then she laughed.

David kissed her. She looked terrific, as always, tall and thin with silvery hair. She was reliably opinionated. She could cut you to shreds if she had a mind to, but she did it with finesse, and her unusual combination of warmth and authority made her the kind of person that people naturally wanted to be around. Abraham Goldman worshiped his wife; David thought she took advantage of him.

The three of them sat at the kitchen table while Lena Goldman cut up raw vegetables for crudités. She asked him why he couldn't move back to Philadelphia, now that Allison was gone. No reason, except that he had a thriving practice. He told them he'd run into Allison last month.

Abraham Goldman smiled. "Why don't you find yourself another woman, David?"

His mother was looking at him as if he needed immediate first aid.

At least they'd stopped asking when he was going to have children. It wasn't that he didn't want children, it was more that Allison and he couldn't get it together long enough to produce any.

Ivan and Maggie arrived at six o'clock. David hugged his brother, who had grown a beard, and kissed his sister-in-law, whose mop of flaming red hair looked even frizzier than usual, congratulated them both on Ivan's research grant.

"I didn't think it would come through, with all the budget cutting going on," Ivan said.

"A hundred thousand ought to keep our two teenagers in designer-torn jeans," Maggie said, smiling.

He asked her where Joan and Molly were. David absolutely adored his nieces, particularly Molly, who called him her special uncle. In fact, David was her only uncle.

"Teenagers," Maggie reminded him. "Joan drives now, and the both of them are profoundly embarrassed to be seen in public with their parents. They'll make an entrance later.'' She headed into the kitchen to help her mother-in-law.

"I'm really happy for you," David said after she'd gone. Despite their differences, and whatever childhood feelings of inadequacy those differences inspired, David liked and admired his older brother.

Ivan put his arm around him. "Thanks. So, David, are you going to tell me why you look like you've been through three days of Chinese water torture?"

David admitted he hadn't been sleeping well.

"Worried about another of your patients?"

David shrugged.

Ivan took his pipe out of his pocket, lit a match to it, drew in the smoke.

"Now, if you'd chosen a sensible specialty—like, say, plastic surgery—you wouldn't be so worried all the time. Take it easy, David."

David looked at him. *He* took it easy. For all his brilliance, Ivan was indeed a laid-back man, thoughtful, contemplative, a typical professor complete with pipe, jacket patches and beard. Maggie was another story, living testimony that opposites attract. She was a kooky redhead, creative, high-strung, explosively articulate on every subject imaginable. David liked her but found that a little of Maggie could go a long way.

The guests had begun arriving now, and the two brothers had to cut their conversation short, but they continued again when Ivan met David at the food table and asked about his divorce.

"So, when are you going to be a free man?" Ivan said, puffing on his pipe, sending a plume of cherry-scented tobacco into the air.

"Allison is stalling for some reason."

"Why don't you go ahead and do it yourself?"

"She left me. Let her do it."

"You know what your problem is, David? Inertia." He lit another match to the pipe, drew in. "Mom said Stan was coming down."

David nodded. "He was going to drive down after a meeting he had this morning."

"How's he doing?"

"Settling once again into his natural state of ex-husbandry. Very much the same except for a few extra pounds."

"Did I hear someone making derogatory comments on my ever increasing corpulence?"

The two of them turned and saw Stan Friedland on his way to their corner. Stan was a large man with a full beard, a lucrative Park Avenue psychiatric practice, and three ex-wives. Indeed, he was getting larger.

"Talk about ESP," Ivan said. "You would pick this moment to show up."

Stan laughed, patted his belly.

"How'd your meeting go," David said.

"That Fleming is a narrow-minded asshole," he said, then headed for the canapés.

David's nieces showed up when the party was in full swing. Joanie, who'd been accepted at Brown, Barnard and George Washington, was very excited about college. Molly, who was fifteen, asked him if he was going to get back with Allison. He told her no, he didn't think so.

"Allison," Molly said, "is a rotten person to leave a wonderful man like you. I'd never leave you if *I* were Allison."

"Don't think I would let you leave."

She smiled, then remembered her braces and stopped smiling. David hugged her. She was a terrific kid.

The party was getting noisy now, groups scattered here and there around the house, talking, laughing, drinking, eating. Stan finally tore himself away from the food table and joined them again.

"Mom tells us you're into ESP," Joanie said. "What kind of stuff are you into?"

"Pagan witchcraft," he said.

Joanie's eyes widened. "No, really."

"Actually, I'm a psychiatrist, Joanie," Stan said, "just like your uncle here. I do have some interest in parapsychology, though. I have on occasion done some experimental work with the Rockham Institute, which is a place where they study this sort of thing."

"Bunch of cauldron-stirrers, if you ask me," Ivan said.

"Daddy!" Joan turned back to Stan. "What kinda of stuff do they study? ESP? Telepathy?"

David was surprised that his niece was interested in this sort of thing or knew anything at all about it.

"Research in all areas of what is called P-S-I, which is the study of all paranormal phenomenon," Stan said. "Telepathy, dreams, ESP, psychokinetics, clairvoyance, psychic energies of all sorts. But the work isn't anything like what most people think. It's highly scientific and systematic."

"You mean no séances or gypsies in turbans with crystal balls?" said Molly, careful not to smile.

"Occasionally you do find people with true ability— what is called a gifted subject. First, you have to weed out the fakers. Most are fakers."

"Most?" Ivan said.

Stan rubbed the bridge of his nose, as if he had defended this particular interest of his on too many occasions. He had certainly defended it enough times with David.

"True psychics are very rare. Psychokinetic ability is even rarer. The research at the Rockham Institute attempts to study these phenomena by means of normal rules of scientific inquiry—objectivity and repeatability. For scientific study, all sorts of alternative explanations—extraneous variables, like power of suggestion, self-fulfilling prophecies, memory lapses and faking—have to be eliminated."

"Once I saw a movie where this guy could explode people's heads. It was neat."

"Fun stuff, Molly. But it's science fiction. The current state of scientific P-S-I experimentation is very tame. Practically dull."

"You mean like predicting those cards with the symbols on them?" Joan asked.

"Zener cards? Well, it's become a little more complicated than that, but basically that's the idea."

"I'd say they're all trying to find something that doesn't exist, except in the imagination," Ivan said.

"That's not *my* problem with it," Maggie said. "My problem is I just don't see how you can apply scientific principles to something that by nature is unscientific. Psychic phenomena are elusive, mysterious, and they're meant to be that way. What you're doing is trying to explain the unexplainable."

Stan laughed. "And Ivan's research on the nature of infinity is explainable?"

"Everything that exists has to operate according to scientific laws, Maggie," David said.

"Unless it *doesn't* exist," Ivan said.

Maggie made a face at her husband. "Oh, don't pay any attention, Stan. These Goldman brothers are just so boring and logical. Professor Ivan here doesn't even believe in himself until he looks in the mirror in the morning. I think the supernatural is like Freud's id.

You know it's there, but there's no damned way you can prove it objectively.''

"I'm not sure I understand, David," Stan said. "Your new patient is schizophrenic. So what's the question?"

The two of them had slipped away from the house and were sitting outside on the patio. It was a beautiful summer night, a clear star-laden sky, a nearly full moon. There was a horde of insects buzzing the yellow porch light. David could hear party sounds from inside: laughter, conversation, the music someone had put on.

"You don't think she murdered this woman, do you?"

Hoping the insects would go away, David switched off the porch light. "No. I really don't think so."

"You're not suggesting that there's some truth to her claims, are you? That she's some kind of a mutation, who can cause things to happen with her dreams and her thoughts?"

"I'm not suggesting anything."

"David, the kind of power required for a thought like that to cause someone else to murder would be something totally unknown. Causation would have to involve telepathy, clairvoyance, psychokinesis, plus some kind of brainwashing by thought transference—all over long distances, unimpeded by temporal considerations. She'd have to be like a radio transmitter, sending out signals complete with delaying factors. She sends out the signal on day one, and two weeks later the 'weapon' gets it and goes out and commits murder. I'd be more willing to accept some form of precognition."

"What kind?"

"No kind, because for one thing, it violates the cause-and-effect rule. Ideally, event A, the thought, should be related to a third party before event B, the consequence. But your Laura reports it after the fact. It's much more like she imposed the specific vision on her anger afterward, as a way of punishing herself—I'm assuming she has a real problem with anger."

"Yes. But putting that aside—"

"It's difficult to put that aside, David. Evidence would have to be a lot more convincing than that for someone like Niles Martin to accept it."

"All right, but hypothetically—what kind of precognition would it be?"

"Well," he said, lighting a cigarette, "it's like Lincoln's famous assassination dream. You can look at it two ways. Does the fact of the actual assassination three days after the dream mean the dream was precognitive, or did the dream cause the assassination?"

"Three ways. Did the dream actually take place?"

"Four ways. If it did, wasn't it just a coincidence? Death dreams are pretty universal."

David told him how lucid Laura seemed.

"Which schizophrenics often are."

"Well, there are other things, too. For one thing, she keeps walking in and out of my dreams. She isn't the main subject of the dreams, but she seems to be always there. Watching or listening, but there."

"Not so remarkable if she's unusually attractive or just plain unusual," he said.

"She's both. But there are other things. Her remarkable quality of empathy, for instance. She never says something negative about anyone, Stan, unless she counters it with some psychological insight into the way they behave. She always has excuses for people, as if she understands what is in their hearts. Her excuses, of course, don't extend to herself. Her standards for herself, for her behavior, for control of her anger and her emotions, are beyond belief.''

"Anything else?"

"Well . . . there's this habit she has. She keeps making guesses about what I'm thinking.''

Stan flicked his cigarette out on the lawn, where it glowed in the darkness for a moment.

"Accurate guesses, I take it?"

"Incredibly accurate. Often she expresses not only my thought but the words I just used to think it with.''

Stan was staring at him. "You know, schizophrenics are top telepathic performers.''

"So you think it's possible she may be able to cause—"

"Cause? No. But there may indeed be something paranormal here. She did know about the ten cuts. Why not have her tested?''

"I suppose I could.''

"Want me to call Niles Martin and set it up?''

"No. Give me another week or two.''

"Why?''

"I don't know. I just have the feeling there's something I'm missing.''

"I say Variety B paranoid schizophrenia. She feels so evil she brings disaster to others by magic. Any Variety A—mistrust or someone plotting against her?''

"Not that I've uncovered.''

"Are you medicating her?''

"Thioridazine. Nothing yet.''

"Still," he said. "Variety B paranoid psychosis. Schizophrenia, or at least some type of schizoaffective disorder. I had a patient once who said she'd turned into poisonous blue smoke. She used to mark out a circle around her, exactly four feet in diameter. Said if I got any closer, I'd be a goner. This one sounds much like it to me."

13

The man walked among Death Witch images; their color was red, the color of power, the color of death. There were so many. How could he choose? He touched them with his fingertips, remembering. Her face.

There was a noise. Quick, now. Act quickly.

Moving among Death Witch images, he stopped. He was looking at a wild animal, clean-picked bones. How very thoughtful of Her to make it so clear. So precise.

Perfect.

14

Patients often began their sessions with a little present for David, some insight or pattern they'd worked hard to uncover and sweated to reveal: "Doctor, I finally realized I'm afraid of men," or "Would you believe I've always hated my mother?"

Laura Wade began her third week of therapy as follows:

"Ellen had to have twenty-five stitches on her wrist and hand. The dog attacked her."

David looked at her for a long moment before he was able to speak. There seemed to be something in his throat, obstructing his breathing, choking him. He poured himself a drink of water from the pitcher on the credenza, gulped it down. She was watching him as he drank. He set the glass down on the desk.

"It could have been worse," she said softly, more to herself than to him, then she covered her eyes with her hands and took a deep breath. When she looked up, her face was composed.

"Tell me what happened, Laura."

"The worst part about it is that it was our dog. I told Zach we shouldn't have a doberman."

"A doberman?"

"Yes. Named Darwin."

Darwin? As in Charles?

"Zach always says we need protection, but I've got the three kids—"

"Aren't they your husband's children, too, Laura?"

"Of course. But I'm their mother and I've always been nervous about Darwin when their friends are around, and we do have a burglar alarm. But Zach wanted the dog, so I kept him in the pen. I almost never let him out, which was cruel—I know that—but I couldn't help it." She was crying.

"But we were all out by the pool yesterday, and Darwin got out of his pen somehow. Ellen was standing by the diving board, in her bathing suit. And then suddenly, without warning, the dog attacked her."

Christ! Was he supposed to believe this? He certainly couldn't ascribe it to faulty memory, or to her imposition of the dream on her anger. This was before the fact. She had told him the tiger dream last week.

Suddenly David's eyes hurt. He took off his glasses and switched on his desk lamp. Laura looked raw in the light, unfinished. Maybe she *was* a multiple personality, rare as that was. Maybe one half was doing things the other half didn't remember. Such as letting the dog out of its pen. Such as murdering Rita Harmon.

He stood up and walked slowly over to the window, aware of her eyes on his back. Morning clouds had given way now to a light drizzle. Mrs. Frangipani was outside on the sidewalk, standing with another woman in a red kerchief. The two appeared to be arguing about something. Mrs. Frangipani was gesturing, making a point. Laura was still watching him when he turned around, her hands folded on her lap. A murderer's hands?

He looked at her. Though he'd never dealt with multiple personality himself, according to the literature, it was common for them to be one personality who knew about the other, or others, while the others were only aware of lost time.

"Laura," he asked, "have you ever had blackouts?"

"No. Why?"

He looked at her. Did that automatically eliminate the possibility of multiples? Maybe not.

"The similarity of your tiger dream and the dog attack could just be a coincidence," he said.

"How many times do these things have to happen for you to accept some explanation other than coincidence?"

"All right, Laura, let's just suppose there is a precognitive element to your dreams—"

"Not just my dreams."

"All right, then, your dreams or wishes or visions.

Causation is an entirely different matter from precognition, wouldn't you say?''

"Absolutely. That's why I'm so scared. I think I really could have gone on with my life, the other way.''

"Let's look at it logically. Causation would have to involve telepathy, clairvoyance, psychokinesis over a long distance, plus some kind of a delaying factor. You send out the signal on day one, and the dog gets it a week later. Think about it. Does it make sense to you?''

"Why not? I've always been telepathic and clairvoyant. I was born that way. It must be my internal structure that gives me those abilities, right? And now my internal structure is altering somehow. As if I have a disease, as if it's all suddenly gone haywire. Why couldn't I do those things if suddenly my powers went out of control?''

"Laura, I find nothing physically wrong with you. Your CAT scan is normal, your blood work—''

She laughed. "I guess I'd have to come in here with electric fingers or with an extra set of eyes for you to believe me.''

"When I see the sparks, I'll let you know.'' She *was* different from most psychotics. She made jokes.

David leaned back in his chair and looked at her. She *did* seem to be changing. Her face was very tired and drawn, her skin almost sallow; she looked as if she hadn't slept in a long time. Her hands were clenched tight—her hands! The paralysis had disappeared. He was reminded of Freud's famous patient, Anna O.

"Laura, are you sure you never have blackouts? Times in your life that you can't remember things, or when you woke up and couldn't remember what day it was, or what you'd done the previous day?''

"Very sure. Why do you keep asking?"

"I thought you could read my mind."

There was a long silence.

"Is Darwin an aggressive dog, Laura?"

"Actually, he was always pretty friendly, even with strangers. But you read all those stories, and I was uncomfortable having him around anyway."

"Was? What happened to the dog?" he asked her.

"Zach shot him."

"*Shot* him?"

She nodded.

"What do you mean? When did he shoot him?"

"Well, Darwin had grabbed hold of Ellen's hand and she was screaming and the kids were screaming—" She began crying again, too hard to go on.

He waited a moment, trying to picture in his mind such a horrible scene.

"What happened then, Laura?"

"Well, suddenly Darwin let go of her. Then Zach came out. When he saw what had happened, he went inside and got the gun—he keeps a gun in the house for protection—and . . . well, he just ordered the dog behind the cabana and shot him."

"Right then and there?"

"Yes."

Silence.

David stood up and went over to the other side of the desk, sat on the edge. The incident was one of the most appalling a patient had ever recounted. How could a man do such a thing, right there with children watching and listening?

"How did you feel when he did that?" he said finally.

"The children . . . are very upset, especially Sammy. I was up with him all night."

"How did you feel about it, Laura?"

"I was upset, too. Of course, I had wanted to get rid of the dog all along, but I . . . well, I thought Zach should have just taken the dog away."

"Of course he should. Weren't you angry at him?"

She hesitated a moment. "Yes . . . I guess I was."

"Don't you know when you're angry, Laura?"

She rubbed her temples with her fingertips, moaned softly.

"I know."

"Did you express your anger?"

She looked at him as if he were out of his mind. "Of course not."

After a moment, she got up and walked over to the window, looked out. "Please help me."

She was obviously aware of how inappropriate her husband's behavior was—and, just as obviously, afraid to express her feelings.

Suddenly she said, "You know what it all reminds me of? Do you remember Freud's famous case, Anna O.? The one who developed all those hysterical symptoms including an arm paralysis?"

David rubbed his eyes, put his glasses back on.

"Yes," he said. "I remember."

He could hear the ticking of the clock. Laura was lying on the sofa, breathing regularly, her eyes open. He looked at her. Could he contact another personality, assuming there was one?

Although terrified at first, she'd been a highly susceptible hypnotic subject. After less than ten minutes, she was deeply under.

"Are you relaxed, Laura?"

"Yes." Her voice was calm, easy.

He took her further down, just to be sure.

"All right, Laura, how do you feel?"

She smiled. "Fine."

"Okay, then, where are you?"

"In your office."

"Good. I want you to put yourself back on to the day of Rita Harmon's murder. When you do this, I want you to talk in the present tense, as if it's happening now."

"I told my children—"

"Picture it happening now, Laura. Tell me what you see. Present tense."

Her expression remained blank.

"It's happening now. You're talking to Rita on the phone. What time is it?"

"Three."

"Where are you?"

"In the kitchen. I'm sitting at my desk in the kitchen. I pick up the wall phone. 'Hello.' "

"What does she say?"

" 'Hi, Laura. I'm sorry, I have to cancel tonight. George wants me to meet him at St. Germain, in Manhattan. Seven-thirty. Shall we do it next week?' I tell her next week will be fine. Rita's thinking that she's going to wear her green silk dress with the plunging neckline and the puffed skirt."

David looked at her. No. This wasn't possible. She was reporting that she read people's thoughts. *Under hypnosis?* Maybe she wasn't really under.

"How do you feel, Laura?"

"Fine. Relaxed."

He looked at her, noted the breathing, the glazed eyes. She couldn't—surely—be faking.

"All right, Laura, now skip ahead a few hours. It's five o'clock. What are you doing?"

She hesitated, then began to speak, very slowly.

"I'm telling Melissa that I'm going to the movies. She says, 'What movie, Mom?' I tell her, 'I'm sorry, honey, I'll take you next time.' She makes a face, then I go upstairs . . . and . . ."

"And what do you do?"

"I lie down on the bed and I fall asleep."

Maybe this was it. "And then?"

"I wake up. And I look at the clock. Now it's six-fifteen. I get up and change my top. The red cotton. I go downstairs, take my bag and my keys from the front hall, say goodbye to the girls—they're in the kitchen— and to Sammy, he's in the playroom, and I tell Darlene I'll be home around ten and to make sure the kids aren't up till all hours. Melissa says, 'Susan invited Courtney and me over tonight.' I say, 'Fine. Have a good time. Do you want me to drive you?' She says, 'No. We'll walk.' I go outside. It's still light out and a little chilly . . . so I go back and I get a sweater, and I come out and open the car door and get in and put my key in the ignition . . ."

If she was faking it was one hell of a performance.

"Where are you now?"

"I'm backing out of the driveway . . . and I go left on Derwin Place, past Ellen's house, and I think I should have invited her but I'd really rather be alone. I've been really upset to see anyone after what happened at the dinner party."

"Where are you now?"

"Turning right on Easterbrook Road. I go under the highway, past Marwell Avenue and past Third Street and then I turn right onto Main Street. I park in a space there, and I go out and start to walk. I look in the window in the shop, and there's a little toy Santa, and I think that's odd because it's summer, and then I go to the next store. It's a men's clothing shop. . . . "

David listened as she described things in the shop windows she passed, then went on to say she headed into the movie at ten of seven and sat there until the movie started, and didn't talk to anyone. When she began to describe the loud rock music that began the picture, he decided he'd had enough. She certainly wasn't at the murder scene, unless she was capable of astral projection in addition to whatever else she was capable of.

It couldn't be multiples, unless they existed at some lower level of her personality, one he hadn't reached.

Of course, even if it was multiples, that still wouldn't explain the dog's behavior in attacking her friend.

As he began to bring her out of it, she said, "I didn't talk to anyone at the movies. Except the ticket taker. But she didn't look at me. That's good."

"Why?"

"Because I don't want an alibi. Because I want them to convict me. Because I want them to put me to death."

After she left, he picked up the phone to call Henry Culligan, but before he'd finished dialing, he changed his mind. If he asked the detective what Rita Harmon was wearing when she died, he'd have to explain why he wanted to know. He'd have to say that Laura thought she knew what Rita was wearing. And if she was right, the detective would take it as proof positive that Laura was guilty, that she was there at the murder scene.

And there was also the possibility that Rita Harmon had changed her mind later, when Laura was out of "earshot," and worn something else.

Then he remembered. He didn't have to call Henry Culligan. Henry Culligan had already told him what the corpse was wearing. "I got a dead woman in the morgue . . . I'll show you her nice green silk dress, all covered with blood.''

David hung up the receiver and put his head in his hands.

On Thursday night, Zachary Wade's limousine pulled up in front of David's office at seven-thirty. David, having spent much of the day preparing for the meeting, still had not come up with a plan for what he would say.

He offered the man a drink, which he refused. He sat down in exactly the same place he sat before. This time the suit was three-piece, dark blue, same quality fabric and cut. He looked at David, raised his eyebrows slightly.

"Well, how is she?"

"Somewhat calmer, but the crisis is far from over. It's possible that your wife is suicidal, Mr. Wade."

"Suicidal?"

"Well, she sees no way out for herself. She believes that her anger has the power to destroy, and since no one can successfully control or deny their emotions—well, you see what I mean. My advice is for you to watch her carefully. Maybe even hide that gun you keep."

"How do you know I have a gun?"

"Laura told me."

"I see."

"Now, I've begun her on some medication, which could help, but it'll be at least a week before we see any change. Assuming we're going to see any change."

"What does that mean?"

"Mr. Wade, for some patients these drugs are a godsend. But you have to find the right medication and the right dosage as well, often a process of trial and error. Unfortunately, there are some people who don't respond to any of them, at all.'' David didn't mention that these people are the ones who often decompensate more and more until they are essentially unreachable, cases in point of madness as it is generally understood. ''I think it's going to take a long time, Mr. Wade.''

He was tapping his foot on the floor. ''What do the two of you talk about?'' he asked after a moment.

''We talk about Laura's feelings, about how she sees things. She told me what happened with your dog, for example.''

He stopped tapping. ''What about it?''

David recounted the dream about the tigers.

''She dreamed a tiger was mauling Ellen's arm, and she thinks *that* was what made Darwin do it? You've got to be kidding.''

''Did she mention the dream to you?''

''Laura never tells me her dreams. People's dreams have never particularly interested me.''

''Does she ever wake up in the middle of the night screaming?''

''Often.''

''What do you do?''

''I hold her and tell her it's going to be all right.''

''When I asked if you'd noticed something wrong lately, you said you hadn't. Doesn't waking up screaming strike you as something wrong, Mr. Wade?''

''She's always had nightmares. Always.''

''Have they increased in frequency of late?''

''Perhaps.''

David was beginning to get really annoyed with him. Didn't he pay *any* attention to Laura? He said he loved her and love required some caring, some attention. He suggested that perhaps he might be more attentive to his wife's feelings.

"She was upset that you took the dog and shot him, Mr. Wade," David said. "Understandably so."

"For Christ's sake, the dog was attacking a neighbor. Just what was I supposed to do?"

"Surely it would have been better to take the dog *away* to get rid of him."

"She didn't say so. How the hell am I supposed to know what she's thinking."

"She's afraid to get angry at you, Mr. Wade. She's afraid of hurting you."

"With her evil powers?"

"Yes."

He stood up. "This is the most unbelievable thing I've ever heard of. What would give her such ideas? It's absurd. . . . "

He seemed much more nervous tonight than he had the last time. He kept walking around the office, pacing back and forth. David decided to play a hunch. He didn't really expect to get a truthful response, but it couldn't hurt to ask.

"Do you want to help your wife, Mr. Wade?"

"Of course I do."

"All right, then. I'm going to ask you something you may think inappropriate, but in order for me to help your wife, it would be best if I know certain things about your relationship with her."

"I have nothing to hide."

"All right, then, do you have affairs, Mr. Wade?"

The man stared at him for a moment, then said, "If you must know, I do not have affairs. Occasionally, I engage the services of prostitutes."

Christ, the man was arrogant. David looked at him. He was tapping his foot again. Yet he'd just said he went to prostitutes casually, offhandedly, as if he were saying he went to Boston.

"Does Laura know about them, Mr. Wade?"

"I've never told her. Occasionally, not often, I find a need for a little variety. The women I pay for are young and beautiful. They do whatever I want, and then they leave. Mistresses and affairs get complicated."

"Are your tastes unusual?"

"Not really. But my wife has never been a very sexual person."

"What does that mean?"

"Well if you must know, she's frigid."

"Sometimes lack of response to sex can lie with both partners, Mr. Wade."

"I figured you would say that. I assure you, doctor, it has nothing to do with my skills as a lover. Sex doesn't appeal to my wife. There are some people like that. Asexual. Not that she denies me. She simply doesn't particularly enjoy it. Never has. Sex is only one small part of life. Laura has many other attributes."

"Like what?"

"Well, for one, she's quite beautiful, don't you think? Of course, she has the mistaken notion that she's peculiar-looking. And she exercises without fail. Of course, so do I. We'll live longer, isn't that the current medical thinking? In any case, my solution to her problem in bed strikes me as a good one. I call on women to come and service me, if you will. I'm not naive. I realize their response is pretty much an act, most of the time. But there are no strings, no attachments, no complications. I'd say that was better than having affairs, wouldn't you? I could have affairs, or engage a mistress, I suppose. In my work, in my travels, I meet many women. As I said, women find me attractive.''

''Why so?''

''By society's standards, I'm an attractive man. Both my physical features and my position. I run a large company. Certain women, often very beautiful women, seem to respond to power and authority.'' He looked at David. ''You can tell me that in your work, in your position of authority, you have never had women attempt to seduce you.''

''Of course I have. It's endemic to psychiatry, not necessarily because of anything I may actually be.''

''Yes. I suppose you *would* say that.''

''Why?''

''Transference. Countertransference. Bunch of nonsense.''

''You don't have much respect for psychiatry, I take it.''

There was a trace of amusement in his face.

''Not particularly.''

''Why not?''

''What's the old saying. 'Those who can't do, teach'? Those who can't live, analyze life.''

David stared at him. It was almost a personal attack, certainly not an answer to the question.

''And you see no point to such an analysis?''

''The world is easily explainable to me, doctor. I am not a man who looks for the kind of hidden meanings in life that you do, for intricate psychological explanations for behavior. Life is what it is. What's the point of trying to figure it all out, making circular and useless psychological explanations, the way Laura does, the way you undoubtedly do? That only leads to worry—believe me, Laura worries about more things than you can ever imagine—and I suppose to what we have here. To this breakdown you say she's had.''

Was he suggesting there'd been no breakdown?

"Mr. Wade, it might help if you showed more understanding of *what* your wife worries about, what she feels. It might help if you didn't put her down so much.''

"I don't put Laura down. She puts herself down.''

David wasn't going to get anywhere with that one. Christ! He didn't like this guy at all. Of course, David didn't have any right to impose the fact that he didn't like the man on Laura, except perhaps help her realize that she didn't have to put up with a man who tried to dominate her the way he obviously did. Unfortunately, David had seen many female patients in his practice with controlling husbands.

Finally Wade said, "Yes. You probably have a point, doctor. I do love Laura, and I want her to get well.''

He was looking at David, the picture of concern and sincerity, but he was still tapping his goddamned foot.

15

"In the midst of life we are in death . . .''

Henry Culligan stood under an elm tree a discreet distance from the crowd of mourners at Fairlawn Hills Cemetery, listening to the Episcopal minister about to commend the spirit of Rita Harmon to heaven, her body to earth. The coroner had finally released her remains for burial; the family had gathered to mourn her. Culligan was a Catholic—lapsed, as he liked to say; the rituals of the service were similar, the spirit was exactly the same.

"O God, whose mercies cannot be numbered, accept our prayers on behalf of thy servant Rita and grant her entrance into the land of light and joy . . ."

Dog-tired, suffering from lack of sleep and a wife who'd just about run out of understanding, plagued with the symptoms of a hell of a cold, stuffy nose, watery eyes, pain-in-the-neck cough. Culligan watched the coffin being lowered into the ground. It didn't help to be standing out in the rain. Fall had swept into the Northeast early, unexpectedly, arriving with a cold front out of Canada that chilled both the flesh and the spirit.

"Make us, we beseech thee, deeply sensible of the shortness and uncertainty of life. . . . "

Culligan's eyes moved over the large crowd. Had to be close to a hundred people. First, he took in the scene as a whole, the roof of black umbrellas, the line of expensive cars along the road, the rows of headstones, the bereaved family quietly standing by. Then he focused on individual faces. Each showed strong emotions to a greater or lesser degree: shock, grief, indignation, fear, confusion.

Except for Laura Wade's. She was standing near the front of the crowd, wearing a black knit dress and a small brimmed hat with a veil. Her husband stood beside her. They were a handsome couple. But, then, so were many of these people. Zachary Wade had his hand on his wife's elbow, supporting her. It didn't look as though she needed his support. She reminded Culligan of a stone statue amidst the swaying crowd. She was not watching the proceedings. She was staring off in the distance, her face only partially obscured by the veil. The woman's face was totally blank.

Three goddamned weeks and he still had nothing on her. The murder weapon was not among Laura Wade's three art knives. The blades were at least one tenth of an inch too long, the jagged edges rendered that type of blade incapable of inflicting damage consistent with the victim's wounds, even if they had been new, which they weren't. They had been used to cut canvases. Period. The prints on her car dashboard were not Rita Harmon's; none of the fibers were a match. Spectroscopic analysis of the sand samples had produced nothing. Shell fragments, sand, rock. No oxidation, no fire. There would be no more search warrants. Not until—unless—he had something specific.

That morning, Culligan had talked to Jonathan Beatty, the department's chief forensic psychiatrist. Beatty had pretty much confirmed everything David Goldman told him about the possible background of the killer. He also said that Laura Wade sounded from Culligan's description like the classic paranoid confessor. Schizophrenic disorder of some type, most likely, Beatty had said, and something about an excess of a certain chemical in the brain called dopamine.

"Apparently she's never had anything like this before," Culligan said. "At least according to her husband and her friends."

"A sudden onslaught of this severity, at age thirty-five?" Beatty said. "I'll bet you find some history of mental illness in the family. Of course, I'd have to examine her myself to give you a professional opinion."

Not likely, unless Hallahan could get someone to issue a subpoena, not very likely unless Culligan could come up with some legally valid reason. The painting, he knew, would never stand up. He'd had five men check out the possibility that she had rented a car with every car rental dealer from Manhattan to Easterbrook. He'd had another two men on the clothes. Each of the eight other guests at Laura Wade's dinner party had been questioned.

None of the dinner guests said much of anything except that Laura Wade's altercation with Rita Harmon had been embarrassing but understandable, given Rita Harmon's penchant for flirting, a fault in particular evidence that night. All of them doubted there was anything to the speculation that Zach Wade had been having an affair with her. Rita Harmon was known to be "all talk," they said. And Zachary Wade seemed to love his wife. Why shouldn't he? She was a beautiful woman; they seemed well matched. In fact, they were an ideal couple.

None of it had turned up a goddamned thing.

David Goldman had called. Laura Wade had described her movements on the night of the murder, under hypnosis. Described them *exactly*. People don't lie under hypnosis, Goldman said. Seemed like a competent psychiatrist, as psychiatrists went.

Even though the housekeeper at the Wade house couldn't confirm the time of Laura Wade's arrival at home on the night of the murder, the facts in the case refused to get in line behind Laura Wade—or behind anyone else, for that matter.

Culligan tried to think what, in this entire morass, he *did* have. For one thing, he had scores of interviews. Over the past few weeks, he and his men had questioned nearly sixty people, many of whom were here at the funeral. Rita Harmon's children. Not a possibility. Her husband. His business clients from Omaha, the maître de' at St. Germain, and two other diners had confirmed that he was at the restaurant until ten P.M., when he left for the morgue. Neighbors. Friends. No one had seen anything. No one knew anything.

Culligan looked over the crowd again, focused on Zachary Wade. A possibility, not a very likely one. What was the motive? Culligan had questioned Wade in the midtown executive offices of Gardners Inc. twice now. The first time he'd arrived early in the morning, before nine, been ushered into Zachary Wade's office suite by a friendly and efficient middle-aged secretary. Wade was on the phone at a sleek black marble desk. Behind him were three large arched windows and a spectacular view of the Empire State Building.

Wade nodded and motioned for him to sit down, continued speaking into the receiver, his feet up on the desk.

"For Christ's sake, Daniel, I thought you said you knew this supplier. What the hell am I going to do with six hundred dozen beach balls at the beginning of September?"

Beach balls?

Wade was quiet for a few moments as he listened to Daniel's response, whoever Daniel was.

Culligan took the opportunity to look around. The office was a study in masculine modernity, everything black and silver or gray, sparsely but expensively furnished. The only truly personal touch was a picture of Laura in a silver frame on the desk, facing him, and three small pictures of each of his children along the credenza next to a computer terminal and screen.

"Tell him to forget it, Daniel," Wade was saying. Then he held the receiver away from his face, looked at it as if it might speak, finally slammed the receiver down on the telephone console.

He shook his head.

"Christ, if that guy wasn't Laura's sister's husband, I'd fire him right now."

"Is Gardners a family-owned business, Mr. Wade?"

"Come on, detective. You probably know more about my finances than I do." He swung his feet off the desk. "Sam—Laura's father—considered taking it public about eight years ago but decided against it."

"He's retired now, I understand."

"Yes. Finally."

"And left it all to you?"

He laughed. "Wrong phraseology, but effectively, yes, he left me in charge. I have the title of president, a small percentage of stock, and all of the work, but the Gardners own this business, detective. Sam Gardner and his wife, and Laura and her sister and brother."

Culligan looked at him.

"Don't think I'm complaining. When I married Laura, I had nothing. Nothing at all. I have very little to complain about, wouldn't you say?" This last comment was made with a broad sweep of his arm.

Well, he could complain that he had a loonytune for a wife.

Zachary Wade pushed a button on the phone console, and his secretary appeared a moment later. "Jane," he said, "I need a cup of coffee." He turned to Culligan. "How about you?"

"No, thanks."

After the secretary left the room, Culligan asked, "Why didn't Sam Gardner leave his own son in charge?"

Wade's face broke into a grin. "Greg Gardner? Christ! The guy's been useless since the day he was born. Traveling around the world with a backpack since the sixties. Probably in Nepal right now, or somewhere equally remote. . . . Thanks, Jane.'' He took a steaming cup of coffee, set it down on the desk. "Now, how can I help you, detective?''

Might as well get right down to it. "Where were you on the night of August tenth?''

"I was here very late that evening. We've got a new store opening in Boston next week. I finished quite late, stayed at our apartment in the city.''

"What time did you go there?''

"About ten. Why?''

"Did anyone see you in the office?''

"Not really. Everyone leaves at five or so. Jane ordered me a sandwich around six-thirty, then I sent her home. I worked straight through until ten.''

"Make any phone calls?''

"A few.''

"And you didn't go out?''

"No. Why would I go out if I had work to do? Am I a suspect?''

"Your wife said you were having an affair with the dead woman.''

"If I was having an affair with her, why would I kill her?''

"Maybe she'd threatened to tell your wife.''

"Come on, detective,'' he said. "Then I could have threatened to tell her husband, and the two of us would have been at a standoff, wouldn't we?''

He was right. There was no way to make sense out of that.

"Can you confirm your wife's whereabouts on August tenth?'' Culligan asked.

"I can't believe our housekeeper didn't hear Laura's car pull in that night after the movies.''

"She said she went to sleep early, and didn't hear anything. Your older girls were out. And your son was sleeping."

He stood up and went over to the window, looked out, then turned around again. "This is ridiculous, detective. My wife is a very disturbed woman, obviously. I was not aware how serious her . . . illness was, nor even that she was disturbed, and she's under a doctor's care now—but I do know that she isn't a murderer. And I do not appreciate your searching my home as if I were a common criminal."

There was more of the same. More that time, more the second time: Laura wouldn't do it, she didn't have memory blackouts so far as he knew; he was not having an affair with Rita Harmon or anyone else; he had no idea why his wife persisted in her "bizarre delusion."

His own story wasn't airtight, but it checked out well enough. The president of a toy company called Panda Inc., headquartered in Boston, had told Culligan he had a long conversation with Wade around six-thirty. Which meant he might have had the time, but in the absence of any reasonable motive it seemed a waste of effort to pursue it.

The funeral was over; the crowd was dispersing quietly, the cars taking their places in a line to leave. Zachary Wade was standing with the victim's husband, speaking in low tones, presumably reiterating his condolences. Laura Wade was already walking toward their car, a long black Cadillac limousine.

Culligan made his way back to his own car and got in. He sat for a moment. A hint of sun was peeking through the clouds now, making the mist-droplets glisten like diamonds on the tidy rows of headstones. The mourners passed.

Culligan started up the engine and pulled in back of the last car in the line of cars leaving the cemetery, an orderly procession, one following another.

He spent the drive considering the possibility that he was going about the case all wrong. Maybe it *was* a mugging, a random one-time thing.

It was nearly six by the time he got home. Betty was miffed, though she wasn't showing it. Culligan had been married a long time, and he could usually tell when and why Betty was pissed off at him. This one was easy. It was Saturday, and he had promised to take the grandkids to the Museum of Natural History. Instead, he'd told her this morning that he wanted, needed, to go to a funeral.

She looked at him and said, "You're going to go to that woman's funeral?"

"I have to," he said.

"Why?"

"I don't know why."

The two of them sat down to dinner, during which she made small talk about their trip to the museum that day and about the grandchildren. Finally, as she was serving him a slice of blueberry pie, she said, "Ozzie Allen called you this morning, just after you left."

"Why didn't you tell me?"

"I suppose I wanted you to myself for a few minutes. Ever since you started on this damned case, I feel as if you're living in another world, Henry. You're up in the middle of the night, you're at work fifteen hours a day—"

"Betty, I've got twenty-four men working full time for almost three weeks now, and we still have nothing.

The papers are screaming about how violent the streets are—''

''They were violent before this murder, and they'll be violent after it. The papers are only making a big deal because the victim was from the suburbs.''

''Maybe so, but Hallahan is on my case every day.''

She smiled. ''Well, tell him to get lost.''

''I tell him to get lost, I'm out of a job. Now tell me, please, what did Ozzie say?''

''He didn't say what he wanted, Henry. He just said it was important.''

Culligan glanced at his watch, pushed away his half-eaten pie and went into the den to make the call.

Ozzie answered on the first ring.

''Know why I haven't been back to you, Henry?'' he said.

''Why?''

''Because I couldn't find out a damned thing. Seems like Samuel Gardner came out of nowhere. So I got to thinking. How does a guy come out of nowhere and start up a business like that? And you know what I found out? I talked to a guy who says he knew Gardner when he was a kid.''

''And?''

''And my guy says his name wasn't Samuel Gardner. Not originally, anyway.''

''He changed it?''

''That he did. The family name was Zophlick.''

''You sure?'' Even if he *was* sure, what did it prove? A man starts a business under a different name than his own. Maybe he didn't think the American public would go to stores named Zophlicks.

''Yeah, I'm sure,'' Ozzie said. ''But do you know *why* Samuel Gardner changed his name?''

''Why?''

"Because in the spring of 1935, Samuel Zophlick's sister was committed to an institution, the Darlington Home for the Insane. One of those places where they used to put the real lunatics. You remember that movie with Olivia De Havilland? Snake pits, they called them. And this place apparently deserved the tag. Run by the state with a minimum of staff. People lying around in chains, people screaming, filth and excrement in the halls, the whole bit. And Sophie Zophlick became part of a huge scandal—a cause célèbre, if you will—for some group called the Committee for Mercy to the Insane, which was working for more humane conditions in those places. It became the headline story of the day."

"*What* became a headline story?"

Ozzie Allen hesitated a moment, then said, "During her stay in that place, Sophie Zophlick was the perpetrator of a brutal murder. If the article on the first page of the June 3, 1937, *Philadelphia Inquirer* can be believed, one night Sophie Zophlick somehow got out of lockup at the Darlington Home for the Insane and took a knife to one of the psychiatrists who worked there. You'd change your name, too, if Sophie Zophlick had been your sister."

16

The Death Witch had sought help, as if there could be help for Her, as if help could save Her. It was a glitch in the Plan, necessitating changes, minor ones, none too troubling. A minor annoyance. In the end she would be defeated, destroyed, forgotten, for he was the stronger. He had the Plan. Maurant said: To win, one must be willing to play the game, ruthlessly and without pity. Sacrifices must be made. One must anticipate in advance what the opponent's next moves will be, and undermine those moves. Sacrifices made for the sake of the end game. The man liked that analogy.

The Death Witch was ageless. She had lived long. Soon, no longer. The man knew Her, but She knew nothing about him. Therein lay his advantage.

They had played a parlor game, a Death Witch power game. Sit there, little one. Sit there and watch. Watch how She knows what you think. See how She tests you. Trust Her.

He laughed, as he prepared for Her coming.

There was no such thing as madness; it was a concept invented by fools—an illusion, an excuse. There was only the absence of discipline, which was a weakness and which could not be forgiven. But there were those among men who did excuse weakness, who pretended to explain the inner workings of another's mind, who spent their lives in such a pursuit: they were the weakest of all.

Weakness, the man knew, was a virus that spread through the body of man, even from one to another. Those who surrendered to weakness had to be destroyed, like rabid dogs.

He was a witness to—and a part of—the worst of it. Tainted blood ran in his veins; he was surrounded by weakness, yet he remained strong. He made no excuses. Neither his past nor his present was an excuse. The past was written, could not be changed. Only the future was his. The weak would rot with Her.

All of life was related, one thing linked to another, all of them spiraling out in concentric circles from a central point. Life, like madness, did not exist in a vacuum. One could not deny one's history.

17

David was on a small motorboat in a vast, smooth sea. The compass pointed due north; he looked in every direction but could see no land. The sea stretched on endlessly. He knew it would soon be dark. Suddenly there was a gull hovering over his head, stopping for a moment in midflight beneath a clear rosy sky. He looked at the compass again and this time it pointed south. Now he could see land in the distance, a white house, a woman.

Closer in, he saw it was Laura. She was wearing a blue silk dress with a wide leather belt slung low at the waist. She shouted, ''No. No. Go back!'' But all he could think of was reaching her, holding her, touching—

David awakened in a cold sweat. The bedside clock said seven-thirty. He was disoriented for a moment, then realized that the alarm was ringing, an insistent, unfamiliar buzz. Usually he awakened just before it sounded.

Christ! He was dreaming about her again. The dream was not explicit, but it was unmistakably sexual. It had been a long time since he dreamed sexually about a patient. Perhaps the dream had been triggered by his running into Allison a few weeks ago. Or was it last week? He was losing track of time. He did know that Allison was the last woman he'd gone to bed with. A psychiatrist didn't have that much opportunity to meet women other than his patients, who didn't count.

He shut the alarm off and headed for the shower. His skin felt sweaty, overheated, as if he had a fever as well as a broken air-conditioner. What did it take to get the damned super to do his job? Not that he really needed the super to fix the air-conditioner now that the weather had turned cool. Turning the cold faucet up to full pressure, he stood there—woozy, off balance, his face turned toward the spray, his skin stinging with the blast of icy water. Was it Thursday? No, Friday. Laura would be coming in today. Was it too early to hope the medication had produced some effect?

She came into the office and sat down, asked if she could open the window. As she moved across the room, he noticed that she looked particularly lovely, her hair brushed back from her face. No, it wasn't the hair. It was the dress. *The blue silk dress.*

He tired to remember what she'd worn to the first session. It might have been white, maybe white wool. Then there was the pink linen thing, next white pants, followed by a tan knit dress. . . . No, he'd never seen this blue dress before—except in his dream.

"I had a dream last night about you," she said.

Oh, Lord. And wasn't it a little early in the therapy for a transference dream?

"In the dream," she said, "I was in my house—we

live on the Sound, you know.'' (No, he didn't.) ''I went into the yard and I saw you coming toward me in a boat and I yelled at you to go back. But you came ashore anyway and I took you into my house and . . . Are you all right, Dr. Goldman?''

No. He wasn't all right. He was sitting there with his mouth hanging open, reminding himself how often people dream of boats and water, common symbols of the womb.

''Go on, Laura.''

''After we got into the house, I looked out the window and saw a huge red bird on a high branch with its wings folded into itself—like a parrot, but huge, monstrous, with a hooked beak. I picked up the phone to warn everyone. I kept dialing, but all I got was a clicking sound. I looked up, and the earpiece wasn't connected to a phone at all but to a long cord with another phone at the end. You were at the other end. Suddenly I looked out at the tree where the bird had been and it was gone. I ran out and saw it lying on the ground, dead.''

What was his parrot doing in her dream? A dream reprocessed experiences, using anything heard, seen, thought or read at any time; the *dreamer's* experiences. So how did *her* experiences, her backyard, her clothes, show up in his dream and how did his experience—his parrot, dammit!—show up in hers?

''Dr. Goldman?''

David looked at her. He was a rational man. He believed there were historical, psychological reasons for beliefs, knowledge, behavior. He believed in natural causal sources for dreams, and he did not believe in mutations. Yes. There was the rare three-legged chicken, the occasional blue lobster. But this? A woman so telepathic that she could take an experience from his mind and process it in hers?

So while she sat there telling him her dream—*their* dream—he sat there trying to muster rational explanations. The best he could come up with was not very good. Jung's theory that certain dreams were located in the collective unconscious, therefore common to all people—which might have covered the water and the boat parts of the dream. Or a snake in the dream, if there had been one. But a *parrot*?

David asked her to describe her house.

"A white colonial, with black shutters—a shore colonial, they call it—with a large roofed porch that runs the full length across the back, facing the Sound."

It was, of course, the house in his dream. Lots of houses looked like that. . . .

"What does the dream remind you of?" he asked.

"Well, it's my backyard. My house. The telephone thing with the cords was strange. The bird—I don't know, it comes from somewhere else. I don't know why it was so big."

She was quiet for a moment.

"Laura, why were you yelling at me in the dream? What were you doing?"

She stared at him, eyes a rich brown, gentle, frightened.

"I was warning you," she said, "but you wouldn't listen."

Almost every psychotic he had ever treated had warned him about one thing or another. You got used to it. But you didn't get used to this.

Could she be setting him up? Could she have broken into his apartment and looked around and come up with the parrot to convince him? No. That wasn't right. Again, she'd be trying to convince him that she *was* crazy, not that she *wasn't* crazy. As a matter of fact, the whole line of thought was at least as convoluted as the craziest thought the craziest psychotic he'd ever talked to might dream up.

She looked away for a moment, shifted her position, crossed her legs. Suddenly he became aware of the shadow of her breasts beneath the blue silk, the outline of her nipples.

What the hell was the matter with him?

She was staring at him again. God. What if she knew the thought he'd just had, felt it, sensed it, sensed his . . . what? The fact that he was thinking about her breasts?

He picked up his pencil, stuck it in the electric pencil sharpener on his desk, held it there until the point was lethal.

"What were you warning me about?" he asked finally.

"I'm a poison," she said. "I destroy people. I'll destroy you, too."

On Sunday morning, David put in a call to Stan to see if he could set up something for Laura with the Rockham Institute. The answering service informed him that Dr. Friedland was in Baltimore for the weekend and hadn't left word when he would be back. Probably he'd gone to visit his mother.

That afternoon David went to the library to do some reading in parapsychology. The West Seventy-second branch had at least fifty books on the subject. They seemed to be of four basic types. First, there were the personal accounts of supposedly gifted psychics—Edgar Cayce, Uri Geller, Eileen Garrett, and the like. Then there were the reference books, compendiums of witchcraft and visions down through the ages. There

were the psychic debunkers. Finally there were the
accounts detailing psychic phenomena in clinical psy-
chotherapeutic practice, including a number of legitimate experimental investigations by parapsychological
researchers, among them Niles Martin.

He wanted to be drawn to the more "scientific"
reports, those less likely to inspire his easily activated
skepticism, but instead he found himself wandering
through the more spectacular but empirically unsub-
stantiated stories of ghouls and witches and curses and
bleeding stigmata. He read bits of Jung, a chapter in
a book by Nandor Fodor, two articles in the *International Journal of Parapsychology*. It seemed there had
been a few cases—without witnesses except after the
fact—in which people claimed to have deliberately
produced malevolent effects via some kind of telepathic power. He could find no cases like Laura's, in
which those effects seemed involuntary, the telepath
not claiming to have hurled his or her venom on purpose.

He spent most of the afternoon in the library reading, normally an activity he enjoyed—and got back to
his apartment caught in a whirl of ghosts, within and
without.

18 David tried, valiantly, to listen to his
two o'clock patient. Darryl Clancy was a referral from
Marilyn Reinhold via Donald Grayson via Rose Sum-
ner. It didn't speak well for his fellow psychiatrists,

passing the man around that way, not that he blamed them. Clancy was just so damned boring. Maybe his colleagues felt there were so many interesting people in the city who got into therapy—bisexual television produces, addicted actresses, agency workaholics, manic-depressive Wall Street dynamos—that it didn't seem necessary to suffer through a patient like Clancy.

An accountant for a small rock-salt distributor in Queens, Clancy was a timid man with a nasal, rambling speaking style, paced to invite the listener to doze off before he got the next word out. Usually the words were about his employer of ten years who paid him $22,000 per, expected overtime without pay, and for some reason had Clancy's undying allegiance. Darryl Clancy was really a nice guy, but his problems were very small.

He was talking about a crush he seemed to have developed on one of the secretaries in his office, trying to work up the nerve to ask her out. David tried some role-playing, which seemed to boost Clancy's confidence, then showed him out after fifty minutes that seemed like three hours.

"Thank you so much, Dr. Goldman." Then, with a wink, "I'll let you know how it turns out."

The phone was ringing. Stan Friedland's answering service: Dr. Friedland has gotten your messages; he's sorry he hasn't been able to get back to you but he's been in Baltimore and will call you when he returns to Manhattan.

"Did he say when that would be?"

"I'm sorry, sir, he didn't. He just asked me to call you."

"Thanks. When you reach him, please tell him it's urgent."

He hung up the phone and glanced at the clock. Five

minutes past the hour. Laura was never late. He got her file out and was just about to put in the tape he'd made of Tuesday's session when the buzz sounded.

It was Laura. Her face was smeary with the remnants of mascara. Worse, she was having difficulty breathing.

He guided her to the couch, helped her take her jacket off.

"There's something in my throat," she gasped out. "I can't breathe."

He looked down her throat, using a tongue depressor: nothing amiss, not that he expected there to be.

She was panting, hyperventilating.

He told her to breathe and count, breathe and count, and counted with her.

"It's all *right*, Laura. Tell me what happened."

He finally got the story out of her. She had been having trouble driving lately, turning left when she should have been turning right, forgetting where it was she was supposed to be going. So she'd decided today to take the train in for her appointment. She parked her car and went up onto the platform above the tracks, where a man approached her. He asked her for the time, said he had a meeting in Manhattan in an hour and was the train usually on schedule. She told him she didn't know, then looked away. He persisted. She thought he was trying to pick her up and told him to go away, which he did, probably insulted.

And then she watched him descend the steps, talk to another woman down on the platform, pace back and forth, back and forth on the platform. She knew he was standing too close, she knew he would fall in. What was worse, the thought crossed her mind that if he did fall, it would serve him right. She realized, she said, that she'd infected him.

Because he fell onto the tracks just as the train came into the station.

"I'm a murderer." The words were choked out. David could barely hear them. There was a queer rasping sound coming out of her mouth.

He got her a glass of water, told her to breathe and count, breathe and count, worked with her again until the panting and rasping eased up.

"There's nothing in your throat, Laura. I know it feels as if there is, but you're not choking, you're having a panic attack."

He got her a Valium from his credenza.

"Laura, this will help you calm down," he said, handing it to her.

She swallowed the pill then whispered. "That's two. Two deaths. More to come. Oh, God, what am I going to do?'

He sighed. "We are going to talk about this. Now, a man actually fell onto the tracks, and the train came in?"

"Yes. Yes. Yes."

"All right, then. He fell onto the tracks after you had the thought that he might fall, that—"

"Not after. *Because*. The man fell because I was annoyed. He was standing so close to me. My God, I never meant to hurt him."

"Did you push him onto the tracks?"

She stared. "Of course not. I infected him. I gave him the evil eye. The Laura hex. It *isn't* what you're thinking."

"What am I thinking?"

"Selective attention. I *didn't* just have the fleeting thought that he was too close to the edge and might fall, then focus after he fell on having had the thought."

David felt like he needed the Valium. "All right, Laura, let's talk about what you were feeling. Were you angry?"

"No. I really *wasn't* angry, just a little annoyed. Or maybe I was."

"Don't impose anger on the situation now, Laura. I want to know if you were angry *then.*"

"Not really."

He hesitated. "Perhaps you were attracted to the man."

"Absolutely not." She got up, moved to the other side of the office. His blinds were drawn. There was a dark striping effect in the room, lines of sunlight on the walls and on her face.

"Tell me, Laura, if you *were* attracted to a man other than your husband, would that bother you?"

"Of course it would."

My God. Here was a woman who worried about being *attracted* to another man, married to a man who felt so justified in hiring prostitutes to "service" him that he had offhandedly mentioned it to a virtual stranger.

"Laura, thoughts and actions are two different things."

"Not for me, David."

"Any chance you could have felt guilty about feeling attracted to the man, then be punishing yourself by assuming the blame for what happened?"

Now she was glaring.

"Are you mad at me, Laura?"

"Only dogs go mad." She said it in a low voice, almost like a growl.

"Where did you hear that expression, Laura?"

"From my father. He used to say it."

"Why?"

She looked at him. "You'd have to ask him."

"Why do you think he said it, Laura?"

"I don't know. I don't *know* my father." She looked away. "My father has all kinds of things in his mind that I could never understand. Especially . . ."

"Especially what?"

A long silence. "There is an image in his mind. The image of a woman. And she's always, always, screaming." She covered her face with her hands.

A reflection of herself? Enough ancient history. He had to help her, and he had to help her now.

"Laura," he said very softly, "tell me what the man looked like."

She stared out the window. "He had blue eyes."

David felt a barely resistible urge to put on his glasses, which he resisted. He asked her to describe her feelings while the man was standing close to her.

"I was annoyed, maybe even frightened. My world is very insulated. I hardly ever speak to strangers. So I guess I was frightened, angry. All right, maybe I was even attracted. He was a nice-looking man."

"Who did he look like? Anyone you know?"

"I don't think so."

"Did he look like me?"

"He was shorter. I mean, he was a perfectly nice-looking man, a businessman in a suit."

"Like me?"

"No."

At this point, it would probably have been helpful to get her to admit her attraction to him, to speak to her about transference, but for some reason David simply couldn't bring himself to do it.

He decided to change the subject.

"Do you like sex, Laura?"

She looked at him. "Not particularly."

"Any sex?"

"Well, the truth is, I've never had sex with anyone but Zach."

"Does he have unusual tastes?"

"Not really."

That was exactly what he'd said. David wondered if he forced her, or was rough, or . . .

"What does 'not really' mean? You're a grown woman, Laura. Does your husband have unusual sexual tastes?"

"You mean perverted tastes, don't you?"

"All right, perverted tastes."

She shrugged. "No. Nothing like that."

"Then what is it you don't like about sex?"

"I don't know. . . . I guess I don't like the feeling of being out of control."

"I see. Anything else?"

Softly: "It reminds me of a machine."

"What kind of machine?"

"A pumping machine."

"And you don't like that?"

"No."

"Laura," David said, "do you know that sex can be gentle and caring and . . . loving?"

"I guess it could be; at least people say it can. I guess it never will be for me."

"Why not?"

"Because . . . well, Zach doesn't know how to do it that way."

"Is he rough with you?"

"Not rough, really." She sighed. "He does everything right, I think. Oh, I don't even know anything about it. What do I know about it?"

"Have you ever watched a sexual scene in a movie?"

"Yes."

"Sometimes it's gentle and loving, right?"

"Yes."

"Then you know the difference. Right?"

She closed her eyes. "Yes. I suppose I do. So where does that leave me?"

"Well, you could try to tell your husband how you feel about sex."

"I have."

"And?"

"He calls me frigid."

What a trap for her.

"He's never tried changing his approach?"

"He doesn't know what I'm talking about."

Why not? Zachary Wade was obviously not a stupid man. Of course, many men had trouble acknowledging, much less discussing, any problem in this area.

"Perhaps you should bring him in here so the three of us can talk about it."

"He would never come."

"Why not?"

"Because he doesn't think there's a problem."

"You mean he doesn't think *he's* got a problem."

"Yes."

Well, at least she'd admitted, however hesitantly, that it wasn't entirely *her* problem.

She glanced at the clock. "I guess my time is up now."

"Will you be all right?"

She shrugged, then stood up, collected her jacket, turned to go. "Thank you, David."

"I'll see you on Friday," he said, watching as she closed the door softly behind her, wondering when she'd started to call him David.

19 "Dr. Goldman, Detective Culligan called again."

The answering service had already given him two messages from Henry Culligan. And it was only Monday morning.

Might as well get it over with. He dialed the number.

"David Goldman, returning your call."

"Yeah, Goldman. Why didn't you tell me about the mental illness in your patient's family?"

"What?"

"You heard me."

"Yes, but I don't know what you're talking about, detective."

"Well, I've been doing a little checking on the Gardner family, *doctor.* Are you asking me to believe your patient didn't tell you?"

"Tell me *what?*"

"That her aunt, her father's sister, was the same thing *she* is. Crazy as hell. Violent. Back in the thirties, this woman—this aunt—killed someone. Pretty brutally, too, just like this one. Now in my book—"

"Detective Culligan, what—How do you know this?"

There was a short silence. David could hear papers rustling.

"I have a copy of the June 3, 1937, *Philadelphia Inquirer,* doctor. It says right here that during the evening hours of June first of the same year, an inmate at the Darlington Home for the Insane, one Sophie Zophlick—that was the original Gardner family name—committed a murder. And you know what else it says, doctor? It says the man she killed was a doctor, a psychiatrist on staff at that place.''

Good Lord. Laura would have told him if she knew. Perhaps her father simply couldn't bring himself to tell her, and had kept it a secret all these years. Possibly it explained his unwillingness to accept anger or excessive shows of emotion in his household—

''Goldman?''

''All right,'' David said slowly, ''if what you're saying is true, and I have no reason to doubt it—''

''Don't.''

''Fine. But even if it is true, it doesn't necessarily have any bearing on Laura Wade's case.''

''Oh, no? What medical school did *you* go to? I spoke with Dr. Jonathan Beatty—perhaps you've heard of him—and he confirmed that there's a substantial genetic component to this sort of thing.''

David had indeed heard of Beatty, who was often quoted in criminal-trial newspaper articles. But surely he wasn't offering a medical opinion on this case. . . .

''Yes, I agree there is a genetic component, but it doesn't exactly work the way you're suggesting, detective. The fact that there is a family history of mental illness—''

''*Violent* mental illness, doctor. Violent behavior. *Psychopathic* behavior. I think the shoe fits, don't you?''

The buzzer was on. David glanced at the clock. Nearly five of three. Laura. ''I have to get off the phone,'' he said. ''My next patient's here. But I *don't* think the shoe fits.''

"All right, doc," Culligan said. "Let's just say the *piece* fits. Just one more piece of the puzzle."

This Culligan was really going after her, keeping close tabs. Maybe he should be keeping tabs himself. He buzzed Laura in.

She was wearing a soft, cream-colored leather coat, which she hung on the back of the door before she sat down. He wondered if he should tell her about her aunt. He had to tread very carefully here. The shock might trigger a total decompensation.

Laura was looking at him with that keen stare of hers. Did something happen to her eyes, some reflection disappear, when she stared that way? Or was it his imagination?

"Culligan called you today, didn't he?" she said.

"Yes."

"He's keeping tabs on me."

Damn.

A flicker of some emotion David couldn't quite identify passed over her face. Satisfaction? Good God! What if she *did* know about her aunt, and had deliberately withheld the information because—

"Probably Culligan thinks I did it," she said. "But it's hard to tell what he thinks."

"Why's that?"

"I don't really know." She lit her cigarette. "With certain people in my life, I'm very in touch, my senses are very sharp. Almost word for word, thought for thought. With others, I get almost nothing. I don't really know the reason."

"Why not?"

"Because there isn't any reference guide to explain it to me."

"Why do you *think*?"

She was taking short, quick puffs on her cigarette.

"The only way I can explain it to you is to describe how minds appear to me. Like a piece of mica. Transparent layers stacked upon transparent layers. But when you put it all together it becomes almost solid. You can only see the top layer, perhaps sense a few of those directly underneath. In certain people, I can sense only the top layer. In others I occasionally get flashes of those layers underneath. You see, as the mica gets deeper and deeper, the images becomes less and less readable. There, underneath, there's no coherence, no structure to put it all together, no language to interpret it, only images, feelings, a jumble of emotions and memories that only get more incoherent as you pass through. In certain people, like Culligan, I get almost nothing. In others, I can almost see through the layers."

The thought occurred to David that if there was such a power, the power to know other people's thoughts and feelings, it would take a tremendous strength of will not to go mad.

"I suppose it's because people's thoughts are organized in different ways," she was saying, "incorporated into their general psychological framework in different ways. And also, because my relationships with different people are different. I've never been able to sense the deepest layers, in anyone." She looked at him. "Until now."

David felt a pulse quicken in his head. "You mean with me?"

She stared at him for a moment, then said, "Do you really want to know this?"

David nodded.

She got up, went over to the sofa, resettled herself and looked over at him, her expression a bewildering combination of clarity and fear. There was a long silence.

Was she going to tell him?

Softly, so softly: "I am a witness to your soul."

I am a witness to your soul.

All week long David found himself guilty of inexcusable lapses during sessions: not listening properly, asking the wrong questions, even interrupting, a most serious blunder, since it could choke off a valuable insight on the patient's part. To make matters worse, he found at the end of each day that he had taken session notes like a novice. Vague, skittery, as unfocused as the note-taker. Each evening David vowed to set his mind aright, only to find he'd done the same thing at the end of the next day. And he simply couldn't decide what to do with the news about Laura's aunt, if anything.

By Friday night he was wound up like a coil. Which didn't help him get through the first "first date" he'd had in thirteen years. It was a blind date, arranged several weeks before by a friend of one of Stan Friedland's ex-wives. Considering what *they* were like, David didn't know how he could have assumed any friend of one of them would be companionable.

The woman's name was Marissa Norell. Short, plump and fairly pretty, she ran one of those drafty Soho art galleries, lived in the East Sixties. They went to an Italian place, and before they'd finished the *zuppa* she informed David that mental illness was essential to artistic creativity. With the arrival of the tortellini came her pronouncement that psychiatry made people too self-involved.

"People should handle their problems, go with the flow," she said, dabbing at her lips with a napkin.

"But what if the flow doesn't go with them?"

"Better to suffer with a crooked flow than be over-self-involved, right?"

"Let me make sure I've got this straight," David said. "You would dismiss the whole profession—*my* profession—because it runs the risk of making the people it's trying to help overly self-involved?"

"Everybody has problems, I only calls 'em as I sees 'em," she said, laughing queerly, as if she had just said something brilliant.

When David said good night to her at the door of her apartment, it was with the fervent hope that he would never lay eyes on her again.

"David, I wanted to call to apologize for the way I behaved the other day."

It was Allison. Actually, over a month had passed since their accidental meeting. He told her he was sorry, too, wondering why she had really called. Certainly not to apologize.

It turned out she wanted him to go to a formal business dinner with her Thursday evening. She was sorry for the last-minute invitation, but she and the man she was seeing had a fight and she knew he would help her out.

"What's the dinner for?" David asked. Had she invented the story about the other man?

"Cancer research. Someone with the bright idea that the advertising community wasn't doing enough charity work set up an organization called the Advertising Community Council. Every year they pick one person to honor. Thursday they're honoring the president of Sherman Bates, the conglomerate holding company for my toy account."

"Is he a philanthropist?"

"Maybe. I've never met him. My guess is they chose this guy because he has so many obligations to call in. At two thousand a table, they need a lot of obligations."

"You don't need an escort for those things, Allison."

"Come on, David. Go with me. You're the only other unattached presentable male I know."

"I was under the impression you thought I was anything but presentable."

"I *never* said you weren't presentable, David."

True enough. "You still haven't told me why you want me to go."

"No reason. I just do. Come on. It'll be rubber chicken and boring speeches but it's for a good cause."

David told her he would.

"Great," she said. "I'll pick you up at your office at seven."

"Seven-thirty."

"We'll miss the cocktails."

"Allison," David said in the tone of voice he'd so often used with her, "you know I'm not through until seven-thirty. Even then, I'll have to change in the office."

"Fine," she said. "Seven-thirty it is. Thanks, David."

Night ghosts.

Sleep was very nearly impossible.

David spent the weekend alone, reading, walking around his neighborhood, allowing himself the luxury of feeling lonely. On Sunday he drove out to a beach on Long Island, spent a few hours watching a storm system approach over the Sound, then headed back to Manhattan in a misty rain that turned into a downpour as he neared the West Side. When he got back to his apartment, he tried to work on a paper he'd started months ago, but found himself unable to concentrate on it. Or on anything else, for that matter. Sitting at his desk by the window, he gave himself a quick review course on the pitfalls of psychiatry, the need for detachment, the potential seductiveness of psychosis and of patients in transference.

None of it helped in the least.

On Monday morning, he was so tired that he slept through the alarm and got to his office late. His first patient, Diane Sagori, was already waiting.

He apologized, brought her inside and shut the door. Whereupon she launched into a diatribe on last night's sexual encounter with a bastard, the latest in a long series. The essential root of her problem was so obvious to David that he was tempted to launch into his own diatribe. With Diane, a patient who knew intellectually why she behaved as she did but was emotionally unable to change without working it out one weary step at a time, it often seemed that his job amounted to nothing but persistence and patience. Meanwhile, he had to listen to a litany of angry projections.

By the time Diane's hour was up, he was convinced he'd made a dreadful mistake in accepting Allison's invitation. All day long, he found his mind wandering away from his patients. His note pad was filling up with more doodles than notes. If he didn't stop this, he was going to lose all his patients, and rightly so.

20 On Thursday morning David hauled
out his tuxedo and headed for work carrying it on a
hanger and munching on a salt bagel from Zabar's.

When he let his last patient out, he found Allison
sitting on the sofa in his outer office, flipping through
a copy of *New Woman* magazine. She was exquisite,
wearing a pale peach shirt-collared gown that set off
her blond hair. So often had she sat in that very spot
over so many years that for a moment it seemed as if
she had never left him.

She looked up from the magazine. "It says here that
sixty percent of the married women in America
wouldn't marry the same guy again if they had it to do
it over."

"Does it say how the men feel?"

She laughed. "Don't be ridiculous, David. This is
New Woman. How the men feel is beside the point."
She dropped the magazine on top of the pile on the
coffee table and stood up.

"You look terrific, very glamorous. Executive," he
told her, suddenly remembering a minidress she used
to have that looked anything but executive. Black silk
with spaghetti-straps and so little fabric that he'd called
it her come-on dress. She insisted on wearing it, bra-
less, to Molly's *bat mitzvah* in Philadelphia; the synagogue ladies were probably still talking about David's
tiny blond *shiksa* wife in her nonexistent dress.

"Thanks."

"Guess I'd better put on my tux." David headed back into his office, closed the door and got himself into the penguin suit he'd left hanging on the back of the bathroom door all day. He tied and adjusted the bowtie, which Allison readjusted the minute he came out.

In the cab on the way to the Pierre, she told him about her new boss, Matt Lawson, "a real pistol" with a great sense of humor and a lot of good ideas. David vaguely wondered if Lawson was the mystery man she'd just had a fight with.

He also wondered how she was planning to introduce him. Or maybe she would just leave him standing there the way she'd often done when they were married. He found out as they made their way into the crowded ballroom and got in line at the bar.

"Hi, Matt," she called, turning to greet a couple about three bodies away. He was a short, bald man of perhaps fifty-five; she was plump, had a pleasant face and was wearing a bouffant cocktail dress that looked just right for a prom.

"Matt Lawson, David Goldman, my husband."

Lawson switched the cigarette he was smoking to his left hand, held out his right.

"Nice to meet you. I thought you two were kaput."

Allison's smile was radiant. "We are. Sometimes, on special occasions, I drag him out of the woodwork." This with a wink at David.

"Aren't we modern, bringing the ex," said the woman. "I'm Margaret Lawson, Matt's wife—current."

Everyone laughed.

"You're the psychiatrist, right?" Lawson said. "You must think we advertising types are terribly shallow and calculating."

"Oh, I don't know," David said. "There are plenty of shallow and calculating doctors."

"It can't be easy to sit and listen to other people's problems all day," Margaret Lawson said. "How do you stand it—I mean, having to know all the answers?"

"In psychiatry," David said, "you're not expected to know all the answers. At least not in quite the same way as, say, in internal medicine. Most psychiatrists spend most of their time trying to help people find their own answers."

'But don't they want your advice?''

"Sometimes. It depends on the patient." The noise level in the room had risen to the point that David felt as though he were shouting. "So, what's this shindig all about?" he said, determined to steer the conversation away from himself.

"Patrick Leary. Philanthropist, corporation president, honoree," Matt Lawson said.

"There must be eight hundred people here," David said. "Who are they all?"

"Everyone who ever sold anything to any of the Sherman Bates companies. Anyone who could be guilted into coming. All the service agencies, all the big toy-store presidents, chain stores, department stores."

"Like Bloomingdales?"

"Bloomingdales, A&S, Caldors, Sears, Gardners."

"Gardners?"

"Sure," he said, "Paragons of business, all."

The lights dimmed several times. David and Allison shuffled into the ballroom with the Lawsons, David's eyes moving from couple to couple in the crowd. The ballroom was a vast sea of white linen and gleaming silver. White-jacketed waiters scurried here and there, as if moving in time to the relentlessly upbeat music provided by a sizable band on the stage. Every seat at their table, except David's and one other spouse's, was occupied by someone from Allison's agency.

David danced with Allison a couple of times; she teased him about his awkwardness, as usual, and he refused to dance with her again until later, after the chicken (which turned out to be surprisingly good), when she begged him for a slow dance.

The band was playing a medley of fifties tunes. The singer had a cool, soothing baritone, and the lights dimmed as the tempo of "Since I Fell for You" slowed. Allison moved closer, drew her fingertips up, played with the hair at the nape of his neck as they danced. Suddenly she kissed him, full on the lips. He looked at her. Was that what this was all about? What an idiot he was.

She smiled.

Well, the sex *would* be great. Certainly that had never been a problem—until the end, that is, when neither of them could tolerate being in the same room with the other.

They sat down when the band launched into a faster number. It was then, as the lights came back up, that he spotted Laura. She was sitting only a few tables away. He could just see her profile, one shoulder, her bare arm. She was wearing a strapless gown of chocolate silk, and had her hair pinned up. Zachary Wade, whose arm was around her, seemed to be involved in an animated discussion with someone on his left.

David couldn't hear a word they were saying, but he could watch. The way she was sitting there, quietly. The play of well-toned muscles across her back. The way he lit her cigarettes, occasionally stopped talking and turned to her as if asking her opinion on whatever was being discussed.

David watched them through the dessert, a delicious sorbet with raspberries, of which Laura took one bite, then laid her spoon down. The waiters were serving coffee. Laura took cream, sipped slowly, demurely. David watched. He had imagined her doing these ordinary things—taking cream in her coffee, talking, eating—but to see her doing them was oddly disconcerting, perhaps because he was watching her without her knowledge. A woman in a short purple dress approached their table, bent down to kiss Laura on the cheek, spoke to her for a moment. Laura turned to look up at her, in David's direction. She had seen him watching her.

"David?" What's the matter?" It was Allison. Her lips were moist, stained with the raspberries.

"Nothing." He could feel Laura's eyes on him.

"You haven't said a word for the past ten minutes."

Now Laura was looking at Allison.

"David?"

Laura was standing now, excusing herself, making her way out of the ballroom.

"I'll be back in a minute," he said, getting up.

As he stepped through the ballroom doors, he could see Laura hurrying down the hall toward the ladies' room. He followed her, stood there moronically in front of the door for a few moments until, finally, she came out.

He expected tears. He got them—along with something more serious, more basic. Fear.

"What are you doing here, David? For God's sake, this is the last place you should be."

"I'm sorry, Laura." For what? "I'm here with my—"

"No! Don't tell me who she is." She rubbed her temples with her fingertips, then covered her face with her palms. "Oh, God, I couldn't help it. I didn't mean it."

"Mean what? What are you talking about, Laura? There's nothing to be afraid of."

"Isn't there?"

They stared at each other for a long moment. My God, what if she—

"What are you doing here, Goldman?"

It was Zachary Wade, standing just behind his wife. Laura straightened up and turned to face him, suddenly very composed.

"I just happened to run into Dr. Goldman, Zach."

Wade pressed his lips into a tight line, then looked at her and said, "Shall we go back, Laura?" He took her by the upper arm, his whole hand encircling the bare dark skin. David watched him lead her through the nearest ballroom door, then stood there for a few moments trying to collect himself.

"David?" Now, Allison. "Who *was* that woman?"

"A patient."

"Small world," she said, taking his arm. "Come on, I think we can get away now. I've put in my appearance. We'll skip out before the speeches."

He put his arm around her, fighting the insane thought that she might need protection.

Allison's apartment was on the East Side. They got there about eleven.

"Want to come in?"

"I could use a cup of coffee."

Seeing so many of their old things in their new surroundings, he felt disoriented and yet somehow perfectly comfortable. She went into the kitchen. He took off the bowtie and laid it on the coffee table, all the while making neutral conversation. "Is this vase new?" "Where's the old brown chair?" He could hear her clanging around in there, calling out answers, getting out the pot, turning on the water.

"How's Bird?" she called.

"Fine."

Now she was standing in the doorway. Her skin was pale, luminescent in the dim light. She moved toward him, reaching up to slip her arms around his neck, kissing him softly. He remembered the way she always nestled up to him when she was in the mood, kissing him first on the lips, then on his neck, then each ear. . . .

"Allison—"

"We're both grown-ups, David," she said softly, "and I'm unattached at the moment. Why don't we get attached, just for a little while?"

Cool.

"Come on, David. It'll be fun."

They stood there, staring, as if they were across the room from each other. Finally, she unwound her arms from around his neck and went back into the kitchen. He followed her, watching her without saying anything. With her back toward him, she said, "It's not a big deal, David."

"Sure it is."

She turned and stood there, looking beautiful, looking at him. There was a long silence.

"I'd better go, Allison."

"You're such a pain. Good God, David, it wasn't an ultimatum, just a suggestion. If you don't want to . . ."

What he *wanted* to do was tell her to run. He *wanted* to tell her to just pack up her things and run, but instead he said, "I'm sorry, Allison. This was all a big mistake."

He backed out into the living room, grabbed his coat and started into the hallway.

"You could still have coffee," he heard her call, just before he closed the door behind him.

21

David got to his apartment about midnight, hung up the tux and stuffed the bowtie into a drawer where it would probably stay for another two years.

He was just about to head for bed when he realized something was wrong, and, almost in the same moment, realized what. The quiet. Where was the screeching and screaming that invariably greeted his arrival?

Slowly, hesitantly, he walked over to the parrot's cage and stood there for a moment peering through the brass bars. The macaw was lying on the floor of its cage, feet up, beak open, as if some trigger-happy burglar had broken into his apartment and shot it down from its perch. Boom. Clumps of red and blue feathers all over the place.

He touched its skin in the bare spots. Pale, stiff. No need to check for a heartbeat. This thing was definitely dead.

Good God! This *couldn't* be a coincidence. But if it wasn't a coincidence, what the hell was it? Had her dream caused his parrot to die, or just foretold its death? Surely she had no conscious awareness that his parrot was dead, nor even that he had—used to have—a parrot. Certainly he had never told her. He hadn't even told her about a wife, ex or otherwise, much less the wife's bird.

None of which mattered one damned bit, since she'd had the dream at least two weeks ago. Which meant the causal explanation would have to include a delaying factor.

The world didn't operate this way.

He scrambled for her case folder, started leafing through, as if seeing it in writing would help. September 2. There it was: The blue silk dress. The white house with the black shutters. The phone. And the parrot.

"I was warning you," she said, *"but you wouldn't listen."*

He could even listen to it again, on tape, in his office.

Was it all true then? Was every single goddamned thing that he, with all his diplomas and his credentials, had been treating as psychotic delusions true? Could Laura have killed his parrot with a mere turn of her mind, with a passing thought, a wish, a dream?

No. There had to be another, logical explanation for the parrot's death, an explanation that didn't make him sound as if he were one of his more disturbed patients. A rare ornithological disease of sudden onset and duration? A bag of tainted birdfood?

It wasn't that he cared about the parrot. Bird was Allison's; he hadn't even liked the thing. It was even possible that subconsciously he'd wished it dead. Conveniently forgotten to feed it? No. He remembered feeding it that morning. It was fine that morning when David left for work. It *squawked* at him.

He could accept some kind of precognitive element to it all, maybe even some telepathy—they would find out when he took her down to Rockham—but this? Supernatural bird murder, complete with a time delay, from eighty miles away? No. This he could not accept.

All right, then, maybe Laura had poisoned the bird to make him *think* she had this power she said she had.

Good God! Now he *did* sound like a nut.

He looked back over the cage. On top of everything else, he had to do something with the damned bird.

He headed for the kitchen to get the *Times*. He spread several sheets of it out on the table in the living room, laid the parrot corpse out on the paper, and folded the sheets up until he had a neat package.

David had once read a book whose main character could, at will and without the need for a match, ignite fires. But Laura Wade's "power" wasn't "at will." What was it she'd said to him, maybe in the third or fourth session? He could see her sitting there, the sleeveless white sweater she wore that day, the tears on her face. "Dr. Goldman, why aren't I entitled to my private thoughts—my little jealousies and resentments, my dreams—like everyone else?"

And what had he answered? Something about how they had to find out why she didn't feel entitled to her feelings.

No point in blaming himself. That was the right response. She *didn't* feel entitled to her feelings.

It was just that his parrot died.

David opened his door and walked down the hall to the trash chute, shoved the parrot package inside, then stood there, waiting for the soft thud as the thing finally hit bottom twenty floors below.

And what about him?

I destroy people, David. I'll destroy you.

* * *

The phone was ringing when he got back to his apartment.

"Hello?"

"David, it's Stan. Sorry to phone so late, but my answering service said you called again and said it was urgent. I was down at my mother's, and I just got back from Baltimore. Tell me what's wrong."

David told him, as briefly and coherently as he could, starting with Laura's dream—*his* dream—and ending with his throwing out the parrot.

"Bird *died*?"

"That's right. Bird died."

Silence. "You know, everything you told me at your parents' party could be explained without resorting to a supernatural explanation. Coincidence, after the fact, misinterpretation, misreporting. But this? I don't know. . . . It *could* be just a coincidence."

"Pretty bizarre coincidence, wouldn't you say, considering her particulars?"

"Still. I told you, David, schizophrenics are top telepathic performers. In standard experimental paradigms with Zener cards and random number generators, they often test significantly higher than your average Joe off the street. There've been a few studies on this by some researchers out in California."

"Then you think it's possible that she caused Bird's death?"

"You might have evidence for precognition, David. You have no evidence for that. At least, I've never heard of anything like it. She'd have to be like some kind of radio transmitter—she sends out the thought on day one, it hovers around in the air for two weeks, then your bird gets it and keels over on day fifteen. Same thing with that murder. Not to mention that it would appear she reached into your mind and dredged up something that . . . well, *I* know how you felt about Bird.''

''Some transference, huh?''

''She would have to have read your mind—and not even your conscious mind but maybe your *sub*conscious mind—to know that you hated the parrot. Then have produced the dream in *her* subconscious mind, which in turn caused the parrot's death. I don't know. That's pretty wild.''

David laughed, but it came out like a sick croak.

''No, wait,'' Stan said, ''I've got it wrong. Her subconscious mind would have to have read your subconscious mind—''

''Are you laughing at me?''

''Not at all. It almost sounds as if you're suggesting that she can make *your* subconscious wishes come true, in addition to her own. In any case, I think you should have her tested.''

''That's why I called you. Do you think you could talk to Niles Martin, and find out if he'll see Laura at Rockham within the next week of so?''

''Be glad to. Where's she now?''

'Connecticut.''

''Does she seem all right?''

''For the moment. I'm not sure how all right she'd be if she knew about this.''

''You think she's suicidal?''

''She sees no other way out for herself. Stan, her explanation for all of this is standard psychotic issue. I told you, she believes she's a walking infection, a poison that sometimes gets out and infects the atmosphere.''

''Have you got some theory about all this?''

"You mean one that would explain it all in psychological terms?"

"In any terms."

"I don't have a theory, just a gut instinct. That if you took away all the specific events that seem to confirm Laura's emotions in the world outside her mind, the poison delusion would disappear. But think, Stan. If it appeared to you that your most private thoughts and emotions were being manifested in public, in horrible ways—murders and accidents and that kind of thing—at what point would you be justified in invoking the causal explanation? The psychotic explanation?"

"Jesus, I suppose you could be called schizophrenic—as in detached from reality—if you *failed* to invoke it." He was silent for a moment, then said, "I wouldn't tell her about your parrot, David. You don't want to be accused of collusion."

"It's not quite as simple as that, Stan. She wants all this not to be true, and yet she desperately needs for someone to believe her."

"You realize, of course, that having her proved a psychically gifted subject wouldn't mean you can stop this thing. What if you take her there and she passes the test with flying colors—predicts cards, makes dice turn flipflops, turns water into wine, for Christ's sake? What then?"

"I don't know. I just don't know."

"All right, David, I'll call Niles Martin."

"Thanks. One more thing: I've got a police detective on my back. He thinks Laura may well have murdered that woman."

"Why?"

David told him about the violent family history.

"So the detective thinks she's a 'bad seed,' " Stan

said. "There was a time when I might have laughed, but with all the latest research—"

"I know. Old wives' tales sometimes have a way of turning out to be true after all. Still, I don't think she did this, Stan."

"But of course you could be wrong?"

"Of course I could be wrong."

"Why else does the detective think she did it?"

"Because she knew about the ten cuts." David paused; he could hear Stan taking a drag on a cigarette.

"Have you thought of any other explanation for that?" Stan asked.

"She could be a multiple. Maybe one personality is doing things the other one doesn't know about. And leaking over certain key information. But I don't think so."

"Well, I guess you'll just have to prove she knew it by . . . some other means."

"I know. That's what scares me."

"How about her attempts to read your mind? Is that still going on?"

"God, yes. I spent a few hours listening to her tapes the other day. Either she has an uncanny ability to guess or she *knows.*"

"How many hours did you spend reviewing her tapes, David?"

"Four. Maybe five. Why?"

"You remember that patient I had last year, the writer—"

"Yes. You referred her to Darnell."

"Because you had a full schedule at the time. Why don't you refer this one to me?"

"Because I've had a few dreams about her. Because I care about her." David's voice sounded hostile, even to him. And he wasn't about to tell Stan he'd dreamed about her every night that week. Nor would he even *mention* what had happened at the charity thing that night.

"You know I'm right," Stan said.

Silence.

"Just how beautiful is this woman?"

"Come on, Stan. I'm not some neophyte intern in need of enlightenment as to the pitfalls of counter-transference."

"Just don't collude, my friend. Her gifts may be fascinating. Don't let her gifts seduce you into believing her delusions."

"I don't need a lecture on objectivity, either, Stan. Do I sound as if I totally believe her?"

"No," he said. "You sound obsessed."

22

Her skin was pale in the moonlight, pale as the sand, the sea, the moon. She had her back turned toward him. He could not see her face; he saw her buttocks, the curve of her hip, her back. There was a small brown mark just at the base of her spine, a birthmark. He touched it with his fingertip. Its surface was smooth and just slightly depressed. He moved one hand up along her back, touching each vertebra in turn. She shifted position slightly. He touched her breast. His hand was shaking. She turned toward him, her face cast in shadows. Now a cloud passed over the moon and she smiled. Her teeth were hard, cold,

gleaming white. Her eyes were all white, all orbs—
like eggs. He opened his mouth to scream.

David awakened with the thought that some part of
the dream was real. Which?

All day long he kept remembering the dream, reminding himself that the truest, deepest desires appeared in dreams—and that he *had* to refer her to
another psychiatrist if he couldn't stop thinking of her
this way. Even worse, what if his obsession with her
was part of the same net of her power? If her wishes
came true, was he one of her wishes? He could just
see it, the Donahue show, the headlines. PSYCHIA-
TRIST CLAIMS TELEPATHIC SEDUCTION BY
SUBURBAN WITCH, LOVE POTION NUMBER
NINE. They would lock him up and throw away the
key.

"Dr. Goldman!" The voice belonged to his
Wednesday one-thirty, Albert Stern, a mean little man
deeply humiliated at having to seek help and given to
acting out his humiliation by attacking David's professional abilities. Stern, who had the hour before Laura,
said, "Do you think you could manage to pay attention to me instead of what's outside the window?"

"You said your wife is constantly picking on you,
Albert. That's why you have trouble controlling your
temper."

"I said a lot more than that. You weren't listening."

David sighed. "Albert, I heard you say your boss
was picking on you. But you're right, I'm not paying
the kind of attention I usually do, and I'm sorry. Next
week, I'll listen closely, and next week let's talk about
you. Not your wife, not your boss. Fair enough?"

After Stern left, slamming the door behind him, David went out for a walk. He hadn't been a very good

therapist this morning. Not even competent. There was a mime performing on the sidewalk in front of Central Park. He watched the man for a while, then got a hot dog before walking back to his office.

Laura came in at precisely three o'clock.

"I'm sorry if our running into each other upset you last night," he said.

Silence.

"Laura?"

"Zach and I went to a charity ball in the city last night."

"When we saw each other there, did you perhaps think—"

"I didn't think anything."

Was this a conscious denial? Last night she had seemed perfectly aware of her reaction to Allison. A jealousy reaction, clearly. But to Laura a jealousy reaction meant disloyalty, and constituted further proof that she was a loathsome person. Did she think that if she denied her feeling, Allison would go unharmed? And what in the world could he say to her? If she really did have the power to affect reality with her emotions, should he not reverse normal therapeutic procedure? Instead of discouraging her from her "psychotic" beliefs, instead of encouraging her to accept her natural emotional responses, shouldn't he discourage that kind of self-acceptance?

He looked at her. No doctor could do that.

"Laura," he said gently, "were you afraid that something might happen to the woman you saw me with?"

"No. I wasn't afraid of anything. You must have misunderstood."

Maybe she really *didn't* remember. Could the

woman who saw him last night have been *another* Laura? A multiple? A murderer?

"Do you really not remember, Laura?"

She said nothing for a moment, then finally whispered, "No, I remember. Your wife is very beautiful. Once I dyed my hair blond. It looked dreadful."

"Laura, you do realize I have a private life outside of my work, don't you?"

"Of course. Why shouldn't you? You're a wonderful person."

"I care about you, Laura. And you may think I'm a wonderful person and I may even *be* wonderful, but you don't know me. You don't even know I have an ex-wife, not a wife." He plunged on. "Laura, your reaction on seeing me with a woman was perfectly normal. You're grateful to me for caring; perhaps at times you even think you're in love with me."

"I love my husband."

"I know that. But in the process of psychiatry, as I'm sure you know, sometimes we tend to transfer our feelings to the one we perceive as caring most about us, the psychiatrist. The transferred feelings may be ones of caring, even love, that perhaps we feel we don't get from the people in our lives." There. He'd delivered his little speech, lesson A on transference. He wished it hadn't sounded so hollow.

"I know Zach cares about me," she said. "He just isn't the kind of man who can put up with the kind of worrying I do. He's a very buttoned-up person. A straight shooter, my father always calls him."

"Your father is a cold man. You told me that way back last January. Is Zach a cold man?"

"No. He's a wonderful husband, a good father. He's reliable, quick-witted. And brilliant, really. Some-

times he can be brusque, but only when I do something wrong.''

''That's like saying, 'My husband beats me but only
when I deserve it.''

''Zach doesn't beat me. He loves me. He's—''

''Don't give me another list of his good qualities.
Tell me if he's available to you, tell me if he cares for
you, tell me if he makes you feel loved. If you're always ready to blame yourself, you won't ever see that
there may be substantial weaknesses in other people.''

She didn't respond, except to look at him, her features slack with despair.

''It sounds to me,'' David said, ''as if you think he
should love you, and that you should love him, whatever the true situation. Now, I'm not saying he doesn't
love you. But how can you judge if you're convinced
that your reactions and emotions and feelings aren't
all right, and everyone else's *are*?''

''I guess I always thought I should be above all
that.''

He looked at her. ''Didn't you once tell me your
father insisted you control your emotions?''

''Yes. My father always seemed to . . . I don't know
. . . avoid me. I remember one time when I was about
eleven, he came back from a long trip and we all lined
up to give him a kiss, and he kissed my brother and
sister and then kissed me—and he turned his cheek
away as I kissed him back. It made me feel . . . I don't
know, like some kind of . . . disease.''

''And he behaved differently toward your brother
and sister?'' Was it something about *her*?

''No. Not really. Just that one time. Or maybe he
did. He always seemed to be watching me, though,
and I could always feel something inside him. Fear,
or something. And there was that image.''

"What was it like, Laura?"

"Me," she said. "It was an image of me, screaming."

David suddenly felt as if time were racing. He had to stop her, to freeze her at that moment, as if she were a videotape on pause. He had to have time to think about it, consider all the possibilities, tell her—or not tell her—about her aunt.

"Do you know what the image meant, Laura?"

"No. I never knew what to make of it. I don't blame my father for the way he acted with me when I was little. He was fearful for me, or maybe *of* me. He did the best he could, I guess. I was a pretty strange child. I didn't know how to deal with my gifts."

"But you never discussed those gifts with him?"

"No. And it's only recently—as an adult—that I've learned to act like everyone else does. I don't blame my father at all. I would have been the same way with a child like me."

"No, you wouldn't, Laura. Look at the way you are with your son. You told me that you bend over backwards to make sure he feels loved."

"I suppose I do have some of the same fears about him as my father did about me. But I doubt he would feel all that loved if he could sense my mind the way I do my father's."

"Have you ever gotten any indication he can?"

"No. I worry about it, though. And anyway, it's different nowadays. People are aware of the damage parents can do."

"*You* are aware, Laura; not people, *you*. Why can't you ever give yourself credit for anything?"

"Because it's never enough."

"One of the things we have to accept as adults is that our parents are what they are, Laura. That doesn't mean the little child inside us doesn't want them to be different. Your father is a cold, distant man. Maybe he had his own reasons. But those reasons aren't caused by anything you are. Or aren't. Nor do they negate your feelings.''

"I love him."

"Of course you do. And you hate him, too. Love him for the good things he's given you, be angry at him for the bad ones—or the good ones he's withheld. Maybe even talk to him about it. And then go on."

She was staring at him. "Fine. You give me permission to express my anger at my father?"

David was on such thin ice that he could all but feel it cracking beneath his chair. He decided to change the subject.

"How do you feel today, Laura?"

She scowled. "If you mean, has your medicine worked on me yet, the answer is no. It just makes me tired."

"And?"

"What is it you think the pills are going to do?"

"Help you, I hope."

"The only way they can help me is if they can stop my feelings. I think things, David—"

"Laura, please don't call me David." He *should* have said something neutral: "It would be better if you didn't call me David," something like that.

She was looking at him as if she'd just been slapped. "I thought you were my friend."

"I am."

"You've been so good to me. . . . ''

She was going to cry. No, she wasn't. And whether she cried or not, all he wanted to do was take her in his arms, protect her, comfort her—suddenly, magically, make it all go away. It was not a thought he'd ever had about a patient, at least not in quite that way. He forced his mind onto a professional track. Self-hatred caused delusions of power. Or was it the other way around? If the power existed, wouldn't the self-hatred follow? Collusion.

"I'm trying to help you," he said. "I'm going to take you down to Rockham. They'll test you—"

"*Test* me? What good is that going to do?"

She had walked to the front of his desk and was leaning over him. He saw a thousand reflections in her irises. (Her eyes were all iris, all orbs. Like eggs.)

"Delusions of power?" she said. "Well, you just tell me about delusions of power the next time you talk to your ex-wife."

Jesus Christ. Was she going to walk in here each time and announce some new horror she had wrought?

David felt a sensation of dizziness, as if he were being whirled about in a game of blindman's bluff.

"I have horrible thoughts inside me, *doctor.*"

"Laura—"

"Can a pill make me stop feeling them? Can a test result make them go away?"

She was hovering over his desk, standing above him, directing the course of the interview as if she were the doctor and he were the patient. He had lost control of the session.

He stood up and looked directly into her eyes. Her expression changed, and she took a step back.

"Oh, God, you feel it, too." Another step. "I'm sorry I've gotten you involved, David. I'm so sorry." She was backing out the door. *"You feel it, too."*

Did she mean she knew he was under her spell? Or did she mean she was under his?

And then she was gone, leaving both the inner and outer doors to his office swinging open.

"Dr. Goldman?" Mrs. Frangipani was standing there, looking alarmed. "Is everything all right?"

A reasonable question, with Laura running out of his office, and him standing there.

He pictured himself running after Laura. Could he reassure her that everything was going to be all right? Fly out the door to his office, past his open-mouthed neighbor and into the street in time to catch sight of her before she rounded the corner on Amsterdam? And once he caught up to her, could he grab her by the hand, whirl her around, take her in his arms and tell her, "There, there, it's all in your mind—well, maybe not completely . . ."

No. He couldn't. But if he didn't, what would she do?

He ran.

The street was about as crowded as it ever got, the afterwork crush. About midway down the block, he saw her standing next to a scrawny city tree. He started to call her name, then realized she wasn't alone. She was standing with a man. With Detective Culligan.

"Do you always make a practice of running out into the street after your patients, Dr. Goldman?"

"No, I . . . what are you doing here?"

"I was coming to see you, of course," Culligan said. "I want to ask your opinion about something."

David sighed. "Laura, will you be all right?"

She looked at Culligan, then back at him. "I want to hear what he has to ask you."

Culligan shrugged. "Okay by me," he said.

David looked at him, then at Laura. Would he allow this? Did he have a choice?

"All right, but we can't discuss it here." He led the two of them back into his office. Laura sat down on the sofa and said, "What do you want his opinion about, Detective Culligan?"

"This family history of yours," Culligan said.

"Detective," David said, "this is my patient. And there are some things that—"

"For Christ's sake, Goldman, I'm a police detective. And your patient is a prime suspect in a *murder* case."

"Then arrest her. Or wait until the two of us can discuss this in private."

"Now you're going to tell me she *doesn't know,* doctor?"

"Know *what*?" Laura stood up and took a deep breath. "If there is something about my family background that you know and I don't," she said, "then it's time I did."

David—exhausted, defeated—nodded his consent.

"All right," Culligan said, "Your father's sister—"

"My father had no sister. My father's family all died when he was very young."

"Mrs. Wade, do you want to hear this or not?"

"Yes."

Culligan cleared his throat. "Your father's sister—Sophie Zophlick—"

"Zophlick?"

"Well, yes. Your father had the name changed. And it seems the reason is because Miss Zophlick was put in a place called the Darlington Home for the Insane—"

"What do you mean insane?"

"Insane enough to kill a man, Mrs. Wade."

Her expression, to David, was a grotesque parody of one of the gargoyles on his building. After a moment, she turned to face him. "You *knew*?"

David nodded. "He told me the other day."

She stood up straight and said, very calmly, "I have to go see my father."

She began walking toward the door.

David started after her. "Are you sure you'll be all right?"

"No, I'm not sure," she said, "but I'm sure there's nothing you can do."

With that, she turned and headed out the door.

"All right, Culligan," David said. "What is it you want?"

"I want to ask you your opinion about the murder—the old murder. You know, the two of them—Sophie Zophlick and the doctor, his name was Elias De-Mane—were found at his home. So I—"

"Wait a minute," David said. "You told me this all happened several years after her commitment. When people were put in those places—I'm afraid I can't do much to defend the state of my profession in those days—they were usually locked up for good. How did she get to this doctor's home?"

"Well," he said, "it seems the two were having a—what did they call it then, a tryst? Of course, now they'd call it what it is."

"How do you *know* this, detective?"

"Spoke to an old man, a doctor who was on staff at Darlington when it happened. Named Emmanuel Kassand. He's in the St. Francis Home for the Aged. Couldn't remember what he had for lunch that day, but he remembered what happened fifty years ago, clear as a whistle. And why not? It was quite a scandal. A man, a doctor ruining his career over a woman—a beautiful woman, I give you that. And a woman described by everyone who knew her as stark raving mad. Kassand said she was a real lunatic. Any of this strike any bells?''

David sighed. ''Symptomatology doesn't carry through that way, detective. Laura's aunt may have been a murderer, but Laura isn't. Certainly not in the sense you mean—in the sense her aunt was.'' Did it matter exactly how she murdered, if she did?

''You'll never find any evidence that she was at the murder scene,'' David said.

''Then how'd she know about the ten cuts?''

''Look, it's possible there may be some precognitive element—''

''Precognitive?'' Culligan frowned. ''I told you I don't believe in all that crap. You know what else I don't believe in? Coincidences. A coincidence is like a little bell in my head. It rings when something's not right, and it keeps on ringing until I figure out how come it's there. And that's *two* coincidences now. The aunt was a murderer. And her niece knew about the ten cuts.''

''That isn't anywhere near enough to charge her, much less get a conviction.''

''Maybe not. But I've got a gong going off in my head at this point. And I'm a very persistent man, doctor. Very persistent, where a coincidence is concerned. And where *two* coincidences are concerned I'm a downright pest.''

PART THREE

Laura:
Vision

23 Her father's house was a stucco and wood Tudor reproduction he'd had built in the fifties, set beyond a cluster of great oaks at the end of a long private road, surrounded by two acres of perfectly manicured lawn. Laura stopped the car in front of the bird bath in the circular driveway, stood before the double mahogany doors, and considered what she would say to him. Her father was old now. He'd had two heart attacks in the past three years. Twice during the two-hour ride that seemed like ten, she'd come close to turning around and going back.

Marie Tate, the Gardners' housekeeper, opened the doors. "Laura. How are you, dear? Your parents are in the living room. I don't think they were expecting you."

No. They wouldn't have been.

The Gardners' living room was all white: plush white silk sofas, white brocade drapes, a white piano polished to a high gloss, white-on-white jacquard pillows. Even the rugs were white, and so thick a person left footprints marking his passage.

Laura stood for a moment in the doorway, looking out on that sea of white. Samuel Gardner was reading.

Marla was picking out Chopin at the piano. They didn't notice her at first.

Once, Laura had asked her mother why she had furnished the room in such a fashion as to convey the message: hands off, don't touch, don't yell, don't get dirty, don't relax, sit up, be still. Marla Gardner, who doubtless thought the comment precocious for an eight-year-old, had answered the question simply: she thought it was beautiful. And indeed it was.

Laura could still remember the decorator waving her arms around saying, "White will be marvelous in here, Mrs. Gardner, with those wonderful French doors over there and these fine moldings. All the finest fabrics, all different textures, all in white. It'll be a deluge of white!"

Stepping into the Gardners' living room was like entering a cloud, or a dream.

The Chopin waltz stopped. "Laura, dear, how are you?"

Her father looked up, then slowly stood. He seemed smaller, more fragile even than when she'd last seen him some months ago.

She endured their embraces. There was a long silence.

"Is anything wrong, Laura?" her father said.

"I. I needed to see you."

"Well, isn't this a nice surprise?" Marla Gardner said. "Where are the children?"

"At home. They started school last week."

"And Zach? How is he?" Sam Gardner's voice had an edge to it, as if he knew this wasn't a social visit.

Laura nodded, and there was another long silence.

"Well, isn't this nice—"

"I found out, Father," Laura said.

He looked at her mother as if pleading for help, for

rescue. Why? Marla Gardner couldn't rescue a cat from the clutches of a mouse. She was a shallow woman, a silly woman.

"Found out what, dear?" her mother said.

"About Sophie Zophlick."

Her father looked as if Laura had struck him.

"I know the whole story, Father. Everything."

"What . . . how did you find out?"

'What's the difference? I did." Laura realized there were tears on her face. She hadn't wanted to cry.

"Laura," her mother said softly, "your father doesn't like to talk about Sophie."

"No, Marla." He touched his wife's arm. "I probably should have told her, I should have told all the children, as soon they were old enough to understand." He was shifting from foot to foot, running his fingers through what was left of his hair.

"Understand?"

"I didn't tell you, Laura, because . . . because I wanted your life to be happy, full of good things—"

"She was a *murderer,* Father! Why didn't you ever tell me?"

"Because it didn't make any difference," he said. "She's dead. They're all dead. It doesn't have anything to do with you. You have a wonderful husband, three beautiful children."

She could feel her father's pain—undefined, unexamined—rising in him like a sea monster. She could feel his guilt. After so long, he still felt guilty. And she was making it worse, dragging out long-buried memories. She covered her ears, the instinctive reaction whose uselessness she'd discovered as a child, but she did it anyway. She didn't want to feel his pain. She wanted to feel hers.

"I want to know why," she said simply.

"Who can say why these things happen?" he said. "Why someone suddenly becomes violent, starts thinking people are talking about them—"

"She thought that?"

"She said she heard them thinking."

"Oh, Lord."

Her aunt had it, too. It was in the genes, passed down from generation to generation like a curse. But Laura had managed to live with it. Why hadn't she?

"The doctors never know why, Laura," he was saying. "What could I have told you? Sophie was stark raving mad. It was so long ago—1935—and my father was dead. My mother didn't know what to do. After a while, she had to have them come and take Sophie away. I was a young boy. She'd tried to hurt me. And after she went to that place, that was the end of it."

"You didn't visit her?"

"I was only a boy, Laura. It wasn't like you went to those places. When they sent people there, it was forever. No one went to Darlington. It wasn't a place to visit."

"No one ever went to see her?"

"You don't visit a monster, Laura."

Monster?

"Laura, I don't know how you found out about it," he said, "but you must try to forget. It doesn't matter."

Laura looked at him, suddenly realizing that Sophie had been a silent, permanent presence in her life, something she had always sensed but couldn't quite bring herself to look for, like a ghost. There was the image in his mind again, that image of the woman screaming. Was it Sophie screaming? No, it was Laura. Dark hair, dark eyes . . .

"What did Sophie look like, Father?"

"I don't remember."

No, he wasn't going to lie to her. Not now.

"You're lying," she heard herself scream. There was almost a physical pain to screaming at him. She was always the good girl. Control yourself, Laura. Only dogs go mad.

He stared at her, then turned and shuffled slowly out of the room. She listened to the sound of his footsteps on the stairs. Her mother, for once, remained silent.

She walked over to the bay window that faced the back lawn. It was dark but she could see the pool, closed up tight for the winter, its patio bare, lawn beyond.

Her father came downstairs a few minutes later and without fanfare or introduction handed her a small picture.

She seemed to be looking at a picture of herself: the same dark hair, the same facial structure, the nose . . . Everything the same.

"Me," she said.

"No, Laura. Her face was fuller. And her nose . . ."

Her anger exploded against her father like lava from a long dead volcano, churning down the mountainside, bubbling, hissing, shooting cascades of fiery hot spray. Now she was Pompei, buried under layers and layers of black sediment, lies and lies and lies.

"I had an operation on my nose, Father," she screamed. "Remember?" She looked back at the photograph, holding its serrated edges lightly between her fingertips as if gripping it too firmly would make it crumble and be lost forever. The girl in the photograph was younger than she was now, perhaps ten years younger, sitting on a stool, leaning toward the camera, mouth smiling, eyes not, one end of a long strand of pearls held between thumb and forefinger. A photograph of a monster. He had kept it all these years.

She looked back up at him, then slowly turned the photograph over. Printed on the back in small, stamped letters were the words "Mitovich Studio. Philadelphia, 1937."

24   Clutching the picture in her hand like some kind of prize, leaving her sixty-five-year-old father standing there like a punctured balloon, Laura stormed out of the house in which she had made her solitary way toward adulthood, the house of the dazzling white living room, the house in which she had tried to kill herself three times. Stabbing (red, on white thighs); drowning (stupid); jumping (third story, got caught in a bush, ended up with a few scratches).

She had wanted only to be normal. To think, to feel, to touch. To see. To be a good person, to marry and have children, to raise them well, and have pleasure from them. Everyone wished, perhaps, for what they could not have. Normality was Laura's dream.

Her circumstances were ordinary enough. Some, most, would call her family wealthy, but her father had made his money after the war, selling ordinary things—hardware, housewares, cosmetics—the sterile mass-produced stuff of a new generation, all shrink-wrapped and packaged and safe. He had a store, then three stores, then ten. She thought even he was surprised by his success.

Her home was very formal—the way it was furnished, the way she was dressed, the way she was carted out for her father's business acquaintances.

She went to school. She had a brother and sister who fought with each other and with her parents. She ate cereal for breakfast. Her mother kept herself busy with her children and with her charities; her father's business kept him busy.

It began when she was very young, with voices and with images. She had a vague memory of herself as a little girl putting her hands over her ears, over her eyes, to block out the funny thoughts and pictures. Her mother always asked why she did it, but Laura couldn't explain. She was three, maybe five, and she didn't have the grasp of language to make her mother understand. She didn't understand herself. It wasn't images she could see with her eyes, or words she heard with her ears; it was inside her mind. She wondered *why* she had to explain it to her mother.

Even after she understood that she heard things other people simply didn't hear, knew things other people didn't know, she couldn't help wondering. *What* were the other words she sometimes heard when people spoke, words that sometimes contradicted what they said aloud? And what were those pictures she saw in her mind? And why did her dreams, her thoughts, seem to tell what was going to happen? She would hear someone thinking about doing something, have a dream or see an image, and then—two days later, or two weeks, or a month—there it would be.

It wasn't just about *people* that she knew, either. She could detect the cry of an abandoned sparrow fledgling in a thunderstorm, of a seagull hunting for its mate.

She could find an underground spring in a field of tall grass. She could tell, always, when it was going to snow. And when they gave her the IQ tests, she always knew the answers, even if the questions were grades ahead of where she was in school. One hundred eighty points. She heard the administer think he had never seen anything like it.

How could she be normal when the first picture she brought home from kindergarten was a perfectly rendered pencil drawing of a galloping horse, so rounded and real it looked like it might gallop right off the page? When all the other first-graders were barely drawing stick figures and she knew about shading and shadow and perspective? No one had told her. She just seemed to be able to form pictures in her mind, then copy then accurately onto the paper.

She heard what people thought about her artistic talent, not just what they said: ''Amazing!'' ''Uncanny.'' ''Bizarre!'' ''Prodigy.'' ''Unbelievable.''

They didn't know the half of it.

It took what happened the summer she was eight to make her understand. That summer, as usual, her mother packed them all up—Laura and her sister Carole and her brother Greg and the housekeeper Marie—and moved them for three months to the house in Barnegat Light, on the Jersey shore, a Victorian house with nooks to explore and trellises and a huge front porch that faced the high dunes. It was wonderful there. Her mother relaxed some of the rules, and the furniture was the old stuff, familiar, demoted to make way for new furnishings consistent with increasing wealth.

That was the year Laura had her new doll, the French one Father gave her for her birthday with hair the color of pale honey. (She named her Gretchen, after a character in a story she'd read.) And that was the year her new friend Annie Spellman came.

There were seashells to be collected with Annie, bicycles to be ridden, and hula hoops, and scooters, and the beach. That was the summer she was given the run of the house and also of the town. The cove. Old Mr. MacGuire, the fisherman. The lighthouse. Unsupervised. Heaven.

It happened on a Saturday in the middle of the summer, when Laura's father had come down for the weekend. That afternoon she and Annie (and Gretchen) were collecting seashells on the beach, just walking and dropping oyster shells and clam shells and sea glass into their buckets. Carole was out on the sand in front of the house when they got back, making another one of her sand castles, complete with turrets and a moat. "Isn't this the greatest castle you've ever seen, Laura?" Then, "Oh, what do you know? You and your baby!"

She was making fun of Gretchen.

Laura stepped on the sand castle.

"Don't, Laura." Carole grabbed Laura's ankles, tripped her, then jumped on top of her, and the two sisters tumbled down. Laura was the younger, but she was taller even then, and she struggled in the sand against her sister, the two of them rolling over and over, spitting, hissing. They were like two cats. Carole was screaming, "You ruined my castle!"

But Laura also heard something else, a subtext to her spoken words: "I'll fix you, Laura." And then: "Gretchen."

She saw in her mind an image of her sister picking up a scissors and chopping away at her beloved doll's hair. And then she saw herself: getting out of bed, feeling something soft between her toes. Honey-colored curls, corkscrew curls lying in a sad pile on her pink rug. She saw herself picking up a handful of the shorn curls, racing around the house looking for her doll—the rest of her. Down the stairs, out the door, around the house, by the shed, down in back by the tall grass, which would lash at her face as she ran through it. Finally she would find the doll in the attic, propped up on the old four-poster bed, her once beautiful hair clipped to the roots, poking out in all directions.

Laura suddenly realized that what she was hearing was what Carole was thinking. And the images? *The images were of what was going to happen.*

"Don't you touch my doll!" she screamed.

Carole stopped fighting and pulled away. "I didn't do anything to your stupid doll."

"You're going to."

"I am not!"

Of course she was. It was exactly what Carole was thinking. But why was she denying it? Didn't she know that Laura could hear?

"What is going on here?" Suddenly her father was standing over them, his face looming against the backdrop of a clear blue sky, her mother behind him. When he spoke, it was in a low voice that seemed to come from the back of his throat. "Little ladies do not fight."

"She ruined my doll!"

'I never touched her doll."

"She was *going* to," Laura screamed. "Punish her for ruining my doll!"

"Laura," he said, "Your doll is right there." He pointed at Gretchen, lying in the sand where Laura had dropped her.

"Punish her!"

"Carole already said she wouldn't do anything to the doll, Laura."

How could she make him understand? "But she's *going* to."

"Why does she keep saying that?" Carole yelled. 'I didn't do anything to her stupid doll. See, there it is, right there! Anyway, it would serve her right if I cut off all her hair."

"There—you see? She was thinking about cutting Gretchen's hair all off."

Eleven-year-old Carole looked at her sister, then turned to their father, said, "She's weird," turned and walked away.

Laura was crying by then. She knew her sister was lying, but there wasn't any way to prove it. She cried and covered her face with her hands and just kept saying that she'd heard Carole thinking it, she'd *seen* her doing it.

By the time she looked back at her father, his face had turned pasty gray, the color of half-cooked pork. Laura could see the fear and grief in his expression; she could feel it. Was it bad to hear people's thoughts?

He said softly, "You heard Carole thinking, Laura?"

She nodded.

He glanced at her mother, and the two of them stared at each other for a long time, eyes locked in one of those silent battles they occasionally got into that were so baffling to Laura and, apparently, so important to them.

Her mother turned to her father and said, "It was just a guess, Sam. Just a guess." She could see her mother was angry with him. Furious, even, which was very unlike her.

She remembered thinking her mother was defending

her, which she wasn't. She was denying. Always denying.

He told her to go to her room.

She obeyed, but as she walked away, she saw in his mind a clear and precise image, the image of a woman screaming. Yes. That was it! She *often* saw that image when he was nearby. The image must come from him. It must be what he was thinking.

She retreated to her room, her little pink world, alone. She got into her pajamas and took her doll into bed, hiding with her under the covers, vowing to her that she would protect her from Carole. Of course, her sister never *did* cut Gretchen's hair, which at the time confused her. But she soon realized that when she interfered in the natural progression of events, she disrupted the flow, which meant she also had the capacity to alter the course of people's lives. She'd headed her sister off from ruining her doll by admitting she knew what Carole was thinking, and, in the process, she'd exposed herself, something she had rarely done since.

Later that night her father sat down on the far corner of her bed. She wanted him to hug her and tell her it was okay. He seemed very sad. He still had red hair then, and he was still young, still gloriously handsome—to her, at least.

"I don't want ever to see you fighting like that with your sister, Laura."

"But I was mad."

"Only dogs go mad." He stood up and turned to go, then stopped and looked back at her. "Only a very bad girl would try to listen to people's thoughts."

She vowed to herself never to be a bad girl again, but she stayed in her room, all night, thinking up all the ways she could hurt her sister, counting them up, adding and rearranging and reordering visions of violence until she fell asleep. She awakened, later, from a nightmare: her sister was going to hurt herself—she was going to fall. She wondered if she should warn Carole to be careful, then she decided it was best not to say anything at all.

Finally released from her room, she was in the kitchen the next morning, just sitting down to pancakes, when she heard the thud. By the time they got upstairs, Carole's ankle was swollen out like a balloon. She was rolling around on the floor, screaming in pain. The doctor at the local hospital said she'd broken the ankle in two places.

At ten, Laura took up painting with a vengeance. Her parents set up a studio in her bedroom to encourage her, but then they complained because everything she painted was dark. When she was eleven, she did a watercolor of a monster she'd seen in a dream. She thought it was the best thing she'd ever done, but when her mother and father saw it, they were horrified. So she tried to please them. She put light and color in her pictures—reds and greens and blues and yellows. And they stopped looking horrified and started giving her compliments. She tried oils, acrylics, pastels. The work piled up, until her room was crammed full and she had to store the excess in the attic.

She spent long hours by herself, painting, reading, or just sitting in her room, immersed in elaborate fantasies of benevolent power. Or she would walk along the stream at the back of the property, follow the path of a doe in the woods, gaze up at the sky, wondering why she'd been blessed with these powers—cursed with these powers.

Once her brother skidded on some wet leaves in the roadway on his motorcycle. Laura had known it would happen all along. She'd seen it in a dream, and she agonized over the knowledge that she could have saved him from a limp he carried to this day.

She wondered why she had to make these choices, to tell people what she'd seen or not. And what did it all mean? Why did she see her father's mind like a sapling in a gathering storm, braced for the onslaught? Why did he say, "Only dogs go mad," and think it even more often than he said it?

Sometimes she thought *she* would go mad, just like her father's dogs.

Why? Why her? It was unnatural to know things before they happened, to feel other people's feelings, to know their thoughts. Her father had told her so.

Sometimes it hurt to know what people were thinking about her, but she learned to accept it, excuse it, or even to ignore it. Now *there* was a gift—to be able to ignore it. Surely she wasn't worthy of knowing things other people didn't know.

Was there some purpose to her life that she didn't understand?

She went to the library and got out science books, genealogy, biology, archaeology. Was she a mutation? Some freak, created by an accidental association between gene and egg, a mixing? Was she a new kind of being? If so, why didn't any doctor she ever went to see anything different about her? Was she a witch, a monster, a god?

She got books on witchcraft and conducted lone ceremonies in her bedroom. Oh, how pathetic she was, with her rods and her herbs and her cards, trying desperately to tap into some cosmic force she had the temerity to think she could control. She read about precognition. Yes! That was it, she knew things before they happened.

The silent, confused child become a somber, terrified adolescent.

One winter morning when she was thirteen, the headmistress called her into the office and told her that the art teacher wanted to arrange a showing of her work. She told the headmistress she didn't want to do it, that she couldn't allow herself to be put on display that way, but it was already arranged. Her parents had agreed.

That afternoon, she tried to kill herself for the first time. About a quarter mile from the house there was a special place where the stream that ran along the back of the property was deep and wide and the bank especially steep. A small natural pool.

The water was colder than she expected, and deeper. There was a kind of warmth to the icy water, though. She seemed to become a part of it, she understood it, she knew where stones lay along the moss at the bottom and where fish had laid their eggs, and where a natural eddy had once taken someone under long ago. Her mind worked backward and forward in time. She floated, looking up at the darkening sky, listening to the chatter of the rushing stream, the rustle of naked winter trees, the sounds in her head. She tried to stay under but her legs kept moving on their own, paddling, drawing her back up to the surface. Deciding she didn't have the courage to kill herself, she clawed her way back to the bank.

When she got back to the house, dripping and shivering, her mother began fussing over her, helping her out of the wet things, and Carole laughed at her and said she looked like a drowned rat, but her father only stared. There was that image in his mind again. She tried to take the image out, examine it, explain it. Who was the woman screaming?

She told him that she had tried to kill herself.

"You don't mean that kind of talk, Laura," he said.

Her mother explained that she didn't want to do the showing.

"Why, Laura," Sam said, "it's a great talent you have. It's an honor. Why wouldn't you want to do it?"

"You'll see, Laura," Mother said, in her soothing voice. "It'll be fun. You'll see."

"It'll be terrible!" she screamed. "My paintings are terrible."

"No, Laura. Your paintings are wonderful."

Oh, yes. She could paint a tree that looked just like a tree. Her demons looked just like demons.

She began to scream at them, trying to get them to understand that she couldn't be put on display like that.

"Laura!" her father said. "Control yourself. You just have a little case of nerves, isn't that right?"

They were standing there watching her, assaulting her with a chorus of thoughts. Each of them was thinking how ridiculous it was for her to get hysterical over something so simple.

"Go away! Just go away."

She ran from them, away from the image in her father's mind, up to her bedroom, first taking a tour of the living room where she marked her path in muddy footprints, dropping lots of nice big drips on her mother's pearl-white rug.

She locked the door, took off her clothes and lay down on her bed. Her mother was probably down there right now, scrubbing the mud out of the carpet.

As it turned out, she didn't have to do the showing after all. She stopped painting altogether, and her parents took pity on her. Anyway, she got pneumonia and had to stay in bed for almost a month, suffocating in her own poison with each new breath of the fetid air.

25 She was in the bath. The photograph lay facedown on the counter by the sink next to the accoutrements of her daily regimen: the perfumes, the lotions, the polish, the powders. She'd put three capfuls of oil in the bath; now she was sloshing around in the water, a liquid womb. She dribbled the water down her arms with the washcloth, watched the way it trickled braids over her skin. When she was finished with her bath, she would be the real live walking, talking windup doll named Laura, all perfumed and scented and pretending to live.

How clearly she could remember Annie's admiration when they were eight: "You heard Carole thinking about cutting your doll's hair? You saw Carole fall in a dream?"

Annie had said that Laura was lucky to be able to hear people thinking, and that it was almost as if her wish had come true. "Like you got revenge on Carole," Annie said.

The two of them had giggled about it all summer, thinking how great that would be, to be able to get revenge by making a wish and having it come true. For three summers in a row they giggled, and made secret lists of everyone they hated, which was just about everyone—their parents, Laura's sister, Annie's brother, the old woman who ran the local grocery store—and all the things they wanted to have happen to them. Annie wanted to have a giant bowl of brussels sprouts come down from the sky and forcefeed itself to her mother.

Then the Spellmans stopped coming to the beach in the summer, which was just as well, because somehow it all didn't seem so funny to Laura as she got older.

"Laura."

There was a sound. Knocking.

She was touching the scar on her thigh, remembering how she had slit the skin with a razor when she was fifteen, watched the blood ooze out. She told her mother it was an accident, that she'd cut her leg shaving.

"Laura!"

Stepping out of the tub, she wrapped a towel around herself, made her voice normal.

"Come in, Zach."

He opened the door and stood there in the doorway, watching her as she began her regimen. He always seemed to be watching her lately. How could she blame him? How could he understand what she had done? To confess like that? He was afraid of the scandal.

Did he think she had killed Rita Harmon? She listened, but there was a roaring in her ears, as if she had suddenly been submerged underwater again. She could hear the rushing sound, she could feel it filling up beneath her skin: she could feel her bones bobbing around. She was drowning inside.

"Laura," he said, "where have you been?"

She had never been able to listen to his thoughts. Had she ever loved him? She'd been so happy when he married her. Had she thought marrying him would make her normal?

No. She couldn't hear what *anyone* was thinking.

Only lunatics heard people thinking. It was in the genes.

"Where have you been?"

Zach was standing behind her as she massaged lotion into her hands. She could see him in the mirror. He had his arms folded across his chest. He looked almost exactly the same as he had when she met him on her third day at Penn. She had been in the library, reading an occasionally intelligible tome called *Introduction to Modern Philosophy*. The assignment was a chapter on existentialism. So much had she identified with it that for hours she sat there immersed. She, more than anyone, knew just how isolated the individual was. Suddenly her orgy of sober but naive self-revelation was pierced by a pair of eyes watching her so intently that the words on the page blurred.

She'd looked up and there he was, arms folded across his chest, eyes—

"I just asked you where you were, Laura. What the hell is wrong with you?"

"I went to my parents'." Was that croaking sound she heard somewhere her voice? "Did I kill her, Zach?"

He stared at her. Then he said, "I don't know, Laura. Only you know that."

"I don't remember killing her."

"Then you didn't," he said. "Unless you have magic killing powers. Do you?"

There was the roaring. Didn't he know she was a monster? She could kill with her mind.

"You drove all the way down to Philadelphia?" he was asking.

She told him why, handed him the photograph.

He held it in his hands. "She's a dead ringer for you, isn't she?"

Yes. A dead ringer.

She was lying in bed, trying to sink into the quilting. She could hear the steady sound of Zach's breathing, of his untroubled sleep, the whoosh of the wind through the eves, the sound of the waves lapping gently at the sand.

Carefully, quietly, she got up from bed and made her way upstairs to the attic, a blind woman in the dark. She stood there for a moment, then turned on a single lamp and removed the cloth from the work on the easel, *Nightmare under the Moon*. The thunderclouds were nearly done. They would be great and dark when they were finished, rolling across a pale yellow moon.

She still had some work to do on the flesh tones of the woman lying naked on the ornate sofa, the claw marks on her face. But the demon in the foreground was complete, the bottom half of its body a woman's hips and legs in warm pink and ocher tones, the top half a creature of fur and claws and teeth, standing over the other, licking the blood from its claws. She picked up a brush, then stopped, laid it down again.

She squeezed her eyes shut, tried to remember if she had killed Rita. Rita had called to cancel their meeting. Laura had gone to the movies, then home to bed. She'd awakened and seen the article about Rita in the paper. No time lost. Every moment accounted for.

But she also remembered every moment of the dinner party: cutting up the vegetables with the caterer, trying to keep the children out of her hair all afternoon, Bob Grandville calling to cancel, Zach wanting sex just before the party. She remembered the way her skin hurt afterward. And the way Rita practically sat on Zach's lap (she hadn't really thought they were having an affair, had she?). The way she had chewed the same piece of veal over and over again, the headache she had, the noise in her head (sometimes there was so much noise it was hard to hear anything). And she remembered looking down at her hands, palms down on the linen tablecloth, nails painted red. She could hurt Rita. Ten fingers, ten slivers, ten marks on that face with her nails, ten thin dark streams of blood oozing from the pale powdered flesh.

She opened her eyes. Of course she had killed Rita. She didn't need to pick up a knife or a gun. She had done it with her anger. It had all changed somehow.

Only dogs go mad.

Had she known there would come this time when she would find herself spiraling downward, falling faster and faster, her mouth forced open by the wind as she whizzed downward until finally she hit the ground, a mass of tissue and bones and flesh?

It wasn't hitting the ground she feared, it was the free fall. And here she was, so far into the free fall that she could hear the whoosh of wind on her face. She searched for a ledge, a rock, a stump to grab hold of.

David, do this: tell me you know what to do, help me find some way to turn my brain off. My brain is skidding over ice, off and sliding, out of control. Put your arms around me, make me safe, hold me until I am well. Just the touch of your fingertips to make me well . . .

She was dreaming.

She was a child again, running down a wide aisle with shelves crammed full on either side, darkness beyond. Dish towels with pictures of cookie jars on them, candy, Sinatra records, toasters, toys. A Halloween mask, a section of screwdrivers, bottles of Prell shampoo. In her father's store, where he always took her on Sundays—but the products were all mixed up on the shelves.

At the end of the aisle, she saw him lying on a cot, a white blur against the dark backdrop, a long thin lump beneath a gray blanket. His skin was pale, fragile. He smiled and put his arm outside of the blanket. His arm was very bony, the fingernails long and ragged, curled over his fingertips. And she was so angry at him, the anger foamed out, black milk overflowing, spilling out onto the floor. She was raging, raging. But she didn't speak. She only did this: she put her palm on his chest to feel the beating of his heart—rhythmic, weak, but steady.

And with the touch of her hand, suddenly there was no sound at all.

His heart was still.

The scream was out before she had opened her eyes.

26

The man heard the roar of the jet engine, the dull thud of the landing gear. He could feel the Death Witch failing now, losing strength, losing will. He was the stronger, and She was beyond the help She had sought.

Someone was speaking to him.

"Fasten your seatbelt, please." He recognized the stewardess. This was her regular route. It did not matter. He was well concealed.

The man smiled back at the stewardess.

"Yes, thank you, Miss."

Miss smiled. He watched her move down the aisle.

Quickly, with a touch, he felt the wig, smoothed his clothes down. All was in place. He had been this way before.

He had chosen his place carefully, cleared the land and built the cabin himself at the edge of the river, where the water was muddy and red and the vines so thick that no light reached the land surface. The river was nearly one hundred miles wide in some places, and everywhere it teemed with life. Creatures that existed nowhere else on earth, all locked together in a preordained cycle of life.

He breathed deeply, sucked in the odor of birth and death, of prey and predator. The Death Witch, the predator. He remembered getting up, slowly in the dark, making his way down the long hallway, bare feet—child feet—padding on the wooden floor, floorboards creaking, the turn of the crystal knob—

The blood. The father, the Death Witch lover, deserved his fate. The father had died of his own weakness. The man excused the father least of all.

He had work to do. He set about bringing the wood he had carefully dried and seasoned into the clearing, arranging it in the proper way. He took a bundle and laid it on top of the wood, lit a match and set it ablaze, stood for a moment, watched the flames envelop the cloth.

Remembering his one act of carelessness, he winced. Though he had planned everything—devoted his life to the Plan—endured through all barriers and suffered through many fools, he had allowed himself that one moment of weakness. And though his carelessness would not alter the Plan's outcome, weakness could not be forgiven—his own, especially. There would have to be punishment. Perhaps he would put his hand in the fire, leave it there until it was a charred stump.

Slowly he brought his hand up to the blaze, felt the scorching heat as the flame began to lick his flesh. Yes. That would do. But later, not now. There could be no such mark now. He withdrew his hand and walked away.

Stage Two would begin very soon, altered slightly, allowing for circumstances. It was time to return, to implement this new stage, in which the Death Witch would be brought down.

27 Stan Friedland was calling to explain the arrangements he'd made for Laura to be tested that weekend and to give David the rundown on the Rockham Institute and Niles Martin.

The institute's central building and thirty-two acres of farmland had been owned by the late E. Marley

Rockham, a billionaire eccentric. A dabbler in the occult, Rockham had spent most of his life in this pursuit, surrounding himself with those who shared his interests, while his family tried every legal trick in the book to have him declared insane and usurp financial control of his estate. Their attempts failed, despite the fact that toward the end of Rockham's life he became convinced he was the reincarnation of an obscure Babylonian king. Niles Martin, who had attached himself to E. M. Rockham in the latter part of Rockham's life, was left the entire estate to establish an institution devoted to the study of the supernatural.

"Martin comes from the world of academics," Stan said. "Monied family, though not so spectacularly as Rockham's. Graduate work in psychology at Columbia and Oxford, research assignment at Berkeley. That's where he became involved in parapsychology. I should warn you, David, the guy's brilliant, but he's a real pain in the neck."

"Why's that?"

Stan laughed. "I could tell you he's proper, pompous, and arrogant, but that doesn't do him justice."

The judgment was confirmed when David spoke to Martin on the phone the next day. He felt as if he and Laura had been granted an audience with the Pope.

"The drive should take you about two and a half hours. Be here as close to eight o'clock Friday night as you can, Dr. Goldman."

"I'll try."

"And, by the way, I should warn you about the gardens."

"Gardens?"

"Yes, We have some rather unusual outdoor gardens on the grounds of the institute."

* * *

David had heard from Laura only once since the day Culligan had confronted them in the street. He'd left messages at her home, several more after she missed her Wednesday appointment, then she'd finally called him on Thursday afternoon. She sounded terrible on the phone, as if she could barely bring herself to speak. He asked her what was wrong but she simply refused to tell him anything other than that she'd gone to see her father. David told her about the appointment he'd made for her. She asked if he would come with her.

"Of course. We'll be staying at the institute for three days. That's how long Niles Martin says the complete battery of tests usually takes."

"All right," she said. "Zach is out of town on business again until Friday night. I'll leave him a note saying I'm going away for the weekend to see Annie."

"Why can't you tell him the truth?"

Silence. "He wouldn't understand."

For once, David identified with the man. He didn't understand either, nor did he know if he was doing the right thing.

"Laura," he said, as gently as he could, "the purpose of therapy isn't to help you lie better."

"My whole life is a lie."

At four-thirty on Friday evening, Laura showed up in David's office wearing a navy pants outfit and carrying a small suitcase. She had a heavy raincoat draped over one arm. The days were cooler now, and wet.

He took a good look at her. Something had obviously happened. Her face was pale and drawn, she hadn't even put any makeup on. He decided to let it go and get started, only partly because Niles Martin was expecting them at eight. The other reason he wanted to get going was because he wasn't sure he wanted to know what was wrong.

They rode along in silence until he asked her if she wanted to listen to music. She nodded. He put in a tape of Mozart, which she recognized right away as Symphony No. 25 in G Minor.

The music engulfed them. Laura closed her eyes, and occasionally David stole a glance at her. Her features no longer seemed as sharp as they had: her high cheekbones were almost gaunt; even her hair seemed to have lost some of its sheen. It was as if she were losing definition, bit by bit, right before his eyes. He knew he was powerless to stop it, may even have been exacerbating it with this little trip by encouraging her delusions.

He tried to concentrate on the scenery whizzing by them, the afternoon light fading into dusk, the orange sun setting over the horizon.

"Are you hungry, Laura?"

"No. But if you want to stop, it's fine."

He pulled off at the next exit and walked with her into Howard Johnson's, where they took a table in the far corner. He ordered no. 5, the fried chicken dinner. Laura ordered a salad, then picked at it when it came.

"Tell me," he said. "Tell me what's happened."

She stared at him, put her fork down, then reached into her purse.

"Would you like to see a picture of Sophie Zophlick? My father gave it to me."

She took out a small photograph and handed it to him. It was obviously very old, but it looked exactly, astonishingly, like Laura. Jesus! No wonder Sam Gardner—

"Quite a resemblance, don't you think?"

David nodded.

244 ■ *Fran Dorf*

"She was committed to Darlington in 1935, my father said. And he never heard from her again. Until the murder. Then everyone heard of her."

David turned the photograph over, looked at the date on the back. 1937. What the hell was this woman doing posing with pearls for a picture in a studio—having a "tryst," as Culligan put it—two years *after* her commitment to a snake pit?

"It explains a lot," Laura said. "The way my father was with me. He must have been terrified, seeing me grow more and more to look like his sister. And now I've . . ."

"You've what, Laura?"

"Killed him." She told him what had happened when she went home to confront her father; she described the dream she'd had that night.

He said, "Having a dream in which your father dies is perfectly natural under the circumstances. You're angry at him for deceiving you. You know that, Laura. Don't blame yourself for having the dream."

"Should I blame myself when he dies?"

Could he tell her father wasn't going to die? The man was in his sixties.

"He hasn't died, Laura."

"He's already had two heart attacks."

"All right, then. The content of the dream is perfectly understandable. The dream was prepared by your subconscious mind from events and knowledge already in your experience, which is your father's heart condition."

She was crying. "I should never have confronted him in the first place. He's an old man. I should have left him alone."

After they got back in the car, he said, "Laura, I'd

like to ask you something. If you could have had anything you wanted, what would that be?''

''I always wanted to be good, but no matter what I did, I never was.''

''Who said you weren't good?''

''I told you, people don't have to say *anything* to me. I know what they think.''

He tried to imagine how much destruction such a thing could cause in a child, in anyone. Did he believe her?

''If I was given vision,'' she said softly, ''why wasn't I given wisdom?''

Yes.

''If only I could have everything back the way it was before.''

''When before?''

''Before it all changed.''

''Was it so good then?''

She clasped her hands together. ''I never expected so much out of life.''

''Did you never want to be happy, Laura?''

''Happy?''

He did not respond. He wasn't even sure she knew what the word meant.

They got off at Exit 8, took a series of back roads, then found the landmark, a row of pine trees, stately in a heavy mist that all but obscured the sign reading Dapplewood Road.

About a mile down, they came to the brick pillars bearing an unobtrusive sign that said Rockham Institute, and passed under two rows of oaks that met overhead to form an enormous arbor. Then, a clearing.

David saw why Martin had warned him about the gardens. They were surrounded on both sides of the long driveway by huge hulking forms, the figures of animals, both real and mythical. A lion poised for attack, a giraffe, a centaur, a bear, what might have been a giant seal with hooved legs . . . and they were sculpted out of *hedges*.

"There must be a hundred of them," Laura said.

They passed slowly through the strange, silent zoo as they approached the huge mansion ahead of them.

"At Longwood Gardens near Philadelphia there was a beautiful topiary garden," Laura said. "But it was nothing like this." She looked at him and laughed. "Do you know how hard it is just to trim a hedge to be round?"

He laughed. "I wouldn't know. The only thing I've trimmed in my adult life is a mustache I had for a few years."

Niles Martin greeted them in an enormous marble-floored foyer dominated by an impressive curving staircase. David could see a portrait gallery on the landing above. And everywhere there were *things*—objets d'art, antiques, curiosities, collections of one sort or another.

"I hope the first sight of our little castle didn't alarm you," Martin said. "One of the few French Normandy mansions in America. Rockham was a stickler for detail."

Martin was very much as David had pictured him: tall, thin, soft-spoken, fully bearded. He was wearing a worn olive-green sweater and a pair of out-of-fashion glasses, granny glasses.

"That's quite a sculpture garden," David said.

"Not precisely the first impression we'd like to convey, but Mr. Rockham's express wishes were that the gardens and the mansion remain intact."

"It would be a pity to cut down those gardens," Laura said. "It must have taken years to create them."

"Twelve years, to be exact. Mr. Rockham brought in an artist from Kyoto." He smiled. "E. M. Rockham was something of an adventurer, in both the spirit world and the real one. Have you had dinner?"

"We stopped along the way."

"Why don't I take you to your rooms, then I'll show you around?"

Taking Laura's suitcase, he led them up the stairs. At the top, the central portrait caught David's eye, a large gilt-framed painting of a distinguished-looking young man with gray hair, a handlebar mustache, and a monocle.

"Meet E. Marley Rockham," Martin said, stopping beneath the painting. "Our benefactor and resident ghost. You'll notice the incongruity of the work. He had it painted in his youth, then called the artist back several times over the years as he got older to change the hair color and add the monocle."

The rooms to which he showed them were small but comfortable.

"Why don't you settle in and I'll go make us some coffee. Think you'll be able to find your way down again?"

Laura said yes, but David wasn't so sure.

"Fine. I'll be waiting for you in the library. It's right next to the front hall."

David's room was expensively furnished, though every piece had a slightly threadbare look. The single window commanded a view of the sculpture garden. Looking down, he saw that the garden was arranged symmetrically, with an outer circle of smaller animals surrounding successively larger and less realistic ones—an elephant with five tusks, the centaur, the seal with equine legs—all of which faced a huge central sculpture that could have been a giant griffin, although he would have to look closer to be sure.

There was a knock at the door. He opened it and joined Laura, who had changed into a pair of white wool slacks and a black sweater. They made their way back through the house, and finally located the library, where Martin was reading in a comfortable armchair in front of a blazing fire.

Martin took them on a tour of the "business end" of the mansion—the dream chambers, the computers, various instruments for measuring galvanic skin alterations, electroencephalographic equipment, audiovisual equipment to induce relaxation in subjects—then led them back to the library for coffee.

David had the impression that Martin realized this huge house was a more appropriate setting for a Frankensteinian chamber of horrors than for a scientific research center—and would have preferred his benefactor's abundant gifts to have been on a smaller scale and in a lower key.

Along with the coffee they got a short history of the Rockham Institute and all the obstacles Martin had to overcome in establishing it. He referred more than once to "peons," an epithet he applied to anyone who failed to believe in what he was doing, including members of his own family and his more conservative colleagues. Eiderman, a skeptical colleague at Oxford, was "a good man, but he had no true vision, no originality. He was a peon." Even E. M. Rockham himself was, in the final analysis, a peon.

"Rockham," Martin said, leaning back in the overstuffed velvet chair and taking staccato puffs on his pipe, "deserved his reputation as an eccentric. He believed, but for the wrong reasons. He searched, but in the wrong way. The man was forever trying to contact dead relatives and ancestors. Sometimes he would run about this house in his pajamas calling to the spirits.'' Puff, puff. ''It was all rather comical,'' he said, without a trace of humor.

David managed to keep from asking why this unenlightened peon had become Martin's benefactor. Actually, despite Martin's manner, David found himself both fascinated by him and relieved that he did most of the talking.

His narrative finally at an end, Martin explained to Laura that he wanted to know as little as possible about her—''so as not to bias the experiments,'' he said.

When she asked why, he launched into a lengthy esoteric explanation about statistical bias and experimental design and analysis of variance. David watched Laura in the firelight, observed the interplay of light and shadow on her face. She was calm, poised. Surely Martin could not guess the desperation beneath that carefully cultivated composure of hers.

''My main goal in establishing this institute,'' Martin was saying, ''has been to bring the field of parapsychological research into the mainstream of psychological thought. P-S-I is a phenomenon that exists. It can be studied as scientifically as any other phemenonon. Now, there are cases of spontaneous P-S-I manifestations that simply can't be duplicated in the laboratory. I'd say ninety percent of the books in this library describe those. But I'm primarily interested in effects that are reproducible, observable, measurable.''

As the evening wore on, David was aware, uneasily so, that even though Martin seemed to be doing most of the talking, the few questions he did direct to David—about psychiatry, about people they both knew

of, about his association with Stan some years back—
elicited far more information about David's personal
life than Laura should have been hearing. Though he
tried to disclose as little as he could without offending
Martin or making it obvious what he was doing, much
of the conversation had him stepping over the line. Of
course, he knew that he was already *well* over the line
in his mind. He was relieved when Martin finally suggested they all go up to bed.

Upstairs, in front of Laura's room, she said, "He
doesn't believe I'm going to be a gifted subject."

"Maybe you'll prove him wrong."

"And if I do, what then?"

She closed the door behind her. David went on to
his own room, stripped off his clothes, took a steaming hot shower and fell into bed, only to lie awake for
what seemed like hours, uncomfortably aware of Laura's presence in the next room. At one point, he heard
her crying softly. He wanted to go to her. Was she
crying in her sleep or was she lying awake as he was,
staring at shapes in the dark?

He could not listen and he could not go to her, for
even if he were to take that dangerous step, he had no
idea how to comfort her. And if he got up or moved
about his own room or went out into the hall, she
would hear him. And so he lay there, suffocating under
the weight of her sadness, forced to listen to her grief,
to imagine it, to feel it, until finally, long after midnight, he fell into a restless and intermittent sleep.

28 After breakfast, David accompanied Martin, Laura and Martha Ivery, the director's assistant, to the East Wing and stood for a moment while Martin settled Laura into a reclining chair, placing electrodes on her palms, over her heart, at her temples and behind the top of the right ear. The electrode wires were connected to a jack box at the back of the chair, which in turn was connected by wires to a polygraph and translated by an Apple II microcomputer in the next room. Next, Martin took Laura's baseline measurements, all the while explaining to her what he was doing.

"These measure eye movement, skin response, heart rate, that sort of thing. We want to see exactly what physiological changes occur."

The first session was to begin with Laura's viewing a relaxation film on the large white screen in front of the chair. "Try to relax," Martin told her, "but don't fall asleep."

"Like meditation?"

He smiled, handed her a set of ESP cards, the standard five cards—star, circle, square, cross, and three parallel wavy lines. "Martha is preparing a whole stack of them in the next room. During the first session she'll be sitting across from you here, turning the cards over one by one. Your job is to concentrate on the cards and see if you can get a picture in your mind of which of the five she's holding up."

David gave Laura's hand a reassuring squeeze, then went back into the other part of the house, stopping at an open conference room door for a moment, to listen to a discussion of the chisquare vs. Pearson coefficient in the statistical analysis of some previously collected data. Then he headed out for a walk on the grounds. It was a spectacular fall day, blue sky, crisp air, the tapestry of leaves flickering in the sunlight. Walking through the topiary garden, he heard the insistent loud whir of a machine, and finally discovered its source: a man using an electric hedge trimmer, standing on a very tall ladder propped up against the bear. He stood beneath the man for a moment, watching him work, then went on toward the heavily wooded section a few hundred yards away.

Living in the city with only the occasional scraggly tree implanted in cement to remind him, he realized he'd forgotten how spectacular a full regalia of autumn leaves could be, the reds and yellows and oranges so brilliant that they looked almost painted. He was reminded of childhood, days after school spent playing in backyards, lungs filled with crisp fresh air; shuffling through mountains of dry, crackling leaves; an impromptu game of touch football; the frantic prowl for candy on Halloween night; the pungent, pleasant odor of burning leaves; the sight of each father tending his own pile in the street. He wondered if Laura had the good memories, too—or had her pain obliterated them all?

It was Sunday, the third night. Through the glass David could see Laura, lying on the cot in Dream Chamber One. Electrode suction cups at her forehead and temples were attached to wires feeding into the terminal box at the head of the cot. A black cable ran from the box into the room in which Martin and he were standing. The East Wing was set up like a wheel, a series of experimental chambers visible through one-way mirrors around the central soundproof observation room.

In another chamber, he could see Martha Ivery. Over the last few days, she and another woman had been working steadily with Laura. Over thousands of trials, Laura had tried to guess, predict, influence or alter the chance course of card sequences, computer-generated pictures, numbers, dice, a machine called a random number generator, and God knew what else. David had no idea whether Laura was succeeding in the effort, nor even what would constitute success. Martin kept saying he would wait until all the results were in to discuss them.

But David did know how difficult it all must be for her, the effort to confirm her power and the desire not to, the indignity of electrodes attached to her body. And, of course, the ever-present fear for her father. To see her that way, hooked up to machines, reminded David of the recurring dream she'd told him the previous January. The one from her childhood: the shock treatments, the falling.

David could hear the hum of the electroencephalograph, printing out the lines that indicated Laura's brain waves and lateral eye movements.

Martin handed him a form from a table nearby. On it were printed spaces for subject, target, dream protocol, judge, date, number, notes. Next to these the judge was required to circle the number that most described how closely a subject's dream fit a target picture, from one of very great correspondence to twenty for no correspondence.

David had to admit he was impressed. "Are all your experiments this exact?" he asked Martin.

"We try to make them as free of bias as possible. The fact is, parapsychology is like no other branch of science. People seem to be rooting for our failure rather than our success."

"I'm surprised, considering the interest in this stuff all over the country these days."

"A few movie stars get interested and suddenly everyone's a channeler. I'm a scientist, not a voodoo doctor. I construct my experiments so that flaws in experimental design can't be used by my *colleagues* to discredit the results."

"How did you get into this line of work anyway?"

He smiled. "I wish I could say I've had a P-S-I experience myself, but I haven't been so lucky."

"Laura wouldn't call it lucky."

"Perhaps not." He looked at David. "Anyway, I became interested probably in the same way you became a psychiatrist. You met someone you admired who became your mentor, you read something fascinating, you by chance became involved in important work. You're interested in the mysteries of life. So am I. It's no different, really."

Walking over to the machine that was now registering a series of tiny unipolar blips, Martin said, "Those are the low-voltage EEG theta waves. She's entering ascending stage-one REM sleep." He pressed a button, leaned into the microphone and said, "Begin."

Martha Ivery drew a large picture from one of several manila envelopes sitting on a table in front of her, closed her eyes, then opened them and stared at the picture. It was a print of Edouard Manet's *The Fifer*.

"We have about twenty minutes before we have to

wake her up and ask her what she dreamed," he said, taking a tape cassette from one of the shelves. "Why don't you tell me what, exactly, you think you have here." He popped a tape into the cassette deck, placed the microphone in front of David, pushed the On button.

David was getting tired of his arrogance. "Why don't you tell me what you think *we* have?"

He stared at David, then went over to the window, where he watched Laura sleeping for a very long moment. Finally he turned around.

"I'd say we have the most gifted subject I've ever seen. Quite possibly the most gifted subject ever tested."

David looked at him, unable to respond.

Martin went over to a table, picked up a stack of computer printouts, leafed through them.

"Telepathy. Precognition. Clairvoyance. These scores are absolutely incredible. Christ! It's almost as if she were *looking* at the targets. As if . . ."

"She has an extra set of eyes?"

"Is that how she describes it?"

David sighed. "She believes she's a mutation."

"A *mutation*?"

"Of course, my first assumption was that she was some kind of schizophrenic. Her reactions seemed clearly psychotic—"

"But *she* doesn't, does she?"

"Not at all."

Briefly, David filled him in on her background, her lifelong belief system, her current primary delusion (could he still call it a delusion?) that her emotions had consequences in the real world. He also described the circumstances of the murder, her confession, his initial treatment of her case as one of depressive psychosis.

"And you say she knew about the specifics of the crime?"

"Not only that, she thinks she *caused* the crime. Then there's this detective—"

"Who thinks she did it?"

"Exactly."

"She could have simply foreseen the murder. Precognition for a woman of her abilities—"

"No. You see, that's just it. In her vision, *she* was ripping the woman's face apart with her nails."

Martin wanted to know what made David change his mind about her. He told him about the shared dream they'd had, his parrot's death.

"Transferential precognition and causation. Is that what you're suggesting?"

"I don't know what I'm suggesting."

"In the mind of a woman like this, the line between precognition and causation must be very thin. Still, though her scores are extraordinary, to cause a stranger to commit murder—"

He was interrupted by a piercing noise, horribly amplified by the sound system, a terrifying disembodiment of a scream, echoing in the chamber. In the mirror he could see Laura, awakened by a nightmare, ripping the tape and the probes from her face, disengaging herself from the tangle of wires.

David sprang to his feet and rushed into Chamber One.

29   She was dreaming:

Swimming in a river with David, in a great dense jungle. On either bank, the growth was so dark she couldn't see beyond the outer edge. The forest was thick with living things: with insects, with snakes, with tiny creatures and huge ones, teeming with unseen life. The vines and fronds broke along the bank, where there was no sun. The water hissed and simmered like a steaming soup, the air was so thick she could feel it on her skin like oil. A group of alligators snapping their great jaws clamored through the white-hot mist. A vibrant humming sound filled the air, the sound of danger.

Still she swam beside him, freed of the pain, feeling only buoyancy, lightheadedness, desire. She heard him laughing, though she could barely see him in the steamy air. She moved still closer, hair swishing along her shoulders, fanning out onto the water. She wanted to feel him with her. She slid her arms around his neck and kissed him, long and deep; felt him urgent against her, loving her. This, then, was the thing that happened between men and women, not the other horrid, brutish thing, the thing of hatred. She felt a stirring between her legs, closed her eyes.

Someone was moaning.

No. It was Zach inside her, beads of sweat trickling down his forehead like small insects, hair slick and wet. Had it been he all the time?

He swam away from her, diving beneath the surface of the water. It was only a moment before she heard him scream, looked for him in the water—now different, horribly alive, crawling with living things. Insects. Worms. Fish circling pools around her. A great river snake in a foaming eddy, flicking its forked tongue.

Again she heard Zach's scream, a wild scream, an agonized scream. She began to swim toward the sound, but with each stroke she was farther away.

His scream echoed through the jungle. "Something's *inside* me. Something—"

He struggled onto the bank of the great river and lifted his flaccid penis, bending over, as if trying to look inside. He could not see them, of course. And even if he could it was too late. The tiny creatures of the river were boring in, attaching themselves with barbed hooks to the intestine, the scrotum, the stomach. The compromised flesh was already beginning to bleed.

She saw him twitch, a graceless acrobat, jumping around in a strange dance among the tangle of liana vines—screaming, crying, dying.

Someone was screaming. She was trying to get away, but something was holding her back.

No, it wasn't something, it was all the wires, the tape, the bonds. She struggled to be free, ripping them from her forehead, from her arms, hurting, pulling skin.

She was screaming, "I killed him, I killed him."

David had his arms around her. He was saying comforting things: "There, there. It's all in your mind. It's only a dream." And she was babbling like a crazy woman, her voice echoing in her head, a voice that sounded like someone else's. Still, in his embrace, her screams became sobs, her sobs became whispers, and finally she was silent, knowing he understood.

But would he understand the dream?

She broke free and ran, out into the garden under a nearly full moon, cloaked in a haze of ragged clouds. Barefoot on the cold green earth, through the fragrant freshly mowed meadow, she ran.

"Laura!"

She heard David running behind her, and she ran on, through the vast moonswept meadow and into the woods beyond, tearing through the tangle of brush. She ran blindly, her arms outstretched lest she run into a tree, branches and unseen things whipping at her face, the twigs beneath her snapping in half, like her mind.

She tripped over a protruding root and tumbled onto a bed of dry leaves.

"Help me, David."

He knelt down beside her on the floor of the forest, put his arms around her, made her feel safe, just for a moment.

"Help me."

But she knew he had no help to give. No comforting words. No reassurance. Still, he was very close. She could feel his breath on her face.

He pulled away.

"Tell me about the dream, Laura."

There was a light.

"Is she all right?" It was Niles Martin, shining a glaring flashlight on the two of them. She could see Martha coming up behind him.

David was helping her to stand. "She's had enough," he said.

She allowed him to lead her back into the house and

help her to lie down. She watched him as he prepared a syringe, with an unsteady hand, first dropping the needle on the floor, then fumbling to unwrap another, then cutting his finger as he broke the neck of the vial.

Yes, she would rest.

David was very gentle with her, lifting her arm, rubbing something cold on her skin. She saw the needle disappear into her arm, which she knew was attached to her body even though she couldn't feel it. "Laura?"

Laura wasn't here. It was only a matter of time before she infected everyone with her poison. She was already in the process of dying, wasn't she? It was only a question of when, of how. If she could control the power, she would will herself to be dead. But she would have to find another way. The punishment would have to be swift and violent, to fit the crime.

She could take the car out on the highway, jerk the wheel, let the car swerve over an embankment. One dull thump, a shattering of glass that pierced her face in a thousand places and then she would sail free. Or perhaps a light snow would begin to fall, an October snow, unexpected and treacherous on the warm asphalt, and the car would skid.

Or the gun in her house.

Or she could jump from somewhere. It would have to be very high. To sail free. To be free of pain. Peace.

The next morning, Laura found David in the library, reading. She stood watching him for a moment before he became aware of her presence.

"Laura." Once she had a doll with blue eyes like his.

"I have to go home," she said.

"Excuse me." Martin was standing in the doorway. "Are you feeling better, Mrs. Wade?"

"We're going to leave now," David said.

Niles Martin looked at her and said, "How long have you known you were so gifted, Mrs. Wade?"

"Always."

He came over to her. "I'd like to convene a conference—"

"A *what*?"

"A conference for the scientific community. These are the most important results in the history of paranormal psychology."

She looked at David. "Please don't let them do that, David. I won't. I can't."

"What the hell's the matter with you?" David said to Martin. "Don't you see Laura's dilemma?"

Martin was glaring. "What's the matter with *you*? You're supposed to be a scientist. You must know what this discovery means to the—"

"I don't give a damn what it means to the world. I care what it means for Laura." David took her suitcase and her hand. "I'll take you home, Laura."

He insisted on driving her all the way to Connecticut. She slept most of the way so she wouldn't have to see his eyes.

It was almost four when they arrived. Her daughters crowded around her as they came inside the house.

"This is Dr. Goldman. Melissa. Courtney."

The two girls greeted him politely, then stood there awkwardly until Laura told them they could go.

After they went upstairs, he said, "They're lovely girls, Laura."

She asked him if he wanted a cup of coffee, which he didn't. They stood in the foyer.

"What are you going to do now?" he asked.

"I don't know. Zach will be home from work soon."

Suddenly he said, "Show me your studio, Laura."

"Why?"

"I just want to see it."

She led him up to the attic. He stopped in the doorway, and she heard him gasp as she turned on the light. Then he was inside, moving among the canvases, his eyes jumping from one to the other, a look of stunned bewilderment on his face.

"Pretty awful, huh?" she said.

He stared at her. "I thought you said painting was a hobby."

"Well, it is."

He shifted his gaze again, this time to the work in progress on the easel.

"Do you mind?" he asked.

Before she could respond, he had lifted the cloth from the canvas and stepped back.

"Nightmare under the Moon," she told him.

He looked at it for a moment, then moved over to the drawing table, where she'd begun a sketch for a new work. It was a fourth attempt. The old man was perfect. But the demon was still wrong.

"Goddammit, Laura," he said, "your work is brilliant. Why the hell don't you do something with it?"

"Like what?"

"I don't know. Take it to an art gallery, or a museum."

"Why?"

"Well, for . . . I don't know what for. To sell them, to share them—"

"Maybe I don't want to share them. Maybe I want to keep them all to myself." She pulled the muslin back over the painting.

"Laura," he said, "you can't really think your work is anything *but* brilliant, can you?"

"I know that technically my work is very good."

"Technically?"

"Well, you wouldn't want to hang one of them in your living room, would you?"

"Maybe I would," he said, lying. "It's unbelievably good, Laura. I say that not because I know anything about art. All I know is how your work makes me feel."

"As if you want to wake up from the nightmare?"

"Well, yes. But that's the point, isn't it?"

She didn't know what the point was.

After he left, having said something about another idea he had to help her—which he didn't believe any more than she did—Ellen knocked on the door.

"Who was that, Laura?"

Laura just stood there, staring at her friend.

"Zach knows, Laura," Ellen said. Her arm was still bandaged; she'd had to give up her job.

"Knows what?"

Now *Ellen* was staring. "Look," she said finally, "I don't give a goddamn who you're sleeping with. God knows, if you've discovered passion after fifteen years of marriage, I'd be the first to congratulate you. But you ought to at least get your alibi straight."

"What are you talking about, Ellen?"

"Zach called your friend Annie. He knows you weren't there."

Suddenly her face was burning hot. *"And he thinks—"*

"I don't know what he thinks," Ellen said. "I know he called me on Saturday to see if I knew where you were. That detective came again, the one who's been asking questions about you. He brought some cops. They questioned everyone in the neighborhood, for the second time. For Christ's sake, Laura, what the hell is going on?''

Maybe she should just turn herself in. No. She would take care of it herself this time.

''Why is that cop asking all those questions about Rita's death?''

She might as well say it, Ellen deserved the truth—she had tried to be a good friend. Soon enough, everyone would know. ''The detective thinks I did it,'' she said.

''You mean because of what happened at your dinner party?''

Laura nodded.

''I told him that you wouldn't—''

''Don't get involved, Ellen.''

''I'm already involved. If you had just told me what was going on, I would have covered for you this weekend.''

''Please stop. This isn't what you think.''

''Oh, no? You go away for the weekend and a strange man drops you off, what do you expect me to think?''

''He's my psychiatrist.''

She was staring again. ''Oh, I see. A psychiatrist with a pickup-and-delivery service. Come on, Laura, I thought we were friends.''

''I'm telling you the truth.''

''How long have you been seeing a psychiatrist?''

''A few months.''

Ellen shrugged, turned to go. ''Well, if you ever want to talk about it, I'm right next door.''

''Thank you, Ellen. I'm sorry. I really am.''

Ellen hesitated, then said ''Your psychiatrist is pretty good-looking for a psychiatrist, and if you were going to have an affair with someone—''

"He's my doctor. Doctors don't have affairs with their patients."

"You'd be surprised what some doctors do. Jason knows plenty who have affairs. But none of them makes house calls."

The house seemed very different now, as if something in it had died. Laura went into the kitchen, where Darlene was preparing dinner, sat down at her desk, looked over her appointment calendar.

She heard a noise in the playroom, rushed in to find Sammy in the middle of the floor. Big, bold strokes of red and blue and green and yellow were marked like slashes all over the wall.

"Sammy! Dammit—"

My God, I could just as easily infect him.

She squeezed her eyes shut, then hugged her son as hard and as long and as tight as she could, and he was crying, too. She pulled away, got to her feet and stared at her son in horror. Would hugging Sammy stop the poison from escaping her, stop the black milk from overflowing? No. she had to run. It hurt even to look at him.

She retreated to her bedroom, tried to sleep and couldn't, then got up and began walking aimlessly from room to room through this dead place until she felt a presence. Zach had come in and was leafing through the day's mail in the basket.

He refused to look at her. Did he really think she would have an affair? Would he just be totally silent, the way he was when he was angry at her, or would he look at her with that look that made her feel . . .

Of course he wouldn't look at her, nor would he accuse her in front of the children. He would wait until later, when the two of them were alone. In front of other people, in front of their children, everything was perfect. Even she was perfect. Zach didn't want anyone to know what a horror he had married.

Melissa and Courtney had come running down. Zach brushed his lips past each of their cheeks in turn. She heard the roaring in her ears again.

"Come on, girls," he said. "Let's go out on the boat."

"Darlene will have dinner ready in a few minutes," she said.

"So it will wait," he said.

"Zach, please." He was so tall and sure, her husband, so blond, so handsome, so perfect. How could she ever have thought she could be a normal wife to him?

"Don't *you* say anything." He had his arms around the girls and was already leading them to the back door.

She went into the kitchen and watched out the back window as Zach took the girls out onto the dock and started up the speedboat. Standing up behind the glass shield, he guided the boat expertly out into the open sound, the motor roaring, the wind whipping his hair back from his face. She stayed by the window watching until the boat disappeared; she watched until it returned a half hour later.

Dinner was interminable, a nightmare of silence and accusatory stares. The children filled in some of the gaps. Melissa had a boyfriend in school; Courtney teased her about him. Laura could barely listen.

"Mom?"

Courtney was speaking to her. "Did you tell Daddy what Sammy did today?"

She had forgotten. She found herself wishing her

daughter wouldn't bring it up, then froze for fear of wishing anything.

"I haven't told him yet, Courtney."

"Sammy *wrote* all over the walls."

"I already scolded him, Zach," she said.

"I hardly think one of your scoldings will cover crayoning the walls, do you? If you were any kind of a mother, you'd know that."

Why was he saying that? She had always been a good mother. Suddenly she felt something she'd never felt from him before. Hatred. She felt it radiating out of him, reaching her, touching her like a soft breeze on bare skin. Of course he hated her.

There was a long silence.

"Sammy, go up to your room," Zach said.

"Zach, I know what you think I did, but *please* don't take it out on—"

"We'll discuss this later, Laura."

He pushed the chair away from the table and stood up.

He was waiting for her in the bedroom, sitting on the chair, looking over some papers. He had some stock certificates for her to sign.

She tried to hold the pen in her hands, wrote her name with an unsteady hand. Her signature had disintegrated into a childish scrawl.

He took the paper from her.

"Laura, I don't appreciate your bringing up private matters in front of the children. Children must not be privy to the failings of adults. At the very least, I demand that."

Of course he was right.

"And now," he said. "I'd like to know where you

were this weekend. I called Annie, Laura. She said she hadn't seen you in *ten years.*''

She would have to tell him. At first she thought she would only tell him certain things, certain parts of it, but as she began speaking it seemed as if she had opened the floodgates. The sea began to spill out. She kept explaining, explaining.

Afterward, he looked at her. ''You still believe you killed Rita with your mind?''

''I don't remember actually killing Rita,' she said. ''Please. I'm telling you what I feel, what I've been living with.''

''Perhaps you *are* some kind of witch,'' he said.

''You believe me?''

''I believe if you believe.''

''I'm afraid for you, Zach.''

''Why for me?''

So she told him about the dream of the river. It was the most difficult thing she had ever done.

There was a long silence, then he let out a long, low whistle. ''Dr. Freud would have had a field day with that one. And what does your Dr. Goldman say about all this?''

''Well, he thinks . . . He took me to the Rockham Institute this weekend. That was where I was. They did all these tests there, to see if I had paranormal—''

''*What?*''

''He's trying to . . . he's trying to help me—''

''By taking you to some voodoo place? Jesus. I don't believe this. You can't even get yourself a sane psychiatrist.''

''Zach, please—''

He glared at her. ''Laura, if you ever see that quack

again, I'm going to have his medical license taken away. In the morning, we'll go see Bill Brindell.''

Oh, God.

30 David drove back to his apartment and got very busy with the weekend mail. He paid a few of the bills that had been piling up, then went out for a walk, barely aware of the city around him. It was raining, a light steady patter on the sidewalk. If only he could reassure Laura, comfort her, comfort himself. But no. He had dragged her down there, put her through all the tests, seen to it that her powers were scientifically confirmed. Even so, Martin obviously thought the idea of her causing a stranger to commit murder was preposterous. Which meant David's believing her was collusion. And if it wasn't collusion, if she really did have the power to affect the world with her emotions, what then?

Worst of all, he was so in love with her it hurt. He could no longer even pretend to be her doctor. His position was hopeless.

At Seventy-fourth Street, it began to pour, and David turned back. There was a strange hush in the apartment; the empty bird cage sat there on its stand, brass gleaming. He took off his raincoat and called Allison.

"Just wanted to see how you were feeling," he said.

"David," she said, "your concern is admirable but hardly appropriate, considering your behavior last week."

There ensued a weird, lopsided conversation in which David kept trying to find out if anything unusual had happened to her, and she kept trying to find out why he wanted to know.

At nine-thirty he lay down on his bed, fully dressed, intending to welcome a long—very long—sleep but still unable to think of anything but Laura. She had refused to tell him her dream. Had it been about him? Had she dreamed that something horrible had happened to him, then awakened, positive that he was a goner?

And those paintings. How astonishing they were, how good. And every one of them clearly, unmistakably, from the same source. David knew that source; he recognized the images. He had heard them, all of them: her fears, her demons, her dreams.

It was as if some unearthly photographer had been at work. In one, there was a lovely field of flowers, a tree, a perfect blue sky: but there, sitting in the middle of the field, crouching amidst the flowers, was a small black figure with white eyes, and claws, and teeth. A demon. And the one she called *Nightmare under the Moon*. Ten claw marks on the woman's face. And the sketch on the drawing table showed an old man with sparse gray hair, atop him another demon, touching the old man's chest—this one in close-up, so close you could see the red rim around the demon's irises. There were, in fact, small demons in every one, and creatures with extended claws, and hellish purple fire, and demons devouring flesh, and blood.

Wandering through this landscape of nightmares, David drifted in and out of consciousness for an hour or so before he finally fell into something only vaguely resembling sleep.

He was awakened by the phone.

"Mr. Goldman." The voice was male, angry.

"Doctor Goldman," he said, idiotically. "Who is this?"

"Zachary Wade."

He sat up in bed, swung his feet around onto the floor, trying to propel himself into some semblance of wakefulness, control.

"Mr. Wade, how may I help you?"

"I think you've already done enough to *help* me."

"I don't understand. What's the problem?"

"I'll tell you what's the problem. Two months ago, I find out my wife is as crazy as a loon, that she's gone into a police station and confessed to some murder she thinks she committed, by God-knows-what method, and then I meet you. This Friday, my wife informs me she's going to her friend Annie's for the weekend. Which is fine with me. She's free to do what she wants; I never interfere. Only during the weekend I get another visit from this damned detective who thinks Laura actually committed the murder. He wants to know where she is, so I call Laura's friend Annie, and it turns out Laura hasn't seen the woman in ten years. Now, I don't like being made a fool of. Not at all. But that doesn't even concern me. What concerns me is that I am left to wonder where the hell she is all weekend. She finally comes back today, and when I confront her, what does she tell me? She tells me her *doctor* took her to some place to test her fucking psychic powers."

"Mr. Wade, the Rockham Institute is a scientifically—"

"You're going to *defend* taking her there? I don't believe this."

"Mr. Wade," David said, lowering his voice, "I realize this has all come as a shock to you—"

"A *shock*? What, may I ask, do you think is wrong with my wife? Your medical opinion, that is."

"At first, as I told you in my office, I diagnosed a schizophrenic psychosis and began treating it as that. But then certain things began happening, which seemed to confirm that there might be something to Laura's so-called delusions after all."

"What?"

"I really don't think we can discuss this on the phone. If you'd like to come in, perhaps the three of us can talk about it."

"With you? I wouldn't come within twenty feet of you."

"Mr. Wade, this is a very complex situation, and your hostility isn't helping."

"What's complex here? My wife is crazy. I'd say that's fairly straightforward. But what *she* is isn't the issue here. The issue is *you*. The issue is that you're supposed to be treating her illness, not encouraging her delusions by taking her to some . . . I don't even know what to call it."

"Then let me explain it to you. I'd like to do it in person, with Laura present and—"

"I'd like never to set eyes on you."

"Look, Mr. Wade, I can certainly understand your reaction. I suppose mine would be the same. But your wife's . . . illness is very complex. If you'd just—"

"My wife doesn't have an illness. My wife is crazy."

"I wish you'd stop throwing that word around. The phrase is—"

"I don't give a goddamn what you wish. It's obvious to me that my wife belongs in an asylum."

An asylum?

"There are no asylums anymore, Mr. Wade."

"A hospital, then. Whatever. Do you know she told me she was responsible for a man's getting killed at the train station last week? No, she didn't push him. She willed him down, or something like that. Now, in my book, that means crazy. Out to lunch. Off her rocker. Nuts."

David suddenly realized that he hated the man, more than he'd ever hated anyone.

"Mr. Wade, if you don't calm down, we can't continue this conversation."

"Dr. Goldman, or whatever you call yourself, this conversation is over. *You are obviously as crazy as she is.* And if you ever come near my wife again, I'll have you arrested."

With that he slammed the phone down, leaving David staring at the receiver, replaying the conversation in his head, only dimly aware that his own behavior on the phone had been almost as reprehensible as Zachary Wade's, that he had responded to his attacks more like a wounded lover than a doctor. All he could think was: "How could she be *married* to him?"

He could understand the man's skepticism, even his hostility. What David couldn't understand was why he had detected in him not one note of sympathy, one shred of compassion, for the woman he supposedly loved. It appalled him, enraged him. His hatred of Zachary Wade grew moment by moment as he paced around his apartment.

It was in that frame of mind that he answered the door some hours later.

Laura was soaked, hair dripping, raincoat sopping, tears flowing.

"I'm sorry, David."

"It's all right, Laura. I said if you needed me—"

"I wanted to warn you."

"The dream was about me?"

"No. The dream was about Zach."

He put his arm around her, led her inside, took off her raincoat and draped it on the back of a chair.

"What do you want to warn me about?"

"I had to tell him," she said. "That detective came back, and Zach called Annie. He found out I wasn't there, and he thought . . . Well, I don't know what he thought, but when I told him about the institute he got angrier than I've ever seen him. He called you all sorts of names. He said I wasn't ever to see you again."

"Laura, you're not a child. Or your husband's possession. This isn't the nineteenth century."

"He said we would go to see Bill Brindell in the morning. He's the psychiatrist we know socially. An awful man."

"It's not up to your husband to decide which doctor you see." She had started crying again. "When you told him, what did he say?"

She sat down on the sofa. "He patronized me. He pretended to believe me."

After the phone conversation David had with him, he found it hard to believe.

"Are you sure, Laura?"

"At first I thought he really did believe me. But then I realized he was probably just . . . humoring me."

"How did that make you feel?"

"I understand it, I guess."

"Don't be so damned understanding of everyone," he said sharply. Then, "I'm sorry. Why don't you tell me about the dream?"

She told him. For a moment he did not respond; speech was obscured by a sweep of reactions, the first being relief that the dream wasn't about him, after all.

Certainly it was the most gruesome and explicit revenge fantasy he'd ever heard. There was no true symbolism in the dream. The wish was out front, manifest and latent content merged.

"Why would I have had such a horrible dream about Zach?" she said. "He's my husband. He's the father of my children."

He wondered if there really was something—some animal, or worm or maybe a parasite—that could burrow inside the penis that way, something she'd read or heard about somewhere. Or was it invented by her subconscious mind and worked out within the water theme so often present in Laura's dreams, as in her life.

"Dreams exaggerate our feelings, Laura. Look at the way your husband behaves, ordering you around as if he owns you. Somewhere inside, you may well resent him, even though you don't know it or accept it consciously. You know a dream doesn't necessarily mean you want what happened in the dream to happen in real life."

"Maybe it does, this time," she said softly. "Don't you see?"

"What?"

"Maybe I dreamed that way about him . . . because of you."

Of course. She was going to tell him she was in love with him. But she wasn't *really* in love with him, was she? It was just transference, and David's own feelings were just . . . He didn't know what his own feelings were.

Weakly, he said, "Dreams dramatize inner life."

"Other people's dreams. Not mine, David."

She stood up, staring at him, eyes dark and huge. "I'm sorry for involving you in all this."

"Don't be. Please."

She reached for her raincoat. "Do you see how dangerous it is to know me?"

More dangerous than he could say.

He couldn't help it; he couldn't help himself. He allowed himself this violation of his life's work and his soul.

Once he had kissed her, it was as good as done. Her lips were slightly salty from the tears. To go on seemed like the most natural thing in the world. He had done this thing in his mind so often that there somehow seemed to be no difference between the thought and the deed. He proceeded mindlessly, like a teenager in a backseat passion.

But the lovemaking wasn't like that. It was sweet, slow, deliberate, as if they'd been lovers for a long, long time.

He took off her clothes, all of them; she turned aside, as if she couldn't bear to be looked at.

David had never been much of a talker during lovemaking. To speak always seemed beside the point, but Laura seemed so beautiful to him that he kept telling her so. He laid her down on his bed, kissing her face, her throat, running his lips along her breasts, finding every part of her, saying everything he could think of that would make her feel beautiful. He felt as if he would never get enough of her, discovering her. He tasted her sweat, basked in her particular smell, explored her body. She had small, wonderful breasts, with very slight stretch marks, and long, beautifully shaped legs. There was a long, rough scar on her thigh.

Her response to him was astonishing. She was almost savage. And through it all, she kept saying, not "I love you, I love you," but "You love me, you love me."

How could she despise and reject herself so, when he loved her? Finally, they both came to a dizzying, mind-shattering climax.

Afterward, she seemed lost within herself, out of his reach, though she was lying next to him. He looked over at her, lying there, one shoulder poking out of the blanket.

He would always remember the feeling of watching himself make love to her, even while he was doing it. Somehow he had been able to separate himself from it, to experience their coming together and to look at it at the same time, like a camera in a close-up. To touch his lips to her breast, his cheek to her belly, and to have the beauty of that skin-to-skin touch—that one moment, that one experience—be the only thing that mattered.

She was stirring now. "It feels as if I flew into a million pieces and then came back together," she said softly. "I never thought I was capable." Then she looked at him and said, "In a way, it reminds me of childbirth."

"How?"

"I guess because it's so all-consuming, so complete. I liked childbirth."

"You what?"

"Not the pain of it, although truthfully I didn't even hate that so much. It just seemed so *necessary* to go through a lot to get so much." She pulled away from him, her dark hair fanning out in wisps on the white pillowcase.

"You like being a mother, don't you?"

"I really do. I don't suppose that sounds very modern. But I like children. They're so eager, so accepting; they don't make judgments about things. Their minds are very different from adults'. They—" She stopped. "You don't want to hear this. You've heard me talk enough."

"I do. I love the sound of your voice."

She kept talking, dreamy talk, going on and on, looking up at the ceiling.

"When I had Melissa," she said, "I really wanted Zach to be there. I asked him, but he said he couldn't stand all that blood and mess. And you know, for Sammy's and Courtney's births I was glad he wasn't there. It was almost as if I had to do it alone, it made me feel so alive, so in touch, so . . ." She hesitated a moment, looking at him.

"Why did you do this, David?"

"I love you. Why do you *think* I did, Laura?"

She laughed a nervous laugh. "I pay you one hundred twenty dollars an hour to—"

"To what, Laura?" He sat up. *"To make love to you?"*

"Well, no, I guess to help me understand—"

"Do you know what I have done? Your husband could crucify me now!" Not content simply to betray her, he laid his own guilt about it on her, too.

"No, he won't—"

"He should. I *deserve* to be crucified for this."

"David," she said, her voice very low, "I've been married to Zach for sixteen years. Not once has he ever made me feel anything like the way you did. I can't condemn you. I want to thank you."

"Oh, God, don't," he said. "I'm supposed to help make your life easier, not more complicated. Certainly not jump into the middle of it. I've failed on all counts."

"I love you," she said. "I never thought there were men like you."

"You think I'm a wonderful man, but you don't

know me. Our relationship has been about you, not me, and that leaves you free to idealize me.''

"But you're wrong. I do know you, David. I know you completely.''

"You mean because you've read my mind?''

"Well, partly, I suppose. Sometimes I don't even make a distinction between what I learn that way and what I learn through a person's actions. Sometimes it's the two combined. But I don't even need to read your thoughts, I know from your behavior. I know that you're kind, and loving, and giving. I know from the way you touched me.''

"I can't be your doctor anymore, Laura," he said. "And I can't go on being your lover.''

"Then be my friend," she said. "Help me.''

He looked over at her lying there in his bed, in his apartment, and felt overwhelmingly tender toward her, tender and protective—and overwhelmingly responsible.

"You see," he said softly, "I *do* love you. And I have no idea how to help you.''

"Don't, David. It's dangerous to love me.''

"I don't believe that," he said with more conviction than he felt.

"Oh, no? Look what it's done to you already," she said.

He had to look away.

"I'm scared, David. Do you know how scared I am?''

He put his arms around her. "Yes, I know.''

"Yesterday," she said, "or was it last night, when I had that dream about Zach, I decided I couldn't live this way anymore. Never knowing when. Always wondering, worrying, afraid to think, afraid to feel. My mind plays games with me, and sometimes I think I really am going crazy.''

"Maybe nothing will happen, Laura. Maybe this one *is* just a dream. Just symbolic. Awful, but symbolic. It only happens sometimes. Maybe this time it won't.''

She laughed. "And maybe you've cured me.''

He suggested a few interpretations of the river dream.

"Zach doesn't deserve to be punished for what I feel,'' she said. "No one does.''

To which David had no answer.

Finally she slept for a while, and he tried to. Mostly he watched her sleep. Moonshadows danced on her face; she took the shallowest of breaths. He drew back the blanket and studied her body, the roundness of her stomach, the contours of her neck and her breasts.

It wasn't her body that had made this the most passionate erotic experience of his life. Was part of it the element of danger, of doing something forbidden? With a woman who wouldn't—couldn't—say no? Something as petty as his knowing that Laura would not judge his performance as a lover? Or was it something else entirely? That he did love her.

He tried to think why. She didn't have any qualities he had ever thought he even liked in a woman. She had allowed herself to be totally subjugated; she was paranoid and filled with self-loathing; she didn't know what she really wanted in life, except to be allowed to live. Indeed, she didn't even seem like a whole person, despite the fact that she apparently possessed powers most people had never even dreamed of. Yet beyond that there was her gentleness, her will to live, her persistence in the face of such a terrible trap. A lesser person would have given up long ago.

He lay his head beside hers, felt her breath on his cheek, slightly sour from sleep and from cigarette smoke. There was a hint of her perfume and another scent, perhaps shampoo. It was as if he could feel her life, her experience, her blood coursing through his body. Along with a loneliness more devastating, more terrifying, than any he had ever felt on his own.

Yes, he was in love with her. He had wanted to make her well, to show her she could be loved, to show her how much he loved her. Had he told himself that their making love would be a good thing?

He touched her skin, traced with a fingertip the contours of that body which had brought him so much pleasure and guilt and pain. She sighed and turned over on her side, and then, in the moonlight, he saw the small brown mark just at the base of her spine. The mark he had touched in his dream.

He was half dozing, half conscious of the predawn street sounds, the garbage trucks bouncing under the window, the faint rumbling of the subway, a light and steady rain drumming on the windowpane.

And another sound: knocking.

He opened his eyes. Laura was sitting up in bed, panting, on her face the same look of terror he'd seen the night before at the institute. She looked at him with eyes that didn't seem to know him.

"I killed him," she whispered. "I killed him."

She'd had the dream again.

He glanced at the clock. Five fifty-nine, and someone was knocking—banging—on the door, banging so loudly that he wondered if Grace Axelrod on the ninth floor could hear it.

He got up, pulled on his pajama bottoms, made his way to the door.

Zachary Wade was standing in the doorway. David was in his pajama bottoms, but what he was really in was absolute panic—heart thudding, adrenaline pumping, mind racing: I'll tell him Laura isn't here. Or I'll tell him she's here, she arrived so late that I offered her my bedroom and slept on the sofa myself.

Before he could tell him anything, the man pushed his way past and headed for the bedroom door.

Christ. It would have been better if he'd walked in a few hours earlier. It would have been better for him to have witnessed their lovemaking than this.

Laura was standing by the window, naked. She had the window wide open and was standing there in the cold night air, looking down at the sidewalk, twenty floors down. The thought that their appearance had saved her from actually jumping crossed his mind.

"Laura?"

She remained motionless as she stared out the window. It was obvious to David that something in her had snapped, that what he'd tried to convince himself might be good was in fact as bad as it could be, as bad as they told you from the moment you got into psychiatry.

Zachary Wade stared for a moment at his wife, then turned and gave David a look of utter revulsion.

"You would take advantage of a woman so obviously disturbed? *What is wrong with you?*"

Later, David would be unable to describe how he felt at that moment. In the course of a few hours he had gone from the most wonderful experience of his life to the worst, by far the worst.

David walked over to her. "Laura?"

She made no effort to cover herself, just kept staring out the window, the curtains billowing out around her as she looked down the wide expanse of Broadway visible from David's bedroom.

"Look at all the people," she said. "So many people."

She didn't so much as glance at either of them. Very slowly, in a whisper, she said, "You have to go home, Zach. Go home and get away from me."

"Come with me, Laura." He moved closer to her.

She lifted her naked arms, clasped her hands over her head, moaned softly.

"Laura?" David said.

Finally, she looked at him.

"Stay away. You'll be hurt by the poison. You were so beautiful to me. I don't want you to get hurt."

Wade closed the distance between him and his wife, put his hand on her shoulder.

"Take the children to my mother's, Zach. No, take them far away, where I can't get them. The children are in danger. Promise me."

"Laura, your children are fine," David said.

She glanced over at him as if she knew neither him nor the language he was speaking.

Zachary Wade helped her on with her bra and panties and slacks. She didn't protest while he put one limp arm and then the other into a sleeve, buttoned her blouse, pulled on her boots. David stood there watching them, paralyzed, a witness to the most shameful moment of his life.

He watched Zachary Wade walk her down the hall, stood while they waited for the elevator.

As the door to the elevator opened, Wade looked at David just once. There was a coldness there, a malevolence he had never seen before, even from the most disturbed patient he'd ever treated.

He said, "I should have known what would happen when one of your kind interfered."

And then they were gone.

31 "You *what*?"

It was the first thing Stan Friedland had said since David launched into his monologue.

"Jesus, David. A schizophrenic. I just can't believe you would do such a thing."

David looked across the desk at his friend. Had he hoped running over to Stan's office with a confession would help?

"Neither can I," he said.

Stan got up and moved over to the window overlooking Park Avenue, then turned back.

"I spoke to Niles Martin this morning. He said she was a gifted subject—incredibly gifted—but that he couldn't find any evidence for gifts of the scope you're suggesting. Which makes her a paranormally gifted schizophrenic, but a schizophrenic just the same. Niles *told* me there was something strange going on between the two of you."

"I—I'm in love with her."

"Jesus, I hope you're in love," Stan said. "How could you jeopardize your entire professional career for anything less? So what do you think happens now? She gets a divorce and the two of you live happily ever after?"

"I thought we were friends, Stan."

He came over and sat down, began filling his pipe with tobacco from a worn leather pouch.

"I'm sorry, David. I really am. I guess I sound angry because . . . because I came so close once with a patient. At least some of my anger is at myself for not seeing what was happening, until it was too late."

"It wouldn't have mattered, Stan."

"I knew you were lonely, but I just can't believe this. Even if she weren't a schizophrenic—"

"But that's just it, Stan. I don't think she is."

"Why not? The symptoms fit. Changes in thought processes. Thought broadcasting. Hallucinations—"

"No hallucinations," David said.

"All right, but you've clearly got delusions of sin and guilt. You've got grandiose delusions—"

"One delusion—that her mind can cause events in the real world. The rest of it isn't a delusion. She's clairvoyant, telepathic and precognitive. We've proven that. But if the delusion of causing things in the world isn't a delusion, where does that leave the diagnosis?"

Stan lit a match to his pipe, drew in deeply. "So it's a depressive psychosis. Where does that leave *you*?"

"But what if it isn't a psychosis at all?" Standing up, David began to pace around the office. "Sure, she's depressed. You'd be depressed, too, in her situation. Think how you would feel if suddenly your most private feelings, your secret thoughts, were appearing in the world, violently. And there was nothing you could do about it."

There was a silence as Stan drew in on his pipe. "You're suggesting maybe I'd go mad, too?"

"I'm suggesting that this may be no ordinary madness. She's certainly not an ordinary woman. Maybe it's a perfectly understandable madness. A reasonable madness."

Stan's pipe had gone out. He laid it in the ashtray and leaned back on the couch, watching as David paced and talked.

"And think how you would feel, Stan, if this happened and your self-esteem was *already* in the toilet. Laura was brought up in a household that may have actually fostered her self-hatred. Remember, her father was deathly afraid that she'd turn out like his sister, who looked so much like Laura it's incredible. And Sam Gardner was afraid of his sister's violence, so any expression of anger—anything even remotely out of control—wasn't allowed. Do you know Laura tried to kill herself at least once that I know of, and they *still* didn't acknowledge something was wrong? Which would tend to give a person the idea that she is unloved, unwanted, that anything she did or felt was wrong."

"Which sets up a psychological foundation for a paranoid delusion of this type," Stan said.

"Forget the delusion. Try to understand. Thoughts and wishes and feelings that you or I would simply accept as part of being human, she absolutely refuses to tolerate in herself. She should be above them. They're unacceptable feelings that further reinforce her self-hatred. The poison delusion has developed and solidified as events keep piling up that prove it. The line between inside feelings and outside events gets blurred, and she feels responsible for more and more bad things. And finally she *is* responsible. It's like a vicious circle. She's so bad for having these bad emotions, these bad wishes, that she infects people with her poison."

"But you're saying she actually *does*, David. You're suggesting a psychological explanation for a parapsychological phenomenon."

David stopped pacing and stood by the window. "Well, why not? She has a psychological framework, like anyone else. Why couldn't her power change the way she says it has?"

"But, David, no one can learn to control their emotions completely. If what you're saying is true, everyone who knows her is in danger. She's bound to have bad thoughts or wishes about everyone she knows at one time or another. It leaves her no way out."

"That's right. She's got very few choices left."

There was a silence. Stan came over to the window where David was standing. "I see what you mean, but look, David, I don't want to debate her choices with you. Going to bed with a patient was *your* choice."

"Maybe not, Stan. Look. She's deep in transference with me, but her loving me is unacceptable to her, of course. But it's *still* her feeling, no matter how much she denies it. It's her wish. She wants me to love her. And it's the subconscious wishes she finds unacceptable that seem to manifest themselves in the world."

Stan was staring at him. "Are you seriously suggesting she telepathically laid an obsession with her on you and then forced you to act on it?"

"I know it sounds crazy. But how can we even begin to understand the powers Laura Wade has? Listen. About two weeks ago I had a dream about her, a sexual dream. And in the dream I *saw* a small birthmark at the base of her spine. I touched it. And it's there, Stan. A small brown birthmark. I saw it last night."

Stan looked at him. "You're saying she transferred the knowledge of the mark to your subconscious mind to produce the dream?"

"Maybe I've made a spiritual connection with this woman. Maybe my love for her gives me access to her soul, through her mind, through her thoughts—without the mask of language or physical processes. Who knows what mysteries and powers love can draw out of the mind, if only we could be open to them?''

''I don't think you should romanticize this, David.''

The phone was ringing. Stan picked up the receiver. ''Yes, Sue. Thanks for telling me.'' He hung up and came back over to David, put his arm on David's shoulder.

''I think you've allowed yourself to fall in love with a patient, and the rest is just rationalizations. What you have to do now is minimize the damage—''

''I can't, Stan,'' David said. Then he told him what happened afterward, when Zachary Wade showed up.

Stan listened, thoughtfully but without comment, until he was finished, then said, ''I wonder what Wade meant by that.''

''What?''

'' 'I should have known what would happen when one of your kind interfered.' ''

''What's the difference?''

''Do you suppose he was referring to the fact that you're Jewish?''

''Laura's family is Jewish. I assumed he was, too.''

He shrugged. ''That doesn't necessarily mean he isn't an anti-Semite. Whatever he meant, it's an odd thing to say.''

''Actually it's about par for the course. You might as well know, from the moment I met him I disliked the man intensely.''

''Any particular reason? I mean, other than the fact that you're in love with his wife?''

David chose to ignore the dig. ''There's just something about him that just seems off to me.''

''What does Laura say about him?''

''From what she told me in session, he isn't particularly supportive or loving. From what I saw myself and from Laura's characteristic defenses, I'd say it's likely she's *underestimating* the problems in the relationship, perhaps rationalizing them, making excuses, denying. For one thing, this woman has gone through her entire life thinking she's sexually unresponsive.''

''You, of course, know better.''

Again David ignored him. ''He tells her that. And of course she'd believe it.''

''She'd have to, since anything wrong is always her fault.'' Stan looked back at his pipe lying on the table, left it there.

''That's right,'' David said. ''Anyway, what's important at the moment isn't what I think of him. It's what he thinks of me that matters.''

''Why's that?''

''Because he called this morning to say he had notified the Medical Ethics Board, and was instituting a multimillion-dollar lawsuit against me.''

32 ''David?''

Lena Goldman was standing in the doorway. She seemed pale, wounded; the look on her face was enough to make him want to run for cover.

''Come in, Mom.''

For the past three weeks David had been barraged by a flood of legal repercussions. A subpoena for him to appear in court as the defendant in a two-million-dollar lawsuit had been delivered last Friday; that

morning a letter had arrived from the Medical Board
of Ethics notifying him of their upcoming review of
his medical license, pending the outcome of an investigation into medical and sexual misconduct. Yet even
as his shame became more and more public, David
had thought he could keep his status a secret from his
parents, assuring himself he'd tell them when he could
figure out what to say, reminding himself that Philadelphia was a long way from New York. Apparently it
wasn't far enough.

"So, it's true." His mother looked around. The
place was a garbage dump: papers and books here and
there, a pile of dishes in the sink, a half-eaten plate of
spaghetti on the coffee table, a few cartons of con-
gealed Chinese takeout lying around. He hadn't even
noticed it. He'd grown accustomed to squalor.

"How could you, David?"

How to explain it to his mother when he couldn't
explain it to himself?

She cleared a space on the sofa and sat down.

"Your father wouldn't come with me. I'm sorry."

David wasn't surprised. His father had always prided
himself on his sense of honor. Duty and honor. He
gathered up some newspaper sections, most of them
unread, from the sofa.

"Stop it, David. Just tell me what happened."

David told her as best he could. There were no
wails, no moans, no where-did-I-go wrongs.

"I think she's only one step away from being in-
dicted on a murder charge," he said.

"Do you believe she committed the murder?"

"No. But the detective in charge of the case probably does."

"Then why doesn't he arrest her?"

"Because he hasn't got any evidence that will stand up in court. You can be sure he's still looking."

"How do you know?"

"Because he keeps calling me. He keeps asking questions. One time he wants to talk about her paintings. Another time he asks me if we ever talked about her habits, where she used to go, who she was friends with. I think he may be trying to find out where she might have put the clothes she wore, maybe the murder weapon. The coroner said it was most likely a scalpel, though they've never found it."

"Where would she get a scalpel?"

"Anyone could get one from a medical supply house."

"Maybe she threw it away."

"She didn't do it, Mom. And believe me, Culligan's had every landfill from Manhattan to Easterbrook checked for a pair of blue pants and all the rest of the things the witness described. They'll never get anywhere that way."

"Why not?"

"Because they're proceeding from the assumption that Laura did it. So they're checking out places she might have gone, people she knew, places she might have put the physical evidence linking her to the crime, given her movements around the time of the murder. But, you see, she didn't do it, so they're barking up the wrong tree."

"How do you know she didn't do it, David? Are you in love with this woman?"

"She's in the hospital."

"David, you haven't answered my question." Then, looking at his face, "Never mind, it's answered. It's amazing that this sort of thing doesn't happen more often."

Was this her way of rallying behind him? Next she'd start blaming Laura for being a seducer of innocent sons, a siren who turned men to stone. Or perhaps this was simply her way of denying the seriousness of his situation.

"Don't you understand, Mom? Psychiatrists don't fall in love with their patients—and even if they do, they don't screw them."

She didn't flinch at his crudeness.

"Don't you see?" he said. "I made things worse. I made *her* worse. It doesn't matter that I'm in love with her, or even that she's in love with me. She's—"

"Why didn't you tell me when I called last week? And the week before?"

He started to cry. His mother reached over and hugged him. Then she drew back and looked fiercely into his eyes.

"You do love her."

"Yes," he said. "I love her."

"I knew you wouldn't do anything like this if you weren't in love with this woman. I told your father, I said, 'David would never do such a thing if there weren't a good reason.' He wouldn't listen to me, but eventually he will."

He asked her how she had found out about it. It seemed she'd heard the news from his sister-in-law, who heard the news from Marilyn Reinhold's mother's friend's daughter, with whom his sister-in-law Maggie had a passing acquaintance. All the way down in Philadelphia. He could imagine that conversation: "Did you hear, your brother-in-law screwed one of his patients? A schizophrenic!"

"Are they going to have a hearing, David?"

"Within a month. My medical license will probably be revoked."

"My goodness, David. What does your lawyer say?"

"What *can* he say? I was caught red-handed, so to speak."

"But . . . is he preparing a defense? I could get Don Graceland."

David shook his head. "Mike Reilly's a competent attorney, Mom. It's his client's competence that's in question here." He looked at her. "I've stopped practicing."

She stared at him. It was true. He'd called every one of his patients, referred them to colleagues. He hadn't been brave enough to tell them the reason, just truthful enough to say that he wouldn't be practicing anymore. A few of them heard, though, one way or another. Diane Sagori had telephoned him at home a few nights ago and called him names for five full minutes. David, it seemed was her best proof ever that all men were fucking bastards.

"How will you manage?"

"I have some money saved." Actually, he had plenty of money, thanks to an aggressive group of investments he'd begun last year with a broker Allison found. He could go on this way for a few years.

"What are you going to do?"

"I don't know."

"Let me take you out to lunch, David."

"No."

"Then I'll clean up."

"It's okay, Mom. Really. I like it this way."

She began taking all the things off the coffee table and piling them up on top of the stack of newspapers.

"What else can I do?"

What could she do? She could stop being so gaddamned understanding.

* * *

"David?"

It was Mike Reilly calling.

"Did you hear? Laura Wade's father died yesterday."

David heard the sharp intake of his own breath. "A heart attack," he said. The words came out unbidden, an automatic reaction. It wasn't a question.

"How'd you know?" Mike said.

"I've already explained it all to you, Mike."

There was a long silence. Mike Reilly was no doubt considering a plea of insanity as David's defense.

David said, "I have to go, Mike."

"Don't do anything stupid, David," Reilly said.

David parked his car in the visitor's lot at Rolling Hills Psychiatric Hospital. The best psychiatric institution in Fairfield County, one of the best in the country. Top physicians, extravagant facilities, highly trained staff. None of which could protect Laura from herself now.

He stopped at the receptionist's desk.

"Dr. Goldman," he said, hoping he wouldn't be asked to show medical identification. "I'm here to see Laura Wade. I'm consulting on her case."

The receptionist checked a list on the desk in front of her. "I'm sorry, Dr. Goldman, I have specific orders that you're not to be admitted."

Orders from Zachary Wade. Could David blame him?

More to the point, was he going to risk being slapped with a harassment suit, in addition to everything else?

"Thank you," he said and turned to go.

He left through the front doors and walked around

to the back of the building, where he found the doctors' entrance. Placing his briefcase on one of the cars
parked near the entrance, he started rifling through it,
as if he were looking for something. A woman wearing a white coat passed by him, smiling. He smiled
back. Her tag said, ''Myra Nordstrom, MD.'' The
moment she was out of sight, David went up to the
door, flashed his ID at an attendant and said, ''Con-
sult. Dr. Nordstrom.''

The man waved David through.

He proceeded up the hallway and turned left, then
followed a sign that directed him to the dayroom. It
was aggressively cheery, with clusters of bright chintz
sofas, floor-to-ceiling bookshelves on one wall, art
supplies in one corner. A number of patients were
scattered around, most of them watching television.
No Laura.

He went on, losing his nerve as he walked aimlessly
through the halls, along with any sense of why he'd
come in the first place.

Finally, in one of the rooms in the hall marked Visiting
Wing, he found her. He stood in the open doorway,
watching. She was talking softly to a stocky, well-dressed
woman of about seventy with carefully teased and sprayed
gray hair, so thin you could probably see right through it
if you looked down on her. She was crying. Laura had an
arm around her shoulders.

David stood there for a few moments. Laura's eyes
were dull—drugged—and the pallor of her skin was
frightening. Finally, she glanced up and saw him.

''David?''

''I'm sorry to disturb you,'' he said from the doorway. ''I just wanted to talk to you, to see how you
were doing, to tell you—''

''Who *are* you?'' the older woman said.

"Mother, this is David Goldman."

"I'm going to call the nurse." She started toward the door.

"Mother, wait."

"Please, Mrs. Gardner, I'll only be here for a few minutes. I just came to see how Laura is."

"How should she be? Her father died less than a week ago."

He looked at Laura, who reminded him of a frightened animal.

"I killed my father, David," she whispered. "They won't let me kill myself. Do you understand? It happened again."

"*What* happened again?" her mother said.

"I killed him, Mother. I told you."

Mrs. Gardner was looking at Laura, obviously horrified.

"They give me so many drugs now," Laura said, "I can barely think. But I can't hear what people are thinking anymore. My mind is so . . . Dr. Roland always wants to talk about you. She says you betrayed me. She says you did the worst thing a doctor could do."

"Laura was fine until she started seeing you," her mother said.

"I've never been fine, Mother."

The woman looked at her daughter as if she'd never laid eyes on her before.

Laura turned back to David. "Zach and I are much better, too. He comes to see Arlene once a week with me. And he's been very nice. He's trying to change. To be more supportive." There was a flatness about her voice, a lack of inflection. As if she were mouthing words.

"Zach's a fine man, Laura," her mother said. "Your

father and I had our difficult times, too, and we got through them. You'll get through yours. A good rest and you'll be fine. I always told your father so.''

''You were there all the time and you never noticed there was something wrong with me. You never even worried. At least Father worried.''

''How would you know if I worried or not?''

Laura looked at David, then at her mother. Was she going to tell her?

''You're right, Mother,'' she said. ''I wouldn't have known.''

''I loved you,'' Mrs. Gardner said. ''Your father loved you. I think he loved you best. What did you want me to do?'' She sank back into a chair. ''I tried, Laura. But you never told us.''

''Would it have helped? You wouldn't have wanted to hear. You still don't.''

Mrs. Gardner looked away.

''You just wanted me to be normal, isn't that right?'' Laura said.

''Is that a crime?''

''No. It's what I wanted, too.''

There was a silence. Finally, Laura walked toward David. ''I persuaded Zach to drop the lawsuit.''

She stared at him for a moment, then leaned over and whispered, ''My father is dead, David. After it's over . . . will you tell them why I had no choice?''

He backed away. She was asking him to explain her suicide to her family.

He took one last look at her, then turned and headed down the hall. By the time he reached the back entrance again, he was practically running.

When he got back to his apartment at half past twelve, the phone was ringing.

"Hello?"

"This is Marla Gardner." She didn't have to tell him that she was Laura's mother. Or that she was furious. "How dare you," she said. "I didn't say anything in the hospital because I didn't want to upset Laura. We've had enough this past month—"

He could hear her starting to cry, then the furor was back. "We're not dropping any lawsuit. We only told her that because she was so insistent about it. She's so fragile now, if you cared anything at all about her, you'd know—"

"Mrs. Gardner, there's no way I could care any more about Laura than I do."

"Who the hell are you? Some sleazy quack who would take advantage of my daughter. Why? Because she's so beautiful? It's disgusting."

"I'm sorry. You must know that. Do you know that my life is in ruins?"

"Do you expect me to care, young man? What do you know about love? Love isn't sex. Love is making the best of things, sticking by someone, making a commitment no matter what. Zach is standing by Laura. I stood by my husband, that poor tortured man. He lived his whole life tormenting himself about that monstrous sister of his, always trying to figure out something he could have done that would have made things different. And then, as Laura got older . . ."

"I do understand, Mrs. Gardner," David said. "I saw how much Laura looks like his sister. In the photograph."

She let out a moan. "That picture! If you want to know the truth, I think getting that in the mail was what killed my husband."

"Wait a minute, Mrs. Gardner." David's head was

spinning. "You mean someone *sent* him that photograph of his sister?"

"That's right."

"Who?"

"I don't know."

"Did *he*?"

"What's the difference? The only thing that matters is that he used to cry over that picture, night after night. And I had to watch him torment himself. So don't you tell me about love. And if you ever bother Laura again, I swear, I'm an old woman, but I'll kill you."

After David hung up the phone, he went out for a walk along Central Park West. The wind chilled to the bone, but he walked to his office anyway, which he hadn't had the heart to go into in weeks.

Mrs. Frangipani was in the vestibule.

"How are you, Dr. Goldman? Have you been on vacation?"

David gave her a smile. "Yes."

Inside, there was a thin film of dust on everything. He opened the door to his inner office, sat down at his desk. If he wasn't to be a doctor, what would he do?

Going into the file, he took out one of Laura's tapes. It was marked August 28. He put it in the machine and sat down to listen to her voice on tape. "I was just thinking of what the thing with my arm reminds me of. Anna O. . . . "

He began taking things out of his desk and piling them on top: pads, pencils, legal pads, a picture of Allison on a beach in Mexico, an opened package of peanut butter and cheese crackers.

On the tape, Laura was talking about her paintings. "No, it's just a hobby. I don't sell my paintings."

His own voice. "Why not?"

"Zach says my work looks like little gothic nightmares."

"What do *you* say?"

"Why would anyone buy little nightmares?"

Little gothic nightmares?

Jesus Christ. He missed it then, and he'd been missing it ever since. He'd been caught up in *her,* but this wasn't about her, at least, not completely.

He flipped off the tape, grabbed his coat and headed out of the office, double-locking the door and leaving his pile sitting there on the dusty desk. With any luck he'd be in Philadelphia by six.

33 It was nearly dusk by the time David pulled up in front of the St. Francis Home for the Aged, a dark, crumbling old building in a West Philadelphia inner-city neighborhood. All the way driving down, he'd kept looking in his rearview mirror, irrationally convinced that the blue Mustang he kept seeing in it was following him, until he took the turnpike exit and the Mustang didn't.

Inside, the building was surprisingly cheery. The halls were pale yellow, with bright nonfluorescent lights.

"Visiting hours are over," said an enormous black woman behind a reception desk.

"I'm looking for a patient here named Dr. Emmanuel Kassand. My name is David Goldman. I'm a doctor, and I've come all the way from New York to see him."

She looked at the wall clock. "I expect he'll be eatin' his dinner now."

"Please. It's very important."

"What's goin' on? Poor old guy—he's ninety-three, you know—don't get no visitors for years. Even his son don't come. And now, last month, he got all kind of people askin' for him."

"Who?"

"Well, you. And that other guy, the one with the glasses. A cop, I think he was."

"Anyone else?"

"No one else."

Of course not. It was too good to hope for.

"I suppose I could take you in," she said, "long as you don't stay too long. Don't want to get into no trouble, now do I?"

Emmanuel Kassand was eating his dinner at a small tray table in the corner of the room. He seemed very fragile; the skin stretched taut over his bones, paper-thin over blue veins. A few wisps of white hair sprouted from the top of his head.

David stood in the doorway. "Dr. Kassand?"

The old man looked up from his meal. A forkful of turkey and stuffing tumbled back onto his plate.

David moved in closer. "Dr. Kassand, I've come all the way from New York to talk to you."

Kassand put his fork down. "Had a cousin there once. Alma. Dead, now."

"Dr. Kassand, my name is David Goldman. I'm a doctor—a psychiatrist."

"I used to be a psychiatrist, long time ago. Gave it up. Became a family doctor. At least there you know what you're dealing with. But the mind! We're like infants crying in the dark when it comes to the mind."

"What made you give it up, Dr. Kassand?"

"Who wants to know?"

David repeated his name, then explained why he'd come. When he mentioned the name Sophie Zophlick, the old man seemed to become more lucid.

"Why do you all want to dig it up now?"

David sat down on the bed. It was the only other place to sit in the room.

"Her niece—her brother's daughter—is my patient."

Kassand looked at him intently, his eyes as narrow as slits. "They brought her into Darlington when she attacked her little brother with a piece of broken glass. At least that's what Elias said. I wonder if it's the same brother."

David nodded. "Might be. Then you know about Sophie?"

"Know? That's all Elias ever talked about. In the beginning she was just assigned to him. We were chock-full of them in those days—the real crazies. You have the drugs now, so it's not the same. We had a place full of lunatics, and only three of us. Dementia—you call it schizophrenia now. That was about when the shocks came in. Seemed to help some of them, calm them down sometimes. Of course, some people it made worse."

"And Sophie?"

"It seemed to help her. Most of the time she was fairly composed, but then suddenly she'd fly into a murderous rage, accuse you of thinking bad thoughts about her, attack you. One time it took four orderlies to prevent her from killing one of the nurses. But Elias was one of the young idealists, all set to change the face of psychiatric medicine. He'd only been at Darlington a few years. Some of the patients were . . . how to say it? . . . not very appealing. I admired him for what he was trying to do. Had he worked a few more years in that place he would have seen things the way we did. A fine man and a fine physician—until he took up with her. Then everything changed.

"That woman destroyed Elias DeMane. He kept running around talking about some kind of power she had, mind power. Said she knew the future, knew what people were thinking. I tell you, Elias became as demented as she was. Deteriorated pitifully. Became obsessed with her. Even used to sneak her out of the place, sometimes. Used to sit for hours and look at that picture he had taken."

"Of Sophie?"

Kassand nodded. "She was something, I tell you. Beautiful girl. Exotic." He was silent for a moment, then said, very softly, "But at the end, her eyes were dead . . . dead eyes. Like a shark's eyes."

Laura's eyes weren't like that.

"He had the portrait taken down on South Street, in a studio. He didn't have his wife anymore—Felicia had died giving birth to their son."

"He had a son? Elias DeMane had a son?"

"Indeed he did. Pretty little boy, looked just like his mother. China-doll face, peaches-and-cream complexion. Henry, I think his name was."

David's legs felt like rubber as he went over to the window, looked out over the street. A woman was passing by wheeling a shopping cart full of groceries, a small child perched on top of the bags in the cart.

"How old was the son when it happened?"

"Young. Four, maybe even three." He snapped his fingers, but the only sound that came out was a scraping noise, skin against skin, like sandpaper. "Or maybe the boy's name was Martin. Can't remember. I lost touch. I guess I didn't want to remember."

"Dr. Kassand, is there any possibility the son could have witnessed what happened?"

He looked at David with a shudder. "A son seeing *that*? Elias was just ripped to shreds. Like a wild animal had done it. And she . . . well, she actually mutilated herself. No. The boy was sleeping. My wife and I offered to take that poor child in, but there was a relative somewhere. Great-aunt, I think. Kansas, maybe. Don't really recall. Maybe Ohio."

"Do you remember the name of the town, Dr. Kassand?"

"Carrelville, Charleyville—something like that."

"You're sure you can't?"

"I'm ninety-three years old, son. It'll happen to you someday. One morning you'll wake up and there you'll be—old. Don't know why I keep on living. Everybody I know is dead."

David thanked him for his help, then turned to go.

"Did I have dinner?" he said.

David pulled the tray table closer to him. The turkey with the mound of gray stuffing looked no better cold.

"My favorite meal, turkey," he said. "Always has been. Thanksgiving. Mary and I sitting around with the kids; everyone coming over. Always get a kick out of it. Don't you?"

David nodded.

"Dr. Kassand? Just one more question. What happened to the picture?"

He looked up from the plate. "The picture of Sophie? I suppose it was there with Elias's things. Maybe it went with the boy."

Again David turned to go, but Kassand called him back.

"Young man," he said, "the name of the town was

Lordsville. Lordsville, Kansas. And the aunt's name was Lucille Dreedle.''

34 A half hour after the Northwest flight landed in Wichita the next morning, David was driving west in a rental car along Interstate Highway 51. It was clear and cold. The corn had already been harvested and there wasn't much activity. The incredibly flat terrain was broken only by an occasional farmhouse, an occasional intersecting road, and, occasionally, a passing car.

Glancing in the rearview mirror, he saw the old silver Impala that had been in back of him for almost twenty miles, but he decided he was being ridiculous when it turned off at the next road. He wondered when his next miniattack of paranoia would strike. Twice at the ticket counter back in Philadelphia he'd thought he noticed a man staring at him.

About three miles west of a town called Pawnee, pop. 10,000, he came to a large, low brick building set back from the road, a school. The Pawnee Regional High School, according to the letters above the entrance.

The man at the Hertz counter had said Lordsville was just south of Pawnee. David found the office, asked a secretary if he might see the principal. Explaining that he was a psychiatrist from New York, he said he was doing research on one of his patients, and that he wanted to check the records.

She asked him to wait, then disappeared into the

office marked Allen Dunning, Principal. After a moment, she led him in.

Dunning was a young man with a high, beaked nose and a bad case of adult acne. David introduced himself, told him he was looking for information on a Lordsville family named Dreedle.

"Lordsville's just down the road a few miles," Dunning said. He had a strong Midwestern accent. "Not much of a town. There isn't even a post office there anymore. And I've never heard of a family in these parts by that name."

"It was about forty years ago."

"Pawnee Regional's the school for the whole township, just built eight years ago. Back then, they had—"

"Do you have the records for back then?"

"I'd have to check in the basement," Dunning said.

"I can do it myself if you don't have time."

"I'll be glad to help."

David followed him into a large room near the building's boiler room. Along the far wall were stacked boxes of cardboard files with dates in bold black marker. The oldest date he could see was 1926.

"Maybe a few years after the war," David told him.

Dunning hauled out the box labeled 1950.

"What was the name again?"

"Dreedle. Henry." David hoped it was Henry and not Martin.

Dunning lifted up the lid, leafed through, pulled out a file. "No. This isn't what you want. This is a girl. Barbara Dreedle." He looked it over. "Average student. Transferred in the middle of eighth grade. Here's the stamp."

"Where'd she go?"

"Looks like Union High School, Topeka."

"Would you try the name Henry DeMane."

He flipped through again. "Not here."

"Would you try another one? Or I'd be glad to look myself."

The two men leafed through more boxes. Nothing. They tried a few more years. Dunning was poking around in 1948; David was beginning to lose hope.

"Here it is," Dunning said, pulling a file out of the box. "Must have been misfiled." He opened it, glanced at the typewritten transcript lying on top of some papers. "Good student, your Henry DeMane."

David took the file, looked at the transcript himself. Good student? All A's, straight through. Until 1950, when the transcript ended, in the tenth grade. Apparently he'd left school the same year as Barbara Dreedle. (His adoptive sister?) There was no transfer stamp on this one, though.

Under the manuscript, David found a two-page typewritten letter, yellowed with age. The letterhead read: Emmett Darwin, MD, Sixteen Main, Wichita, Kansas.

June 8, 1945

Mr. Donald Billingsly
Principal
Lordsville Grammar School
Lordsville, Kansas

Dear Mr. Billingsly:

As of this date, I have conducted a comprehensive psychiatric evaluation of your student, Henry DeMane. In view of the behavior and disciplinary problems you've had with him, I can certainly understand your insistence that his aunt bring him to me.

The subject is a twelve-year-old male, tall for his age, well-built, with attractive features and no physical defects that I could discern. In terms of sexuality, he is post-latent. He scores high in the gifted range on the Stanford-Binet.

In addition to the intelligence test I also administered the Thematic Apperception Test, a new diagnostic test developed at Harvard. I won't go into the specifics of the results; suffice it to say there was an extremely violent, aggressive thread running through all of the stories the boy produced for the test. His stories were cruel, some also bizarre.

The boy is so low in remorse that none shows up on any of these tests. He apparently feels no need to conform to what's expected of him, and, concurrently, neither seeks nor needs approval from others. I'm not surprised that you described him in your letter as a loner. It is highly significant that his TAT stories indicate no degree of nurturance whatsoever, a construct that describes the need to help and love others.

Frankly, I have never seen a boy anything like him. At twelve, he is incredibly sure of himself; poised, charming, knowledgeable in areas one would not expect of a boy his age. Even more disturbing, the negative traits that lie beneath the surface—boredom, hostility, rage, possibly paranoia—are not apparent in conversation outside a therapeutic setting. In view of the violence his aunt believes he witnessed as a boy, it is possible that he is fixated at a very early stage of development, which could lead to criminal behavior of the type you describe (the fire in the boy's room at school, the decapitation of the goat, etc.). Though he would not admit his responsibility for these acts, he did make the general comment, "What harm was done?" He also said that while he did attempt to

force his young adoptive sister to have sexual in-
tercourse with him, she really wanted him to do it,
that girls always say no when they mean yes. We're
talking about a twelve-year-old boy here, and a
nine-year-old girl!

He has no memory of that night, at least none
he would acknowledge, although Mrs. Dreedle
says he had terrible nightmares until the age of
six or seven. He refused to be hypnotized. He
also refused to discuss his dreams, saying he
didn't have any.

I would have to undertake a long-term analysis
before commenting along more specific diagnostic lines, but I would say that the pattern could
scarcely be more alarming. If you have *evidence*
that it was this boy who committed these crimes,
perhaps you could force the aunt to act and perhaps forestall the escalation of petty vicious behavior into crimes whose consequences are far
worse than the death of small animals. . . .

There was more, including a recommendation for immediate psychoanalysis, following a brief hospitalization. The letter, like a second, brief letter responding
to the aunt's rejection of this proposal, and accusing her
of being an "ostrich," whose pity for the boy was mis-
guided, were signed Emmett Darwin, MD.

Christ. The fucking guy had named his *doberman*
after that psychiatrist.

"Is this boy your patient?" asked Dunning, who
had been reading over David's shoulder.

"No, but I believe he's married to my patient."

Underneath Darwin's letter lay a report from a gym
teacher describing Henry DeMane as totally undisci-
plined, despised by the other boys, and prone to vio-

lence. The teacher, not surprisingly, refused to have him in class anymore.

David didn't need to read another word. Of course, the TAT and other such tests—like the general tone of Darwin's letter—seemed dated today, but the picture that emerged was frighteningly clear. Cleckly had described the signposts of the psychopathic personality as early as 1941, and though Darwin made no mention of Cleckly in his letter, Henry DeMane fit Cleckly's profile: the superficial charm, the high intelligence, the undeveloped conscience, the absence of remorse, anxiety, guilt. As did the crimes of which he was accused—setting a fire, cruelty to animals, attempted rape, along with the inappropriate rationalizations.

They headed back upstairs to Dunning's office. David's brain was reeling, not with answers but with more questions. How had Zachary Wade connected with Laura? Had he married her with the intention of doing what he'd been doing? And what, exactly, *was* it that he'd been doing?

Dunning agreed to photocopy the contents of the file. David stood quietly by the machine, watching him, struck by the simplicity of Wade's motives. Revenge, pure and simple. Because, certainly, Laura's aunt killed his father. Because, probably, he'd seen her do it.

Dunning handed over the Xeroxes. David thanked him for his time, headed out to his car—then found himself laughing. Zachary Wade thought he was dealing with an ordinary person. But Laura Gardner Wade was no ordinary person. Far from it. Her aunt had apparently had the same gifts and gone mad all by herself. Funniest of all, Wade—mad as a hatter himself—thought he was dealing with ordinary madness in his wife. He didn't, couldn't, know.

PART FOUR

Madness

35 The man began practicing the kill of the Death Witch at Aunt Lucy's house, on small animals mostly. As a young boy, as an adolescent, he understood nothing and made no attempt to hide himself. He was lacking in both discipline and character, flaws that arose from making excuses. He was pitied; even Aunt Lucy pitied him. (The poor traumatized child!) He was inundated with their attempts to help, which were worse.

The school counselor sent him to the only shrink doctor she could find, who asked him a lot of personal questions and tried to get him to talk about why he was so angry all the time, and what he remembered about his father's death (as if he would have told anybody), and whether he wanted to screw his mother, which he thought was hilarious, given the circumstances of his mother's demise. She had died giving birth to him, and was therefore irrelevant. The shrink doctor was an intellectual pygmy, lost in a sea of stupidity, Freud his only port. Later, he brought that pale and insipid man a pile of dogshit in a box, which he wrapped up with a bow and a ribbon and red flowered wrapping paper he stole from Aunt Lucy. He told the shrink doctor it was a present from her. *Why do you do those things?* was what they always said to him. *A bright boy like you.* The shrink doctor told them he was insane. Hah! What did they know about madness?

He never mentioned the Death Witch.

He left not long after that—a person without a history, whose mother (appropriately) had died giving him life. He became a vagabond, a wanderer, traveling all over the world, here to there and back again.

He took odd jobs. He learned several languages. He studied art in France. Once, in Amsterdam, a woman told him he fucked like a robot. He hit her across the mouth. She asked him to leave, which of course he did. She was unclean, anyway, and that he couldn't stand.

In the spring of 1955, he hooked up with Nadia Maurant, a rich woman with nothing to do except drive around Europe in her Mercedes. She took him on a trip across Scotland, a wet and useless country, in which he came down with pneumonia, and then she took him to her brother's clinic outside Geneva. The man felt a certain kinship with the Maurants, their circumstances being somewhat similar to his own. When Claude was six and Nadia fourteen, their mother had run off with an Italian (gruesome people, almost as bad as the Jews; it was not surprising Freud was a Jew), and their father had killed himself. Of course, Claude and Nadia were left with piles of money, while he was left with nothing. Which would make his victory all the sweeter, when it came.

The man had admired Claude Maurant, whose

talents were many and varied. Before opening his clinic, Maurant had been a highly regarded member of the French underground during the war, a specialist in sabotage. His skill as a plastic surgeon was only surpassed by his skill at chess and his knowledge of explosives. It was at Maurant's hand that the man learned the value of the sacrifice, the discipline of the knife, and the importance of planning an operation, surgical or otherwise.

Maurant had already done his sister's face twice, but she was still old, and fucking her was like death. After his recuperation, when the man told her he'd had enough of her, she begged him to stay, crying down on her knees in a room at the clinic. An ugly scene, not one he would ever repeat. Women, except whores, were all victims.

He told Maurant, who was not surprised. Why should a young, attractive man spend time with a useless, broken-down woman? Sometimes he thought about Maurant now, a fine figure of a man, a physique precisely defined, no soft edges, no flab. Sharp, like his scalpel. Once the man kissed him, and found his lips warm and sweet. But by then he had found his place by the river, halfway across the world, and he needed the money to acquire it—while Maurant intended to stay where he was. It was just as well. He could not afford to become too attached.

By the time he was thirty-one, the pittance his father had left him was gone. Without money a man had to resign himself to mucking about in the filth with the rest of the creatures—attractive only when one was young. With money, a man could choose when, where, and for how long he would make his forays into the grime. He could enjoy the difference between a whore he paid twenty dollars for and one for whom he paid five hundred.

The man did not know what drew him, well-seasoned but not yet well-heeled, back to the city of his birth. Though he was a methodical man, he had no plan, no particular *reason* for returning. Nor did he waste time trying to analyze such moves. You were what you were. You did what you did.

It amused him that such a methodical person should have planned his life around a coincidence. Sometimes he thought about that—what would, or wouldn't, have been, had he not driven out of the city that day; had he gone to one of the northern suburbs instead of the southern suburbs; had he not taken that particular turn, stopped in that particular diner on that particular road.

It was one of those old-fashioned places with gleaming chrome counters and waitresses with pads and ocher uniforms. When She walked in, he was sitting there sipping his coffee, nibbling on a dry piece of cake. At first, he could do nothing but watch Her—fascinated, astonished. He sat in that diner at least an hour after She left, then drove back to his shabby room, where he examined his pathetic collection of memorabilia and confirmed what he already knew to be true. He asked questions—discreetly, but of the right people. Day after day from a hidden place, he watched as She arrived at school with Her sister, the two of them in their little blue uniforms. He found out what he needed to know. He planned his operation.

It would take time, of course, to set up so daring a masquerade. Time to construct a history, fabricate a life, get a formal education, obtain—Maurant's contribution—a new face. He took his new name, which meant "The Lord has remembered," from the Bible. (He allowed himself that one moment of bitterness, for the Lord surely had forgotten him.)

To live beside the Death Witch and not be tainted by Her would be the ultimate test of his character.

36

She was used to the routine. At first, she tried to make them understand about the poison; she screamed and raved like a crazy person, she banged her head against the walls—to scramble her brains so her dreams wouldn't hurt them, so her thoughts wouldn't get them—but they put her in one of those white jackets so her arms couldn't move and she was strapped down to the table. Then they took her out of the jacket and increased her medicine so she didn't have the energy to bang her head against the walls anymore.

It wasn't such a bad place. They made everything so easy. In the mornings a nurse brought in a tray with her medicine. Then she had breakfast and some activity, maybe sketching out on the lawn, or painting (she tried to paint but her arm shook too much). There was a piano in the dayroom. And lunch, where she sat sometimes with Angela, who said she was really an Italian countess.

It was funny. There were some people whose thoughts she'd never been able to make sense of. It was like that a lot with the people in here; their thoughts were all confused, noisy, their mind maps full of detours and holes. Like Angela's.

After lunch there was more medicine, then an afternoon session with her doctor, or her group, or with Zach and Arlene, then showers (supervised, of course), then dinner. Sometimes someone picked a fight with her over the size of her portion, but mostly everyone just sat there taking teeny bites like her sister took and not looking at her. They had enough troubles so they didn't need hers, too. And then maybe she did a little reading before bed, or watched TV, and then she slept. She had a nice private room with a view of the lawns. All around her were nice bright colors, feel-good colors, nice cheerful nurses, nice doctors. Even the orderlies were nice. Except she could hear them thinking sometimes. Not like the patients.

But none of them knew how much danger they were in.

She had even murdered her father.

They let her out for his funeral. Had it rained that day?

She thought it had been a wet, gloomy day, and that he was buried near a large oak tree in the Mount Laurel Cemetery, and that a rabbi named Tannenbaum said Samuel Gardner had been a wonderful husband and father and a great philanthropist; but she couldn't be completely sure because she wasn't present. There was a body there who looked like her, all dressed up in a nice dark dress with a hat on its head purchased especially for the occasion, a body for everyone to hug and kiss and give sympathy to, but they were hugging thin air, a mirage in a Givenchy dress. She was transparent; if they looked they could see right through her skin. And she kept thinking that she ought to make a speech apologizing for causing all these people to be brought together on such a sad occasion and that it would be pretty funny when this transparent being got up in front of the synagogue and made a speech and there were words—noise, sounds—coming from the pulpit but no source. She may even have laughed aloud at this thought; Carole, who was sitting next to her during the eulogy, glared at her. Mother didn't notice.

The doctors were afraid she was going to commit suicide, so they didn't let her have anything sharp, and permitted smoking only in the dayrooms, and kept all the windows locked. And she thought she would find a way to do it, anyway. But then the first day went by and she put it off because, really, she was a coward. And they kept her so doped up that pretty soon she forgot why she wanted to kill herself. Her insides were rotting anyway, so it might not be necessary.

Sometimes they let her have visitors.

Her mother came. All Laura could say was, "I'm sorry." And all her mother could do was cry, and say, "You'll feel better soon."

David stayed away, after that one time, because he knew. He was the only one who knew, and she was glad he didn't come. He'd already risked himself for her—to try and make her a person—but only God could turn water into wine.

Her sister came once and looked at Laura as if she were a mad creature. So Laura, obliging as always, made a scary face at her. But she wasn't sure the muscles were working right, because the drugs made her face numb, so she probably only looked funny, not scary. At least that's what Carole was thinking.

Her brother was somewhere in Zanzibar by now.

She knew they were all talking about her. She heard them thinking. Poor Laura, had a nervous breakdown. She thinks she's turned into poison. Not turned *into* poison, *is* poison. Has always been poison.

They wouldn't let her see her children. She cried every time she thought about them.

One afternoon she got into a long conversation with Sue Ellen X, who wouldn't tell Laura her last name— if she told, Sue Ellen said, they would find her. When Laura asked who ''they'' were, Sue Ellen X said they were always playing music in her head to try and distract her. Laura *heard* that music from inside Sue Ellen's head, laughed out loud and said, ''Vivaldi and Pink Floyd.'' Sue Ellen was furious that Laura knew, accused her of being in cahoots with them. Then Sue Ellen tried to attack Laura, but when she started to fight her off, the orderlies restrained her and a nurse gave her another pill.

Mustn't tell them. Mustn't say anything about it, just go back to being the way she was before. Keep it to herself. If she let them know she could still hear their thoughts, she would never get out of here.

She had a new doctor. Her name was Arlene, she was nice. She had a short haircut, very severe. She said David had betrayed Laura, but she didn't feel betrayed, only sad. Zach had agreed to come in and have some three-way sessions. Anything to help her get well. Arlene told Laura it was just the illness that was making her think dreams and thoughts came true, that she could control the illness if she kept taking the drugs, the ones that mushed her brain. Laura said she believed Arlene, and after a while, maybe she did. Maybe she was mistaken. Maybe she'd never heard thoughts. Maybe she never knew the future. Maybe she wasn't a witch at all, just a pathetic shell of a woman with nothing inside except melting mush.

She dreamed:

She was running through the house, looking for Sammy. There was a strange silence in the house, a stillness, and no furniture at all. Just empty rooms, as if no one ever lived there. She kept running and running, but she couldn't find Sammy. She looked in the bedroom and in the kitchen, she even went up to her studio, but the room was empty. Even her paintings were gone. When she looked out the window—at the back, at the pool, at the Sound—all she could see was pool water and sea water, glistening in the sunlight. And so she ran back into Sammy's bedroom and sat there in the corner of his room, empty except for his cat George, curled up in the corner, fast asleep.

She reached out to stroke the cat but suddenly she was falling, falling. . . .

She woke up screaming; they gave her another pill.

Now Arlene would want to know what she'd dreamed, and Laura would have to tell her. But she would also tell Arlene that she wasn't afraid the dream would come true. She'd tell Arlene she was cured. Then Arlene would let her out.

She had already decided how she would end it: falling would bring relief from the pain.

The only thing was, she couldn't let Laura sleep until then.

37 David noticed a peculiar odor in the hallway as he got off the elevator, carrying the mail and his overnight bag. It smelled like someone had just burned soup on the stove. He fumbled with his keys in the lock, finally pushed the door open about an inch before he realized he'd dropped a couple of envelopes near the elevator. He set down the bag and backtracked to retrieve them.

He was picking the letter off the floor, maybe thirty seconds later, when it happened. A horrifying, ear-splitting explosion. The door of his apartment burst outward with a force so violent, a noise so deafening, that he was knocked to the floor.

And then, silence. Around him on the floor were pieces of glass, plastic, splinters of wood. When he collected himself, he realized he was, essentially, unhurt. His lip was bleeding and his arm hurt like hell, but he was all right.

"Christ almighty! What the hell—" His neighbor, Mindy Stewart, had rushed out of her apartment, along with several others from down the hallway. "Dr. Goldman, are you all right?"

David tried to stand but got dizzy and had to sit back down again.

"I think so," he said. "My arm is hurt." His voice sounded like he was speaking from the bottom of a well.

Mindy looked over at the huge gaping hole in what used to be the outer wall of David's apartment.

"My God. What in the world happened?"

Her voice sounded miles away.

A few minutes later David managed to stand. He walked over to the hole and peered in. The totality of the destruction made him dizzy again. There was almost nothing recognizable left, just jagged edges of things, pieces, bits. Most of the Sheetrock was gone, exposing the bare boards and beams. The sliding glass door was shattered; the room was filled with the groaning of a cold breeze whipping through the living room. There was a kind of burning smell. And the silence. The stillness.

David stepped inside and shuffled through the wreckage aimlessly. His neighbor was following him around in silence; two or three other neighbors were peering in through the hole.

He found the bedroom relatively intact. In the bathroom, he took a look in the mirror, what was left of it. The cut on his lip wasn't too bad. Must have bit it. But, Christ, his arm hurt. He found a shirt in the closet, whose door was black with soot but actually in place and, with Mindy's help, he fashioned himself a sling.

Then he went over to the phone by the bed, picked it up. It was dead. He sat down on the bed.

"Would you do me a favor, Mindy? Would you call the police?"

"I think Mrs. Harrison already did that."

"No," he said. "I want you to personally call Detective Henry Culligan, at the Tenth Precinct, and tell him what's happened. I'd do it myself, but I'm feeling a little woozy."

* * *

Detective Henry Culligan was just about to head over to Twenty-fifth Street and Tenth Avenue to question a possible suspect Compton had turned up in the Garcia case. Sitting at his desk, finishing up some paperwork first, Culligan realized that he was feeling better than he had in months. Lilly Dunleavy had suddenly called that morning and said she'd changed her mind about being hypnotized. Her psychiatrist said it might be a good way to get rid of the nightmares she was having. At one o'clock, Culligan had an appointment with Doug Gray and Lilly down at Police Plaza.

Thank God for psychiatrists.

Of course, you couldn't say that about Laura Wade's psychiatrist. Funny thing, that Goldman had seemed like a good guy, for a shrink. Still, you never could tell.

But at least now the Harmon case might get moving again. Three months after the murder, the investigation was at a complete standstill. They didn't even have a *lead* on a suspect; the case against Laura Wade was nowhere. In fact, he almost felt sorry for the woman. She was like a walking plague. First, Goldman goes and gives her a romp in the downy billows, then she gets sent to the loonybin, not that she didn't belong there, and then, to top it all off, her father dies. Of course, Laura Wade wasn't his problem. Rita Harmon was. And, right now, so was Emmanuel Garcia, even if he was a two-bit junkie shot in a drive-by a few nights ago whom the world was probably better off without.

Culligan was just putting on his coat when the phone rang. He picked it up. "Culligan. Tenth."

"Detective Henry Culligan?" The voice was female. "My name is Mindy Stewart, and I live at 210 West Eightieth Street. There's been a bomb here."

"Why are you calling me? Did you call 911?

"Someone did, but Dr. Goldman asked me to call you personally—"

"David Goldman?"

"It was his apartment that was bombed. He's okay. I think. Considering. I don't know why he asked me to call you."

"I'm on my way," Culligan said. The Garcia suspect would have to wait.

It took Culligan nearly twenty minutes to cut through the traffic from the precinct to the upper West Side. An ambulance was parking in front of the building. The paramedics were loading up a woman who'd been cut on the forehead by a shard of flying glass from the explosion on the twentieth floor.

A crowd of people was milling about in the hallway in back of the barricade when Culligan got off the elevator. The bomb squad had already arrived. Culligan showed his ID to the officer standing there, then went up to the gaping hole in the wall and peered into the apartment. It was a complete wreck. Must have been a nice apartment once.

David Goldman was silently watching the bomb squad at work, his arm wrapped in an Ace bandage and immobilized in a sling.

Detective Roger Ramirez, who was the only officer Culligan recognized, looked up from where he was working near what appeared to be the frame of a sliding glass door.

"Henry, this guy says he won't talk to anyone but you. The paramedics tried to take him to the hospital but he refused. Said he would wait for you."

Ramirez shrugged, then turned back to his work.

Culligan stepped over the jagged edges at the bottom of the hole and went up to Goldman. "Okay, Goldman, this isn't my beat, as they say, but I'm here. You okay?"

"My arm is hurt. I think it's only a sprain."

"How do you know?"

"I'm a doctor, remember?"

Culligan nodded. "So. What the hell happened here?"

Goldman stared at him for a moment. "Zachary Wade tried to kill me. That's what happened."

Culligan looked at the man.

"He must have had me followed," Goldman said. "It wasn't my imagination, after all. And when the guy following me saw where I went, he called him. He knew I was getting too close—"

"To his wife, from what I hear."

"You heard about that?"

"Of course I heard about it. Got yourself in a whole heap of trouble, from what I hear. I'll admit, it *does* look like Wade might've had a *motive* for killing you."

Goldman frowned. "His motive isn't what you think, detective."

"Oh, no? I'd be pretty mad if you'd bedded my wife. Course, I don't think I'd pull something like this, but I might—"

"Detective, listen! This isn't about jealousy. This is about revenge. This is about Rita Harmon. This is about a madman."

"Goldman, you're going to have to explain what you're talking about."

Goldman sighed. "Detective, do you know why you thought Laura Wade murdered Rita Harmon? The answer is because it *looks* like she did. And do you know *why* it looks like she did? Because it was set up so it would look that way."

"By who?"

"By her husband."

"So you're saying not only that Zachary Wade pulled this but he's the perp on the Harmon case, too?"

"Does Laura Wade *seem* like the kind of woman who could have murdered someone?"

"Well, she seems screwed up, that's for sure."

"Screwed up, as you put it, is one thing. Psychotic is one thing. Delusions are one thing. I'd say for a woman with Laura's gifts, for a woman who's been living with that man for fifteen years, the fact that she *isn't* psychotic is a minor miracle. But a true psychopath is a completely different animal."

"But Wade keeps saying his wife would never do such a thing. He certainly doesn't *seem* to want us to convict her, doctor."

"He doesn't."

"Now you've lost me. I thought you said he wanted us to think she did it."

"He doesn't care what you think, really. He set the whole thing up for *her*. He wants *her* to think she did it."

"I thought you said—"

"Look, Culligan, I'm sure you're a fine detective. But there's no way you could have ever figured this one out. Because you don't—and you never would—have access to all the facts. I'm the only one with access to all the facts. Laura Wade's facts. So you're going to have to bear with me for a moment. Because Zachary Wade killed that woman, and Zachary Wade set this up, as sure as I'm standing here."

"But why would Wade kill Rita Harmon, even if they *were* having an affair?"

"Forget the affair. This doesn't have anything to do with an affair. This has to do with Sophie Zophlick."

"Laura Wade's aunt?"

Goldman had suddenly turned pale. "I just need to sit down."

Culligan followed him into the bedroom, which didn't look too bad. Which showed the guy who set the bomb was no amateur.

Ramirez came to the bedroom door. "Looks like a real professional job, Henry."

"What's that mean?" Goldman asked, sitting down on the bed.

"Means the explosive device was set by an expert, a guy who knew exactly what he was doing, how much of a charge to set so he didn't blow out the entire building, how to rig a delay to the door, and also how to keep us from tracing it out." Ramirez went back into the other room.

"I'll tell you," Culligan said, turning back to Goldman, "you are one lucky bastard. How'd you manage to not get killed here?"

"I—I don't really know. I dropped some letters down the hall, and when I went back to get them . . ."

He shook his head. "Like I said, a lucky bastard."

Goldman was digging into his shirt pocket with the hand that wasn't in the sling. He grimaced as he pulled out a small stack of folded papers.

"You all right?" Culligan said. "Maybe you should have that looked at before you—"

"Not now. Read this letter." Goldman handed him the papers.

It was a Xerox of a letter dated June 8, 1945. Emmett Darwin, MD, Sixteen Main, Wichita.

"What the hell?"

"Read it."

Culligan scanned the letter.

"DeMane? Isn't that the name of the doctor the Zophlick woman murdered?"

Goldman was rooting through the drawers of a night table next to his bed.

"It's his son."

"Kassand didn't tell me he had a son."

"You didn't ask," Goldman said, producing a small vial of pills from a drawer, then heading into the bathroom.

"I don't get it," Culligan said, following him. "You hand me a forty-year-old letter about a twelve-year-old who was a disciplinary problem back in the forties. His name was Henry. Happens to be my name."

"I'm not talking about a disciplinary problem, detective," Goldman said, downing two pills with a plastic cup he picked up from the floor and filled with water. "I'm talking pre-psychopathic. *Read* the letter. I'm talking total amorality. I'm talking about a boy turning into a man who could have committed that murder, without even a twinge. Who could have done this, for Christ's sake, or at least hired someone to do it."

"You're saying Zachary Wade and Henry DeMane are the same person?"

"That's right. Now listen. There was the first murder, when Sophie Zophlick killed her doctor. That much Kassand told you, right?"

Culligan followed him back into the bedroom.

"Right."

"Well," Goldman said, "it as much as says right there in the letter that the little boy, Henry DeMane, witnessed that murder. Imagine it. He saw his own father cut up with a kitchen knife. And then he watched the murderer, Laura's aunt, take a knife to herself. Pretty traumatic thing for a four-year-old to see, wouldn't you say? Any psychiatrist will tell you it could make him hate women, especially a woman who looks just like Sophie Zophlick. I don't suppose you've seen the picture of Laura's aunt, detective. I have. The resemblance is astonishing.''

"Maybe it *would* make the boy hate her. Go on.''

"Well, after his father was murdered, Henry was shipped off to live with the Dreedles, in Lordsville, Kansas. It appears the adoptive parents developed a permissive attitude toward the boy's early antisocial behavior, because of what he'd been through at the age of four.'' Goldman handed him another letter. "The aunt said as much to Darwin, even used that as justification for not getting him the psychiatric help he needed.''

"So?''

"So. An attractive child whose acts of violence are met with permissiveness gets no help whatsoever in connecting cruelty, say, with its consequences. The consequence of punishment doesn't befall him because he can always manipulate his parents by playing to their sympathy. Poor orphaned boy. And such a terrible thing he saw. And look how sorry he is. The consequences of a guilty conscience, he doesn't even *feel.*''

Goldman sat down on the bed again. "Look, Culligan, I've never claimed to be an expert in criminal psychology, but I know this much. Psychopathic behavior almost always follows a set pattern in a person, a series of steps. It usually starts out early, in childhood. Small behaviors that seem minor, but if you know what you're looking for, they're very telling. Maybe the kid sets a fire or two, or maybe he pulls the wings off flies. His behavior is cruel, impulsive, deviant. I'd say slicing the head off a goat, which is what that letter from Emmett Darwin suggests he did, is pretty cruel, wouldn't you? I'd say attempting to rape a nine-year-old and then claiming she wanted him to is cruel, wouldn't you? I'd say his attitude—'What harm was done?' that's what he said to Darwin—indicates a lack of moral conscience, a complete absence of guilt feelings.''

Goldman handed him another piece of paper. It was a copy of an old high school transcript.

"Looks like the kid transferred out in the tenth grade," Culligan said.

"No. They stamped the transfers. This one just ends. No stamp saying he transferred. Maybe he just took off at sixteen and wandered around for a while, and maybe he showed up in Philadelphia ten or so years later with a new name, a new identity. And when Laura came of age, maybe he married her.''

"And Sam Gardner made him head of that business?''

"Why not? It's a family business, detective. There wasn't anyone else. Laura certainly wasn't interested, nor was her brother. And her sister is an architect. So Wade worked his way in, and up.''

"Sounds like a lot of maybes to me. For Christ's sake, if the kid was twelve when this letter was written, that would mean he's . . .''

"Fifty-three.''

"There you go. Zachary Wade doesn't look a day over forty-three, maybe four.''

"You've heard of plastic surgery, haven't you? And exercise? The guy's a fanatic.''

"I still don't get it, Goldman. What does Rita Harmon have to do with all this?''

"But that's just it. She's got nothing to do with it. *Laura's* the one he wants to punish. Just for being, just for *existing*." Goldman sighed, looked at him. "Detective, did you ever play chess?"

Now, the man really *had* lost him. "Yeah. When I was a kid."

"Did you ever sacrifice a bishop to get a queen?"

"Goldman—"

"The thing is, we—the both of us—came into the game not in the beginning but when it was well under way. Rita Harmon only died as a means to an end."

"What end?"

"Zachary Wade is trying to drive his wife mad. And doing a thorough job of it, wouldn't you agree? What he's doing, you see, is setting up events so that suddenly his wife's personal nightmares appear to be coming true. And that's where we come in. Rita Harmon's murder is his *pièce de résistance*. Three months ago, at a dinner party, eight witnesses see Laura Wade accuse Rita Harmon of coming on to him. Yes, she was angry at Rita Harmon. She even thought of scratching at her face. Have you ever been angry at someone, detective? What would you think if two weeks after you thought an angry thought, the object of your anger suddenly died?"

"A normal person would assume—"

"But that's just it. Laura Wade isn't a normal person."

Culligan looked at him. "You got a real thing for her, don't you?"

Goldman looked him straight in the eye. "All right, I've got a thing for her. But think about it, detective. In order to drive someone mad you'd have to find out your target's unique weaknesses, personality faults, fears. And then you'd play to them, work with them, use them. And what are Laura's particular weaknesses? Well, for one, she has precognitive visions.

But suddenly the visions don't seem so passive anymore. Suddenly it looks to her like she's somehow crossed the line from merely seeing the future to creating it. And that leaves her no way out, that leaves her guilty, because the events come directly out of those little emotions we all have—those jealous thoughts, those angry thoughts, those fears, those unacceptable dreams. Can you stop an emotion? Can I? No one can.''

"But why would she suddenly come to the conclusion that she put a hex on Rita Harmon's murderer?"

"Because her husband spent fifteen years laying the groundwork for the delusion to develop. And what's the delusion? That she's worthless, evil. So evil, in fact, that she can kill people with her poison.''

"What kind of groundwork? Does he beat her?"

"Absolutely not. He's far too smooth for that. He has to convince the world that they're the perfect loving couple. No. Psychological cruelty can be much worse. When they're alone, he tells her she's incompetent, he berates her, he wears her down, he destroys her ego, which is in the basement to begin with. He's cruel to her. Maybe humiliates her. Or worse, he's indifferent to her. Fifteen years of cruelty and indifference, detective. Think of it.''

"How could any woman live with a man like that for years on end?"

"Most women wouldn't. But Laura believes herself unworthy of life, let alone love and kindness.''

Culligan took off his glasses, pulled a handkerchief out of his pocket and began to clean them. "My wife wants me to quit this damned racket," he said. "She was bugging me about it last night, again. Says it makes me a nervous nut. You think I'm a nervous nut, doctor?''

"Detective . . ."

Culligan put his glasses back on. "And you know what I told her? I told her I would, which is a lie, but it's a nice thing to think about. I'm sure not quitting until I figure out what's going on in this goddamned case."

"Don't you see? Laura Wade *handed* him a way to drive her mad. Just by being who she is."

Culligan lit up a cigarette. "I'll admit, it does make some sense. But how does he know what to do, what fears to use? Does she tell him?"

"No. Both of them told me she never talks to him about these things."

"Then how . . ." Culligan looked at him. "Of course. She *paints* them."

David Goldman let out a long, deep sigh.

"That's right. She paints them. You saw that painting on the easel, *Nightmare under the Moon*. She's the demon licking the blood from its claws, ten claws. Don't you see? He used that painting to know exactly how to commit the murder so Laura would think she was responsible for Rita Harmon's death."

Culligan stared at him. "And if anyone—like, say, a detective—ever saw the painting, he'd think she was, too."

"Did you by any chance look through Laura's *other* paintings?" Goldman asked.

"Pretty gruesome stuff."

"Did you happen to notice the painting of the tiger? The one attacking the woman?"

"I don't really remember."

"It was there. I saw it myself. Laura Wade *paints* her fears, her personal demons, her nightmares. And the tiger attack was one of her nightmares. She dreamed that a tiger would attack her friend. She told me about it in a session; I have it in my notes. And on tape.''

''You guys tape your sessions?''

''Sometimes. And a few weeks later, the Wades' dog—a doberman—attacked the same friend. And between the time of the dream and the time of the attack, she painted it. Wade sees the tiger painting. He stages the dog attack. He may even have trained, no, he *did* train the dog to bite the neighbor. Unusual behavior for a dog of that kind, a doberman, who in a frenzy of attack might easily *kill* a person—to get out of his pen and run up to a specific person—and bite her on the right hand. Why didn't the dog really *attack* her? Because dobermans are smart animals. They can be *trained*. And Wade trained the dog to do exactly what he wanted it to do. He staged that attack completely and wholly for his wife's benefit. And then there's the matter of her father's death.''

''Yeah, I read the obit. You gonna tell me Wade staged Sam Gardner's death of cardiac arrest?''

''Detective, you know as well as I do, that there are ways to stimulate cardiac arrest. Chemical ways. And that if no one suspects anything, the body goes into the ground without further examination.''

Culligan looked at him. Christ. If Goldman was right, Wade had to be the most cold-blooded killer he'd ever come across. Smooth. Convincing. Just the right amount of indignation. Or maybe Goldman was the arrogant one, to suggest such a thing after having bedded the guy's wife.

''So you're saying Wade knew his wife was angry at her father and took advantage of that, too. Are you going to tell me why she was angry at her father?''

''Yes, I am. You see, Sam Gardner never did tell Laura about her aunt. And after *you* told her about it, she confronted her father and they had a terrible fight. She had a dream one night, in which—''

''He had a heart attack.''

''In which she touched her father's chest, which caused a heart attack. And I saw one of her paintings. Actually, a drawing, a sketch for a painting. It was of a demon touching an old man's chest.''

Culligan took a deep drag on his cigarette, drew the hot smoke into his lungs. ''I suppose I could get the body exhumed and get an autopsy,'' he said. ''Christ! Do you know how hard that would be? Do you know how bureaucracies work? In this case, two bureaucracies, both the New York and the Philadelphia police departments. Not to mention the fact that an exhumation order requires a lot more than conjecture, which is all you have.''

Goldman was staring at him, shaking his head. ''In any case, there might not even be anything to find. Because in addition to chemical means, a heart attack in a sixty-five-year-old man might also be stimulated in other ways. Say, by upsetting him.''

''How?''

''Well, it seems Sam Gardner showed Laura a picture of Sophie Zophlick. Gave it to her, in fact, at her insistence. And I found out the other day that Sam Gardner hadn't kept that picture over the years. Certainly not. He spent his life trying to forget he *had* a sister, not keeping mementos of her. Someone sent the photograph to him, within the past few months.''

''Wade?''

''Who else? Sam Gardner said he lost touch with his sister after she was committed in 1935. But the date on the photograph was 1937. It has to have been taken at the instigation of Elias DeMane, Henry

DeMane's father. And he had it among his things. After his death, it must have gone with the boy.''

Culligan ran his cigarette under water from the faucet in the sink, then threw it in the trashcan. ''I'll admit it does hang together. But where's the proof? Where's the evidence linking DeMane and Wade?''

''Well, I . . . You're the detective. I was hoping *you'd* figure out how to prove all of this.''

Culligan glanced out into the other room, where the bomb squad was still working, then looked back at Goldman. ''Well, we might get lucky here, for one thing. Have you got something else?''

The man stood up, looked at him. ''You said once that coincidences bothered you. Here's a coincidence for you. The name of Zachary Wade's doberman was Darwin. Ring any bells, detective?''

Culligan glanced back at the letter he was holding. ''Emmett Darwin, MD. The dog could be named after him. He could also be named after Charles Darwin. Or no Darwin at all. Just a name.''

''Maybe, but I don't think so. This guy hates psychiatrists. I grant you many people distrust psychiatrists, but how many people truly hate them? You know what he said to me once? He said, 'I should have known what would happen when one of your kind interfered.' ''

''Interfered?''

''Pretty odd thing to say, don't you think, even if my own behavior wasn't . . . exactly . . . proper? Doesn't that suggest something to you?''

''Possibly. Why don't we ask the dog who he's named after?''

''Very funny. The dog happens to be dead.''

''That's right, it wasn't in the pen the second time I went up there. What happened to it?''

"Zachary Wade shot it."

"He *shot* the dog?"

"With a thirty-eight he keeps in the house. For protection."

"Yeah, I saw it. He has a license for it."

"No doubt."

"Why'd he shoot the dog?"

"Because the dog attacked the neighbor."

Culligan looked at him. "I'd shoot a doberman who attacked my neighbor, too."

"Tell me, would you shoot the dog right there by the pool, with your three children and your neighbor's children watching?"

"Well, no, I suppose not. But Wade doesn't seem . . . I mean, he's arrogant as hell, but he runs that business, been running it for years. Tell me how a guy that crazy runs a phenomenally successful business?"

"We're not talking about a psychotic individual here, detective. Very often psychopaths don't suffer from debilitating hallucinations, or delusions that psychotics suffer from. Except for the one delusion, of course."

"Which is?"

"That anything they do is justified."

Culligan hesitated. "I agree, shooting a dog in the presence of your children indicates a certain cruelty. Stupid, even brutal. But what does it *prove*? It's not even against the law."

"Can't you see the correlation between shooting the dog that way and the murder? And *this*?" Goldman said. "The arrogance? The reckless disregard for what's right and what's wrong? Can't you see that a man who might do that and this, might also slice up the face of that poor woman, slowly, as if he had all the time in the world, right out there on the street corner, where anyone could come along?''

There was a certain correlation. But it wasn't a legally usable correlation. Still, unless Laura Wade had committed the perfect crime, leaving no shred of physical evidence, Goldman's scenario was the only possible explanation for her knowing about the ten cuts. And there was *this* mess to consider. Of course, this *could* be a disgruntled patient. Who the hell knew?

Culligan turned back to Goldman. ''So what's Wade going to do to her now?'' he said. ''Murder her?''

''No, I think what he's been planning to do all along is to convince her that she has no way out, that eventually her poison will wipe out everyone she cares about. No way out—so she takes her own life. With Laura's history, which already includes suicide attempts, it's like taking candy from a baby.''

''I get it,'' Culligan said. ''Consumed by guilt, she kills herself. Case closed. Not a loose end in sight. Not only is the bereaved husband above suspicion, not only has he got his revenge, he gets her money too. Plenty of that.'' Culligan got up. Now it was his turn to pace. ''You know what?'' he said. ''I bet he never even considered the fact that she might walk in and confess to the murder. Maybe he saw it as a setback, at first, but then he decides he can work with it after all. It gives him a fallback plan.''

''What do you mean?''

''If she doesn't kill herself, maybe he produces a piece of physical evidence that will give us what we need to convict her. There are ways to transfer a print from one object to another. Boom. Away she goes for life.'' Culligan looked at Goldman. It still didn't make sense. "But why's he doing all this to his wife, when she isn't even the one who killed his father?"

"You're giving me logic," Goldman said. "I'm giving you madness."

Culligan walked over to the window and looked out. It was very far down to the street . . . Wade's alibi certainly wasn't airtight. His office building was very close to the murder scene. Maybe he called Harmon and told her to meet him. No, that didn't work unless they were having an affair. So maybe Wade knew where Rita Harmon was going that night, too. But how? Of course. Laura Wade told him at some point during the day, informed him she'd canceled her meeting with Rita because Rita was going to St. Germain. But how could Wade have fooled him so completely? He'd interviewed the guy twice. Maybe because Culligan wanted Laura Wade to have done it, since he couldn't think of any other explanation for her knowing so much about the murder. Maybe he'd *allowed* himself to be fooled.

"So, are you going to arrest him?" Goldman asked.

"Not so fast," Culligan said. "I can't march in and arrest a guy without any proof. Let's just wait and see what the bomb squad turns up. Also, our witness finally agreed to be hypnotized. This afternoon."

"Hey, that's a good idea."

The man looked shocked. So what did he think the NYPD was? A bunch of morons?

There was a silence.

Suddenly Goldman said, "Zachary Wade's adoptive sister! Her transcript was in the files, too. Her name was Barbara Dreedle. I didn't copy the file, but I remember it said she transferred to a school in some other town in Kansas, I think it was Topeka. Maybe she'd be willing to identify him."

"Maybe. Okay, look. Why don't you get over to the hospital and get your arm set? I've got my interview to do. All this is gonna take some time to check out. Meanwhile, if what you're saying is true, right now Wade thinks you're dead, and that may work to our benefit."

"Then you believe me," David said. "Thank God for that."

"It's not a question of belief, Goldman," he said. "It's a question of evidence." He walked over to the door. The room was packed with officers now. The media had arrived.

Culligan recognized Sergeant Detective John Alonso.

"Hey, John."

Alonso came over. "Hey, Henry. What are *you* doing here?"

"I was personally invited by the victim," Culligan said. "Let's get someone to give this guy in here a ride to the hospital. And I think it would be a good idea not to tell the media what happened. Let's just tell 'em details are sketchy."

"Sure thing. Why?"

"It's a long story, John. I'll run it down for you just as soon as we get Dr. Goldman out of here." He turned back to Goldman.

"You know, Goldman, if what you're saying is true, he's had this whole thing planned out to the nth degree, but I think pulling this was his mistake."

"Why?"

"Because he's gotta know he'd be the first one we'd think of with a motive to do this."

Goldman shrugged. "But he doesn't have any choice."

"I warn you, doc, if you've got me started on a wild goose chase, I'm going to arrest you."

"For what?"

He grinned. "For obstruction of justice. Impeding an investigation. Giving false information to the police. I can think of something real good. Trust me."

38

Doug Gray's melodious voice could have given him a second career on radio. Small and trim, with bushy red hair, he seemed younger than Culligan remembered him. His left hand was missing a finger. That, Culligan remembered.

Lilly had brought her boyfriend with her. Gray told him to wait outside, ushered Culligan and the girl into his office. Culligan wondered if Lilly would be susceptible to hypnosis at all, considering all the noise outside Gray's office. He could even hear the girl's boyfriend talking to someone.

Once they had all sat down, Gray spent some time preparing Lilly. He reminded her that her participation was entirely voluntary, and that she could leave at any time or refuse to answer any question she didn't want to.

"I thought under hypnosis I would be . . . well *forced* to answer whatever you asked," she said.

"Not at all. You'll be perfectly aware of what you're saying, Lilly," Gray said, then he proceeded to explain just what he would be doing.

"A witness to a traumatic event often suffers what's

called traumatic amnesia, in which case, they're unable to recall certain details that hypnosis can bring to consciousness.''

"But I remember it," Lilly said firmly. "I have dreams about it all the time. Nightmares.''

"You'd be surprised at how many little details go with any event, Lilly. The conscious mind can't possibly deal with all information available at any given moment. You might say hypnosis helps push all the details—too many for anybody to remember under normal circumstances—from the subconscious into the conscious.''

He began with a series of eye exercises, then took out a small silver ball bearing on a string and suggested that she concentrate successively on relaxing each part of her body. After a little over half an hour, Lilly seemed to be in a deep trance. She was lying on the couch with her eyes open.

Culligan glanced at his watch and turned on the tape recorder.

Doug Gray began speaking into the microphone.

"The date is November second, and the time is one-thirty P.M. This is Douglas Gray of the Chief of Detectives office, Hypnosis Section. With me is Detective Henry Culligan of the Tenth Precinct. We're here to interview Miss Lilly Dunleavy. . . .

"All right, Lilly, I'm about to use the standard deepening procedure I explained to you. I want you to count to ten, very slowly, and I want you to picture yourself in a well. With each count you are further down the well. Think of yourself as deeper down the well with each count. Picture it in your mind. Say 'deeper' as you float down the well. Now begin.''

In a slow, relaxed voice, Lilly began to count.

"One . . . deeper . . . two . . . deeper . . . three . . ."

Another minute, and Culligan would have been under himself. The man knew his business.

When Lilly finished counting, Gray said, "Now I want to take you back to the day of the murder. Think back to the night of August tenth. You are working late in the office. It's summer, the air conditioning isn't working. It's very hot. Picture yourself sitting at the desk. Picture everything. What you're wearing. What articles are on the desk. Picture yourself sitting there, as if you're there now."

There was a long silence, then Gray said. "You're sitting there, at the desk, Lilly. What are you doing?"

"Typing the report. It's taking forever. I have to keep staring at the monitor. My eyes hurt."

"How are you sitting?"

"My shoes are off. It's hot, my back hurts. . . . "

Culligan listened as Lilly described getting up from the chair, walking over to the window, seeing the two figures in the street—one prone, the other kneeling.

"What's the prone figure doing?"

"Just lying there. She isn't moving. Her feet—I can see the high heels—are in a funny angle . . . sort of twisted."

"And the figure that's kneeling?"

"I . . . can see a knife. He begins slicing at her face. It reminds me of carving. One . . . two . . . three . . ."

Culligan looked at Gray as Lilly counted up to ten. It was remarkable, though there wasn't anything really new in the description, except her memory of it. Gray didn't seem the least bit concerned. He continued prompting, always careful not to plant any details in the witness's mind.

"Okay, Lilly, what does he do then?"

"He stands up and turns around. Now he's facing me. . . . He's holding the knife in his hand."

"Which hand?"

"The right."

"What does he do?"

"He puts the knife in his pocket."

"Which pocket?"

"The one on the right side of the jacket."

"What does he do then?"

"No. It's at the same time. He puts the knife in the pocket and at the same time he starts walking. He's walking very slowly toward me."

"Describe his clothes."

"Jeans. Dark coat—short. Bomber style. A ski mask."

"Picture the ski mask, Lilly. What color is it?"

She narrowed her eyes, as if she was actually seeing the mask. After a moment, she said, "I can't tell. It's too dark."

Damn. There was nothing new here. Of course it was early, but according to Alonso, the bomb job in Goldman's apartment was a model of precision. It was an eighteen-inch homemade pipe bomb filled with gunpowder and scrap metal, old-fashioned, but not a stray fingerprint on it, or anywhere else in the apartment. They *had* found a print of *Laura* Wade's in the apartment, though, on the windowsill in the bedroom. Culligan had correlated it in the computer himself. But they couldn't arrest Zachary Wade just because he seemed to have a motive.

"All right, Lilly," Gray was saying, "the man is walking. Now what does he do?"

"He . . . he walks."

"And?"

She hesitated a moment, straining. Then she said, "And he opens the door and gets in, on the driver's side."

Doug Gray looked at Culligan. "What does he get in, Lilly?"

"A big car. It's there, on the street. It's parked."

"What kind of car?" Gray asked.

"A big car. A very long, very big car."

"What color, Lilly?"

"Black. It's a Cadillac."

Henry Culligan looked at Gray and grinned from ear to ear.

David Goldman sounded panicked on the phone.

"They let Laura Wade out of the hospital this morning, detective."

Culligan hesitated, wondering if he should tell him. "How's your arm?"

"Hairline fracture. Not too bad. Detective, Laura is in danger. You've got to do something."

Culligan decided he would tell Goldman what the witness remembered; he owed the man that much. "I just got back from interviewing the witness, Goldman. She suddenly remembered something that seems to confirm your theory."

"What?"

"A limousine at the scene of the murder."

"A *limousine*?"

"I think it's a first."

"How could she forget a limousine?"

"You're the shrink. You know what trauma can do. Plus, there's a lot of limousines in Manhattan these days. I hardly notice them myself anymore."

There was a long silence. Then Goldman said, "I'm

going up there. Believe me, detective. Laura's in danger.''

"Let me give you your first lesson in police work, doctor. You gotta be patient.''

"Kind of like psychiatry," Goldman said.

Culligan laughed. "I suppose it is, at that.''

"Why did you become a cop, detective?''

"You gonna analyze my answer?''

"No," Goldman said. "Just curious.''

"Never gave it that much thought, to tell you the truth. Dad was a cop. Two uncles were cops. Even my sister's a cop. Guess you could say it's in my blood. Irish blood. What's in Jewish blood?''

Now Goldman laughed. "Psychiatry, I suppose. And patience.''

"I hope so. Don't go sailing up there, doc, thinking you're gonna save the day. Wait for us to get there.''

"I think I can handle Zachary Wade, detective.''

"How? Get him to lie down on the couch and ask him about his mother?''

"Detective—''

"I'm warning you, Goldman, while you're up there saving the day, you might just get yourself killed.''

39

David glanced at his watch. Four o'clock. Where the hell was Culligan? Though he hadn't mentioned it, he was already in Easterbrook when he called the detective. It had taken him about two hours to have his arm looked after. He'd called

Rolling Hills from a pay phone at Roosevelt Hospital and found out Laura had been released, but when he couldn't reach Culligan after that, he'd headed up to Connecticut. It had been almost an hour since he'd spoken to the detective from a pay phone just off the highway at the Easterbrook exit.

David looked back at Laura's house, across the street and one house down from the shrubbery he was standing behind. There had been no movement on the street for nearly half an hour, the only sound that of waves lapping gently at the private beaches so close by. The house itself was silent. Laura's Mercedes was parked in the driveway; the limousine was behind it. Where the hell were the kids? They should have been back from school by now.

He decided he'd waited long enough.

Slipping through the open iron gate in front of the house next door, he headed into the backyard and across the grass to Laura's back property. He could see the pool, covered up tight for the winter, and the small stretch of beach. There was a dock off to one side, a red speedboat parked beside it. The boat from David's dream.

He made his way around the side of the house, went up to a window and peered in. It was the dining room. Empty. Christ! His arm hurt. He'd decided he needed to be completely alert for this and hadn't taken a painkiller since the one he took from his drawer hours ago.

He found Laura at the next window. In the kitchen, all gleaming chrome and heavy blond oak. Laura was sitting on a chair, her body pale and slack as a lump of dough.

Zachary Wade was standing across the room in front of a counter, arms folded across his chest. His expression was hard to read. Amusement? Anger?

David could read his lips.

"You don't deserve to live, Laura. Witches don't deserve to live."

He'd arrived right in the middle of it. And still no sign of Culligan or his men. He had to divert Wade, stop what was happening. Culligan would surely come soon.

He banged on the window. They both turned and saw him at the same moment. Zachary Wade's jaw dropped open, but he recovered from the shock in seconds, shoved Laura aside as she moved to open the door.

He could hear them arguing.

He ran around front to the garden, found a rock about the size of a softball, ran back to the kitchen window. Laura was sitting down again on the chair, looking up at her husband.

David smashed the rock through the window.

"Let me in!"

In a moment the door swung open and David was face to face with Zachary Wade. He was standing there, tall, confident, just the way he'd looked the first time David saw him. He made the slightest of bows, then stepped aside to let David pass, kicked the door shut easily with his foot. Shards of glass were spread out across the floor.

"Sammy's missing," Laura whispered, sinking back into the chair. Then, even softer, "It happened again, David. I dreamed he was missing, and now he's gone." She put her head in her hands and moaned. "My baby, my baby . . ."

David turned to face Zachary Wade. In his entire life, he had never been so incensed. Sammy was the man's *son,* his flesh and blood. He was using his own son to destroy his wife. And the worst part about it was that he probably didn't even *need* to. Laura had already decided to take her own life; David was sure of it. As soon as she got out of the hospital. Maybe even this very day. Zachary Wade's plan had succeeded.

"What have you done with him?" he screamed, louder than he ever thought he was capable of screaming.

Wade didn't seem to respond to either the volume or the tone of David's voice.

"What have *I* done? The kid is missing, that's all. Probably nothing. Probably wandered off from that four-thousand-dollar nursery school. And those people just let him go. I told her he'd find his way back." The words rolled off his tongue; not a single facial muscle betrayed the lie. His mask remained cold, firm, immobile.

"What have you done with him?"

Laura was looking back and forth from David to her husband, tears rolling down her cheeks, her hands furiously kneading the fabric of her sweater.

"What are you talking about, David?" she said. "It was *me*. It's *my* fault. I infected Sammy."

"No, Laura. He *took* your son. He wants you to think your dream has come true. He's got Sammy somewhere."

She stared at him. "What . . . what do you mean?"

"Laura," David said, "did you call the police?"

She stared at him. "The police can't find Sammy. It was me—"

"Laura, think! Shouldn't your *husband* have called the police?"

She looked at him. "He knows the police can never find—"

"Laura, this man doesn't love you. He's never loved

you. Your entire life with him has been a charade. Your powers are good. They're a very special gift. He made you see yourself as evil, but it's what *he* is. Laura, he's completely mad.''

"Mad?'' Wade said. "You fuck my wife, then you come in here and call me mad?''

David held out his arm. "You tried to kill me.''

"If I tried to kill you, then why aren't you dead?''

David moved toward him. His feet made a crunching noise as he walked on the glass-strewn floor.

"You had it all planned out, DeMane, and it was pretty good, too, but planting a bomb in my apartment, that was your big mistake.''

Wade stared at David, expressionless for a moment, then said, "My big mistake was that I didn't kill you the moment I laid eyes on you.''

Suddenly he grabbed David's jacket collar and pinned him up against the wall.

"Now you listen to me, you little fuck. You come near my wife again and I *will* kill you.''

David had a vague sensation of drowning; he couldn't breathe, he was strangling, struggling. It felt like Wade was pressing his entire weight against David's arm. The pain—

"Zach, stop it!'' Laura screamed.

"Go upstairs, Laura,'' Wade said. "I'll take care of lover-boy here.''

"Zach—''

"Laura. Go upstairs.''

If was a fifteen-year-old dance they were doing. He pushed her down; she was up again, stronger than he thought; he pushed her down again. But this time the music had stopped, and she wasn't dancing. She stayed put.

"Let him go, Zach.''

Inexplicably, he released his hold on David and stepped back. David could see tiny beads of perspiration standing out on his forehead.

"Tell me, how did it *feel* to touch her?" Zach Wade said. "Did you fuck her and fuck her until you were blue in the face? Till you thought your prick would fall off, so cold in the Death Witch?"

David looked at him. There was an odd, deathly pallor to his face.

"Death Witch?"

"Why, yes. You've met her. Of course, this one's a pale imitation of the first. The first one played nice little games. Let's-guess-what-we're-thinking games—"

"You're a madman," David screamed.

Wade laughed. "What an arrogant fool you are, just like the rest of your kind. How could you dare call me mad when you see what I've done here? Just look at her. I can create madness right here in my laboratory. I have. She wouldn't have lasted the day."

Slowly Laura turned to her husband and fixed him with a dark penetrating stare, her eyes boring in.

David looked at her. She had to know. She had to understand. "Laura, think! Listen to his words, his thoughts. Listen. For God's sake, for the first time, really *listen.*"

She squeezed her eyes shut, covered her face with her hands.

"No!"

"Laura, you've got to. You've got to listen to him."

"No."

"Laura, when he killed the dog, *what did you think*? What do you think *now*?"

David stood there for a moment, watching her close her eyes against the truth. But when she opened them,

she was looking directly into his eyes, her face con-
torted in the agony of recognition. Finally. She *knew*.

"You hate me, Zach," she whispered. The words
were an elegy. Infinitely sad.

"Hate you?" he said. "I hate no one. Least of all
you."

She looked at David. "How could I not have
known?"

"You didn't want to know, Laura," David said.
"You denied it. You didn't listen."

"No. With him I just didn't hear."

David turned back to Wade. He was sitting down
now on the desk, calmly, legs crossed, as if he were
a guest in a neighbor's kitchen. Only, he was aiming
a .38-caliber pistol right at David's face.

"Zach?" Laura said, softly. "Have you hurt
Sammy? You haven't hurt him. You wouldn't—"

"Shut up. I have to think."

David considered attempting to grab the gun. If he
could just pick the right moment. He looked back at
the man, sitting there, staring at him, aiming the
weapon at his head. What the hell was he thinking?
Physically, David was no match for him, even without
a fractured arm.

"Now," Wade said, "why don't the three of us sit
down. We can have a little talk."

"Where is Sammy? Where have you got him?"

"Sit down!"

"Laura, where are the girls?"

"They're at a friend's house." She was leaning
against the sink, looking at her husband as if she'd
never seen him before. Slowly, she approached him,
bent over him, her face very close to the gun.

"Why, Zach?"

"Why what?"

"I felt it," Laura said, backing up a step. "I always felt it, but I never understood what it was."

"Henry," David said, as calmly as he could, "put the gun down. You don't want to do this. You know you don't want to do this. We can help you. We can—"

Wade began to laugh a high, shrill, childish laugh. Then he stopped. "You think you can trick me, trip me up. Well, you can't. This is my party, and I've waited fifteen years for it. Can you imagine fifteen years with this woman, this crazy, frigid bitch—"

"What did I do, Zach?" Laura said softly. "What did I do to you?"

He was staring at her. "You killed my father."

"Zach, it wasn't me! It was Sophie. She's—"

"Shut up!"

She drew away from him and whispered, "You killed *my* father."

He looked at her, smiling, amused. Then he looked at David and cupped his hand around his mouth, as if he were about to share a private joke. "Bad ticker. Didn't have to." He stopped smiling. "But the two of you, on the other hand . . . I'll have to think of something real good for you, shrink. I know. How about I hook you up to that electric outlet over there? Shock you out of existence." He chuckled. "Electric shock therapy. How about that?"

He was silent for a moment.

"What have you done with Sammy, Zach? He's our son."

"Pity he has you for a mother."

"Where is he?"

He looked at her. "Quite simple, really. All I had to do was wait until you had one of your bad-thoughts that always upset you so much. Sure enough, you dropped one into my lap the other day during that non-sense with your new shrink doctor.''

"I told you about my dream in the session,'' she said.

He looked at her, smiled. "Of course, I was partial to the original plan,'' he said, looking now at David, "in which the Death Witch kills herself, but it seems I'll have to make allowances for a change in circumstances. It's just a question of how. These things must be done—''

"You killed Rita!" Laura screamed. "You used my paintings! You made me think—''

"The paintings!'' he said, smiling broadly. He got up, moved toward them. "The paintings. Why don't we all go upstairs and take at look at the paintings? Yes, I think that's an excellent idea. Maybe once we're up there we can have Laura do one of her little gothic nightmares. Maybe a picture of a pair of lovers. Dead lovers. Lying there in all their naked glory. Think how complete the circle would be. One kills the other and then kills herself. Perfect!''

He closed in, shoved the gun into David's side.

"Now move.''

Laura's studio was flooded with afternoon sunshine. The paintings were all there, just as David remembered them. Just as shocking, moving, disturbing. The fire. The tiger. *Nightmare under the Moon* was still on the easel. It looked more shadowed than he remembered, the figures eerier, more sharply drawn, more real. The blood on the demon's claws was a deep purplish red. David looked around. Tacked onto the drawing table was the charcoal sketch of Laura's father, with the demon at his chest.

Wade ordered them to sit on the floor, then rooted

through a pile of sketch pads on a table, pulled one out and handed it to Laura. Taking a charcoal pencil from one of the easels, he threw it at the pad. It bounced off and landed by Laura's feet.

"Now draw!"

"Zach, you can't be serious!"

He aimed the gun at David's head. "Draw!"

"Draw what?"

"I've already told you. Two dead lovers." He began pacing the floor around them, circling them like a tiger closing in for the kill, keeping the gun aimed at David's head.

Slowly Laura picked up the pencil and with a trembling hand made a flowing line on the paper. And another. Within moments she had created the outline of a woman lying on her back, eyes closed. The woman was naked, with one arm extended out and the other bent over her heart. The woman looked like Laura, of course. Had she not, in canvases all over the room, always been painting herself? Sometimes with claws, sometimes with teeth, but always herself?

Wade came over to inspect the drawing. "Very good. And now the other."

In a few moments, she would be finished. In a few moments he would kill them, and then leave them there with the sketch. David had to do something. Maybe he could try to reach the little boy.

"Henry," he said, "it must have been a terrible thing for you to see your father—"

"Don't you talk about my father!"

David looked up at the man towering over him. Yes, that was it.

"But you *want* to talk about it, Henry. No one ever talked about it, isn't that right? You *loved* your father. You *needed* him. No one ever understood that."

"My father was weak. Death Witch lover. Not a man at all." Wade had turned to face David directly now; there was a growling sound coming out of his throat.

Slowly, David stood up and faced him. "Henry, your father loved you, too—"

"I do not want your pity."

"Henry, you need my pity. You deserve it."

"I deserve nothing." The hand holding the gun was wavering.

"You were a little boy. No little boy should have seen so much blood."

Wade was making another sound now between clenched teeth, part cry, part howl. And there was yet another sound.

The wail of a siren.

Zachary Wade stood frozen, gun still in hand, sweat pouring from his brow. Listening, he cocked his head to one side like an animal, then whirled around, and—with a last look at Laura that David would never forget—was out the door. Down the stairs.

David ran after him, Laura close behind. But by the time they got down to the back door, across the lawn, and onto the dock, they both realized they were too late. They heard the roar of the speedboat, heading out onto the open sound.

The two of them stood there on the dock, watching the boat move farther and farther out until it shimmered like a tiny red jewel on the metallic surface of the water.

"I know where Sammy is, David," Laura said suddenly. "Zach didn't kill him. Not yet. I saw it in his mind."

David put his arms around her, gathered her in. The

two of them stood there on the dock before the open
sea.

They turned, and suddenly they were face-to-face
with Henry Culligan, and behind him a sea of police
uniforms.

40 Three months later, David pulled up
in front of Laura's house and found Sammy outside,
all bundled up in a snowsuit, sitting under the bare
beech tree, playing with a fleet of plastic trucks in the
snow.

"Hi, Dr. Goldman."

David trudged over to him, knelt down and looked
him right in the eyes. Laura's eyes, deep brown, almost black.

"Sammy, would it be okay with you to call me David?"

"All right, David, but you're not my daddy."

"Of course not, Sammy. I know that."

The boy went back to his trucks, zoomed one around
in front of him, then looked up.

"Where *is* my daddy?"

Suddenly the events of the past months came back
to him. David saw himself standing on the dock watching Zachary Wade speed across the sound; rushing
into the hotel room with Culligan and his men, finding
Sammy, scared but unharmed; the long manhunt for
Zachary Wade beginning with a call to the Coast Guard
and ending with a trail gone dead at Kennedy Airport

on a plane to South America; finding out from Culligan that Barbara Dreedle Moore had confirmed Wade's identity; trying to explain it all to Laura's children; seeing their anger at both of them, and Laura's gentle, persistent attempts to win them back; both of them testifying before the AMA Board of Ethics; the board's decision not to revoke his license.

"Where *is* my daddy, David?"

"Your daddy was very sick, Sammy," David said. "He was so sick he couldn't be here with you anymore. He had to go away."

"What kind of sick?"

David had explained it to him so many times, yet he would explain it to him again, as often as he had to. Whatever harm Zachary Wade had done to the children, well, they would deal with that in their own time, when they were ready.

"Was my daddy sick like with the measles?" Sammy said.

"In the head, Sammy. With something that gets into the mind somehow and makes a person do bad things."

"But why did he take me to that place and leave me there all by myself?"

"I don't know why, Sammy. I doubt if *he* even knows."

"Sammy, come on in now," Laura called from the doorway. "It's getting cold." Standing there, she looked more beautiful than he'd ever seen her. She'd made a lot of progress over the last months. So many things to be sorted out, so much pain to be confronted, so much denial.

"Sammy?"

He said, "Aw, Mom. Don't worry so much," but he grabbed his trucks and headed inside.

She opened the door wide for David to come in.

"Niles Martin called again, David." she said.

"And?"

"And I'm thinking about his proposition. It's a hard thing for me to share my secrets with the world."

"I know it is," David said. "Speaking of your secrets, how is the new work coming?"

"It's finished. Want to see it?"

They climbed up to the attic. Once inside, she had him stand about three feet back from the easel while she slowly lifted the cloth from the painting.

David looked at the work. It was extraordinary, as good as anything she'd ever done, a painting of great richness and depth, containing none of the demon imagery in her other work yet evoking the same elemental emotions, the same solemnity, the same sense of both nightmare and reality—created by a delicate, almost imperceptible blending of shadow and light with layer upon layer of pigment.

It was a dark work, the spacious panorama of a wide muddy river and its bank under the dome of threatening, thunderstruck sky. The landscape, solemn and mysterious, was rendered entirely in blacks and browns and deep greens. Within the thick dark tangle of vines and moisture-laden fronds spilling into the mud at the river's edge, one could sense rather than see creatures of all shapes and sizes and varieties, all watching, waiting, perched on every tree branch, crawling along the jungle floor beneath the foliage, in the water itself.

"I call it *Morning*," she said. "Technically, it's pretty good, don't you think?"

David put his arm around her. She was a special person, Laura Wade, to be so gifted, twice gifted. Yet both of her gifts arose from the same vision, didn't they? All she needed was to remove the blinders, to give herself the courage to open that extra set of eyes.

"You're still painting your dreams, aren't you?"

"This one should be psychiatrist-approved, David," she said. "Doing it helped me come to terms with my anger."

"I'll tell you one person who hasn't come to terms with his anger. Henry Culligan."

"Because Zach got away?"

David nodded.

"But he didn't get away, David."

He looked at her. "How do you know? Did Culligan find him?"

She laughed. "How is it that the man I love is so thick?"

"You must really be getting better if you're calling me names."

She pointed at the painting. "He's there, David. I saw it in my dream."

David looked back at the canvas, wondering, not for the first time, if he understood anything at all about people, about madness, about life.

Near the center of the painting was the focal point: a tiny image, swimming in the water, the small figure of a man with blond hair and delicate features, a perfect likeness. The creamy white flesh tones of the man's skin were painted almost lovingly. He seemed to glow with a radiant light from within, as if he were the single light source that illuminated the entire scene from the water. He was gazing upward toward the sky, his arms extended over his head, palms up, as if to seek salvation. But his mouth was gaping open in a soundless, agonized scream.

41 Doctor Raoul Mendez was very proud of his new X-ray machine. It had come only a month ago, brought to his clinic by truck from Manaus, a long, arduous journey over difficult terrain through the rain forest. Stupid bureaucrats. The Mendez Clinic was doing important work here. These people needed the modern medicine Mendez brought to them, even if it came in the form of a one-room hospital with barely running water and a twenty-year-old X-ray machine.

Of course, the X-ray machine wouldn't help the man in the far cot. A couple of local Indians had brought him in that morning, dragged him from the muddy banks of the river, where he had been sprawled, delivered him to the door of the clinic and then run away, leaving him outside on the dirt in front screaming in pain.

He was a very unfortunate man.

Mendez wiped the back of his neck with his handkerchief. It was so hot in this place at this time of the year, steamy and oppressive, almost more than Mendez could bear. But he had been here almost two years now and was getting used to the sounds of the jungle at last: the unseen slitherers, the screech of the birds, the howlers, the hum of the insects, the patter of constant rain.

He glanced at the nurse, then over at the man writhing around in the cot, entangling himself in the sweat-soaked bedclothes. Mendez had restrained him with ropes at the wrists and ankles, but still he twisted and turned about, senseless with pain. There were burn marks on the skin where he fought against the ropes in his delirium. His piercing screams added to the ever-present chorus of jungle noise.

Mendez put one of the X-rays he'd taken up on the light box. It was a picture of the man's chest cavity. Several small dark spots were visible on the lung.

"I have never seen anything like this, Rosa," he said, speaking in his native language. "Look. There. On the right side. There are three of them."

Mendez replaced the plate with another. "And look, here. There are several of the parasites here, in the intestine. And there, in the kidney. *Candiru* is a nasty creature. Look here, in the testicle. This is how it entered. Look how it swells the flesh."

"He must have taken in a pregnant female, doctor," the nurse said. "He has lost so much blood. He is hemorrhaging badly. Is there nothing we can do?"

"Once I performed surgery, removed one from a man. But this! This is impossible. There is too much tissue involved. Too many sites of attachment."

There was a gasp from the doorway.

Mendez looked over at the girl who'd been standing there for several hours now, watching. Her skin was dark, smooth, young. A child-woman.

"What do you know about this?" Mendez said.

"I'm a good girl," she said. "I always do as I am told."

"Who tells you?"

She pointed at the man on the bed. "He tells me. He's been coming here for many years. I keep his house clean. I—" She broke off, looked away.

"You what? Tell me."

The girl hesitated. "I do what he wants me to do. And then I leave him. He gives me a few cruzados."

Mendez looked at the girl. She was no more than fourteen. "Do you know who he is?"

"He never told me his name. He said he had no family, no country, no people."

"Where does he live?"

"In a small house. It is very near here. He built it many years ago. Four months ago, he came again. He said this time it would be for good." She hesitated. "He is a cruel man."

The man was screaming out words now, fragments of thoughts. Thank God, he didn't seem conscious, Mendez thought. No one could stand such pain. What was he saying? The doctor understood some of it; he had learned English when he was a boy. Something about wild animals, clawing, killing. Mendez listened: "Daddy, I was dreaming. I heard sounds. Down the hall. I went. I turned the knob. Daddy. Daddy. There is so much blood."

Senseless words. Something from his past.

The man was calmer now. He was taking short, agonized breaths, moaning. Mendez felt his distended stomach. His flesh was pale greenish in color; his breath smelled foul.

Suddenly the man opened his eyes, began struggling to sit up. "Let me go. I must kill Her."

The doctor moved closer. "Who?"

"Death Witch," he whispered, then sank back into the bed and closed his eyes.

Mendez turned to the child-whore standing in the doorway. "What do you know about this, girl?"

"He has always talked of this demon Death Witch," the girl said. "He is the only one who can destroy her. He has a special way, he says, but the Death Witch is

very cunning. She kills the Mind Kill. The Evil Eye.''
She shrank back in fear.

The doctor looked at her. The natives had many legends in this part of the Amazon, many fears. This girl had disgraced her tribe, sold herself to this man. But she still had a primitive mind and would believe in such tales as a Death Witch.

But this man was a foreigner. He would not believe.

''He told me the Death Witch had tainted him,'' the girl was saying. ''He said he had to make a cleansing. In the river.''

''Foreigners have no respect for the river,'' Mendez said. ''Did you tell him not to swim in infested waters?''

''I warned him about *candiru.*''

The man's eyes flew open again.

''For God's sake, he's awake now, doctor,'' the nurse said. ''Give him something for the pain.''

Yes. A little morphine. It would get worse for him as the night wore on, as the creatures bored in deeper. Morphine would help the man die easier. Mendez began to tell the nurse to prepare a shot, then stopped. The man was staring at him. There was something disturbing about his eyes, those intense green eyes, the whites now laced with a fine web of red as the blood vessels began to burst, something even beyond the pain, something cruel, without compassion. Without life.

As if the man were already dead.

Mendez backed away.

''Doctor?''

''I'm sorry, Rosa,'' he said. ''We cannot afford to waste our morphine on the dying. We have little enough for the living.''

Raoul Mendez slowly drew the curtain around the man's bed. Outside the clinic, a howler monkey screeched.

ABOUT THE AUTHOR

Fran Dorf received a master's degree in psychology from New York University and now lives with her family in Connecticut. Her first novel, *A Reasonable Madness,* is an alternate selection of the Literary Guild and the Doubleday Book Club.

SPELLBINDING THRILLERS . . .
TAUT SUSPENSE